# THE RETURN OF THE OSPREY

OSPREY TRILOGY

# THE RETURN OF THE OSPREY

*AN INTERSTELLAR ADVENTURE*

BOOK TWO

# DJ Albrecht

Water Valley Press

**Water Valley Press**

Published by Water Valley Press
2086 Vineyard Drive
Windsor, CO 80550

Bible quotations are taken from the <u>World English Bible</u> - a Public Domain Book.

ISBN13: 978-0-9600265-3-1

Cover design by Brandi Galuzzi   https://brandigaluzzi.myportfolio.com

Printed in the United States of America

# Acknowledgment

This story is a work of fiction. But I must acknowledge that it is inspired (at least in part) by the resourceful and talented employees of NASA, some of whom it's been my good fortune to know and work with.

# Contents

# Contents

# The Escape

*"Often you escape by going where those chasing you are unwilling to go."-*
*Michael Westen [Burn Notice]*

## Mars Detention Outpost Delta

Jacques's mind was racing. What woke me up? Was it the food door clicking closed? His heart jumped. Quietly he swung his feet to the floor, stepped to the door, and opened the food box. He looked at the badge and a small piece of paper lying in the food box. Finally! My ticket out of here, he thought while scratching his bushy beard.

The plan, days in execution, was simple. Jacque would exit the prison as a janitor. Each day he had received a note with instructions, which he memorized and flushed down the toilet. The badge was the final item to arrive. It signaled that tonight was the night. Jacques quickly gathered a razor and moved to the sink. Lathering his face, he began to shave off his beard. As he shaved, he went over the plan in his mind. *There'll be a janitor's cart somewhere nearby. As soon as someone bumps into my door, I'll use my badge to unlock my cell. I'll find the janitor's cart and push it past the guard to the break room. A distraction in another wing of the prison will be in progress to draw attention away from me. This should be a piece of cake.*

1

After shaving, Jacques removed his prisoner jump-suit and donned a janitor uniform. *Lucky for me, both prisoners and janitors wear the same kind of shoes.* He climbed back into bed and pretended to sleep.

He heard the footsteps of a guard making the hourly rounds. As the footsteps passed his cell, he heard a distinct bump of something hard against his door. He rose, taking one last look around the cell. The note said, don't be late. There was a nagging feeling that he forgot something, so he looked more closely a second time. *Time's a-wasting,* he thought. He placed his badge against the latch side of the door, anticipating the click of the lock opening; n*othing*. He gave the door a slight budge. It didn't move.

*What? Is the chip on the badge screwed up? Think, man, think. Wait a minute! Of course, the inside of the lock must be shielded in case a prisoner gets a badge. What to do? I'd reach through the food box, but the outside door is locked shut. Or is it?*

Jacques opened the inside door of the food box and pushed tentatively against the outer door. It wasn't latched! Jacques grasped the badge and stuck his arm through the passage, waving the badge in front of the cell door latch. Relief washed over him as he heard the latch click to the open position.

He opened the door and stepped out into a lava tunnel lined by a series of cells. The builders of this "facility" carved cellblocks out of several natural lava tunnels. This provided a secure jail and protected both the prisoners and personnel from the cosmic rays ever present on Mars. *There it is*, he thought, as he saw the janitor cart just to his right. He took hold and pushed it down the tube. *Almost there! The diversion must be in full swing up in cell block A. I can hear it all the way down here. So far, so good.* Jacques crossed the intersection of the three tubes, each one comprising a "cell block." He was two steps away from the break room when he was stopped by a shout.

"Hey, you!" a guard yelled at him. Jacques slowly pointed at himself and shrugged. "Yes, you. I'm talking to you. Get your sorry ass over here."

*Crap!* Jacques thought as he turned slowly toward the guard.

The guard eyed him intently. "Do I know you? Never mind. Get up to cell A4. The inmate there got food poisoning. They're treating him right now and are about to take him to the infirmary. He's tossed his cookies and has diarrhea. You need to clean it up pronto."

"But my shift's over," Jacques replied.

The guard glared at him. "I don't care."

"I need to meet someone — it's urgent," Jacques explained.

"Quit wasting my time. That cell stinks, and we'll not put up with the stench until the morning shift. The faster you get to work, the sooner you can leave for your 'urgent' meeting."

"Yes, Sir." Jacques began pushing his cart toward cell A-4. He was careful to look down as he passed the guards and the EMTs, who were removing the sick prisoner.

*The stench is worse than what that guard said*, Jacques thought. He worked as quickly as he could to clean the floor, bed, toilet, and sink. *Bet whoever planned this little distraction didn't count on me being part of it. I'm going to be sooo late!*

Finally, with the mess cleaned, Jacques stored the janitor cart and approached the final prison door. Even though the guard waved him through, his heart was racing. *Twenty minutes late. This'll never do. I hope I'm not too late to catch my ride.*

Outside the prison, Jacques found himself overlooking a park-like area. It was about the size of a football field and descended gently into a bowl. He guessed that straight ahead, on the other side of the park, was a gated lava tube that led to where the actual Delta 1 colony was located. To his left was another gated lava tube that probably led to the prison staff's living quarters. Snuggled against the lava outcroppings, the park's exposed side was enclosed by a partial geodesic dome structure that extended over the meadow to form its roof. The dome was built of stainless steel and plexiglass, with a covering of ice. This gave an airy feeling to the park while reducing exposure to cosmic rays. He smelled pine needles. Looking around the park, Jacques saw several small stands of neatly trimmed evergreens. The park also featured a lawn of moss and many raised beds of growing vegetables.

A voice in his head said, *Quit gawking and get moving. You're late!* Jacques turned toward his right and followed a path that led through a stand of trees to an obscure door. Next to the door was an RFID reader and a keypad. To gain access, one needed to have the correct badge and key in the valid code, which changed daily. Jacques swiped his badge over the chip reader and keyed in the code that he remembered from the note that came with his badge. Nothing! He tried again. Still nothing. *Crap! Think, think. What was the code anyway?*

*Was it 2463 or 6324 or… if I don't get this right, I'm toast!* Jacques had already tried both combinations with no success. *Wait, I forgot to swipe my badge when I keyed in the second combination.* This time he did both. To his relief, the door unlocked. Jacques opened the door and squinted at the brightness of the lights. He entered the prison's service hanger. It was big enough to hold three large starships. Currently, no such vehicles were present. Jacques saw an assortment of half-track service vehicles, hovercraft, and small pursuit aircraft. *Jeeze, I'm a full half-hour late,* Jacques fretted. He dashed behind Halftrack #8, as the note had instructed. No one was there. *What now? No one ever told me who my contact is!* He picked up a nearby broom and started to sweep, trying to fit into his janitorial role.

"Hey, you!" Someone yelled across the hanger to get his attention. *Here we go again,* Jacques thought, as he answered, "Yes, Sir."

"You're late," the Sergeant said as he walked over to Jacques. "This is no way to start your first night. Follow me, and we'll find the captain." Jacques followed him to a large office on the far side of the hanger. When they arrived, several other maintenance people were leaving. The Sergeant introduced Jacques. "Hi, Captain. Here's the new janitor, Sir."

The Captain said, "Hmph. Being late is no way to start your new job. Sergeant, take him over to Hovercraft Station #3. I noticed that the floor over there is in desperate need of mopping."

"Yes, Sir," the Sergeant replied. "Come with me," he said, looking over his shoulder at Jacques. Just as they arrived at the hovercraft station, a tall, husky fellow quickly grabbed the Sergeant from behind and applied a sleeper hold. The Sergeant flailed, trying to get leverage and break free. But the attacker was too large and strong. Soon, lack of oxygen to the brain left the Sergeant limp. The attacker lowered him to the ground, tied his arms and legs with zip ties, and gagged his mouth. After rolling the Sergeant under a workbench, the assailant opened the hovercraft door and motioned for Jacques to get in. Once inside, he motioned for Jacques to sit in the right seat as he slid into the pilot's seat.

"You're late!" The attacker challenged.

"I hear that a lot lately," Jacques said.

"What? Whatever. The boss won't be happy."

"Had to clean up a—"

"Save it for the boss. We need to boogie," the assailant interrupted. He spoke into his radio, "Traffic Control, this is employee 673682 requesting permission to take hovercraft 492 out for a test spin."

"Hey, Chuck, did the Sarge okay this?" Traffic Control asked.

"Yep, and he said I should've started a half-hour ago," Chuck answered.

"Good enough, I'm opening the door. When it's fully up, feel free to leave. Just stay well away from the frontier. Understood?"

"Understood," Chuck answered.

Jacques jumped at the sound of alarms and red lights flashing.

"A little jumpy, are we tonight? That's just the notice that a flight door is open. It's a safety precaution. They aren't coming for us yet," Chuck said.

"By the way, Chuck is just my cover name. You can call me Dimitri." He eased the craft out into the night.

"Why're we taking just a hovercraft?"

"Don't ask. I'm getting you out of here, aren't I?"

"Don't we need a spaceship?" Jacques asked

Dimitri continued flipping switches and started communicating with Traffic Control but didn't answer Jacques's question.

"You know ... something that actually flies?"

Dimitri took a deep breath and hit the accelerator. The hovercraft swept forward with a vengeance.

"I have a question, Chuck, ... err... Dimitri," Jacques said.

"You've got a lot of questions. What is it?"

"Why'd you take the time to tie up the Sergeant? You could've just killed him."

"Yeah ... but strangling someone takes more time than you'd think. Besides, if this little adventure goes south, I'll only face an assault charge, not murder."

*This better not go south,* Jacques thought.

"Switch on the toggle marked 'com,'" Dimitri said.

Jacques complied. The voice of Traffic Control could be heard speaking with other vehicles.

"Who's Traffic Control talking to?" Jacques asked.

"Researchers, travelers between Moon Base Alpha and Moon Bases Beta and Charlie. Mostly civilian traffic. OK — now's when the fun begins." Dimitri made a sharp turn and accelerated. Shortly after completing his turn, a warning alerted Traffic Control. "WARNING! WARNING! THE FRONTIER BORDER IS BEING BREACHED. Sentries intercept the intruder."

Jacques laughed. "We're going in the wrong direction to be intruders."

"You're laughing now, but the party's over once the pursuit ships arrive."

"STOP! STOP! YOU ARE ENTERING A RESTRICTED ZONE," a sentry drone warned.

Dimitri said, "Here, take over the ship while I occupy those little buggers. Steer toward that slot canyon over there." He hopped out of his seat and made his way to the back of the ship. Climbing into the port side gunner's station, he started shooting at the drones.

"You got it," Jacques said as he grabbed the controls and began flying.

"Damn those buggers, they're too quick dodging my energy bursts. Drop into the slot canyon so they'll have less room to maneuver."

Jacques accelerated the craft into the slot canyon.

"Hey, a little smoother, man! I can't line up my shots."

"Excuse me," Jacques rolled his eyes. "I'm keeping us from decorating a wall."

"Quit complaining and fly smoother. Yeah, like that. Hey! I just got one of those buggers! Yes! Another just lost a wing to the canyon wall."

Two other security drones hit the canyon wall, trying to evade Dimitri's fire.

"Take that, you little bugger," Dimitri gloated as he shot the last drone out of the sky. "Go ahead and set this baby on the ground, Jacques. That was easy."

"Yeah — too easy, if you ask me."

"I'm not asking, chump. Just set her down."

"Really?" Jacques asked.

"This is where the boss wants to meet us."

Before Jacques could reply, a middle-aged man in a NASA flight suit appeared in the pilot's seat that Dimitri had once occupied. The man was looking straight ahead and seemed not to notice Jacques.

Jacques jumped and said, "What the Hel—"

"Oh, don't mind him," Dimitri interrupted, "that's just a hologram of the Boss."

"Could've fooled me."

Upon hearing the exchange, the hologram looked at Jacques. "You're late."

"I had to clean up a mess left by your planned distraction back at the prison," Jacques complained.

"You two being late could've ruined this whole endeavor," the boss said.

"We lost our escorts anyway, Boss," Dimitri said.

"The sentry drones are nothing compared to the pursuit ships. They'll be waiting for us as we exit the canyon," the boss said. "Jacques, go take over the starboard side guns. You'll both have to keep firing at the pursuit ships if we are to survive."

Jacques took up his gunnery position. "Who flies?"

The boss said, "I'll fly remotely."

Jacques felt the ship lift and shoot forward. He was pushed hard against his restraining harness as the ship got up to full speed and blasted out of the canyon. *Just like a bat out of Hell,* he thought.

Just as the Boss said, they were waiting, and their initial blasts took out the ship's shields. But the Boss was flying too fast to be brought down. Soon the escaping vessel was several lengths ahead of the pursuit ships as they turned and followed. The chatter from their pursuers could be heard clearly over the ship's speakers. Occasionally, a transmission would be aimed at their craft. "Halt! Set your ship down. You can't escape!"

"Take careful aim, boys," the boss said. "These pilots will be harder to hit than those pesky drones."

The ship rocked and pitched wildly as the boss maneuvered to avoid the pursuing ships' fire. Jacques and Dimitri aimed carefully, but their ship's pitching and rolling kept them from scoring any hits. Fortunately, their firing and the boss's maneuvers kept them safe for the moment. *We can't keep this up much longer. We need to find shelter soon,* Jacques thought as he felt a ball of fear knotting up in his stomach.

Jacques glanced forward and saw only an open barren landscape ahead. "Feeling a little exposed back here," he said.

"Not to worry," the Boss said, "I have a plan." With that, he made a hard turn, angling toward a small bluff in the distance. The pursuit followed and drew closer.

The speakers came to life again. "WARNING! WARNING! YOU ARE ENTERING A HIGHLY RESTRICTED ZONE. TURN BACK NOW!"

An annoying alarm sounded. Jacques looked at his console and saw a red radiation alarm was blinking. He glanced at the radiation meter. *Wow! The radiation meter is off the charts.*

"Ah, Boss, we have wandered full speed into a radiation zone," Dimitri said.

The boss just laughed. "What's a little radiation among friends?"

The pursuit leader was heard over the speakers saying, "These clowns are flying us into the radiation field. It's time to pull out."

"Roger that," was the reply given as the pursuit ships pulled up and set their course for home. Their leader hovered at the radiation boundary to guard against Dimitri and Jacques circling back.

"Go ahead and fry your hearts out, you fools," he said.

The alarms grew louder as the boss flew even further into the radiation field.

The boss chuckled. "The secret to any successful escape is to be willing to go where the pursuit won't follow."

"What about us?" Jacques asked. "We're the ones getting fried!"

Together Jacques and Dimitri jumped out of their seats and dove for the ship's controls. But they couldn't change the ship's relentless drive into the radiation.

The Boss laughed and said, "Nice try, but the ship is totally in my control. You shouldn't have been so late, Jacques."

Hovering at the radiation boundary, the pursuit leader sent one last message to the ship, trying to escape. He thought, *By my calculation, you'll be fried in three more minutes. I guess your boss was more interested in seeing you die than escape.*

# On the Bleeding Edge

*"What's the difference between obsolete and cutting edge? Obsolete works."-*
*Nicholas Negroponte*

### Eleven Months Earlier - Saturn's Moon - Mimas

The yellowish-brown orb of Saturn was stunning as it came into view, dominating a canvas of deep space black. The Osprey was creeping in low orbit around Mimas.

Captain Matthew (Matt) Dirksen keyed in a unique code that gave him access to the USS Osprey's mission orders. "Our orders are to locate the US Space Corps fleet. We must then switch on our cloaking device to hide us as we move through the fleet and reveal ourselves directly behind its command ship. Sounds simple enough. Any questions?" Hearing no questions, Matt said, "Switch to stealth mode, Chief Torres."

"Aye, Sir," Chief Petty Officer Joshua Torres said.

"Commander Maalouf and Lieutenant Gonzales, keep a sharp eye out for the star fleet's picket ships. As soon as you see one, we'll activate the cloaking device."

"Aye, Sir," Commander Barnabas Maalouf and Lieutenant Marci Gonzales replied in unison.

"Ah, Sir?"

"Yes, Sergeant Smith," the captain replied.

"What's a picket ship?" Master Sergeant Marc Smith asked.

"Picket ships are small, high-speed starships that patrol the flanks of a star fleet's formation to keep intruders like us out."

"Thank you, Sir."

"Sir, I see the star fleet," Marci reported while looking at a pattern of bright specs of light not too far ahead. "That's a large fleet!"

"You're right. Unusually large. Thanks, Lieutenant. Any sign of a picket ship?"

"None, Sir. Shall we engage the cloaking device anyway?" Barnabas asked.

"Good idea, Commander. I expected we'd encounter a picket ship before we got this close to the fleet," Matt said.

"Sir," Josh said. "Perhaps we could stay in stealth mode a little longer, as it makes us look like a drone if they do sight us," he suggested.

"That's a good thought, Chief. However, I suspect that the picket ships are expecting a drone visit before we try to penetrate the fleet formation."

Marci said, "Sir, I just intercepted a fleet message. It seems a picket ship is out of position and is speeding back to its proper station."

"Hmm, we may have already passed the path of the picket ships. Chief, go ahead and activate our cloaking device on my mark," Matt said.

"Aye, Sir."

"Four, three, two, one, MARK."

"Engaging full cloak now, Sir," Josh said.

"What the hell?" Marci said. "My screen just went totally blank!"

"Mine too, as has my visual," Barnabas agreed.

Marci exclaimed, "I've lost my visual too! What the hell did you do, Torres?"

"Nothing. I just switched our cloaking device on. Now, all our outside sensors have stopped responding," Josh answered.

"So, we are flying blind?" Matt asked.

"Affirmative, Sir. No one can see us, but we can't see anyone else," Josh said.

"Not good, Sir," Barnabas added.

Matt frowned. "Thank you for stating the obvious, Commander Maalouf. Reduce to half speed and prepare for a full stop. This cloaking device is a piece of crap."

"It's cutting-edge technology, Sir," Josh corrected.

"Cutting edge, my ass. It's worse than a piece of crap!" Matt responded.

Barnabas chuckled. "You know what they say: the difference between obsolete and cutting edge is that obsolete works."

"Not funny, Commander. On my mark, bring us to a full stop. When we're stopped, turn off that damn cloaking device and return us to stealth mode."

"Aye, Sir."

"Lieutenant, when we come back to stealth mode, chart a course to intercept the fleet's command ship."

"Aye, Sir."

"Commander, bring us to a full stop on my mark. Three, two, one, MARK."

"Coming to a full stop, Sir."

"Turning off—"

Josh was interrupted by a shudder and screeching metal.

The Osprey began to rotate slowly. The collision alarms sounded as Josh brought the Osprey back to stealth mode.

"What the hell just happened?" Matt asked.

"We collided with another vehicle, Sir," Josh said.

Matt clenched his fist. "Obviously, Chief. Where'd it come from?"

"From the angle of impact, I think it flew into us," Marci said. "Though the cloaking device renders us unseen, we can still be hit by objects flying through space."

"I get they didn't see us. Why didn't we see it?" Matt asked.

"Sir, I think that this cloaking mechanism works both ways. It makes us undetectable and also kills our ability to see anything around us," Barnabas said.

"Electronically or visually, Sir," Josh added.

Matt was amazed. "Seriously? The thing that hides us, blinds us?"

"Sad but true, Sir," Josh said.

Matt began to shake. "Dammit! Why didn't your simulator pick this up, Chief?"

Josh grimaced. "We've no previous experience to go on in building the simulation, Sir."

"Confirm all compartments sealed, Chief. Tell me what you see, Commander. Lieutenant, tell me what you hear on the radio," Matt said.

"The cargo hold lost pressure. All other compartments are undamaged, Sir," Josh reported.

"Rear camera shows we've been hit by a small spacecraft. It appears to be hung up on our positioning thrusters, Sir," Barnabas said.

"I'm intercepting a radio transmission from the picket ship USS Shark. They're reporting that they hit an unseen object. Their bridge is severely damaged. They're trying to power through to break free of their obstacle and preparing to abandon ship," Marci said.

"The obstacle would be us. Chief, forget stealth mode. Bring us back to normal mode. Lieutenant, radio the Shark. Request that they reverse power. Tell them that if they need to abandon ship, we'll pick them up. Sarge and Gunny, prepare to pick up boarders through the forward portal."

"Sir, the Shark responds that they are reversing engines and ask us to accept their crew of four," Marci said.

"Very good. Commander, please stop our rotation."

"Aye, Sir."

"We're lucky the Shark is such a small ship, or she would've cut us in half," Josh observed. "Guess we're not reaching our objective, Sir."

Matt said, "I need to start calling you, Captain Obvious, Chief."

It took over an hour to free the Osprey from the Shark's wreckage and collect the crew from the ill-fated picket ship.

"Maalouf set us down on Mimas at your first opportunity," Matt ordered.

"I'm aiming for Herschel's Crater, Sir," Barnabas replied. "It's my nearest spot."

"Torres, McDermott — when we land, I want you prepared to go out and inspect the damage," Matt said, as the Osprey shuddered from its landing on the icy moon.

"Well, this little escapade didn't go as planned. This cloaking device is pretty worthless as it stands," Matt said.

"The brass won't be too pleased, I suppose, Sir," Marci said.

"Not in the least, Lieutenant," Matt said.

"That's the risk of being on the leading edge of technology, Sir," Barnabas said.

"More like the bleeding edge of technology, Commander," Matt sighed. "Now, Chief and Gunny, get out there and check out how bad the damage is. See if we can get this bird home."

When the inspection and a couple of repairs were completed, Josh signaled to Gunnery Officer Hilda McDermott. She followed his lead, and they floated just above the Osprey. They paused for a few seconds to admire the beauty of Saturn as it rose into view over the craggy wall of Hershel's Crater. Saturn, adorned with a pale-yellow hue, and surrounded by its rings of shimmering pinks and shades of gray, was breathtaking.

Josh took a deep breath and let it out slowly. "Our inspection is complete. As long as we keep out of the cargo bay, we should be good enough to make it to the repair center on our Moon."

"Sure about that, Chief?" Matt asked.

"Yes, Sir," Josh said. Seeing Hilda, he added, "Quite the view, isn't it, Gunny?"

Hilda said, "It sure is, Sir. Never thought I'd get to see Saturn from this angle. It doesn't get better than this."

"That's enough for now," Matt said. "You've both done well. Now get in, so we can get this bird home."

A feeling of déjà vu came over Josh as he spoke into his mike, saying, "We're on our way in, Sir."

Josh noticed, as he entered the ship's bridge, everyone was already at their stations. "Welcome aboard, you two," Barnabas said. Marci nodded at them and turned to face her station.

"To your stations. Let's get to it," the captain ordered.

He nodded to Barnabas, who began speaking with Mission Control

"Mission Control, Osprey. We've completed our inspection. It looks like the Osprey will hold together long enough for us to reach our Moon-based repair center. Over."

"Osprey, Mission Control. Very good. Go ahead with your pre-flight check. Over."

"Flight control, Osprey. Computers synced and no critical warnings," Josh said.

"All green on my console," Marci reported.

"Flight control, Osprey. Engines, maneuvering thrusters all good," Barnabas said.

The Return of the Osprey

Matt nodded. "Good! Let's get underway. "Begin with a 20 percent burn on my mark, Commander."

"Mission Control, Osprey. We are beginning our departure protocol. Over."

"Osprey, Mission Control. Godspeed. Over."

Matt saw a smile break out on Barnabas's face as he brought the Osprey out of the shadows of Mimas's mountains and aimed her home. Matt did not share his crew's relief. *What is it?* He thought. *Danger to the ship? No, Torres's repairs will hold. The inevitable hassle of an accident investigation? No. Admiral Robinson? That's it. Robinson is acting coy and unusually interested in the Osprey and her crew. The Admiral keeps hinting that he wants us to be part of a top-secret and essential operation. Robinson's anxious to make use of our cloaking device. He won't be pleased to hear of this little setback.*

His thoughts were interrupted by Marci. "Sir? I have a question."

"Huh? What is it, Lieutenant Gonzales?" Matt asked.

Marci lowered her voice. "Did you notice something strange about the task force we were supposed to sneak in on?" she asked.

"Not particularly. Why?"

"It had too many troop-transport ships. If our priority is to catch a pirate and his spaceship, why would we need so many transport ships?"

"To capture his planet or moon base, I suppose," Matt said.

"It only takes a couple of transports for that, Sir. But over a dozen? They're planning on something much bigger, I think."

"Like what?" Matt asked.

"I dunno. The Chinese just laid claim to several of Jupiter's moons for mining purposes. The President isn't too happy about that."

"Good point, Gonzales. I'll speak to Captain Wright about it when we get home."

Matt's mood grew darker. *The Lieutenant is right. Things aren't adding up,* he thought. *Whatever this means, my gut says it can't be good.*

# Setting the Perfect Trap

*"A goal without a plan is just a wish." - Jeff Rich*

## Johnson Space Center – Houston, Texas

The nondescript waiting room outside Admiral Justin Carter's office was hot and muggy. Senior Captain Lewis Wright thought, *Perhaps it's just me. Still, I bet the admiral's grumpy assistant cranked the heat up, just to add to my misery.* Lewis had been summoned to explain what happened to the Osprey in the sky above Mimas. *Even with a full-blown investigation into the incident, Carter wants to see me,* he thought. *Judging from his assistant's condescending attitude, Carter probably wants a piece of me for authorizing the cloaking device test that caused so much grief.*

The assistant frowned. "The admiral will see you now, Captain."

Lewis got up and nodded at the admiral's assistant. *Somebody this grumpy doesn't deserve a verbal reply.* He stepped forward and entered the admiral's office.

Admiral Carter looked up from his desk. "I read Captain Dirksen's preliminary incident report. It's not at all encouraging."

18

"No, Sir, the performance of the cloaking device is quite disappointing," Lewis said. "As with all new technology, it's a work in progress."

"Progress needs to come quickly, Captain. Dirksen'll need that device working for his next few assignments, I suspect."

"I'm not sure it'll be ready that soon, Sir. What assignment do you—"

Admiral Carter raised his hand before Lewis could get any further. "No, my office will never do, Son." He got up and put an arm around Lewis's shoulder. Directing his junior officer to the door, Carter continued, "We need to take a walk, just you and me, where the walls don't have ears."

"Uh … yes, Sir," Lewis replied, glancing back at the admiral's assistant. With satisfaction, he caught the assistant's disapproving scowl. The admiral led him down the hall toward a checkpoint. There, he had to empty his pockets and submit to a body scan. Once through the checkpoint, they turned right and walked down another hall that had windows overlooking a private courtyard. They entered the courtyard. Its prominent feature was a noisy fountain and numerous trees.

The admiral selected a table near the center of the courtyard and motioned for Lewis to sit. "This area is scanned for listening devices four times a day. Here we can speak plainly and not be overheard."

"A regular cone of silence, Sir," Lewis quipped as he braced for what the admiral had to say next.

"Something like that. You may be wondering why all this extra secrecy."

"The question did cross my mind, Sir. Now, regarding the incident with the Osprey—"

"Not quite yet, Wright. This is far more important."

The admiral smiled at Lewis's questioning look. "I'm sure you've heard it said, 'a goal without a plan is just a wish.'"

Lewis wondered where this conversation was going. "Meaning?"

"Meaning, I'm tired of wishing we could catch Jacques Beauregard's mole here at NASA. I've concocted a plan to catch that SOB."

"What plan?"

"This plan is so secret that I'm only sharing it with you."

"Doesn't any plan concerning Jacques Beauregard need to be approved by Admiral Robinson's select committee, Sir?"

"It does, and it will. But part of the plan — the part only you and I know about — is the trap I intend to create. It'll expose Beauregard's mole inside NASA."

"I'm all ears, Sir."

"Good. I'll start with my premise, which is that the mole is someone on the very committee that approves any effort to catch the pirate."

"That's pretty high up on the NASA food chain, Sir. You think the mole actually ranks that high?"

"I do, and I intend to prove it to the rest of the committee."

"How?"

"The plan is simple. We'll send four scout ships to four different suspected hideout regions. Only you and I will know the exact flight plans for each scout ship. Each scout captain will open their respective orders only after they've taken off and are several hours into their trip."

"Sealed written orders. Now that's old school, Sir," Lewis observed. "Just one problem. Don't we have to share the flight plans with the committee?"

"Bingo! That's where the trap is set. Each committee member will be given one legit flight plan and three bogus flight plans. There's a different scout ship flight plan per committee member. The orders look

20

identical except for the one legit flight plan. If the pirates harass one of our scout ships, we'll know they got its flight plan from the mole."

"Potential targets, Sir?"

"Good question. Our intelligence team thinks that the four most likely places for a base of operations are either among a cluster of Atira asteroids or a cluster of Amos asteroids."

Lewis leaned forward. "So, you're sending each ship to a different location that the intelligence team thinks could house the pirates' base of operation. But, on the orders that you give to each committee member, three of the four locations are falsified."

"You got it. Great plan, isn't it?"

"Yes, Sir. Uh, what if a scout ship just happens upon some pirates nowhere near their actual destination?"

"Not likely. Each of the four destinations has confirmed pirate activity. No activity in other regions has been reported for months. It's a chance we'll have to take."

"Which scout ships do you have in mind?" Lewis asked.

"The Hawk, the Falcon, the Condor, and of course, the Osprey."

"Ah, Sir, about the Osprey."

"What about the Osprey?"

"Well, it's still out of service, and Admiral Robinson is pissed."

"What's the holdup?" Carter asked. "I thought the repairs are completed."

"They are, Sir. Only, the investigation into its accident isn't finished."

"Damn. I didn't know that. Okay, I'll pull a few strings. I want the Osprey's crew in on this plan I'm hatching."

Lewis shook his head. "I'm not sure Robinson will agree. He's recently become concerned about what happens to the Osprey and her crew."

"As he should be. He needs the Osprey for a 'top secret' mission that's being planned. Of course, the task we're discussing takes priority."

"Good to know," Lewis said. "Do you think he's the mole?"

"Why would you say that?"

"I dunno," Lewis said. "It's just that he was all fired up to catch that Beauregard guy, but now not so much. He seems preoccupied. That's got me wondering why.

"He's on my list of suspects, but I'm not so sure. I know that he's been given a different set of marching orders, for sure. I can't share what they are at this moment, only that they include the Osprey."

"Why do I feel uneasy about that?" Lewis asked.

"First things first, Captain. We need to catch us a mole. Off the record, my money's on Silvertongue."

"Why?"

"He gets too much enjoyment whenever Robinson fails to catch that guy."

"So, it's a game to him?"

"Quite possibly. Silvertongue doesn't seem to appreciate how dangerous Beauregard is."

"Could be Admiral Hornsby, Sir. Hornsby is always worried about NASA losing funding. With Beauregard still on the loose, D.C. seems more than willing to keep the funding level that NASA wants."

"That's a thought," Carter mused. "The time for speculation is over. We've got a plan. The perfect plan, if I say so myself. Now it's time to execute."

In his mind, Lewis began to play out the plan proposed by his admiral. *Is it perfect? Can it even be executed? What are we forgetting?*

"A couple of questions first, if I may, Sir?"

"Fire away."

"Actually," Lewis said as he organized his thoughts, "three questions. First, what if a couple of committee members compare orders? Won't they find the discrepancy?"

"Who, besides Morris, knows enough about NASA flight plans to catch that level of detail?"

"Good point, Sir. Next question. Aren't we just setting up one of our scout ships to get taken out?"

"Our best intelligence indicates that the pirates can field six to eight ships max. The pirates'll need to cover each of the four possible targets. By covering each possibility, the pirates will muster a two-to-one advantage, at best. I like those odds given the skill of each of our crews."

"Last question, Sir. What if the pirates intercept one of our vessels because we just happened into their zone of operation? Not because of any intel slipped to them?"

"It's a risk we must take. We need to take out this mole, whatever the cost."

"I hear you, Admiral," Lewis said, still he couldn't help a nagging thought that they were overlooking something important.

# Ambushed

*"You've got to be very careful if you don't know where you are going because you might not get there." - Yogi Berra*

### Somewhere Along the Van Allen Astro Belt

The pursuit was on. The Osprey was tracking a contact weaving through an Atira asteroid cluster. It is just inside the orbit of the Earth. (Asteroids with this type are referred to as Atira or Apohele asteroids). The Osprey occupants were too busy to notice the reddish-brown, grey, and black objects racing by them as they weaved among a field of multicolored and dramatically shaped asteroids.

"Faster, Commander. We can't lose him," Matt drummed his fingers on his console.

"Aye, Sir," Barnabas said as he made a quick adjustment to just miss an asteroid. "Pretty smart of the pirates to hide along the Van Allen Astro Belt orbiting the Sun just inside that of our Earth's."

"Yeah," Josh agreed, "it puts them close to Earth and gives them hundreds of places to hide."

"Cut the chitchat," Matt commanded. "Lieutenant Gonzales, can you make out what kind of vehicle she is?"

"No, Sir. The distance is still too great," Marci said.

"Sir, I think that if we turn 'stealth mode' off, we'll have better range on our sensors," Josh said.

"Sure about that, Chief?" Matt asked.

"No, Sir. But, it's worth a try."

"We're not making any progress this way, Chief. Do it." Matt ordered.

"Done, Sir." Josh keyed in the correct commands.

"Makes us a bigger target ... if anyone's planning an ambush, Sir," Barnabas said.

"Point taken, Commander. Chief, raise our shields, on our sides and the rear."

"Aye, Sir."

"Good. Lieutenant, can you make out our contact now?" Matt asked.

"I can, Sir. It's an older, pre-raptor class interceptor. One of ours."

"Strange. None of our spacecraft should be anywhere near here," Matt said.

"Could it be a pirate ship? I heard they got their hands on a couple of our interceptors," Josh said.

"Hold on!" Barnabas exclaimed as he braked and maneuvered into a hard S-turn to avoid a sizable asteroid. The Osprey sprung into an open space between asteroid clusters.

"Damn! I think I lost him," Marci said.

"I can pick up speed ... now that we are in between clusters," Barnabas said as he accelerated.

The Osprey shuddered, and alarms screamed. Barnabas quickly flew her down and to his right.

"We've got three bogeys on our tail, Sir!" Marci exclaimed.

"Sir, they're giving us steady fire. Our shields are down 40% already!" Josh reported.

"Distance?" Matt asked.

"They're firing from about one klick off, Sir," Marci said. "Looks like they're standing off, trying to wear our defenses down."

"We need to close the gap. Commander, bring us about and head directly into the lead ship. Lieutenant, focus all your return fire on the lead ship," Matt ordered.

"Do we have enough firepower to take him out, Sir?" Josh asked.

"No, but we'll get their attention," Matt said. "Chief, override the crash avoidance systems, prepare for impact, and send out a distress signal.

Barnabas executed the course change. "Headed straight at the lead ship, Sir."

"Good, Commander. Steady as she goes."

"Ah … the old game of chicken," Barnabas said as he held his course. Marci began firing at the lead starship. This apparent suicide maneuver unnerved the three ships. The lead ship jerked up and to the right as the other two vessels fanned out, fearing they would be caught up in the collision. But Matt, trusting Barnabas's skill as a pilot, wasn't paying attention. "Chief, how close is the nearest asteroid one mile in size or larger?" he asked.

"At this speed, we are 30 minutes away, Sir."

"As soon as we pass our attacker, activate our cloaking device and set our course for that asteroid," Matt ordered.

The Osprey vibrated as it passed through the thrust of its attacker's engines. "Cloaking device activated, Sir," Josh announced.

"We're blind again," Marci groaned.

"Good. Commander, accept the course as set by the Chief. Hopefully, we'll find a hiding place on that asteroid," Matt said.

Barnabas smiled. "Hopefully, no one wanders into our path before we get there."

"Or a stray asteroid," Josh added.

Twenty minutes into their blind run toward the asteroid, Matt said, "Chief, put us in stealth mode. Let's see where we are."

"Aye, Sir."

"We're going in too fast. I need to slow up," Barnabas said.

"Lieutenant, scan the asteroid for a crevasse, canyon, or crater," Matt said.

"Nothing on this side, Sir," Marci said.

"I'm slowing to give us a view of the other side," Barnabas said.

"Yes, I think there's a spot dead ahead," Marci said

Josh agreed, "I see it too."

Matt nodded. "Commander, head for that crevasse and prepare to land."

"Aye, Sir."

The crevasse quickly opened into a slot canyon.

"Hit the retro rockets, Commander," Matt ordered.

The crew felt their restraints pressing against their bodies as the retro rockets kicked in.

"Done, Sir. I'm getting our rate of descent under control."

"Good, Commander. Chief, where are our pursuers?" Matt asked.

"Looks like they're just entering this cluster of asteroids, Sir. Even though we turned on the cloaking device to keep them from seeing us. They probably guessed where we'd head."

"Understood, Chief. Commander, do you see a clearing anywhere?"

"I think so, Sir."

"Good. Calculate your distance to landing, and hold steady, reducing your speed only enough for a hard landing," Matt said.

"Yes, Sir."

"Time for us to disappear again," Matt said. "Chief, activate the cloaking device."

"Done, Sir."

Matt saw sweat break out on Barnabas's forehead. "Feeling a little challenged, Commander?"

"More than a little, Sir. I'm landing this bird blind with that cloaking device on."

"We need to keep those pirates from seeing us," Matt said. "I've got faith in you."

"Look on the bright side, Commander," Josh interjected. "No one'll see us crash."

Barnabas grimaced. "Thanks for the reassurance, Torres."

"We're not going to crash," Matt said, glaring at Josh.

Just then, a jolt caused the ship to groan and pushed everyone hard into their harnesses. The Osprey slid a little way, then tilted to a stop.

"Hmm, that wasn't as hard as I thought it'd be," Barnabas sighed.

Marc smiled. "Kinda like coming in on a wing and a prayer."

"More like a blindfold and a prayer," Marci corrected.

Josh groaned. "I think we busted a landing gear."

"Think anyone, other than the pirates, got our distress signal?" Hilda asked.

"Not sure, Gunny," Josh said.

"Okay. Other than a broken landing gear, we're still in one piece, but I'm sure the bogeys are flying overhead searching for us," Matt said. "Chief, make sure that we keep the cloaking device on."

"Yes, Sir."

Matt looked around. "Everyone, I want a damage report, now."

"Sir, we still have no shields," Josh reported. "I'm not sure we can recover them. Other than that, our systems seem to be intact."

28

"We'll need to sit tight and wait for the searchers to move on," Barnabas said.

"How long, Sir?" Marc asked.

"Not sure, Sarge," Barnabas replied. "I bet they guessed we came into this canyon but can't find a crash site. So, they'll be poking around for a while. They may even leave a drone or two behind just to keep an eye on things. In either case, we can't afford discovery or a running battle with no shields."

"You're right, Commander," Matt agreed.

"I hear a 'but' coming," Barnabas said.

"I don't like waiting," Matt said. "We're blind as long as that cloaking device is on. And I hate being blind."

"What if one of the pirates lands here just to double-check?" Hilda asked. "We'll never see them until it's too late."

"That's why I don't like being blind," Matt said.

### NASA Conference Room, Houston, Texas

"What the hell! What do you mean the Osprey's lost? That's unacceptable. Just unacceptable!" Special Security Advisor to the President, Vice Admiral Dennis Robinson's face became beet-red as his rant continued. "I'll have your head on a platter, Wright! When I'm done with you, you'll wish you had never been born!"

The stage upon which Robinson was performing was a flat-beige NASA conference room. His audience: Captain Lewis Wright, Senior NASA Mission Controller; Admiral Justin Carter, Skunk Works Program Manager; Dr. James Silvertongue, Special Counsel to the President; Admiral Gerald Hornsby, Commander of the Astronaut Corps, and Admiral James Christopher Morris II (known to his friends as JC), NASA's Interplanetary Program Chief. All were unimpressed.

29

*At this rate, he's going to have a stroke before he finds that platter for my head*, Lewis thought.

Silvertongue's mellow voice broke in. "Now, calm yourself, Dennis. Please, let's give the good captain here a chance to explain himself. Now tell us, Captain Wright, why did you purposefully put the Osprey in harm's way?"

Admiral Carter cleared his throat. "Gentlemen, it wasn't —"

"Begging your pardon, Sir," Lewis interrupted, thinking, *I can't let Admiral Carter take the fall for this!* "Our best intelligence thought that the risk to any one of our scouts was minimal."

Robinson jumped to his feet. "Minimal, my ass! Best intelligence? Crap intelligence is more like it! What the he—"

The sound of Admiral Hornsby's hand slamming the table interrupted Robinson. "Dammit! Stop shouting and grow up, Dennis. We all know that chasing that damn pirate is a risky business. Shit happens, but we carry on."

Robinson said, "Easy for you to say, Gerald. You didn't have a top-secret mission go down the tubes because some snot-nosed captain put its essential resource at risk!"

Hornsby didn't back off. "There'll be plenty of resources at your disposal, James, so calm down."

Robinson shook his head. "No. Not for this mission, and Wright knows it."

Silvertongue spoke up. "Gentlemen, let's try and put this back in perspective. The captain has said that the Osprey is only a few days overdue, and we may have received a distress signal from her. She could still show up. What are you doing about this situation, Captain?"

"We're putting together a rescue task force at this moment. It'll be launching by the end of tomorrow."

Robinson banged the table with his fist. "What the hell are you waiting for? Launch it now!"

Lewis felt his anger rising. "You don't just hop in a couple of space frigates and take off like you would a car, Admiral. It takes at least twenty-four to forty-eight hours to recall the crews and to provision the ships, Sir!"

Silvertongue stood. "Okay, okay, we've got a plan. Let's let the captain do his job and, hopefully, save his reputation. We'll reconvene for another update in—"

Robinson interrupted. "While he's 'saving his reputation,' let Wright chew on this. Word on the street is, Beauregard has a mole running around NASA. I say it's Captain Wright!"

The room went dead silent. "Stop smirking, JC!" Robinson exclaimed. "I'm not kidding. As Senior Mission Controller, Wright knows everything that goes on here. I'm warning you, Wright. When they find the Osprey's wreckage, I'm bringing you up on charges."

"What charges? What are you talking about, Dennis?" Silvertongue asked.

"Espionage, for being Beauregard's mole." Robinson stared hard at Lewis.

Red-faced, Lewis leaned forward. "You sorry son of a—"

Carter interrupted Lewis by placing an unseen grip on his elbow. Lewis glanced at Carter and closed his mouth. Then he stared right back at Robinson but held his tongue for a moment. He finally spoke. "You're wrong, Admiral." He said while thinking, *Where the hell are you, Matt?*

# Springing the Trap

*"The devil fools with the best-laid plans." - Neil Young*

### Slot Canyon on an Unknown Asteroid

Matt drummed his fingers on the console. The crew had just finished taking a break to relieve themselves and grab some nourishment. Matt stopped drumming. "Waiting's over. Sarge and Gunny, suit up and see what's out there."

"Yes, Sir," they replied.

"Keep a low profile, you two," Matt added.

Suited up, Marc and Hilda grabbed some camouflage parkas and their guns.

"Why are you taking your gun?" Marci asked Hilda.

Hilda winked. "I'm a Gunnery Sergeant. It's what I do."

"Sir?" Marci asked, "How'll we know the pirates have moved on without turning the cloaking device off?"

"Good question, Lieutenant," Matt said. "Any ideas?"

Barnabas said, "I have an idea, Captain."

"Go ahead."

"Why not set out our distress beacon?"

32

"Wouldn't that defeat the purpose of the cloaking device by giving away our location?" Marc asked.

"Not if I disabled the transmitter," Josh said. "Our beacons come with both a transmitter and a receiver. We could use the receiver to intercept the pirates' transmissions."

"Good idea, Torres," Marci said. "Don't forget the cloaking device still blocks our ability to pick up signals from the distress beacon itself."

"You're right, Lieutenant. Permission to suit up, Captain," Josh said. "I'll go out with the beacon and monitor it from outside, then relay my findings through the Sarge or Gunny."

"Permission granted … after the Sarge and Gunny get a feel for the land and find out if we have any pirates lurking about."

The canyon had a rough, flat floor about as wide as a football field. Its walls ran almost straight up. Using their low-vision goggles, Marc and Hilda could discern that the canyon opened several hundred yards ahead.

"Looks like we landed just before we lost the canyon," Hilda said.

"Yeah, it should be easy to set up the rescue beacon just outside the canyon," Marc said. "Damn, what's that light coming down the canyon? A drone, maybe?"

"That's my guess. Let's lay low. I'll set my timer and see if it makes another pass."

As soon as the drone passed, Hilda jumped up.

Marc tugged on her shoulder. "Down, Gunny! Here comes a second one."

Back in the Osprey, Matt listened to Hilda's report. "Two drones making a pass every half hour?"

"Yes, unfortunately, Sir," Hilda said.

"That sucks. Where's the Sarge?"

"He stayed outside to keep an eye on things. He and I have a bad feeling about this place."

"Good thinking, Gunny," Matt observed.

"Why are they keeping such a close eye on this asteroid?" Marci asked.

"Could be they knew that this is a good hiding place," Barnabas answered. "I suppose they know these asteroids pretty well."

Matt said, "I bet they're watching for any asteroid that is large enough to hide us. They're casting a net of drones around where they think we're hiding."

"Kinda like casting a fishing net with us as the fish," Josh mused.

"Right, Chief," Barnabas agreed. "Seems like all we can do is sit tight until they gather in their drones and head home. I just pray that they don't get more curious than they already are."

Matt thought for a minute. "Our cloaking device leaves us blind to what's going on. But turning it off exposes us to those damn drones. Chief, it's time to get that beacon set up. See if you can find out what kind of drones those are and what their search plan is. Gunny, have the Sarge cover him. I want you to hang out by our open portal to relay anything they say over their com system."

Just beyond the canyon exit, Josh settled in by the modified rescue beacon. He just had time to drape the beacon and himself with some camouflage netting before the drones flew by. "Hey Gunny, tell the captain that those drones buzzing us are stolen from NASA. Same as what we have, only an older version."

"The captain wants to know if you're hearing any pirate chatter?" Hilda asked.

"Yeah. Tell the captain that the ships that attacked us plan to leave if they don't find anything soon. Crap! They're leaving the drones behind for another thirty hours before calling them home."

Hilda was off-line for a while. Then Josh heard her say, "Hey Torres, the captain's pretty excited. He wants you to grab the beacon and get back to the ship ASAP. Says he's got some ideas he wants to run by you."

Back on the ship, Matt called the crew together. "All right, everyone, listen up. Chief Torres, brief us on where we stand."

Josh cleared his voice. "Here's the deal. The drones will report anything that moves except another drone that belongs to their battle group."

"How do they know another drone belongs to their battle group?" Hilda asked.

"Good question, Gunny. They recognize each other's identifying signals by way of unique sim cards. That's also how they respond to external commands. Each sim card, and its backup sim card, have a battle group identifier. The battle group leader, probably one of the pirate spaceships, gives each drone their search assignments. It then calls them home when their assignments are completed. I think the two drones, passing over our canyon, are here because someone saw us enter but not leave."

"Great! Do you have any good news, Chief?" Matt asked.

"The good news is, while the drones are in the canyon, their signals are blocked. So, they must loop back over the asteroid to signal the battle group leader their status and whether they see any changes in the canyon or—"

"So, we're stuck here until those drones are given the command to head home," Matt interrupted.

"Looks as if, Sir," Josh said.

"This sucks. If we stay until the drones are recalled, we'll lose our chance to find the pirate hideout," Matt said. Then his eyes brightened. "Unless we sent one of our drones along with theirs to show us the way."

Barnabas shook his head. "Sadly, it would be recognized as an intruder because it doesn't have a pirate's sim card. We—"

"Maybe we can use one of their drones to locate their base for us," Josh said.

"What do you have in mind, Chief?" Matt asked.

"We could grab one of their drones and use its sim card in place of our drone's sim card. Then our drone will follow all the pirate protocols with their sim card, and Our backup sim card will broadcast on our wavelength where the drone is going."

"That would be genius, Chief," Barnabas said, "if only you knew how to capture a pirate drone without shooting it down."

Matt spoke-up. "Maybe we can just modify one of our drones."

"We still need the pirated drone's sim card, Sir," Josh said.

Matt said, "The fact that the drone signals are blocked by the canyon is just the ticket. Gunny, I want you and Sarge to shoot the trailing drone as it comes by. Just take out its propulsion unit in the rear. We want to harvest its sim cards."

Hilda smiled. "I get to shoot something after all. Cool."

"Let's do this. Hurry!" Matt admonished.

Barnabas noticed the urgency in Matt's voice. "What's up, Captain? You sound a bit nervous."

"Call it a gut feeling. I agree with Gunny. I don't feel good about this place."

"But with our cloaking device, they can't see us, Sir," Marci said.

"Technically, yes, Lieutenant," Matt agreed. "But if they even think we're holed up here, they can just bomb the hell out of this canyon, and we're done for. We don't—"

Gunny interrupted. "We got it, Captain!"

"Good work. Now bring what's left of it here so the chief can work his magic," Matt commanded.

Josh surveyed the wreckage. "This is pretty messed up. The primary sim card is toast. I hope I can salvage its backup." Time seemed to drag as Josh worked on swapping the sim cards. Finally, he turned his finished work over to Gunny to launch.

"That'll be our little gift to them," Josh said. "It'll follow all of its battle group command orders while sending us a signal telling us where the battle group goes when it's recalled."

"Okay, Chief, you're a genius. Now we have our very own mole that'll tell us where the pirate hideout is," Barnabas said. "If our luck holds, we only need to sit here for no more than three days, and we'll be on our way home."

Marci smiled. "Don't you love it when a plan comes togeth—"

"Hey gang," Hilda interrupted. "We've got company!"

"Hold that thought, Lieutenant," Matt said as the crew piled out of the Osprey to see what was happening. They saw that behind them, inside the canyon, a pirate lander was touching down. The lander's door opened, and a dozen or so pirates emerged.

Marc, who was positioned on a rock pile fifty yards from the Osprey, said, "We're going to need bigger guns. Chief, grab some RPGs. I'm going to try and draw their fire away from the Osprey."

"I'll grab them," Marci said as she hopped back into the ship.

Matt yelled, "Keep them at bay, guys, while I figure out how to get out of here." Under his breath, he said, "So much for our luck holding."

"We've got this, Sir," Hilda replied while wincing at the sound of gunfire echoing through the canyon.

Barnabas was transfixed by the sight of tracer bullets flying through the canyon and ricocheting off rocks all around Marc. Matt broke the spell by shouting, "Get aboard, Commander! We've got to get out of here without exposing where we are, or the entire pirate force will surround us in no time!"

"Don't they already know where we are?" Barnabas asked.

"No. If they did, they'd be shooting at us instead of Sarge. If they get tired of shooting at him and send some random tracer bullets toward us, they'll be sure to see the tracers bouncing off the Osprey. Then they'll know where we are for sure."

"Perhaps we could switch from cloaked to stealth mode. That makes us appear as if we are merely a drone to the enemy," Barnabas said.

"The pirates would know that we aren't one of theirs and be on us in a heartbeat," Matt replied.

"Yeah, you're right, Sir," Barnabas agreed. "Maybe—"

"Captain," Josh interrupted. "What if we used a pirate's sim card to disguise ourselves?"

"I don't follow," Matt said.

"I can use it to modify one of our drones, just like I did to the one we just launched. I can secure it to our ship and communicate with it via our old legacy com port. Commander Maalouf can use it as his eyes and ears to guide us home while we keep our cloaking devise on."

Matt thought for a minute. "Hmm … that could work. We'll need another pirate sim card."

"There's one flying past us every thirty minutes," Barnabas reminded him.

"Good Call," Matt said. "Gunny, tell the Sarge to retrieve the other pirate drone."

Hilda smiled. "I'm on it, Sir."

Marc wasn't so sanguine. "You're kidding. He wants me to shoot down the second drone, then run out and get it with those pirates shooting at me?"

"Just be careful to shoot it, so it crashes closer to us than the pirates. Nothing to it," Hilda said.

Marc shook his head and took careful aim. As the second drone came into view, he fired. The drone spiraled downward and hit the ground halfway between the advancing pirates and the Osprey.

"Crap, I fired too soon!" Marc exclaimed.

"That sucks," Hilda observed.

"You think?" Marc said as he moved toward the drone wreckage. "Cover me."

Moving was difficult with the reduced gravity of the asteroid. If Marc pushed off too hard, he'd fly up in the air, making a perfect target for the advancing pirates. If he moved too slow, the pirates would be at the wreckage before he could safely retrieve it. Hilda surveyed the situation. Her first shot would expose her position. The pirates had spread out too far for her to be effective with a rifle. The lander also looked like it was about to bring its weapons to bear on Marc. She looked up and found an overhang at the top of one of the canyon walls. *Here goes nothing,* she thought as she fired the RPG at the overhang.

Hilda was momentarily transfixed by the results. A flash of light was followed by a slow-motion rain of smoke, dust, stones, and large rocks drifting down onto the canyon floor. Debris covered the lander, pirates, and Marc. Pirates scrambled to return to their lander, which was a mistake. Hilda's second RPG shot was aimed in the direction of their lander. It struck just in front and to the right of her intended target. The impact set the lander on its side and shattered the cockpit windshield.

Marc dodged several boulders as he grabbed what was left of the drone. "Hey Gunny, I meant 'cover me' figuratively, not literally," Marc huffed as he made his way back to the Osprey.

"You're welcome, Sarge," Hilda said while admiring her work. "I just took 'cover me' to a whole new level."

Back on the Osprey, Matt urged, "Do your thing quickly, Chief."

Josh took a skeptical look at the pile of lander wreckage. "I hope at least one of the sim cards is still good."

"Hurry, guys!" Marc yelled as he watched a second lander arrive behind the first. Marc grabbed one of Hilda's RPG launchers, reloaded it, and moved back to his old position.

"Don't get too far from the ship," Hilda instructed as her field of vision cleared. She could see the debris settling and the pirates streaming out of the second lander. "We need to create more cover."

"I've got an idea," Marci said as she hustled toward the rear of the Osprey. Soon she emerged from the Osprey with two canisters.

"What are those?" Hilda asked.

They're smoke and chaff canisters. We eject them when we're flying ground support on a planet. They foul up visual and radar vision. That's what you want to do, isn't it?"

"You bet, Lieutenant." Hilda grabbed each canister and flung it toward the advancing pirates with all her strength. Assisted by the reduced gravity, the canisters bounced halfway between the Osprey and the advancing pirates. Hilda took careful aim with her rifle and fired. There was a flash with chaff and smoke obscuring the entire canyon from sight.

"Good shot, Gunny! Oh crap," Marci said.

"What?" Hilda asked.

"Look behind us. There's another pirate lander coming in behind us!" Marci exclaimed. "It'll block the canyon opening."

"Shit! we've got to move," Hilda said. "Hey Sarge, we gotta go. Now!"

Not hearing a reply, Hilda looked at Marc's position. He was lying face-down on a rock pile. "Marc, do you hear—"

Josh's voice cut her off. "All set, Captain. "I've got the sim cards switched, drone in place, and we're hooked up through the com port."

"Okay, back to the ship, everyone," Matt ordered. "We've got to boogie!"

Marci slid into her station as a weapons officer. "Ready here, Captain."

Barnabas buckled up. "Set to go, Sir."

Matt said, "Good. Here's the plan. Maalouf, I want you to replicate the drone's normal path that Sarge just shot down. Hopefully, the pirates won't notice its delay in coming out of the canyon."

"Roger that, Sir," Barnabas said.

"Counting down to take off," Matt said. "Five, four, three—"

Hilda's voice interrupted. "We can't leave yet. Marc's down!"

"Crap, he's on the other side of the canyon," Josh added.

"Lifting off, Sir," Barnabas said, concentrating on his flying.

"We gotta wait for the others," Josh said as he jumped into the open portal door.

"No time left here." The sound of bullets ricocheting off the Osprey lent urgency to Matt's voice.

Josh held out a hand to Hilda, who grabbed it and clambered aboard. "We can't leave, Marc," she implored.

"I'll drift to his side of the canyon. Okay, Sir?" Barnabas asked.

"Good idea, Commander. Do it. Chief, Gunny, when we get over the Sarge, drop down and retrieve him," Matt ordered.

The Osprey moved into position just over the prone figure. The sound of bullets bouncing off her hull picked up in intensity.

"This sucks!" Josh exclaimed. "That pirate lander outside the canyon has a clean shot at us."

"Not if I have my way," Marci said. "Permission to fire my weapons, Sir?"

"You'll be firing blind, Lieutenant," Matt said.

Barnabas said, "I'll rotate the Osprey to point in the general direction of that pirate ship as I drift over to where Sarge is."

"I like it. Make it quick," Matt answered.

"I'm lining up on the target now," Barnabas said. "My compliments to Torres. That drone he set up is working well."

"I'm firing my weapons now," Marci said. Hearing no sound, she continued, "I'm afraid I missed."

Using their attached drone to sight in on the target, Josh said, "You're five degrees high, Lieutenant."

Marci made some adjustments and fired again. This time she was rewarded as her target blew up in a fireball. She smiled at the sound of debris bouncing off the Osprey.

Barnabas's monitor abruptly went blank. "Hey, Chief, my monitor went out! I've lost contact with our drone."

"Working on it, Sir," Josh replied.

The number of bullets bouncing off the Osprey trailed off. Hilda hopped down and lifted Marc to the portal. Together, she and Josh wrestled him through the portal door. Finally, Hilda hopped aboard, and they shut the door.

"All in, Sir!" Josh called.

"Hit it, Commander!" Matt ordered.

Slowly the Osprey began to move forward out of the canyon. Josh fiddled with the controls of the drone. "Jeeze!" he exclaimed. "It looks like the entire pirate fleet is descending on us."

A loud screeching sound of metal scraping against metal filled the cockpit. The Osprey began to shudder and rotate.

"What the hell?" Matt asked.

"We must've side-swiped another ship. We'll have to go to stealth mode to see what's happening," Josh said.

"Can't you tell by the drone we've just attached atop our ship?" Matt asked.

"No, Sir," Josh responded. "We caught whatever we hit with the side or bottom of our ship."

"Damn it!" Matt exclaimed. "We're not going stealth. We'll go to normal mode on my mark. Hopefully, our sudden appearance will surprise them long enough for us to make our escape. Ready. Five, four, three, two, one, MARK!"

"Cloaking device is off, Sir," Josh reported.

The sounds of collision alarms confirmed Josh's words.

"Turn those damn alarms off," Matt commanded. "Chief, take a snapshot of our surrounding field-of-view."

"Aye, Sir," Josh said.

"Commander, can you untangle us before we're boarded?"

"Reversing thrust now, Sir," Barnabas said.

The Osprey screeched her complaint at Barnabas's maneuvers. Finally, the two ships parted.

"Full speed straight ahead, Commander," Matt ordered.

The Crew was pushed hard back into their seats as the Osprey accelerated.

"Do you think we can outrun them?" Marci asked.

Barnabas shook his head. "Bogeys are approaching from each side and in front of us. I doubt we can outrun all of them."

"Anyone got good news?" Matt asked.

"We're surrounded, Sir," Josh said. "The ships that were leaving our asteroid turned and are heading our way!"

Barnabas shook his head. "Out of the pan and into the fire we go."

Matt gave a bitter chuckle and said, "I was asking for good news, not clichés. Chief, do you think they've had time to plot our course?"

"I do, Sir," Josh answered. "They're converging awfully fast!"

43

"Good. I've got those jokers just where I want them. On my mark, activate our cloaking device and bring our ship about. Turn ninety degrees to our starboard side. Here's hoping that they won't guess we've changed course. Five, four, three, two, one, MARK!"

The ship's screens went blank, and the crew felt themselves being tossed about by the Osprey's sudden change of direction.

Matt's knee began to bounce. He asked, "Chief Torres, is our drone still attached and working?"

"It is, Sir."

"What do you see?"

Josh said, "It looks like the whole fleet and all their drones are altering course to pursue our last known direction, Captain."

Matt said, "What're you waiting for, team? Let's join the pursuit."

Barnabas asked, "What are the odds this little trick will work, Sir?"

"Slim to none, and slim just packed his bags."

## Space Station Freedom

Aboard the Space Station Freedom, the duty sergeant called the bridge master from his station. "Sir, I'm overlooking docking port C, and I've got some kind of practical joker out here with a drone."

"What's up, Sergeant?" the bridge master replied.

"This guy's asking permission to dock his ship."

"Permission to dock a drone?"

"Yes, Sir,"

"Whatever. Go ahead and grant permission."

"Yes, Sir," the sergeant replied. He sent a 'permission granted' signal, then spilled his coffee, as a full-sized Osprey sprang from nowhere in front of his eyes.

The bridge master, who was still watching, chuckled and said, "Should've known it'd be you, Captain Dirksen. Who else would ride in with a drone sitting on his wing?"

"Good to be back, Sir. Requesting permission to make it to the repair hangars on our moon."

"Feeling a little beat up, are we, Captain?"

"Yeah, Sir. It's worse than it looks," Matt replied.

"How's your crew?"

"Thanks for asking. One of my crew has a concussion, and I'd like to get him checked out ASAP."

"I'll need to OK this with Captain Wright first."

"Understood, Sir. When you're finished, patch me through to Captain Wright on a secure line, if you will," Matt said.

"Will do, Captain, and welcome home."

Josh spoke up, "Uh, Sir, while you're waiting to speak with Captain Wright, I have a question."

"What?"

"How'd you know mixing with the pirate drones and fleet while using the pirate sim card as a cover would work?"

"I didn't, Chief," Matt answered. "I just thought of what I'd do if I were in Beauregard's place."

"That being?"

"I'd send my drones to the most likely escape route. When the trail got cold, I'd command the drones to fan out. That's when I figured we could safely clear out," Matt explained.

Josh gave a low whistle. "That's pure—"

"Genius." Lewis, who'd just come online, interrupted. "Good to hear you're finely made your way back."

Matt said, "Some friend you are. Your little adventure almost got us killed."

"I love you too, Matt. What did you find?"

"You'll love this, Lewis. We got one of our drones mixed in with theirs. It should lead us to their hideaway."

"Excellent, my friend. Now you and your crew are confined to the Osprey until further notice."

"What? You gotta be kidding. Sergeant Smith needs medical attention, and we need to get the Osprey over to the repair hangar on the moon."

"Sadly, this is no joke. Officially, the Osprey and its crew are still lost. We can spirit a medic aboard to check on the sergeant. But, no repairs, at least until we catch our mole."

"How long will that take?"

"Not long if all goes as planned. Wish us luck."

## Johnson Space Center, Houston Texas

The heat and humidity of a southeast Texas summer were lost on the occupants of the labyrinth of buildings that comprise Johnson Space Center.

"Why is it that when it's hot outside, NASA has to crank the air down to near freezing?" Admiral Carter complained.

"I'll have someone check out the HVAC system, Sir," the captain of the guard answered.

They were standing in a non-descript hallway just outside an equally drab conference room. The sign on the door read "Conference Room A." It was five minutes past the hour, making Captain Wright late.

Carter took a couple of deep breaths to settle his nerves. He was on the verge of trapping the NASA mole that had plagued their efforts to catch Jacques Beauregard for months, if not years.

"Are they all assembled?" he asked the sergeant of the guard.

"Mostly, Sir. We have Dr. Silvertongue, Admirals Robinson, and Hornsby."

"What about James Morris?" Carter asked.

"He must have slipped by me when I wasn't looking. The last time I peeked in, he was sitting at the far end of the table, engrossed in his tablet," the Sergeant said.

"Captain Wright?"

"I haven't seen — oh, here he comes, Sir."

"About time, Wright," Carter said as he returned Wright's salute.

"Apologies for being late, Sir," Lewis said. "I made sure the outside of the building is secure."

"Fair enough," Carter said. "Once the traitor's exposed, we can't let him escape. Do you both understand?"

"Yes, Sir."

"Go ahead, Wright," Carter said, "go sit at the other end of the table."

"Yes, Sir," Lewis said as he entered the room. Lewis found a seat next to Morris and said, "Good morning, Sir."

Morris, who was writing something on his tablet, looked up. "Hi, Captain. Pardon me for not shaking hands. I'm fighting a rather nasty cold," he said as he blew his nose.

"Understood. Thanks for NOT sharing," Lewis chuckled as he took his seat. Morris returned to writing on his tablet.

In the hallway, Carter gave his final instructions. "Sergeant, don't forget — no one leaves this room. And have your men ready to storm the room and grab the traitor when I expose him."

"Will do, Sir."

Admiral Carter took one more deep breath, nodded at the Sergeant, and entered the room. As he entered, he heard the low rumble of thunder signaling an approaching storm.

"Gentlemen, thank you for clearing your schedules to be at this important briefing. Please close the door, Sergeant," Carter said. "As you know, I drew up orders to send four scout ships to investigate possible hiding places for the pirate Jacques Beauregard. Well, we've received word from three of the four scout ships, and it contains some good and some bad news."

The room began to murmur with speculation.

"We already know that Captain Wright tops the list of suspects," Robinson said.

There was a ripple of laughter.

Carter smiled. "Nice try, Dennis. Now, where was I? Oh yes — first, the bad news. Three of our scout vehicles came up empty-handed. The fourth, the USS Osprey, was ambushed on the way to their search location. We received a distress call from her, stating she was under attack. She hasn't been heard from since."

The murmur grew in intensity. Admiral Carter raised his hand and said, "Let me finish."

"Did our rescue task force get underway?" Admiral Hornsby asked.

"Yes, it did. The force is following her distress beacon signals at this moment," Lewis said.

"What is the good news?" Admiral Robinson asked.

"We now have an idea as to where the pirates are holed up," Carter replied. "Even better, we know who Beauregard's mole is."

A chorus of voices rose almost in unison. "Who?"

"In due time," Carter said, "in due time. First, let me tell you what we did. Each of you received a copy of the orders and flight plans. But they're not identical. Each copy had three bogus flight plans and the proper flight plan for one search vehicle. Each of you got the right flight plan for a different vehicle. Hence, whoever had the right flight plan for the Osprey is the one who is the mole."

"Now wait a minute, Justin," Robinson said. "How can you be so sure it's someone in this room? One of the pilots or crew members could have slipped the info to Beauregard."

"The orders and flight plans, given to each pilot, were sealed and not to be opened until hours after their ships launched," Carter said. "Only the ones in this room — your committee, Admiral Robinson — saw these orders. You'll recall that you require us to pass any plans to take down Beauregard through this committee for approval."

"So, you don't even trust me," Robinson fumed. "I'll have your hide, you arrogant son of a bi—"

"You're welcome to my hide, but only after I have Morris's," Carter responded. "He's the mole!"

Morris laughed nervously and said, "Nice try, Carter. This little game with the orders you're playing doesn't prove anything."

"Oh yeah?" Carter said. "You thought it safe to pass the orders on because it involved multiple plans and ships. But you got sloppy. You used the same frequency in transmitting your data to the pirates once too often. We've been monitoring it, and what do you know? Your unique copy of the orders was picked up, just hours before the search teams launched. Grab him, Security!"

The security team rushed into the room. Morris stood up. Lewis jumped up and grabbed at Morris but only caught air. The Sergeant tried to tackle the standing image but only managed to upend Morris's chair.

Morris laughed and said, "Give it up, Carter. As you can see, they don't make holograms like they used to. Don't waste too much time looking for me. 'Cause the next time you'll see me will be in hell." Then his image disappeared.

# Battling Ghosts

*"War - An act of violence whose object is to constrain the enemy, to accomplish our will."- George Washington*

## Traveling Toward the Suspected Pirate Hideout

**B**arnabas shook his head in disgust and thought, *"So, we're going to war with the pirates;* he felt uncharacteristically grouchy. There wasn't one specific thing causing his mood. He just felt that things were not right. He was sitting in the pilot's seat of the Osprey, waiting for the task force to form into a battle formation. They were located near the last known position of the spy drone released by the Osprey when it was hiding on an asteroid.

He recalled the excitement in Matt's voice upon returning from a meeting with Captain Lewis and Admiral Carter. He and Matt were having breakfast together at Doug's Diner, a greasy spoon joint just a couple of blocks from NASA. Barnabas chuckled at the thought. *The captain was so excited, he addressed me by my first name.*

"Barnabas, we're finally going after Beauregard and his gang."

"For sure?"

51

"Yep, the spy drone we released found its way to the pirate's hideout. At least that's what the analysts at Langley believe."

"Sweet."

### Last Known Location of NASA Spy Drone

The cluster of asteroids stood out from the black sky like gray river rocks under a spotlight. The Osprey's flight crew prepared for battle as the whole task force approached the suspected pirate base amidst the asteroids.

The Major was, as Matt suspected, full of unrelated questions. He asked, "Why must we wear these awkward spacesuits and helmets? Isn't the bridge pressurized?"

"It is, Major. We wear the suits, so if we are hit in battle, and the bridge is suddenly depressurized, our suits will protect us." Marc answered.

"How?"

"External sensors on our suits sense if the outside pressure drops and activates the pressure system in the suits."

"Tell me about the crew, Sergeant."

Marc said, "No disrespect, Major, but I'd be more willing to discuss the crew if I had a better idea why you're so curious."

"I'm not at liberty to say much. Only that there is a hush-hush mission being planned. My boss, General Krackawhip, is considering using the Osprey and her crew to support this Army mission. She knows nothing of the crew."

Marc took a long breath, "Major, likewise, I'm not at liberty to say much about the dark missions performed by the Osprey and her crew. I can give you a quick background of each crew member and why they were handpicked by Captain Dirksen."

The word "handpicked" caught the Major's attention. "Go ahead. I'm listening."

"Hilda McDermott, the redhead sitting next to you, is not just a well-respected Botanist, which qualifies her to be a mission specialist. She is also an ex-Marine gunnery sergeant. As a gunnery sergeant, McDermott taught small arms marksmanship and advanced hand-to-hand combat techniques. She holds a black belt in Taekwondo. I like to call her the smiling assassin. She earned the silver star for her exploits during the Asteroid conflict."

The major nodded. "And Captain Dirksen talked her out of retirement?"

"The captain can be very persuasive. He wanted both of us to guard against potential boarders."

"Boarders in space? You're kidding."

"I kid you not. Just like the brigands, who sailed in the days of sailing ships, pirates love to board vessels and fight hand-to-hand."

"Okay. So, Gunny has the credentials to repel boarders. What're your credentials?"

"Before becoming a Geologist, I was a master sergeant in the Special Forces. My specialty was explosives. I also hold a black belt in karate. I'm a veteran of the Asteroid conflict, during which I had more than my share of up-close-and-personal fights with the enemy."

The major cocked his head. "Medals?"

"A couple. Mostly, I'm still alive and in one piece. Your next question is, 'why pick two old farts to repel boarders?' The answer is that Captain Dirksen wants NCOs that proved themselves to be aggressive and not squeamish when things turn ugly."

"Understood, Sarge. No one wants a 'young gun' with no combat experience in such a small unit if they can help it. But why are you and Gunny the only soldiers onboard? What if you're boarded by the enemy?"

"This ship is designed to funnel unwanted boarders into an area that is covered by two gun positions. These positions create a deadly kill zone, where any uninvited guests must pass through to get to the bridge. If needed, Gunny and I scramble to our stations from where we operate those guns remotely."

"Then you two should be there now."

"No, Major, now we are needed on the bridge to provide more eyes on the battle zone. Captain's orders, Sir."

The Major sat back, frowning, "The general won't be impressed."

"And I should care because …?" Marc shot back. Hilda, who was listening in, shook her head. *A less senior Noncom would never take a chance answering this Major the way Marc did*, she thought.

"I'll ignore your attitude, for now, Sergeant. Tell me about the others."

"Lieutenant Commander Barnabas Chidi Maalouf is our mission pilot. His specialty is flying long-haul freighters. He flew troop transports during the Lunar War and was awarded the 'flying cross' during the Asteroid conflicts."

"So, he's good?"

"Let's just say, Major, that when the battle starts, grab your air-sick bag. Some of the moves he'll pull are simply amazing — just hard on the body."

"What about her?" the Major pointed at Marci. "She's beautiful. Why she's—"

"Out of your league, Major," Marc interrupted. "First Lieutenant Marci Gonzales is our weapons officer. She may look like she stepped out of a fashion commercial, but her flying handle is 'Ice Queen.' It matches her personality. She finished top of her class at the academy and completed Top Gun training. Her weapon systems skills are impressive. She flew, with distinction, toward the end of the Asteroid Conflict. She also flew fighter cover for your unit's failed raid on Beauregard's old hideout. She took out two pirate fighters and saved troop transport Charlie's ass as it returned from the raid."

The Major winced. "I was on that transport."

"Then you owe her your life." Marc pointed at Josh. "There's Chief Joshua Torres. He's our technical flight officer. His job is to keep all our flight systems up and running. He also handles our shields and defensive weapons. He knows this class of cruisers so well, he led the team that developed the Osprey simulator. As an NCO, he was responsible for all the Academy's flight simulators."

"Is your captain any good?"

"Best damn captain in the fleet. He flew combat missions during the Lunar War and the Asteroid conflicts. He also taught at Top Gun. So, there you have it, Major. As good a crew as any in the fleet."

"We'll see, Sergeant. We'll see."

As ordered, Matt held the Osprey back to watch the battle unfold. It was a spectacle of flashing lights, glowing energy shields, and spaceships locked in a deadly dance across the black backdrop of space. Four pirate frigates rose from among the asteroid cluster to meet the task force. The Osprey's crew listened to the radio traffic. They heard that one task force frigate was dispatched to guard the troop carriers. They placed a landing party on the asteroid housing the suspected pirate base. Somehow the landing party could not locate the first base. It had disappeared before their eyes. The troop carriers took them to a second location with the same results.

The view became cluttered as the pirates released dozens of drones to attack the task force ships. With all the firing going on during the battle, surprisingly few hits were scored by either side. Barnabas wondered, *are we fighting an imaginary fleet or what?* His thoughts were interrupted by Lieutenant Gonzales.

"Captain?" Marci asked. "Do you think it suspicious that a fifth pirate frigate is standing off and making no effort to join the fight?"

"Where?" Matt asked.

"Look at the far end of the battle zone. Use your range finder's magnification, and you'll see it."

"I see it now, Lieutenant. It looks as if it was relegated to the back of their formation, like us. Why do you think it strange?" Matt asked.

"For one thing, it's a frigate, not a drone, Sir. The admiral herself said she uses drone feeds for a battle zone overview. Wouldn't you expect the pirate to at least go into stealth mode and look like a drone?"

Barnabas agreed with Marci. "Lieutenant Gonzales is right, Sir. The way the battle's going against the pirates, why's that frigate holding back?"

"Chief Torres, patch me through to the Admiral on a secure link," Matt said.

"You've got it, Sir."

Barnabas was becoming anxious. Being a passive observer wore on his nerves just as much as it did on his captain's. *I've got a bad feeling something's not right. Beauregard is too intelligent to be caught in the open like this. His fleet's too passive. They maneuver, but their firing is ineffective. If I didn't know better, I'd say we're fighting ghost ships. This must be a diversion. I bet he's planning to strike us where we don't expect it.*

With the secure commlink finally up, Matt began speaking with the vice-admiral. He left his link open to Barnabas so he could hear the conversation.

"Ma'am, Dirksen here. I also have my second in command patched in. We've noticed a pirate frigate located on the fringe of the battle zone. It's barely moved, which makes us curious as to why it's holding back. Also, it's not attempting to hide its presence."

"Yes, we did observe it earlier. But haven't been tracking it. You say it hasn't made any effort to engage us?"

"That's right, Ma'am."

"We're locked in a strange battle. It sounds messy, but we aren't taking significant hits, nor are we damaging any of their ships. This is beginning to feel like a ruse."

"A ruse with holograms, Ma'am?"

"Maybe. If so, the holograms are far more sophisticated than anything I've seen before. We need to gather in our landing craft and reassemble. These maneuvers may be designed to distract us from the real target. If there're no major changes, we'll visit that frigate."

"Request permission to check out the lone frigate, Ma'am."

"What do you have in mind, Captain?"

"We'll skirt the battle zone and work our way behind him. Then we'll sandwich him in, Ma'am."

"It's a good plan. Permission granted."

*At least we finally get to do something*, Barnabas thought.

"Commander, set a course around this mess and put us on course to come behind Marci's frigate," Matt ordered. "Chief, when we're almost there, take a snapshot of the pirate's position. Then, Lieutenant, activate the cloaking device. I want to start this excursion by going dark."

"Aye, Sir," both Marci and Josh said.

Barnabas smiled. "Aye, Sir, now we're talking."

"A smile, Commander?" Matt asked.

"Yes, Sir. Life's a journey—"

"And we're about to take a side road," Matt interrupted.

## Behind Enemy Lines

"We're in position, directly behind the pirate frigate, if my course was correct, and it hasn't moved," Barnabas said.

"Thank you, Commander," Matt replied. "Chief, take us from dark to stealth mode, on my word. Five, four, three, two, one, GO!"

"Switching to stealth mode. Now in stealth mode. All systems are online, Sir." Josh said.

Barnabas jumped as the pirate frigate appeared immediately in front of the Osprey. *Crap, it must have drifted back some after we took the Osprey dark,* he thought. "Sir, I think we're too close to our target to start shooting safely."

"You think, Commander? You have my permission to move us straight back for a couple of hundred meters," Matt said.

"Yes, Sir. I'm moving us backward now .... Now at 200 meters, I'll be stopping—"

But the Osprey did not stop. "You said you were stopping, Commander. What's going on?" Matt asked.

"I don't know, Sir. She's not responding," Barnabas said. *This can't be happening again,* he thought, as he set the engines to full-forward. The Osprey shuddered, and he eased off the throttle. The Osprey picked up speed, still traveling in reverse.

"Do you need help, Commander?" Matt asked.

Drops of sweat formed on Barnabas's forehead as he struggled with the controls. "Yes, Sir! She's trying awfully hard to roll."

Matt grabbed his controls. Working together, they kept the Osprey from flying completely out of control. Still, they could not keep her from accelerating at an alarming rate, slamming the occupants hard against their harnesses. *Been here before, and it wasn't much fun then,* Barnabas thought, as he struggled against the Osprey's twists and turns. The craft itself groaned under the pressure. Barely staying conscious, Barnabas saw streaks of colored lights passing by the vehicle's windows. *This is like flying backward into exploding fireworks,* he thought while fighting the urge to throw up. As quickly as it started, the ship decelerated, slamming its occupants against their seats.

"What's happening?" The Major asked, after retching into an air-sick bag.

"Wormhole, Major. You'd best reach for a second bag. This could be intense," Marc said.

Finally, the Osprey was spat backward out of the wormhole and came to a complete stop.

"I hate going through wormholes!" Hilda declared.

Her voice broke the silence on board the Osprey. Its crew members were composing themselves from the unexpected trip.

"Backwards, no less," Marc agreed.

The Major began to retch into his air-sick bag again.

"Where are we?" Marci asked.

"I've no idea, and I sure don't like the looks of our welcoming committee," Barnabas said. "It seems we're surrounded by pirate cruisers."

"Captain, I count four bogeys in total on my sensors, and we're in the dead center of their formation," Marci said.

Barnabas felt a chill run up his spine as he heard Matt say, "Dammit! It's a trap, and we backed right into it!"

# A Surprise

*"No one is so brave that he is not disturbed by something unexpected."*

*- Julius Caesar*

### Unknown - Other Side of a Wormhole

Matt frowned and commanded, "Chief, take us dark now!"

"Activating the cloaking device, Sir."

"I'm sure those bogeys spotted us before we went dark," Barnabas said.

"Take us straight up half a click, Commander," Matt said.

"We're flying blind, Sir," Barnabas said, reminding Matt that the Osprey was still in cloak mode.

"I'm aware we are. Just moving in case, the bogeys are targeting our position."

"Did I see right? We're looking at four heavily armed spaceships?" Josh asked.

"They're Charlie class heavy cruisers," Marci said.

"Good eyes, Lieutenant," Barnabas said.

Hilda asked, "Why didn't they just blast the hell out of us when we first came out of the wormhole?"

"I'll bet they were expecting us to be one of their ships, running from our task force. They'd let it pass by. Then they'd welcome our ships in turn," Barnabas said.

Matt nodded. "You're right, Commander. They're just hanging out on this side of the wormhole to take our guys out. Jacques will lead our guys on a chase through the wormhole. They'll come out on this side right into the middle of the kill zone set up by these jokers."

Marc gave a low whistle. "Doesn't seem like a sporting way to fight. The odds are all in their favor."

"We'll just have to level the playing field," Matt said.

Barnabas said, "Four of 'em to one of us. Interesting challenge, Sir. We've practiced one-on-one and one-on-two at a time, never one-on-four at a time. What're you thinking?"

"I think we'll execute the way we practiced one-on-two. Then we'll simply improvise."

Marci said, "I only have one regret, Sir."

"That would be?"

"There are only four bogeys out there. If there were a fifth, I could make Ace in one battle."

"You forget — another bogie will come screaming through that wormhole, at some point, during our engagement."

Marci smiled at the thought. "You just made my day, Sir."

"Questioning the odds, Commander?" Matt asked when he saw Barnabas shaking his head.

Barnabas smiled, "I am, Sir. It doesn't seem like only four bogeys are enough to make it a fair fight."

Matt chuckled and thought, *I wish I had the same confidence as Maalouf*. Then he said, "Chief, are you ready to take a snapshot of our surroundings?"

"Yes, Sir."

"Good. Now, just like we practiced, when we switch from cloaked to stealth, shoot the snapshot to everyone's monitor. Lieutenant, on my word, switch to stealth. Commander, once you confirm the snapshot, go dark. Then move the Osprey directly behind the snapshot of the nearest bogie. When we're in position, give the word. Upon the Commander's mark, Lieutenant put us back in stealth mode. I'll target the bogie. Once I do, Lieutenant, you give him hell."

Matt's directives were met by a chorus of "Aye, Captain."

Matt took a deep breath, "Okay, on my word — five, four, three, two, one, GO!"

"Switching to stealth mode. Now in stealth mode," Marci announced.

"Location and proximity snapshot is taken," Josh said. "Image on its way."

"Image received," Barnabas reported. "I'm switching cloaking mode back on … and … We're dark now. I'm moving the Osprey toward our new position now, Sir."

The sudden acceleration of the Osprey threw everyone hard against their seats. As the minutes slowly ticked by, Matt could feel the tension on the bridge rising. *I sure hope our target doesn't move much.* He felt his heart start to pound. He fought the urge to ask how much longer. *It would never do for me, as ship's captain, to express nervousness. Still …."*

"Are we there yet?" Josh asked in a kid-like voice.

Barnabas broke into laughter. "Only a hundred miles to go, Kid."

Matt could feel that exchange drain his tension. He chuckled along with other crew members. The Osprey screeched to a stop, throwing the crew against their harnesses.

"We're positioned directly behind the snapshot of our first bogie," Barnabas said.

"Bringing us into stealth mode, Sir," Marci said. Again, time seemed to slow down. Finally, Marci said, "We're in stealth mode. All systems are online."

Matt fed the snapshot coordinates of the bogie into the targeting system. Then he visually confirmed his aim. To his relief, the bogie had moved very little. Matt ran a slight adjustment and said, "Give 'em hell, Lieutenant!"

Marcy started firing her weapons at the rear engine of the bogie. Matt watched in awe as the engine compartments of the bogie glowed orange-red and began falling apart. His plan worked! They had caught the bogie with its rear shields down.

"Direct hit!" Marci exclaimed as she changed her fire control and zeroed in on a second ship.

The crew cheered, and Barnabas said, "Great shooting, Lieutenant."

Alarms went off in Matt's head. *They'll see where the shooting is coming from. We've got to move!* "Chief. Shields up! Take a snapshot of our surroundings! Lieutenant, ceasefire! Make us dark after we get that snapshot! Commander, turn hard to port and gun it!" He was almost shouting his commands. *God, I hope I'm not too late*, he thought.

The Osprey shuddered from impacts. But Josh got the shields up in time to absorb the hits. Matt's anxiety was relieved by the jolt of the Osprey accelerating out of harm's way.

"Snapshot is taken, Sir," Josh said.

"Changing from stealth mode to full cloak, Sir," Marci said.

"Good. Once we're fully dark, Commander, change course to drop us thirty degrees off our current course."

"Aye, Captain," Barnabas said.

"Next, we'll finish off that second bogie from the side if we need to. Commander, bring us around to the side of the second bogie, based on its last snapshot position."

Matt took a deep breath and exhaled slowly. His head was spinning with the possibilities and questions about where all the pirate ships were. *Calm down—one thing at a time. Just follow the same plan this time around. Take the rest of them one at a time. You can do this,* he calmed himself.

His thoughts were interrupted by the Osprey's sudden deceleration. "We're in position, pointing at the side of our bogie if the snapshot's correct, and he hasn't moved, Sir," Barnabas said.

"Good, Commander. Okay, everyone, second verse same as the first. We'll follow the same pattern as before. Lieutenant, you're up first."

"Bringing us into stealth mode, Sir," Marci said. Matt started to drum his fingers, caught himself, and stopped. Eventually, Marci said, "We're in stealth mode, Sir. All systems are online."

Matt fed the snapshot coordinates of the bogie into the targeting system. Then he visually confirmed his aim. "We're spot on. Fire at will, Lieutenant! Chief, start a series of snapshots. Sarge and Gunny assess the damage to the first bogie if you can see it. Commander, check on the final two bogeys."

Marci started firing her weapons into the side of the pirate ship. At first, her fire seemed ineffectual. *He must have side shields up,* Matt thought, "Give it all you can, Lieutenant. Same spot."

"His shields must be up, Sir," she said. Without warning, the side door flew off the pirate ship, debris escaped through the hole, and the cargo bay began to glow red.

"Good shooting, Lieutenant. Now disengage. Chief, throw our shields up and take the last snapshot. Commander, take us straight up, now!"

"But Captain—" Marci started to object.

Matt interrupted, "We've done enough damage to knock it out of this fight. Take us dark immediately."

"Aye, Sir," Marci said. "Taking the Osprey dark now."

"Don't worry, Lieutenant. I'm counting that as your second kill today," Matt said.

The Osprey began to shudder from many hits. Yet the shields held.

Marci smiled as she announced, "We're totally dark now."

"Good. Commander, take us back to our original position."

"Aye, Captain," Barnabas said.

"That should give us a little breathing room. Damage report?"

Hilda said, "Sir, the first bogie is drifting and on fire. The Sarge and I saw several escape pods descending toward a cloud-shrouded planet."

"Good. That's a definite kill for the Lieutenant. Commander?"

"Sir, one of the two remaining bogeys is tracking us as best it can. The other is staying at its station, guarding the wormhole exit."

"Hmm ... Chief, let's replay, and analyze all our snapshots."

"Aye, Sir. It looks like that third bogie's looking for us, in stealth mode. It's pretty much locked in on our signature even though it's only the size of a drone," Josh said.

"Or is it calculating where we are when it sees us firing on the other drones?" Matt wondered.

Josh said, "That's got to be how they find us, Sir. It looks like when we fire, they move directly toward us and begin firing. Then when we go dark, they stop firing. They hold up and wait for us to show ourselves."

"Same pattern both times, Chief?"

"Yes, same pattern both times, Captain."

"Space fighting 101, everyone — never repeat your attack pattern a second time," Matt said. He was now in his zone as captain of a fighting ship. His thoughts were clear and uncluttered. The whole battle was slowing down in his mind. He was thinking several moves ahead. "Here's what we're going to do. We're going to look like we're repeating our first pattern. But—"

Barnabas's chuckle interrupted him.

"And the source of your amusement would be, Commander?"

"But we'll play a little game of chicken with bogie number three."

"Damn, Commander. How the hell did you know?" Matt asked.

"Sir, we've flown together too many years in too many battles. You've made the game of chicken an art form."

"Well, you're right, Commander. Are you ready for it?"

"You bet, Sir," Barnabas replied. "If the good Lieutenant shoots straight, I won't even flinch."

Just then, the Osprey decelerated, pitching everyone against their harnesses. "We're in position, Sir," Barnabas said.

"Good, Commander. Slide us behind the bogie that, according to our snapshot, is guarding the wormhole."

"Aye, Sir."

This time, Matt calmly waited for the Osprey to gain the proper position. "Bring us to stealth mode, Lieutenant."

"Aye, Sir."

Once all systems were back online, Matt fed the bogie's snapshot coordinates into the targeting system and visually confirmed his aim. As he suspected, this bogie was holding its position guarding the wormhole exit. Matt ran a slight adjustment and said, "Lieutenant, fire at will. Chief, raise our shields and start taking snapshots of our surroundings as they relate to that third bogie."

Marcy started firing her weapons into the rear engine of the stationary pirate ship. "I'm hitting the target, Sir, to no effect."

"That's okay, Lieutenant. I figured he'd have his shields up. Besides, we're saving him for later. Right now, I want that third bogie."

"You got 'im, Sir. He found us from our shooting and is starting to hit us with his weapons."

"Good. Snapshots, Chief? Lieutenant, ceasefire, and take us dark."

"Snapshots taken, Sir," Josh said.

"Changing from stealth mode to full cloak, Sir," Marci said.

"Good. Once we're fully dark, Commander—"

Barnabas interrupted, "Change course to send us straight at the third bogie, Sir."

"Excellent, you read my mind."

"Yes, Sir. Great minds think … ah you know the rest." Under Barnabas's coaxing, the Osprey leapt forward, heading straight for the third pirate ship.

Losing its target when the Osprey went dark, the pirate ship stopped firing and slowed, waiting for its next chance to engage. Using the last set of snapshots, Barnabas projected where the pirate ship would be when he arrived in front of it. "The trick is to be close, just not too close," he said.

Matt said, "Here's the plan. Lieutenant, on the Commander's mark, take us from fully cloaked to normal. No stealth mode this time. Commander, remember to factor in the time it takes to get all systems back online. Chief, at your first opportunity, bring up our front shields. As soon as our systems are online, Lieutenant fire directly at their bridge with everything you've got. Keep firing, no matter what you see. When you can no longer fire at their bridge, go after their rear engines. Commander, we're in your hands."

A big smile spread across Barnabas's face. "Aye, Captain. Buckle up, everyone. We're almost in position." This time there was no stopping. Instead, there was a slight acceleration.

Barnabas said, "Lieutenant, on my mark, deactivate our cloaking device. Three, two, one, MARK."

"Deactivating now, Commander. Systems will be online in five, four, three, two, one. We're online." Marci began firing.

"Shields up," Josh said. Then he gasped at how close they were to the enemy ship. "Commander, aren't we a little too—"

"Close to engage?" Barnabas interrupted as he accelerated. "Not for a friendly game of chicken."

"Crap, I forgot!" Matt exclaimed as he lunged to deactivate the Osprey's anti-collision system.

Marci also gasped but continued firing at the enemy's bridge. The sudden appearance of the Osprey, flying headlong toward a head-on collision, stunned the pirate captain. He was slow to reactivate all his shields and to start firing at the Osprey. Instead, he followed his instinctive reaction to make an emergency turn up and to the right. His move was just in time to avoid a fatal head-on crash. As hoped, it also exposed his unshielded underside to Marci's firing, which cut through the bottom of the engine compartment and engines. All this was done while the Osprey was so close that the pirate ship's debris bounced off its hull, sounding like rain on a tin roof.

"Well flown, Commander. Circle behind. Lieutenant, ceasefire and take us to stealth mode. Chief, bring up shields all around. Sarge, Gunny, damage report on that bogie," Matt said.

"Sir, the bogie is drifting. It looks like the engine compartment is on fire. The engines have significant damage. They'll not be running any time soon. There's debris floating in front of the bogie. The lieutenant must have blown holes in the bridge. I see escape pods leaving the ship."

"Your third kill of the day, Lieutenant. Good shooting. Time to get after that last bogie," Matt said. "Start taking your snapshots, Chief."

"Aye. Uh, Sir? I can't locate the final bogie," Josh said.

# The Capture

*"All warfare is based on deception." - Unknown*

## Unknown - Other Side of a Wormhole

Matt glared and Josh. "Hell and damnation!" The words slipped out of his mouth. He hadn't intended for that to happen. The surprise of losing sight of his last adversary caused the words to escape his lips.

"Did they go dark?" Marci asked.

"No, Lieutenant. That model cruiser doesn't have a cloaking device," Matt said.

"Maybe they jumped into the wormhole to escape," Josh said.

"They may be slimeballs, but they're no cowards. No, they're here and are hunting us right now," Barnabas said.

Matt agreed, "The Commander's right. And until we find them, they have the advantage. Be sure our shields stay up, Chief. Are you sure you don't see anything?"

Marci said, "I see nothing, Sir. Oh wait — I see a swarm of drones heading our way. Do you think he can go into stealth mode?"

Matt said, "The Lieutenant's right. I forgot — they can't go completely dark, but that model cruiser is the first one that can go stealth. I'd bet a cup of coffee that bogie is in stealth mode, following its drones in. Commander, get us behind what's left of bogie three, now!"

Hearing the urgency in Matt's voice, Barnabas accelerated the Osprey, slamming the astronauts against their seats. They were then pushed against their harnesses as he maneuvered hard to put the stalled pirate vessel between him and the oncoming swarm of drones.

"Couldn't we just go dark?" the Major asked.

"That's what they want us to do. Even if we're fully cloaked, we're still here, and the drones will blindly bounce off us. All that pirate has to do is wait for the bouncing drones to give our position away," Josh said.

The Osprey got behind the disabled pirate ship just as the swarm of drones arrived. As soon as they started bouncing off the cruiser, the last pirate ship opened fire. The Osprey crew were amazed at how damaging and unmerciful the pirate's firing was. They could see that a few escape pods (that had been slow to leave) were destroyed.

"No time to gawk. Commander, dive like we just bounced off that bogie. After we've cleared this mess, book it to where we can safely fire on the back of the drone swarm. I'll bet that's where the bogie is hiding."

"Aye, Sir."

The Osprey crew was jerked around with such violence that the Major needed a third air-sick bag as Barnabas guided the Osprey through a series of maneuvers that simulated a ricocheting drone. Then he accelerated toward the back of the diminishing cloud of drones. Everyone heard the metallic slap of a couple of drones striking the Osprey.

"Do we release our drones, Sir?" Marci asked.

"That's a good idea, Lieutenant. Release them now and send them toward the rear of the pirate's pack. We'll circle and flank them instead of going in behind them. When you see them bounce and fly erratically, you'll know where to aim."

"Aye, Sir."

"Shield status?"

"Up and at 100 percent," Josh said.

"Good. When we engage, direct most of our shield power to our front. This'll be a head-on, brute force fight."

Marci began firing. "I've found the range and am hitting the bogie. Of course, its shields are up, so I've not hurt it yet."

"Keep it up, Lieutenant," Matt urged.

The Pirate vessel turned into the path of the Osprey and began returning fire. "We're taking hits, but our shields are holding, Sir," Josh reported.

"Good! Commander, keep us on course to pass the bogie on our starboard side."

"Will do, Sir. We're approaching our kill zone," Barnabas said.

"Kill zone?" the Major asked Marc.

"It's the area that is so close to the target that if the target were to explode, we'd go with it," Marc answered.

Marci asked, "Should I keep firing, Sir?"

"Yes, and I want you to continue firing while we pass through the zone, Lieutenant. Concentrate on their bridge. If we strike home there, we shouldn't get hurt too bad by the debris."

"Aye, Sir."

"Why take such a risk? Why not standoff and fire from a distance?" the Major asked Marc.

"There's a second spacecraft heading this way. If our captain doesn't end this soon, we'll be fighting two enemy spaceships instead of just one," Marc said.

"That makes sense."

71

"Each ship's captain has a preferred way to fight. This is Captain Dirksen's," Marc said. "Of course, Major, pirate captains have a different preferred way of fighting."

"What's that?" the Major asked.

"Hand-to-hand," Marc answered.

Barnabas said, "Bogie's pulling up. I think it's trying to protect its bridge by passing over us."

"Captain, they're too close for my angle of fire to have any effect," Marci said.

"Understood, Lieutenant. Ceasefire."

Just then, invisible hands pushed the two spacecraft together. The Osprey's crew heard a thud and felt a tremor as both ships locked up.

"What the hell?" Matt asked.

"Tractor beam, Sir. From the pirate ship. It's locked us together," Josh reported.

"Crap! They're not supposed to have one. Must be retro-fitted," Barnabas said.

"Sarge, Gunny, prepare to repel boarders," Matt said.

"Boarders?" the Major asked.

"We need to welcome some uninvited guests," Marc answered the Major as he pushed himself toward his battle station.

"We're in position, Sir," Hilda reported.

"Good. We've got to end this fast 'cause we're running out of time. It won't be long before Beauregard comes blasting through the wormhole, and we'll be fighting two bogeys at once," Matt said. "Everyone, switch to personal O2. Chief, bring our life support system down and kill its connection to our cargo bay."

"Done, Sir."

"Sarge, Gunny, take the boarders out from your defensive positions. Then immediately mount a counterattack," Matt ordered.

"Your plan for our counterattack, Sir?" Hilda asked.

"Improvise," Matt replied.

Marc laughed, "Typical officer. Tells us what to do and 'lets' us figure out how to go about it."

Hilda said, "That's why he needs us. We know how to improvise."

The Osprey shook as the pirates blew open the top hatch, which fell to the floor with a resounding thud. The tractor beam force kept the pirate ship and Osprey so tight together, there was no decompression of the Osprey's cargo bay. The boarding party dropped several chemical grenades into the bay.

"We've been breached, and the pirates have dropped in gas," Hilda reported.

"Hold your fire until the smoke clears and the landing party's in the cargo bay," Matt said.

"Roger that, Sir," Marc said.

As soon as the gas cleared, a landing party of a half dozen pirates dropped into the cargo bay. Marc and Hilda cut loose with a devastating rain of bullets from their positions, covering the unlucky pirates. All of the first boarders caught in the crossfire were killed.

"Time to improvise, Gunny," Marc said as they met in the corridor just outside the cargo bay. He tossed her an RPG (rocket-propelled grenade) launcher, just like the one he was holding.

"Going old school, are we?" Hilda said, as she grabbed the RPG launcher and opened the hatch to the cargo bay.

They jumped through the doorway. As Hilda secured the hatch behind her, Marc found a cargo strap and used it to restrain himself. "Follow my lead," he said.

As Hilda strapped herself to the bulkhead, Marc fired his RPG straight through the open hatch into the pirate ship above. The explosion reverberated through both vessels. It was matched by a second explosion caused by Hilda's RPG. The combined damage of the RPGs fractured the pirate's hull with a gaping hole. The sudden decompression swept every loose body, living or dead, through the pirate's breached hull into space. As soon as the pressure in the cargo bay dropped to zero, Marc and Hilda reloaded their RPGs and pushed themselves into the pirate ship's midsection hallway. Marc fired an RPG at the door that he hoped led to the tractor beam generator. Hilda followed suit. Again, the combined explosions had the desired effect. The pirate ship began to drift away from the Osprey. The duo quickly dropped to the top of the Osprey and grabbed hold.

"Sarge, Gunny, head to our port side portal. We'll leave the light on," Matt said. "Chief, you know what to do. Lieutenant, resume firing as soon as they clear the kill zone. This time, concentrate on their engines."

Josh opened the external portside door. Then he pushed himself to the portal and waited. Once the duo had entered the portal chamber and secured the exterior door, Josh opened the interior door and welcomed them back onboard.

"All aboard, Captain," Josh said.

"Thanks, Chief. Buckle up, all. Commander, tail that bastard as close as you can until the Lieutenant takes him out. Oh, and Chief, when you get a chance, bring our life support system online, less the cargo hold, so we can get back to cabin air."

Try as he might, the pirate could not outmaneuver Barnabas. With his shields also damaged, he could not deflect Marci's firing.

"The bogie's engines are glowing red, Sir," Marci said. "There're the flames. Oh, wow — what a beautiful explosion. Their engines are gone."

"Good shooting. Now take out the bridge and the life support system just above and behind it. Between the bridge decompression and loss of life support, the crew will have a little over an hour — two tops —

74

to evacuate and make it to safety. They'll have no choice but to give up the fight like the others," Matt said.

Marci continued to fire until debris was seen coming from the pirate's bridge.

"Four bogeys down, Lieutenant. Just one short of an Ace. I'm pleased with your work," Matt said. "Also, well done, Sarge and Gunny. I like the way you two improvise. Commander, move us to the initial position of the first bogie. We will wait for Mr. Beauregard to arrive and give him an appropriate welcome."

"Such as?" Barnabas asked.

"Such as, once two of us confirm that the first ship through the wormhole is not one of ours, Lieutenant Gonzales starts firing directly at the bridge and life support system. Until it decompresses."

"Their shields?" Marci asked.

"He's expecting four friendly ships on this side of the wormhole. I'm guessing that all his energy will be given to his rear shields," Matt said. "Commander, hold our position as it relates to Beauregard's ship. I'll try and negotiate a surrender. If he doesn't buy it, we'll maintain contact, engage, and continue to engage until the task force arrives."

"Roger that, Sir. What do you plan to say?" Barnabas asked.

"I plan to let Lieutenant Gonzales's shooting do most of my talking."

"Well put, Sir," Barnabas said. Marci just smiled and said nothing.

"Chief, aside from keeping our shields up, contact and orient our ships as they arrive. I'm sure they'll be wondering what just happened and where they are."

"Aye, Sir," Josh replied.

"Sir, I spot a bogie coming out of the wormhole," Marc said. "It's not one of ours."

"Can anyone else confirm?" Matt asked.

"I can, Sir," Marci said. "I have the range. It's definitely the one we got behind just before being sucked into the wormhole."

"Then fire away, Lieutenant."

"With pleasure, Sir. Here's hoping its shields are down."

They were. Within seconds, debris was flying out of the bridge. Matt thought he saw the pirate ship shudder as Marci concentrated her fire on the life support system. Finally, the pirate ship's shields came up, and she switched to stealth mode. Marci ceased her firing but continued pinging the vessel with her range finder. The pirate ship moved quickly to its right and began to drop below the Osprey. Barnabas matched it move for move, guarding it, much like he would a basketball player.

"Chief Torres, patch me through to all known pirate frequencies."

"Done, Sir."

"Monsieur Beauregard, this is Captain Matthew Dirksen, of the USS Osprey. As you know, we have your range. What you don't know is that my weapons officer destroyed your four cruisers. For the moment, it's just our two ships. If you wish to continue the fight, I'll be happy to accommodate you. Just remember, the rest of our task force will be arriving shortly. Those odds do not bode well for you. If you choose to surrender, ping us three times with your range finder, and drop your shields."

Just then, the task force leader's ship came through the wormhole. When Josh told the task force leader what just happened to her craft and who the Osprey was facing, she moved her frigate below and to the rear of the pirate's cruiser. Then she activated her range finder, actively pinging the pirate's rear shields.

The pirate's progress slowed as he seemed to assess the battlefield. Then, the pirate ship's engines died, its shields came down, and the Osprey was hit with three distinct pings.

"Congratulations, Capitaine Dirksen. I, Jacques Beauregard, surrender my ship to you."

"Thank you, Monsieur Beauregard. I must defer to my superior, Admiral Garrison. She is the leader of our task force. She'll be sending a boarding party to assist with your evacuation."

With that, the Osprey pulled back a distance. From there, her crew watched a boarding party take control of Beauregard's ship. Josh kept busy contacting and orienting other task force ships as they arrived. Each one appeared out of the wormhole differently. But they all ended up in the same space. Josh had to urge them to move quickly, out of the path of the trailing ships. All the ship commanders were, at first, disoriented. Some were defiant and unbelieving. All were air-sick. There was one near miss, as a transport vessel was slow to move out of the path of a frigate.

When all the task force ships were safely through the wormhole, Josh leaned back at his station, exhausted. "Whew! I'm glad that's over."

Barnabas chuckled. "Keeping your day job, Son? Not wanting to become an Air Traffic Controller?"

"Felt more like a lifeguard at a swimming pool, trying to get crazy kids out of the diving zone," Josh said. "This task is definitely above my pay grade! I—"

A message cut Josh's comments short. "Admiral about to board the Osprey," it announced.

The message was followed by a hologram of Vice-Admiral Garrison appearing on the bridge. "Well played, Captain Dirksen. You had me worried when you failed to check in with me. Now I know why."

Matt saluted. "My apologies, Ma'am. We were unexpectedly distracted."

"I see. From the four pirate hulks' condition, I'd say you've put your time away from our initial battle to good use. Good shooting, Lieutenant Gonzales. You almost made Ace. As for you, Chief, I need to remind you that your job description includes a clause which states, 'other duties as assigned.' I believe that gives no regard to your pay grade."

"You heard that?" a distressed Josh asked.

"Every word, Chief. You forgot to kill your mike before speaking with your commander."

"My bad," Josh groaned and clicked his mike off.

The admiral turned back to Matt. "It's been said that 'All warfare is based on deception.' You've just taken deception to the next level. I'm impressed."

"How'd you fare on the other side of the wormhole, Ma'am?" Matt asked.

"When we finally got a clear picture of the battle zone, we knew it was a ruse."

"What gave it away?"

"Our ground troops finally found several installations. One was an abandoned staging area. It wasn't set up with any kind of permanent housing. The other was controlling a lot of the holograms we were fighting. The final installation was the center controlling the dozens of drones we had to fight. The pirates were shifty. The drones were real enough and dangerous. All the pirate ships, but one, were holograms. We finally took out the one real frigate and the station controlling the holograms. That left only the pirate cruiser. We gathered our ground troops, lined up, and took after it. My ship was almost on top of it when it just vanished."

"We didn't follow. We held up because we thought Baregaurd had a special cloaking device like the Osprey. We began a careful search with our sensors. Then a drone appeared, sending out a distress signal. It claimed to come from the Osprey. We began to follow it and ended up getting drawn into the wormhole. Once I got a feel for what was happening here, I sent a drone back to notify the supply ships. They followed. Don't worry, Chief. You won't need to play traffic controller anymore."

"What are our orders now, Admiral?" Matt asked.

"For now, patrol the area in case of any more surprises. I'm sending one frigate to follow the landing craft and escape pods to see where they'll land. My guess is that's where the pirates' actual base of operations is located. Once the supply ships arrive, I'll organize an assault to take out the base."

"Sounds good, Admiral. Although, I'm wondering why you don't act surprised at finding that wormholes exist," Matt said.

"When you've been at this game as long as I have, you'll find a lot of things don't add up the way you thought. I'm signing off for now. Again, Captain, well done."

"Thank you, Admiral," Matt said as he reflected on all that just happened.

His thoughts were interrupted by Josh. "Captain, I'm running through the database of star systems and think I've got a hit."

"A what?"

"I think we're in the Kepler 186 Star system. The planet below us seems to be Kepler 186f, Sir," Josh said.

"Really? That star's over 500 light-years from Earth," Marci said.

"Yeah. Here it says: 'Kepler 186 is in the constellation Cygnus, 550 light-years from Earth."

"Seems this little wormhole we've been through carried us a lot farther from home than we thought," Barnabas said.

Matt asked, "Are you sure?"

"Kepler 186 is a Red Dwarf star. It's relatively cooler than our Sun. It has five planets. Kepler 186f is the only one in the inhabitable zone. It's slightly larger than Earth. Judging from the cloud cover we see, it must have lots of water," Marci said.

"How're you suddenly the expert on these things, Lieutenant?" Matt asked.

"It's covered in most astronomy classes. This is the first Earth-like planet ever discovered. While more have been located since, this is the first, Sir."

"Do you think when this operation is over, we might drop in and check it out before returning home, Sir?" Hilda asked.

"I can't promise. If we can wrap things up without further damage, I'll see what I can do, Gunny."

The Major, who was quiet as the Osprey confronted Jacques Beauregard, spoke up. "Captain, I need to speak with you. Preferably in private."

Matt replied, "This battle's not over yet, Major. We're only paused—"

"I understand, Captain. I'm asking on behalf of your mission controller and my general."

"In that case, follow me to the Crew Compartment." Matt released his harness and pushed himself off the bridge.

"Damn name-dropper," Marc said after the captain and Major had left the bridge.

After a brief period, Matt returned without the major. "Chief, patch me through to Admiral Garrison on a secure link."

"Aye, Captain. Is everything okay?"

"Will be when I speak with the admiral."

"She's on the line now, looking for you, Sir."

"Hi Admiral, you wanted to speak with me about a message?" Matt asked.

She answered, "Our techs figured out how to send and receive signals through the wormhole. Understood?"

*How'd they do that?* Josh wondered.

She continued, "Mission Control wants to speak with you directly. So link up with them as soon as possible."

"Will do, Ma'am," Matt replied. "Chief, hop on and work with the admiral's tech to patch me through to Captain Wright."

Josh's conversation with the other techs went something like this: "Hey Chief, Torres here. Tell me what to do to get patched through to Mission Control. Yeah. We're configured on our end. Do your magic. Perfect. Thanks, Chief."

The conversation, and Josh's informality, versus the captain's formal, almost stiff manner, brought a smile to Barnabas's face. "Well done, Chief," he said.

"Thanks, Commander. I'm linking Captain Wright in now, Captain."

The crew couldn't hear what Lewis Wright was saying. They did hear Matt's side of the conversation.

"What the hell is going on, Captain Wright?"

"I gathered that, from what your Major Jerk told me."

"You bet I don't trust his word. I don't even like the bast—"

"Calm down? How can I? You're pulling us out with no reason!"

"Yeah, I get that. What I don't get is what could be so important that we can't be allowed to finish this—"

"No, I agree that the task force can finish up without our—"

"Yes, the Osprey's been damaged. But it's minimal."

Hilda and Marc exchanged knowing looks, Barnabas chuckled, Josh rolled his eyes, and Marci shook her head. A gaping hole where the top hatch used to be, a cargo compartment in disarray, a partially compromised life-support system, and no way to access the engine compartment without taking a spacewalk was hardly their idea of minimal damage.

"You're taking the major's assessment over mine? He's a wimp."

"No, it's the task force leader's assessment?"

"She saw that? Crap."

"What could possibly be so important that it can't wai—"

"Yes, I understand, Sir."

"But—"

"Aye, Sir, We're on our way home."

Matt sighed, "Chief, patch me through, on a secure link, to the admiral. I need to tell her we're being required to return to base and to wish her success. Commander, when I'm done speaking with the admiral, take us home."

"Aye, Sir," Barnabas said. "This doesn't sound good."

"No, it doesn't, Commander. No, it doesn't."

Marci said, "Looking on the bright side, Sir, they know us on a first-name basis at the repair depot."

"Not funny, Lieutenant," Matt said.

"Not even a little, Sir?"

"Not even, Lieutenant."

Barnabas opened his mouth to agree with Marci. Catching the captain's look, Barnabas thought better than saying anything. *Methinks that we're heading into something worse than the captain is letting on.*

### Doug's Diner - Houston, Texas

"It was one heckuva battle, if I do say so myself," Barnabas said.

The Osprey's pilot and her captain were back in Houston. They were just finishing up a hearty breakfast at Doug's Diner.

Matt smiled. "Best piece of flying I've ever seen, Maalouf. You certainly outdid yourself out there."

"Admit it, Sir — the whole crew did well, and Gonzales is the best weapons officer I've ever seen."

"Yeah, I'd take this crew anywhere."

"To hell and back?"

"Absolutely, to hell and back."

Lifting his coffee, Barnabas said, "Here's to the Osprey and our crew. Best crew and best bird ever."

Matt raised his cup to tap that of Barnabas. "Cheers to the Osprey and our crew."

"So, off the record, how'd your meeting with the brass go?" Barnabas asked.

Matt shook his head. "It was strange. The brass didn't seem to be nearly as happy as I expected."

"Even after we-single handedly took out four pirate ships and captured Jacque Beauregard himself?"

"Yeah. Captain Wright was the only one who acted genuinely appreciative. The admirals were preoccupied with 'a future project' and barely interested in my report."

"It must be big if Admiral Robinson is barely interested in the capture of his nemesis, Beauregard. I thought it had become personal between those two."

"So did I. The thing that bothers me is something I overheard as our meeting was breaking up," Matt observed.

"That would be?"

"I overheard Admiral Carter telling Wright that they were both being called back to DC by the President."

"That's a bad thing, Sir?" Barnabas asked.

"In my experience with the military and NASA, I've found that no good ever comes from getting called back to DC."

# The Mission

*"No good ever comes from getting called back to DC." -*
*Captain Matthew Dirksen*

## King George Tavern – Georgetown, Washington DC

The three men sat huddled at a secluded table. They were dressed casually enough. But their haircuts and demeanor gave them away as military.

"What! You've gotta be kidding!" Lewis exclaimed. "There's no way in hel—"

"Shh, lower your voice, Captain," Admiral Carter admonished. "This is a public place, after all."

Lewis composed himself. Looking past the two admirals sitting across from him, he saw Today's News Channel's (TNC) breaking news ticker. It read: "BREAKING NEWS JACQUES BEAUREGARD CONVICTED OF PIRACY SENTENCED TO LIFE IN PRISON ON MARS."

Lewis looked back at Carter. "You can't be serious?"

"We're unquestionably serious. This mission comes straight from the top. The President's Security Council wants the threat neutralized," Admiral Robinson said.

Lewis leaned forward. "This is wrong on so many levels that I don't know where to begin. First, how do we even know they're a threat? Second, does our technology even stand a chance against—"

Carter interrupted him. "Easy, Son. I understand your concern, given the circumstances. Still, we must obey our orders."

"You may, not me," Lewis said. "I'll resign before being part of this debacle."

"Your point is taken, Captain," Robinson said. "But, now that you know what this mission is, you can't just resign."

"What?" Lewis asked.

"What my friend means is, even if you remove yourself, the mission will go on," Carter said. "We'll appoint someone to fill your place. Of course, they won't have the same passion for keeping your crew safe. If you don't participate, more lives will be at risk. Think of the institutional knowledge we'll lose if you walk away. Don't forget, you're only responsible for the landing fleet and the transports with their crews. If the troops you land are in over their heads, it's on the Army. Not on you."

Lewis shook his head. "With all due respect, Admiral, that's small comfort if this whole effort goes south," he said.

Robinson frowned. "Hmph. Let's get back to the captain's objections. They have some merit and need to be addressed. First, it's not our call whether or not they're a threat. The President's Security Council believes their mere occupation of this space and disregard for our way of life makes them a threat. The Security Council believes we must display an overwhelming show of force to gain their respect. We need to send a message that shows that we're a force to be reckoned with in no uncertain terms. Best case scenario, they'll concede to our wishes."

"Worst case scenario?" Lewis asked.

"Not your worry, Captain," Robinson replied. "Don't be impertinent."

85

"Sir, I only ask because I don't think we have the technology to pull it off."

"Ah, your second question," Robinson said. "We didn't. But, fortunately, now you're wrong. I'm speaking of the skillful way the Osprey's crew utilized their cloaking device to capture Jacques Beauregard. We're deploying it throughout the task force for this operation. The enemy can't harm us if they can't see us."

*So, it's 'the enemy' now. Not just a threat,* Lewis thought. "Who came up with that stupid line?" He asked.

"Our top military strategists," Carter replied.

"Did they forget that when cloaked, we also can't see the enemy?" Lewis asked.

Robinson replied, "I've been assured that the engineers fixed that problem with a slight software tweak."

Lewis rolled his eyes. "A slight tweak, my ass. It'll take a lot more than a—"

Robinson's hand slapped the table. "Son, you need to adjust your thinking fast and climb on board. We've been practicing our landing for months, and we've got just the right general who'll give us success!"

Lewis raised an eyebrow. "General?"

"General Roberta J Krackawhip," Robinson said, with a straight face. "She's a regular 'kick-ass' sort of soldier. Just who we need to pull this off."

*She ought to hit it off with grumpy old Admiral Hornsby,* Lewis thought. "Just the same, Sir, I don't hold much hope that this expedition will succeed."

Robinson frowned. "This expedition isn't your concern, Captain. As I said, you're only responsible for getting the landing armada in and out safely and providing covering fire, if needed. The rest is up to General Krackawhip."

Lewis said, "I'll need to brief the transport captains on our destination."

Robinson held his hand up. "No, that'll never do. This is way too secret for that. We've been rehearsing—"

"Without my knowledge, as supposed mission controller," Lewis interrupted.

"Don't be thin-skinned," Carter said. "You were preoccupied with capturing a pirate and mole until now. Please continue, Dennis."

Robinson continued. "We've been rehearsing for an unknown target. We'll get the armada underway before each transport captain opens his secret orders, which reveal the actual target. You know that this isn't an unusual protocol."

Lewis leaned forward. "I'm not even to speak with Captain Dirksen and the Osprey's crew? Given—"

Robinson broke in, "Especially not Captain Dirksen and his crew."

"Sir, you're forcing them into an awkward and unique—"

"Hell no!" Robinson hissed. "That's an order. Their role is key to our success."

Carter nodded his head in agreement.

"Is that understood?" Robinson asked.

"Yes, Sir. I understand," Lewis said as he felt his throat go dry.

"Excellent!" Robinson said. "Let's order up. I'm starved."

### Hobby Airport – Houston, Texas

"Why so glum, buddy?" Matt asked as Lewis climbed into his car. "You look like you're about to send your best friend to the gallows."

Lewis thought, *If you only knew,* but said, "Sorry Matt, I can't talk about it."

"That can't be good. It sounds like you're about to ruin everybody's day."

"Something like that. How'd you guess?"

"Simple deduction, my friend. You've just returned from Washington. We both know nothing ever good comes from getting called back to DC."

# Preparations

### Bruce's Biker Bar – Houston, Texas

Matt paused to let his eyes adjust from the bright Houston sun to the dimly lit and raucous biker bar. He noticed the smell of stale beer and leather and thought, *This is a strange place to meet my crew.* Walking across the room, he sensed a motion to his left. He ducked as an empty mug sailed past his head, crashing against the rock fireplace. There was a momentary lull in the noise. The patrons paused to see if this was the prelude to a fight. Seeing nothing unusual, the crowd returned to their noisy endeavors. Matt also looked for the source of the flying mug. At the corner of the bar sat Hilda, Marc, Marci, and a dejected-looking Josh.

Matt walked over to his crew. "Beaning your CO with a beer mug, Chief, is no way to advance through the NASA ranks."

Marci smiled. "Don't mind him, Sir. He's got a new girlfriend."

"Not funny, Marci, Err, Lieutenant," Josh said.

"I think it's funny," Marci said.

"The general's taken a real fancy to the Chief. She's asked for him by name to help train her landing craft pilots," Marc said.

Hilda said, "Word has it that she can't keep her hands off of him."

"Not funny, McDermott," Josh complained.

"I think it's funny," Hilda replied.

"Chief, you look like you've 'been ridden hard and put up wet,' to borrow a phrase from the Old West," Matt said.

Josh lifted his head. "What do you mean by that, Sir?"

"Simply put, you look worn-out."

Marc held his nose. "He even smells like a wet horse."

"He's planning to drown his sorrows, Sir," Marci added with another smile.

"Son, it'll take more than that 3.2 beer in front of you to do the trick," Barnabas said as he joined the group.

Marc put his finger to his lips. "He started with something stronger, Commander. We've switched drinks on him."

"Things can't be that bad, Chief. You've only finished your first week of training with the general," Matt said.

Josh rolled his eyes. "You don't know the half of it, Sir. She made me land a landing craft under live fire simulation, as an example. Then she made me ride with every other landing craft pilot, as they attempted to land on a hot landing zone, taking live fire."

"So?" Matt asked.

"So, each effort involves zigging and zagging and rolling up and down, finished off by a hard landing."

"That doesn't sound too bad," Matt said. "You've been through worse in the simulator."

"You forgot — this is when the live fire is simulated by live fire instead of the simulator, Sir. My ship was the only unscathed one on the first attempt."

"Good for you," Barnabas said.

"No, Sir. That means I had to ride with each of the other pilots as they repeated the exercise until they also landed unscathed. Some even splashed into a lagoon instead of landing onshore."

"I Didn't know that our landing craft could survive underwater," Marci said.

"Lucky for me, they can if you don't go too deep. I'm telling you, it was a nightmare. Some pilots took a half-dozen tries. I was ready to toss my cookies more than once."

"Lucky for you, the live rounds weren't lethal. You wouldn't have any cookies to toss," Marc interjected.

"Ok, what am I missing?" Matt asked.

"Ever since you went to meet with the accident inquiry board, the general has kept us practicing the landing non-stop. At first, she wanted to do it when every ship had full cloaking activated. We warned her that flying with the cloaking device activated is flying blind. It took two wrecked landing craft to convince her that we were right."

Marci pointed at Josh. "Our very own Flyboy here convinced her to land using stealth mode instead."

"Now General Grumpy Pants has the hots for him," Hilda added.

"That explains a lot," Matt said.

"Like what, Captain?" Josh asked.

"Like, why General Krackawhip backed my request to promote you from Chief to Ensign. It would never do, her cavorting with an NCO and all," Matt grinned.

"Not funny," Josh said.

"I thought it was funny." Matt motioned to the others, who smiled and nodded their agreement.

"Seriously. The brass promoted you to Ensign." Matt slapped a gold collar bar and an epaulet, with a single stripe and single star on the bar, in front of Josh.

"How's that, kid? You're now a fleet officer," Barnabas said.

"What?" A stunned Josh said. "For real, Captain?"

"Matt replied, "Yeah, I got tired of calling you Chief."

Barnabas said, "It was all the captain's doing."

"Along with General Krackawhip," Matt added. "She may be eccentric, but she's a good judge of character."

Marci smiled, "If recommending Torres for promotion is any evidence, maybe not so much."

Matt winced. "Ouch. That's harsh. Say, Chief, I mean Ensign, you need to lay off that beer. We have a special training assignment tomorrow."

"What? Tomorrow is our day off," Josh complained.

"Not anymore," Matt said. "General Krackawhip just informed me that she doesn't want to board her landing craft in our cargo/launch bay like everyone else. The general wants her craft to launch, then pull up to our portside doorway. She'll spacewalk, from our ship to hers, in front of the entire landing fleet. Then she'll give a hand signal to the fleet before dropping into her landing craft hatch."

"You're kidding, Sir," Barnabas said.

"I kid you not," Matt replied. "She says she's carrying on the ongoing legacy of the 203 Air Calvary."

"Hell, no. Krackawhip's just showboating!" Marc exclaimed.

"Yep," Barnabas said.

"To what good is this, other than stroking her ego?" Hilda asked.

"I agree it takes chutzpah. But the general is a highly decorated and successful officer. I would expect no less," Matt replied. "That said, this is a difficult maneuver. We want to get it right."

"You're letting her do this, Sir?" Marci asked.

"I fought, without luck, to keep her off my bridge. I know I can't stop this," Matt said. "It presents us with a problem that we must solve."

"Problem?" Barnabas asked.

Matt cocked his head. "I figure that we'll have no more than twenty minutes — thirty tops — from when we reach the landing zone till we begin landing, or we lose the element of surprise."

Barnabas frowned. "That's not much time to form up and watch the general do her Peter Pan interpretation."

"Which is why we need the practice tomorrow. This maneuver has to be perfect," Matt added.

"Did Mission Control okay this?" Marci asked.

Matt nodded. "Sure did. Captain Lewis signed off on it personally. I believe his words were, 'When it comes to the general, pick your battles carefully.' So, here's the deal. Sarge, take the ensign home and sober him up. It's your responsibility to see that he is ready to fly first thing in the morning. The rest of you, get some rest. You'll also need to be ready to go in the morning," Matt said.

As everyone filed out of the bar, Barnabas tugged on Matt's sleeve. "Any word on where we'll be landing?"

"I still don't know. The NASA brass is being tight-lipped. I expect that I won't find out until we're already underway."

"Any ideas?"

"There are a couple of hotspots in the Solar System. In cases like this, I ask, where's the worst possible place we can get sent?" Matt said.

"You mean the one place where we were told never to return?" Barnabas asked.

"Yeah, Commander, that's crossed my mind."

"What's our chances of success if that's where we're sent?"

"Do the words 'snowball in hell' ring a bell?"

# The Assault Begins

*"The only way to discover the limits of the possible is to go beyond them into the impossible." - Arthur C. Clarke*

### Low Earth Orbit

The Earth stood out as a brilliant blue orb against the black velvet curtain of space. Matt spent only a moment taking in its beauty. He looked at the feed from the Osprey's rear camera and saw the other transport vessels heading into low Earth orbit. His mind came back to the business at hand. "Ma'am, the transports are assembled in the formation you requested."

"Very good, Captain. Proceed," the general ordered as she left the bridge to make her final preparations before the assault.

Matt spoke into his headset, "Captain Dirksen to the task force commanders — Prepare for departure. Follow our lead."

Matt nodded to proceed. Barnabas nodded back.

"Mission Control, Osprey. The task force is assembled to the general's satisfaction. We're ready to commence our departure protocol. Over," Barnabas said.

"Osprey, Mission Control. You're cleared to depart. What are your coordinates? Over."

"Mission Control, Osprey. Our Earth-related coordinates are 25.0000° N, 71.0000° W. Over."

"Osprey, Mission Control. You're cleared to depart from your current coordinates. Over."

"Mission Control, Osprey. We copy. We'll begin our burn on my mark: five, four, three, two, one, MARK. Commencing burn. Over."

"Osprey, Mission Control. You're clear to adjust your heading to match your flight plan and begin with a 40% burn for departure. Godspeed. Over."

Matt said, "Commander, continue the burn and set course to follow our flight plan with the rest of the Armada."

"Osprey, Mission Control. Halt your burn 10 minutes early to facilitate the transfer of the general to her landing craft. Over."

"Mission Control, Osprey. We copy. Over," Barnabas said.

"Now is as good a time as any to open our orders." Matt reached for his console and tapped on the file marked 'Operation Strong Arm.' As he read it, his face went pale.

"What is it, Captain?" Barnabas asked.

Matt released the orders so his crew could read them on each of their monitors. He said, "See for yourselves."

Barnabas frowned, and Marci gasped. Josh said, "Crap! This can't be right, Sir."

"I'm afraid it is."

"Sir, we can't go back. We were told never to return," Josh said.

"Sadly, yes, we're being ordered to return. I wondered if this would happen." Matt said.

"You didn't know, Sir?" Marc asked.

"No. But I'm not surprised. I got suspicious from the way Captain Wright kept acting since his return from DC."

"What're we going to do, Sir?" Marci asked.

Matt raised his eyebrows. "Just what we are ordered to do, Lieutenant. There's a whole Armada out there, waiting to follow our lead. Not to mention a general on board, just waiting to take names and kick butt."

Josh began, "Isn't there—"

Matt interrupted him. "No more, Ensign. We'll be heading back to the wormhole. Only God knows what'll happen when we get there. In any case, know that it's been a privilege serving with you. Now to the business at hand. Commander, when we reach the mouth of the wormhole, we'll pause to unload our landing craft and to allow the good general her opportunity to make a grand gesture of leadership. Then we'll as ordered, lead the Armada into the wormhole to face whatever's on the other side."

"Sir, that's not all. We're ordered to provide fire support for our landing parties," Barnabas said.

"You have a problem with that, Commander?"

Barnabas shook his head. "Not if you order it, Sir. I'm just thinking our previous hosts won't take kindly to our returning with guns blazing after they told us in no uncertain terms to stay away."

"The Commander has a point, Sir," Marci agreed.

"Did I say anything about guns blazing? Lieutenant Gonzales, be sure all our offensive systems are off-line before we invoke our cloaking device and head into the wormhole."

"Yes, Sir. Does this mean we ignore the 'covering fire' portion of our orders?"

"Not at all, Lieutenant. I figure that we're already being watched. Bad enough that we'll be trespassing. No need to provoke our hosts by acting like we'll be shooting at them," Matt said.

"I'm confused, Sir. Are we not going to provide fire support?" Marci asked.

"What I'm saying is that, if necessary, we can bring our systems online, Lieutenant."

"Just like last time, Captain?" Josh asked.

"Yes, Ensign. Just like last time, when all our command and control systems died."

"Based on our previous experience, something tells me that there'll be no firing by anyone on our side," Barnabas said.

"Well put, Commander," Matt agreed.

"Sir, I'm ending our burn, per Flight Control instructions," Barnabas said.

"Very well, Commander. Lieutenant, inform Flight Control we're unloading our landing craft and preparing to transfer the general to her command shuttle," Matt ordered.

"Shuttle commanders, prepare to depart," Josh announced. "The cargo doors will open in five minutes. Corporal Brady, report to the bridge immediately."

The corporal moved quickly to Josh's station. "You wanted to see me, Sir?"

Josh nodded. "Yes, Corporal. It's time to prepare the general for her transfer. You'll follow after her transfer is complete. Understood?"

"Yes, Sir. The general is already suited up, floating in the portal chamber, and ready to go."

"Very good," Josh said.

"Ensign Torres, the shuttles are away," Marci reported. Looking out her window, she added, "The shuttles from all the transports are forming up. Looks like all will be set to transfer the general in about two more minutes."

Josh motioned toward the crew compartment. "Best grab your spacesuit and get ready yourself, Corporal."

"Yes, Sir," Brady said as he moved aft to get his spacesuit. Just then, the Osprey lurched to the starboard, causing the corporal to hit the emergency escape lever. BANG! Everyone jumped at the sound of the portal's external hatch opening. The general, looking at the corporal through the window of the inner portal door, was blown backward into space by the portal's decompression.

"What the hell just happened?" Matt asked.

"I hit a lever by mistake, Sir," Brady admitted.

Josh snickered. "I know that sound. I think you just blasted your general into space."

"Osprey, Mission Control. Please report your position and status. Over."

Matt nodded at Marci, who said, "Mission Control, Osprey. We're just about to transfer the Gen…Whoa! What the—"

"Would you look at that, Sir," Hilda started to laugh. "The bitc—er, general, is flying butt first. Oops. She just bounced off her landing craft's windshield. She's waving and kicking, like a toddler throwing a temper tantrum." Hilda practically choked her last words out. She started laughing so hard, tears were coming to her eyes.

"Not funny, McDermott," Matt said, as a smile spread over his face.

"With all due respect, Sir, now that's funny. I don't care who you are," Barnabas said, trying to control his laughter.

Marc's shoulders were shaking from his laughter.

"Sarge, don't be laughing at the general," Matt chided.

"Sir, I'm just laughing at a thought that crossed my mind. The general would be the perfect date for Admiral Hornsby. You should introduce them after she court-martials the corporal."

Matt smiled at the idea, despite himself.

"Okay, everyone, let's get someone out there to retrieve the general. Once she's recovered, we'll begin the assault, on my mark," Matt said. He clicked on his mike. "This is Captain Dirksen, speaking to Landing Shuttle 1. Please retrieve the general. We'll commence operations as soon as you have—"

The Osprey's unexpected acceleration interrupted Matt's transmission.

"Commander," Matt barked. "I said on my mark!"

Barnabas replied, "I didn't do anything, Sir!"

"Then bring us to a full stop, Commander!"

"We are, Captain!" Barnabas insisted.

"Not sounding good," Marci said.

*Not again, damn it,* Matt thought, as he remembered a similar trip.

The Osprey accelerated on its own, first twisting to the right and then to the left. Its motion pinned the hapless corporal (the only one not buckled in) against the storage compartment bulkhead. The Osprey threatened to tumble out of control while still picking up speed. Each astronaut was jerked alternately against their harnesses, then deep into their chairs. The craft itself moaned and screeched with the stress. Barely staying conscience, Matt saw a kaleidoscope of colors passing by the Osprey's portals. Matt joined Barnabas in fighting to regain control of the ship. Finally, they stopped the rolling tumble and righted the craft as it continued speeding onward. Other than keeping the Osprey from rolling, Matt and Barnabas had no control. The Osprey continued in this state for another half hour. Then, as suddenly as the wild ride started, the computers died, and the ship quickly decelerated, slamming its occupants against their harnesses. The corporal managed to grab a handhold to keep from being thrown against a forward bulkhead. The rear of the craft lifted as it was kicked forward by an invisible force. For a moment, it seemed the Osprey's tail would flip ahead of its nose. Finally, the Osprey slowed up, righted itself with a violent lurch, and began to descend, floating back and forth like a leaf falling to Earth. The craft came to rest with a thud. The entire ship shuddered one last time, and the ceiling panel, just behind the Commander's seat, fell to the floor.

Matt looked around. "Ensign, get a barf bag to the Corporal before he pukes."

"Too late, Sir," the distraught Corporal said as he retched one more time.

"You're cleaning that up first thing, Corporal," Matt said.

Hilda looked out her window. "Damn! Is there any way to get back to Kansas?"

Josh shook his head. "I have a bad feeling that the feathers just hit the fan."

"Yeah, Ensign. A few tossed cookies by the corporal is nothing compared to what we just fell into," Barnabas added.

# Déjà vu

*"...'Forward, the Light Brigade!' Was there a man dismayed?*
*Not though the soldier knew Someone had blundered.*
*Theirs not to make reply, Their's not to reason why,*
*Theirs but to do and die. Into the valley of Death*
*Rode the six hundred..." - Lord Tennyson*

## Mission Control Houston, Texas

Another sultry day dawned across Houston as operation "Strong Arm" was getting underway. The beauty of a Gulf Coast sunrise was lost on Lewis as he monitored the operation's progress. Lewis stood toward the small mission control center's back, where he could view all the flight control stations. He nodded toward Vice Admiral Carter as the vice-admiral walked over to stand next to Lewis.

"I've been dreading this day ever since you briefed me, Admiral," Lewis said.

"Me too, Son," Carter said as he took a deep breath. "Theirs but to do and die."

"What?"

"Tennyson."

101

"You're not helping," Lewis said. He raised his voice and asked the Communications Officer, "What's the status of the task force?"

"The task force is forming up in low Earth orbit. They should be positioned in their proper formation within a few minutes, Sir."

Time seemed to drag on, causing Admiral Carter to say, "This is a long 'few minutes,' Captain."

Lewis nodded an acknowledgment. Finally, Osprey's channel crackled to life.

"Mission Control, Osprey. The task force is assembled to the general's satisfaction, and we're ready to commence our departure protocol. Over."

"Osprey, Mission Control. You are now cleared to depart. What are your coordinates? Over."

"Mission Control, Osprey. Our Earth-related coordinates are 25.0000° N, 71.0000° W. Over."

Admiral Carter winced and looked down.

Lewis glanced at the admiral. *I know what you're thinking, Admiral. I have that same sinking feeling,* Lewis thought, as he nodded to the Launch Controller.

"Osprey, Mission Control. You are cleared to depart from your current coordinates. Over."

"Mission Control, Osprey. We copy. We will begin our burn on my mark: five, four, three, two, one, MARK. Commencing burn. Over."

Lewis said, "Flight Control, Captain Lewis here. Is the rest of the task force following the Osprey's lead?"

"Affirmative, Sir," was the reply. "Our observation posts see the task force maintaining formation. All looks well so far."

"Freedom Control, Mission Control. Do you have eyes on the Osprey? Over."

"Mission Control, Freedom Control. We copy. Yes, Sir, we have her in our sights and are receiving telemetry readouts. Everything looks normal. Over."

Lewis looked at Carter, "The crews should be opening their orders about now."

Carter gave the nod.

"Flight Control, inform the Osprey to stop their burn 10 minutes earlier than the flight plan shows," Lewis instructed. He looked at Carter and lowered his voice. "That'll give the general time to make her grand departure, Sir."

"Osprey, Mission Control. Halt your burn 10 minutes early to facilitate the transfer of the general to her landing craft. Over."

"Mission Control, Osprey. We copy. Over."

"Osprey, Mission Control. Report your position and status. Over."

"Flight Control, do you still have a visual?" Lewis asked.

"Yes, Sir. We have a visual of the entire task force. It looks like the general's landing craft is almost in position for her transfer from the Osprey."

"Mission Control, Osprey. We are in position and just about to transfer the Gen—Whoa! What the—"

"Osprey, Mission Control. Repeat your previous transmission."

"Oh my God! Captain, Sir, you'll never believe what I'm seeing!" The flight control officer exclaimed.

"What?" Lewis asked.

"The general just got ejected from the Osprey, butt first. She just bounced off her landing craft windshield. Someone's going to have to space-walk and pick her up."

"Now that's funny," Lewis laughed.

Carter smiled. "Captain Dirksen'll have hell to pay."

"I know, Sir, but it's still funny," Lewis said.

"Guess Captain Dirksen knows he's in trouble. He just disappeared," the flight control officer chuckled.

"Osprey, Mission Control. Do you copy? Over."

(silence)

"Osprey, do you copy?"

(silence)

"Sir, we've just lost our communication with the Osprey," the communications officer reported.

"Sir, we've just lost all telemetry from the Osprey," the flight control officer said.

"Any automated distress signals?" Lewis asked.

"No, Sir."

"Sir, the tracking stations are also reporting they lost visual contact with the Osprey," the communications officer said.

*Matt must have kicked the cloaking device on too soon,* Lewis thought. "Check with Freedom Control," he replied.

"Yes, Sir. Freedom Control, Mission Control. Do you guys have a visual of the Osprey? Over."

"Mission Control, Freedom Control. Negative, we've lost visual. Over."

"Freedom Control, Mission Control. Any sign of the rest of the task force? Over."

"Mission Control, Freedom Control. We copy. Yes, the rest of the task force appears to be intact. Including the general who, oh wow, she's flailing away like a drowning swimmer! Only the Osprey is gone. Over."

"Freedom Control, Mission Control. I copy. Thank you. Over."

Turning his attention to his control center, Lewis asked, "Can you confirm Freedom Control's report?"

"Yes, Sir. All our tracking stations report that only the Osprey disappeared," was the reply.

Lewis looked at Admiral Carter, who gave him a thumb-down motion. "Mission Control, Captain Wright here. Notify the task force to abort the mission." As an afterthought, he added, "And get Rescue One launched to help reel in the good general."

"Yes, Sir. Ah, … Sir?"

"What is it?"

"No one on the assault team is responding."

"Have they disappeared also?"

"No, Sir. We still have them on visual. We just have no telemetry or radio communication. It seems the entire armada has powered down and is just drifting."

Lewis said, "Get a second rescue craft launched, pronto! Let's get that armada home ASAP."

Turning toward Admiral Carter, Lewis said, "Why does it feel like déjà vu all over again? We never should have agreed to this mission."

The admiral shrugged and said, "We had no choice, Son. We must follow orders, no matter how foolhardy they are. Think Tennyson's 'Charge of the Light Brigade.'"

"I'm afraid the Osprey's crew is going to meet some extremely pissed-off creatures for returning against their orders. You're right in quoting Tennyson."

"That about sums it up, Son. I wish I could offer more hope. But I think the Light Brigade was in better shape than the Osprey."

# Change of Plans

*"No battle plan survives contact with the enemy." - Colin Powell*

### Somewhere on Portae

Marci gave a low whistle as she looked out the window. Except for the night sky, this was not the same place the Osprey had landed on her first trip. Across the deep purple sky, curtains of green and yellow lights still danced to a silent symphony. However, there were no red topiary trees or peacock feather trees. For that matter, there were no precious stone cliffs except at a distance. Instead, she saw a variety of columns, like those crafted by ancient Greeks and Romans. These were made from Jade, Onyx, Topaz, Opal, Ruby, and Sapphire. Instead of supporting structures, they defined semi-circles in the dim lighting. Marci thought she could make out a variety of spacecraft, standing by some of the columns. A little further away, she saw what appeared to be lights from aircraft landing, and departing, much like you would see at a traditional airport. Her view was highlighted by vertical streaks of brightly shining lights.

"Uh … Captain? We have visitors," Marci said.

"Who?" Matt asked.

"There're several columns of light, Sir. And they don't look friendly."

"How can light not look friendly?" Matt asked as he looked out the window. "Oh, I see what you mean, Lieutenant."

Barnabas also out his window." Columns of light? These look more like threatening columns of flames like you see during a catastrophic forest fire."

"You will all dis-arm yourselves and step out of your ship," a deep voice declared. The voice sounded more like thunder or an ocean wave crashing than an actual human voice.

Matt took a deep breath. "You heard the voice. Leave all your weapons on the Osprey and go to the portside anti-chamber. When the portal door opens, we'll step out and line up in front of the flames."

When the door opened, the somber group did as Matt asked. Corporal Brady was the last to leave the ship and line up.

Matt used his hand to shield his eyes from the intense heat. He said, "We're the crew of the USS Osprey. I'm Captain Matthew Dirksen, the commanding officer."

"I am the Vilicus (Overseer) of the Custodes: watchman here at Portae." The voice, which was coming from the leading fiery column, said. "My friends call me Uwriyel. You may call me Taxiarchis. "Using your terminology, I am the commanding officer of Portae."

Sweating profusely, Matt asked, "Portae?"

"Portae is the name of our custos turris (guardian tower) or what you would call an outpost or watchman's station. Enough with the formalities. Who is this one? He wasn't with you last time," the voice demanded.

"This is Corporal Chuck Brady, Sir," Matt replied."

"Why did he disobey my order to disarm?"

"No, Sir, we all dis—" Matt stopped when he saw a stunned look on Chuck's face.

"Sir, I forgot my backup service revolver," Chuck said as he watched the gun lift itself out of his ankle holster and fall to the ground. A stream of light shot from one of the fire columns and hit Chuck. He closed his eyes, dropped to the ground, and immediately began to snore.

"Was that necessary?" Matt asked as he wiped his forehead.

"Yes. This conversation does not concern the corporal, and he disobeyed my orders. As did you, when you returned to Portae, despite our warning to stay away."

"If it were up to me, Sir, we'd have stayed away. However, my superiors ordered us to return and accompany others."

"Others who are armed," The voice corrected. "Did they think an obsolete invasion force would impress us?"

"My government's leadership isn't known for its intelligence, Sir."

"That's obvious. Do you think the argument that you are merely following orders justifies your actions?"

"No, it does not. And we are prepared to accept our consequences, Sir," Matt said, with more conviction than he felt. "Before we hear what your plans for us are, please tell me what's become of those we were accompanying."

Hilda gave Marc a nudge with her foot and nodded toward the columns of flames. Marc noticed that all the light columns, except the one in front, were becoming more like beams of light than towering flames.

"Oh. The invasion force — that's what you call it — is drifting by the wormhole entrance. I suppose your leaders will retrieve them in due time."

Matt sighed his relief. "Thank you, Sir."

"The real question is, what are we going to do with you." The voice was now less thunderous. "As it turns out, we've been expecting you.

We've been instructed to send you to help with a grave situation in your Solar System. One perpetrated by your fellow sons of Adam."

"Situation?" Matt asked.

"Yes, I believe that is the word you would use. You'll be helping some other Solar System inhabitants who are in danger. Hopefully, you will help stop the Evil One. But, first things first. You must rest and be refreshed.

"Stop the Evil One? Could you be a little more specific about the danger and what we are to do, Sir?" Matt asked.

"No, my instructions are to tell you what to do. It's up to you to figure out how to do it when the time comes. Until then, we can give you some rest and refreshment to fortify you for the tasks ahead. If you'll just enter the gate to your left. We will reconvene here when your rest period is over."

"What about the Corporal?" Matt asked.

"We will put him back into the ship. There he will continue to sleep until it is time for you all to leave."

The group followed Taxiarchis's instructions and walked to an eight-foot gate that looked like it was made of solid pearl. As they approached it, it swung open on its own. They passed through and stopped to admire what lay before them.

"Spectacular, just as I remembered!" Hilda exclaimed. "It looks like a crater of colorful glass transformed into a garden. Wait — it's not as large as our garden was."

"No, it's not the same. It is more colorful and smaller," Matt said.

"You're right," Hilda agreed. "The walls around it are not as tall. Ah, there's a waterfall over there to the right."

Marc knelt to feel a patch of moss. "The meadow looks like it's covered with red clover and patches of thick moss scattered about. Look at the ring of outcroppings. They look like they're carved out of ruby."

109

Walking over to a stream of water running from the waterfall through the middle of the garden, Marc took a drink. "Wow! The water tastes great. Just as I remembered."

Josh found some small pools of golden amber liquid against the outcropping next to the garden gate. He tasted the fluid. "Captain, here's the ale that you enjoy."

Matt said, "Good to know, Ensign. Be sure and lay off it this time."

While exploring the garden, the crew found a wide assortment of fruit, which they gathered. The team sat for a meal together.

"What do you make of all this, Sir?" Marci asked.

"I'm not sure, Lieutenant," Matt said. "What do you think, Commander?"

Barnabas looked thoughtfully at the sky. "I'm surprised that we don't seem to be on the outs with the powers-that-be. They're treating us more like guests than as prisoners. I'm intrigued by what kind of task they expect us to do."

"That worries me, Sir," Marc said. "Especially the way they blocked our task force as if it were merely a bunch of flying toys that they didn't want to deal with."

"You've got a point, Sarge," Hilda yawned. "Can we discuss this later? I can hardly keep my eyes open."

Matt nodded. "Gunny has a good idea. Let's find someplace comfortable and rest awhile. I'm sure our hosts want us to be well-rested."

The group spread out to select patches of moss on which to rest. Barnabas caught Matt's sleeve and whispered, "I feel uneasy about all of this. It's too peaceful.

Matt agreed, "Like the calm before—"

"The storm," Barnabas finished Matt's sentence.

"I was going to say before all hell breaks loose."

"As in a helluva storm?"

"Something like that," Matt said.

Barnabas agreed, "Yeah. But what kind of storm? That's what I'm nervous about."

"Me, too. If I knew what we're going to face, I could plan for it. Right now, I'm clueless. We both know just winging it has never been my style."

Hilda thought she would lie down to rest, but she found herself wandering near the edge of the garden. That's when she saw it. It was a curious reddish-colored mineral. *How interesting. It's just outside my reach,* she thought. Ignoring the warning to stay within the garden, Hilda started to take a step out. A hand touched her, and she jumped back. It was Marc.

"You startled me. What're you doing?" Hilda said.

"I'm keeping you in the garden. You know the rule."

"It's just a step or two outside. I'm not bad for making this slight exception. Am I?

"Breaking a rule here doesn't make you bad. It makes you dead."

"What do you mean, Sarge?"

"That mineral you're reaching for is Cinnabar. Just touching it can harm you."

Hilda pulled her hand back. "Really?"

Marc shook his head yes. "No joke. Wait. Did you see that?"

"See what?"

Marc ducked, pulling Hilda down with him. "Look over there."

Hilda looked in the direction where Marc was pointing. She saw a figure disappear behind the waterfall. "Who is it?"

"I think it's one of the pirates."

"Here? That doesn't make sense. Does it?"

Marc didn't answer. Instead, he jumped up and said, "Hey, stop!"

They both ran after the mysterious figure. "We've got to catch that guy. I'm sure he's one of Beauregard's spies."

The chase was on. They followed the fleeing man. He ran on a trail that led out of the garden and into the heart of a crevasse. A second man appeared ahead of them. Hilda began to gasp for breath. The trail split into two. One man took the barren path, headed up the side of a cliff. The other took the route that descended into a lush green valley. Hilda and Marc followed the second man. The further they ran, the denser the vegetation became.

"We're gaining on him," Marc said.

The trail took a turn and opened into a meadow beneath the cliff. Marc ran through an arch made of two tall trees leaning together. Hilda calculated that a few more steps and Marc would tackle the one they were chasing. A shot rang out, and Marc dropped to the ground. Hilda drew her Glock and looked in the direction of the sound. At the top of the ridge stood the man who had taken the barren trail. He was pointing a gun right at her. Hilda heard three shots. She noticed the sound came from her gun, which was aimed at the shooter. He grasped his chest and fell off the ridge. She turned and fell on her knees in front of Marc's lifeless body.

"Marc! Marc!" she screamed. Someone was shaking her shoulders.

"Wake up, Gunny," Marci shook Hilda.

"Is Marc okay?" Hilda asked in a groggy voice.

Relief washed over her when she heard Marci say, "Yeah, he's over there talking to Ensign Torres. From the way you sounded, you were having a bad dream."

"I was. It was a beaut."

Marc's head nodded. He felt a tablet slide off his lap onto the floor. Did anyone notice he'd dozed off? For that matter, where was he? Marc casually bent over to pick up his tablet. He was sitting at a desk in a classroom, complete with a whiteboard in front. It was the kind of classroom that is commonly found in a single-wide prefab building. He was one of a couple of dozen students. Most of whom were intent on what the lecturer was saying.

*This place is familiar,* he thought. *I just can't put my finger on it. Wait. It's a classroom at the explosives training facility I attended years ago.*

The room was familiar enough. Still, something didn't seem quite right with the picture. Then it struck Marc. He was clad only in his boxers. Everyone else was clothed normally. Only Marc was nearly naked. A flash of embarrassment came over him. No one else seemed to notice his lack of attire. The instructor's nasal voice caught his attention.

"PETN is a whitish explosive chemical that has a distinctive bluish tinge. It is one of the most powerful explosive chemicals in our arsenal. It contains nitro groups which are like that in TNT. But the presence of more of these nitro groups makes it explode with more power. Despite its power, it's difficult to detonate this chemical alone. So we use it in combination with TNT or RDX. A variant of this chemical, PETN-A, is many times more powerful than PETN. It's interesting because certain experiments show that its release of energy may be controlled. Also, theoretically, the right kind of environment might create this chemical from another energy source."

*Talk about Déjà vu. I remember part of this lecture,* Marc thought.

The instructor droned on, "PETN has relatively low toxicity and has medicinal properties, such as a vasodilator."

"What's that?" the student in front of Marc asked.

"That means it can widen blood vessels. So, it's used to treat angina — don't worry, you won't explode."

Marc didn't laugh. He was trying to figure out how he could escape and get dressed. The room grew dark as Marc nodded off again. When he came to, he found himself back in the garden and, thankfully, fully clothed.

Josh wandered across the garden after dining on fruit and freshwater (no golden ale for me, Josh thought). He found a patch of moss, furthest away from the garden's waterfall. Marc was there, already fast asleep. Josh reclined on the moss and watched the light show in the sky. Silent curtains of green and magenta light danced quietly across the black canvas. He never tired of watching them sway back and forth. Josh began drifting off to sleep when he noticed a singular beam of light separate itself from the heavenly show.

It drifted down until it stood by his side. "Good evening Josh."

"Vigilo, it's good to see you again."

"It's good to see you as well," Vigilo replied.

"I don't suppose you're dropping in just to say hi for old times' sake," Josh said.

"You're right. I have a task for you, my friend. To carry out this task, Taxiarchi has given you a new name. It's Qui Admonet."

"One who warns?"

"Yes, Qui Admonet, you must give a warning to the people of the Red Planet. And once again, if you don't: sanguis eorum sit super manus."

"Their blood is on my hands," Josh responded

"Only if you don't warn them. If you do warn the people and they choose to ignore you, then their blood is NOT on your hands."

"Now you're scaring me," Josh said, recalling a similar conversation.

"There's no reason to be frightened. I'll help prepare you. Will you do this?"

Josh frowned. "Sounds like I've no choice. You remember what happened the last time you told me to warn my friends. It didn't turn out so well."

"That's why you and I are taking a little trip into the cave."

Josh began to tremble. "Please, not the cave."

114

"It's not the same cave that you think. But it's where you must face your fears."

As they talked, Josh realized they were now standing in a sizeable misty cavern. "Look to the center and tell me what you are seeing."

Josh looked hard into the mist, "I see a garden with a beautiful woman. She's conversing with a graceful reptile. They seem to be having an intense discussion beside a tree full of red fruit. What're we seeing?

"We're looking into the distant past, where your ancestors were deceived by the same one who you must oppose."

"Who is it?"

"It has been known by many names through the ages — Father of Lies, Great Destroyer, Great Accuser, or simply the Evil One. It's about to pay a visit to the Red Planet. It wants to strike a deal with the inhabitants there. If they accept the deal, they will suffer endless grief. Watch. And remember, he can't hurt you."

Josh peered into the mist. The scene had changed. There were two great stages. Each had a backdrop that looked like an imposing clamshell. Below the platforms were a dozen thrones, on which a variety of creatures sat. Some looked familiar to Josh. Others didn't. Behind the thrones was a great throng of creatures, both human-looking and non-human. On the far stage, a tall and imposing man stood in a magnificent cape. He looked like an emperor from the Roman empire. He was dazzling the crowd with his speech. Josh couldn't quite hear what he was saying. The reaction of the audience confirmed that his words were being well received. Somehow, Josh knew this man was evil. The orator stopped mid-sentence and looked directly at Josh. His stare sent a chill down Josh's back. With one hand, the orator beckoned Josh. He felt himself being drawn into the scene until he was standing on the nearest stage. *Remember, he can't hurt me*, Josh thought.

"Just what do you have to say?" the orator demanded.

"Don't believe him!" Josh yelled without thinking.

"Who are you to question me?" the orator shouted. He raised both hands and motioned at Josh. This released a great ball of energy aimed directly toward Josh, who flinched, but continued to yell, "Don't believe him! Don't believe—"

The energy burst over Josh, shaking him and shaking him. "Wake up, Ensign, wake up!" It was Marc shaking him awake. "You're having a bad dream."

"Oh, sorry, Sarge. Did I wake you?"

"By screaming, 'Don't believe him?' Naw. I was looking to get dressed anyway."

"What?"

"Nothing."

Barnabas settled down to rest near the waterfall. He couldn't relax. The captain's words about "the calm before all hell breaks loose" left him on edge. The waterfall also intrigued him. He knew that this was a different garden. Still, this waterfall looked just like the one he remembered from their previous trip.

Enjoying the sound of the water, he nodded off. Barnabas found himself walking behind the waterfall. Just as he suspected, there was the entrance to a dark cave. His mind screamed at him, *Don't do it!* But, he was compelled to enter anyway. *At least this isn't the same cave we were in during our last visit*, he thought. The thought did little to ease a sense of fear that was creeping over him. *Why am I afraid?*

He heard a brushing sound above him. He froze. His ears strained to make out what caused the noise. The cave split into several tunnels. Barnabas chose the one on the left. He could hear a stream running somewhere, far below him. The tunnel had opened onto a narrow ledge. His foot slipped on some loose stones, sending a couple over the side. He heard them bouncing on their way down for a full minute. *Be careful now. I think it's time to head back.* Just as he turned, he caught a glimpse of motion at the mouth of the tunnel he'd just left. He hurried forward, as fast as he dared, along the ledge. To his relief, the ledge led into another path that headed uphill.

Barnabas hurried up the path and felt his fear subside. Then Barnabas heard something scurrying across the ledge he had just left. He began running, falling, and scrambling to get away. He didn't know what it was, but he could sense danger. Barnabas got caught in what seemed to be sticky ropes. He pulled out his knife and began to hack. Finally, he broke through and kept trying to run up the tunnel. The incline was steep. He felt like his boots were made of lead. His legs ached and whatever was following was catching up. Barnabas could feel its hot breath on his neck.

Just as he was about to stop, he saw the light. Gasping for breath, he came to the mouth of the tunnel. It was at the top of a cliff. It had to be at least ten stories tall. Barnabas swung to his right, trying to stick to a narrow ledge, only to find himself tangled in another web of sticky rope. Barnabas began to hack again. This time he slipped and rolled on his back, caught by the web. As he looked up, he saw what had pursued him. At the entrance to the tunnel was a man-sized spider. It hopped down just over Barnabas, who worked to get free. The more he struggled, the more tightly the ropes held him. *I guess this is it. When it comes in for the kill, I'll catch its eye with my knife.*

But the spider looked up, distracted from its prey. At the same time, Barnabas heard a thumping sound, like a helicopter. He felt a breeze rocking him. He followed the spider's gaze to see a flying scorpion, also about the size of a man. *Oh great, I get to watch two disgusting creatures fighting over who gets to eat me.* It was an epic fight. The spider tried to get in close and grab the scorpion's stinger. But the scorpion's ability to fly kept it just out of reach. Then the spider tried to shoot its web-making rope out to entangle the scorpion. That wasn't successful either. The scorpion dove in and clipped the spider's legs with its oversized pinchers. The scorpion also gave the spider lightning-quick strikes with its stinger. Try as it might, the spider could never get a grasp on the scorpion's tail to inject its poison.

Barnabas could see that the spider was slowly losing. When it finally folded what was left of its legs and died, he turned his attention to the scorpion. It was hovering over him, looking into his face. Oddly, its head looked like that of a human with bug eyes. Barnabas felt a sudden wave of calm sweep over him as the beast's pinchers came up against his body. *This ought to be quick and hopefully painless,* he thought. He heard the snapping of web ropes as the scorpion's pinchers cut them away from his body. The scorpion cut Barnabas free too quickly. He started to fall. Before he could react, even to scream, he felt himself wrapped around the waist by one of the scorpion's pinchers. Together, they descended slowly until Barnabas was safely on the ground with the scorpion facing him.

"Who are you?" Barnabas asked.

"I'm called the Protector. I was sent to help."

"I owe you one, Protector. Can you stay and talk?"

"No, I must be off. Take care," the scorpion said as he flew away.

Barnabas sat down, only to realize he was sitting in the garden. Coming to his senses, he thought, *What a strange dream.*

# The Red Planet

*"It's going to be a bummer if Mars turns out to be like us." - Newt Gingrich*

### Somewhere on Portae

The dark blue-purple sky gave way to a pink morning, typical for Portae. Marc joined Hilda in her search for ripe persimmons. They were walking along, munching on the smooth orange fruit, when Hilda stopped abruptly and gasped.

"What is it, Gunny?"

Hilda bent over and began to pick pods from the ground. "It's peyote pods like the ones I got last time we were here."

Marc laughed. "Gunny, you're incorrigible. Didn't that stuff cause enough trouble the last time you collected it?"

"That was then. This is now. You know I didn't get to keep any of it. I still want to try that experiment I mentioned."

Marc just smiled and stared at Hilda.

Hilda caught his look. "What?"

Marc shook his head. "You …. You amaze me."

Hilda cocked her head. "Are you hitting on me?"

Marc was silent.

"You are, Sarge," Hilda accused. "You're hitting on me."

"I'm not hitting on you. Just stating a fact, Gunny. You amaze me. I feel comfortable around you as a friend. Yet you're friendly and distant at the same time."

"It's my life's two-part philosophy of relationships. Part one, keep your distance."

"What's part two?"

"Have an exit strategy."

"That's encouraging," Marc said, with more than a hint of sarcasm in his voice.

"I'll confess, Sarge. Since we've met, I'm starting to rethink my philosophy."

"Now, who's coming on to whom?"

"I'm just saying, I enjoy your company. With you, I feel that I can just be myself."

"I know what you mean, Gunny," Marc said. "I feel the same toward you. For years I've stayed emotionally detached. I suppose going through the number of battles we did, and losing companions nearly every day, getting too close to someone is something to be avoided."

"I guess we're a lot alike," Hilda observed.

Marc bent over to help Hilda pick peyote pods. "It's not a bad thing, Gunny."

Elsewhere, Marci and Josh were feasting on various berries in the garden when Marci caught Josh looking in her direction. "What are you looking at?"

"Just enjoying the view," Josh said absent-mindedly. "I mean, the view over there," he stuttered, blushing, pointing at an attractive emerald outcropping located just over Marci's shoulder.

Marci gave him a skeptical look. "Whatever you say, Torres."

Josh cleared his throat. "I saw my friend last night."

"The one you call Vigilo?"

"Yes."

"It's funny. I didn't believe you before. Now I do. Did your friend say anything?"

"He gave me a name that means 'one who warns.' He said that I'm supposed to warn the inhabitants of wherever we're going."

"Sounds ominous, Torres. Where do you think we're going?"

"He said something about the Red Planet. Other than that I'm afraid that I'm clueless, Lieutenant."

"That you are," Marci teased.

After breakfast, the astronauts assembled in front of the Osprey for one last visit with the watchers. They were comforted to see that the lights standing in front of them this morning were beams, not flames.

After a minute or two of silence, Taxiarchis spoke. "We are sending you to the Red Planet. Its inhabitants are contented, ingenious, and fulfilled. Now evil forces, of which they are unaware, are at work. They are both intelligent and naïve. Because of this, they will soon be in danger of losing all that they hold dear. The Evil One will try to lull them into complacency and seal their doom."

Taxiarchis continued, "You need to assess the situation. Then you must warn the inhabitants of the danger they are in. You may only assist them if they ask. Finally, you must do battle with those who represent the Evil One. The Evil One is also known as the Great Deceiver. This name is well deserved. He has already tried to deceive some of you. So, take care. Not all will be as it seems." The beam seemed to turn toward Josh. "Remember, Qui Admonet, you must give a warning to the people of the Red Planet. If you don't: sanguis eorum sit super manus."

Matt gave Josh a strange look, then turned toward Taxiarchi. "Would you consider traveling with us, Sir?"

"Trust me. We would go with you if we were allowed. Because it is your brother, sons of Adam, who opened the door to this threat, it must be sons of Adam that end it. We are constrained to leave their fate in your hands. Godspeed, and do not fail."

"Sir, we need a little time to go through our pre-flight procedures," Matt said.

"Understood. When you and your crew are ready, we will begin," Taxiarchi said. "Remember your dreams and remember — not all will be as it seems."

The crew boarded the Osprey and buckled themselves in at their respective stations.

"Let's get this show on the road," Matt said. He shook a groggy Chuck Brady, who was just waking up. "Get up, sleepyhead. To your station, Corporal. We've got places to go and people to see. Commander, start the launch procedure."

As Barnabas began running through the pre-flight procedures, Marc pondered, "Hmm … Red Planet and innocent inhabitants. One of our colonies on Mars must be in immediate danger."

Hilda agreed. "Yeah, it all seems to fit. Good thinking, Sarge."

"You remembered your peyote?" Marc asked in a low voice.

Hilda smiled and patted her thigh pockets. "I'm keeping the good stuff close by."

Marc laughed

"Trying to concentrate here, kiddos," Barnabas said.

"The Commander's right, you two. We're trying to launch," Matt said. "But, for the record, I'm thinking the same thing about our destination, Sarge."

"You're not helping, Captain," Barnabas complained.

Ignoring Barnabas, Matt said, "I just had a thought. Commander, we'd best take off in stealth mode. We're not sure where we'll end up, so it's best to keep a low profile until we figure it out."

"Good call, Captain," Josh added. A stern look from Barnabas caused him to turn back to his console with a simple, "Aye, Sir."

With the pre-flight preparation finally completed, Matt gave the "all clear to leave" sign. The Osprey took to the air, seemingly on its own. This time, the Osprey flew for a while with a purpose. Soon, it picked up speed and entered the wormhole with a vengeance.

"I'll never get used to wormhole travel," Josh said.

"Airsick bag ... please," Corporal Brady said.

The Osprey's departure from the wormhole brought her into a low hover over a reddish-brown planet. A loud and annoying alarm sounded.

"What's the problem?" Matt asked.

Josh scanned his console. "It's a radiation alarm, Sir." He glanced at the meter. "And the radiation meter is off the charts!"

"Kill that alarm! We don't need to announce our arrival to the entire neighborhood," Matt snapped.

Josh entered the commands. "Done. Should I raise our shields now, Sir?"

"Good idea, Ensign. Lieutenant, scan to see who or what is firing on us! Commander, prepare to go dark."

"Sir, scanners aren't picking up anything. I don't think we're being attacked."

Josh said, "Sir, uh, at the rate of radiation we're receiving, we've got just over 5 minutes to escape, or we'll fry."

Barnabas shook his head. "Maybe, Ensign, but why would the watchers send us directly into danger?"

Matt slapped his console with his hand. "I've got it! Sarge, break out your spacesuit. See what its radiation detector reads."

Marc disconnected his harness and scrambled to where his spacesuit was stowed — no small feat when one is weightless. "This doesn't make sense, Sir. My suit isn't showing anything more than background radiation."

"Check the other suits," Matt instructed.

"All the same, Sir. They only show background radiation."

"Hmm. Our radiation sensor is external to the ship. Correct Ensign?"

"That's correct, Sir. It's set to detect Gamma rays, X-rays, and the higher energy range of ultraviolet light," Josh replied.

"All the radiation that constitutes the ionizing part of the electromagnetic spectrum. Right?"

Josh agreed, "That's correct, Captain. The radiation is bombarding our external sensor so hard that I don't understand why the sensors inside aren't registering anything. Uh, two minutes before we fry."

Matt nodded his head thoughtfully. "Unless the rays hitting our sensor don't have enough energy to penetrate the Osprey's hull."

Josh said, "That could be true if they're at the low end of the Gamma Ray spectrum —"

"Or at the higher end of the ultraviolet light spectrum," Barnabas interrupted.

"In English, please," Hilda said.

"Basically, exposure to ionizing radiation will cause us harm. But, some kinds of ionizing radiation are more easily stopped than others. Whatever is hammering our sensor is being stopped by the Osprey's hull. So, we shouldn't fry anytime soon," Barnabas said.

Matt said, "Sarge, go ahead and monitor the radiation on your suit. Just in case. The rest of us need to get oriented. What do you see, Lieutenant?"

"The terrain is reddish-brown. I see some light brown dunes with a few dark brown streaks. I guess that's what they call slope streaks."

"I see a couple of craters. And some hills that are all wrinkly like an elephant's knees," Hilda added.

"I see a crevasse or canyon's edge to our starboard," Barnabas said.

Matt asked, "Can anyone spot anything unusual or manmade?"

"Captain, I think I see a glimmer just at the horizon-line to our port," Hilda said.

Marci said, "Oh, wait, Sir. There's a shuttle leaving the crevasse."

"Speed and bearing?" Matt asked.

"It's headed due east, traveling fast enough to pass us in three minutes," Josh said. "Should we go dark, Sir?"

"Yes, activate the cloaking device for three minutes. Then reset to stealth. I think we should tag along for a little bit."

"Aye, Sir. Cloaking device activated," Josh said

"Sir, I've compared where I think we are with a map of Mars. We appear to be in the middle of a restricted area," Marci said.

"Does it say why?" Matt asked.

"Yes, Sir. Due to excessive radiation."

"So, some of the rocks nearby must be giving it off," Marc said.

"Three minutes is up, Captain," Josh reported.

"Good," Matt said. "Put us back into stealth mode, Ensign. Commander, follow that lander."

Barnabas said, "Aye, Sir. I'm following it now."

"Who are these guys? Who, in their right mind, would be hanging out in this area?" Josh asked.

"Ask your captain," Barnabas said. "He's got us hanging around here."

"Not funny, Commander."

"I thought it—"

"There it is, Sir," Marci interrupted. "It looks like a Mark 4 lander, a generation older than ours."

"Excellent, Lieutenant. Let's keep a little distance behind it, Commander. Lieutenant, look for a quality landing spot. We may have to set down quickly."

"Sir, I've picked up a starship on the ground," Josh said.

"Where?" Matt asked.

"Looks like it's the source of the glimmer Gunny saw earlier. The lander is heading straight for it," Josh reported.

"Found a spot from where we can observe the starship, Sir. It's in a shallow crater just before we reach the starship's site," Marci reported.

"Good work, Lieutenant. Commander, come in low and set us in that crater," Matt said.

"You got it, Sir."

"Gunny, Sarge, breakout your EVA suits. When we land, we'll go dark, and you two will become our eyes," Matt Said.

"Aye, Sir," they responded.

Marc hesitated. "Uh, Sir, wouldn't our terrestrial suits be better?"

"Under normal circumstances, yes. But, not knowing what kind of radiation we're dealing with, well, you know the rest," Matt said.

Once outside and positioned behind the ridge of the crater, Marc looked back at the Osprey. "This is amazing, Gunny. From here, you can't even see the Osprey. If we're not careful, we'll walk right into it on our way back."

Hilda wasn't paying attention. She was focused on the activity between the landing craft and the spaceship in front of her. "Looks like everyone's using their terrestrial suits and bubble helmets. The radiation must not be that potent."

"Or they're limiting their exposure time, Gunny."

"Unbelievable, Sarge. Come take a look. Turn on your visual magnifier," Gunny said.

"Whoa. It looks like those guys are transferring stuff from the lander to the spaceship. Must be fragile, the way they're so careful."

"Explosives, perhaps? Sarge?"

"You're right. I bet it's explosive. Not good!"

"It gets worse. Look at who's directing the transfer. It's Jacques Beauregard!"

"No, Gunny. It can't be. He's in prison. Damn! You're right. That is him!"

Upon hearing the news, Matt exclaimed, "Hell, and damnation! Doesn't that guy ever go away? Switch us to stealth mode. I want to see this for myself."

"Done, Sir," Josh said. "He must've escaped. That's not good."

"No kidding, Captain Obvious," Matt said.

Josh winced at the sarcasm and cleared his throat, "What I mean, Sir, is that he's got to be part of the danger Taxiarchi talked about."

Barnabas said, "The Ensign has a good point. With the number of times he's escaped, he makes Houdini look like an amateur. We need to keep a close eye on him."

"He's sure to make trouble for the colonies up here," Marci added.

"Shall I call this into NASA, Sir?" Josh asked.

"For the moment … no. I want to gather more intel and get a better feel for what's going on before sounding the alarm."

"Roger that, Sir," Josh said. "What about that shuttle?"

"As much as I hate to leave, we need to find out what's happening in the crevasse, where the lander came from," Matt said.

"What if we grabbed the emergency lander in our cargo hold and used it to follow the pirate lander?" Barnabas asked.

"Hmm. Might work. I'll have to think about it," Matt said.

127

"You may want to think quick, Sir," Marci said. "It looks like they're wrapping things up out there."

"Crap!" Matt exclaimed. "Let's do it. Lieutenant, take Ensign Torres, Sarge, and Gunny. Get our lander fired up and follow the Pirate lander. Keep a low profile. Whatever happens, don't get spotted. Get in as close as you can. See what they're up to and what they are pulling out of the crevasse. Remember, don't draw attention to yourself. Now get a move on it!"

As the group prepared to leave, Barnabas asked, "Are you sure about this, Sir?"

"No, Commander. I'm not, but I've little choice. I don't want that crazy pirate outta my sight, and we have to know what's cooking at that crevasse."

"It'll probably be a witch's teakettle," Barnabas observed.

Matt sighed. "That or worse, Commander. That or worse."

# The Mine

*"You can observe a lot by just watching." - Yogi Berra*

## Above Mars

**M**arci had little trouble tracking the pirate lander. It seemed to be unaware of her presence. As a precaution, she kept her lander in stealth mode. Soon, they were approaching the rim of the chasm. Josh let out a low whistle. "Looks more like a narrow canyon, Lieutenant."

"Reminds me of the Grand Canyon, under a full moon. Only without vegetation," Hilda commented.

"You're right, Gunny. Keep your eyes peeled for some kind of ship or complex," Marci said.

Hilda pointed, "Over there, Lieutenant. On a shelf about a hundred meters below the lip of the canyon on the opposite wall."

"I see it," Marc said.

"See what?" Marci asked.

"It looks like a couple of igloos and the burnt-out remains of a third," Hilda answered. "Why igloos?"

"They're ice-covered domes. They're commonly used on Mars to protect against cosmic radiation. We'll settle the lander on this side of the canyon, just below the horizon," Marci said.

Marc said, "Over there, behind the burnt-out igloo, is that a cave? Or maybe a mine entrance?"

"Could be, Sarge. When I get this lander down and covered, we'll take a closer look," Marci said.

Once the lander was positioned on a ledge and backed into a shallow cave, Marc asked, "What's the plan, Lieutenant? Do you want Gunny and me to reconnoiter the site over there?"

"Not yet, Sarge. Something's missing over there, and I want to take a closer look from here. Ensign, magnify what we see on the command screen."

"Aye, Ma'am," Josh said. "What're we looking for?"

"Where's their ship? Ah, there it is to the right, back in the shadows," Marci said. "Enhance the image, Ensign."

"I see what you're saying, Ma'am. It's near a parked landing craft," Marc said.

"Incoming vehicle!" Josh exclaimed.

"Where?" Marci asked.

"It's coming out of the canyon," Josh answered.

"Very good, Ensign. I see it now."

"It looks like it's landing by one of the igloos," Hilda said.

Marci watched a small crew of workers in terrestrial suits transferring containers from the lander to one of the igloos. "It looks like they are using the ship as their barracks and the igloos as their workspace."

"They're not nearly as careful with those drums, of whatever it is, as they were with the ones they were transferring to the spaceship a little while ago."

"Which means this stuff isn't as potent before it's processed?" Marc asked.

"That's what I'm thinking, Sarge," Marci said. "we need to take a closer look."

"As in a landing party, Ma'am?" Marc asked.

"Yes, Sarge. As in a landing party of you and Gunny. Grab your terrestrial combat suits and gear up. We'll wait until dark and fly you over to that ledge just above and to the left of the camp. Then you two can do your 'ninja owns the night' thing."

### The Pirate's Mining Camp

Hilda spoke into her mike, "The lieutenant told me to remind you that we've got exactly four hours before we're picked up."

"Copy that, McDermott. She's becoming a regular mother hen," Marc said.

"Yeah, she's a go-getter. I bet she'll be moving up the chain-of-command soon."

Once off the wall, they made their way among the shadows closer to the encampment.

"Mine or huts?" Marc whispered.

"I'll check out the mine," Hilda answered.

"Sounds good. I'll get the igloos. Let's meet against the cliff by the landers in two hours. Then we can check them out along with the starship."

"Roger that. See you in two." That said, and blending with the shadows, Hilda eased her way quietly to the mine entrance.

Losing sight of Hilda, Marc looked for anyone who might see him cross the open space between the cliff and the first igloo. *That's a lot of exposed territory to cover*, he thought. Marc aimed for a stack of drums located at the rear of the first igloo. Checking one last time and not seeing anyone, he dashed across the open space to a small spot between the stack of drums and the igloo. When he got there, he realized that the ice-protected igloo was glowing from the lights inside. *Crap, I didn't think this through. This is like shining a light on myself,* Marc thought. He glanced around for a less exposed spot. Finding no place, and with his heart beating faster, Marc decided to move a couple of drums to visually cover his position. *Crap, these are heavy. I hope no one hears them scraping the ground,* he thought. Then he started to chuckle as he remembered, *there's not enough air here to carry sound anyway, you moron.* A movement to his right caught Marc's eye. He froze first, his heart racing, then he hit the ground. *"Who is it*? He wondered. Rolling over, he thought he saw a shadowy figure flying overhead; *who can fly around here*? Looking at his timepiece, Marc realized he'd tarried too long. He quickly dashed to the second igloo and repeated his process of spying out what was happening inside. A quick look at his timepiece showed that Marc finished with five minutes to spare. He'd not seen anyone guarding the mining camp, or just wandering around outside, all night. *So far, so good.* Marc coiled himself for a quick dash to the shadow of the cliff and the prearranged meeting spot with Hilda. Taking one last look around, Marc made his dash. He arrived with a sigh of relief. A touch to his shoulder sent a chill down his back. He started so quickly, his feet left the ground. Marc turned to see Hilda smiling.

"Why Sarge, you're as jumpy as a long-tail cat in a room full of kids on pogo sticks."

"Damn, Gunny! You scared the bejeebies out of me."

"Gotta get moving, Sarge. We need to check out the landers and that space transport," Hilda said as she casually walked into the open toward the vehicles.

"Hold it, Gunny! You'll be spotted."

"Not a chance. No one wants to even be out at night."

"Really?"

"It's true. I overheard a couple of guys talking in the mine. They didn't finish their work before dark. As hungry as they are, they're not going outside and back to the space transport until morning."

"Why?"

"Everyone thinks this place is haunted or inhabited by flying beasts. Oh, here we are. How do you want to handle this? Sneak into the loading bay? Peer through the windows?"

"I've got this, Gunny. Step aside and watch the master at work."

Marc put a cell-phone-looking device up to the wall of the space transport. Then he placed a sticky disk on the corner of a window. When Marc finished, Hilda asked. "What the heck is that gadget?"

"It's a 5th generation RF-Pose device."

"What's that?"

"Invented just after the turn of the century. The first-generation RF-Pose was a basic laptop-sized radio transmitter. It beamed radio waves that passed through walls but were reflected by human bodies because of their high water content. Computer algorithms analyzed the reflected waves to create stick figures on a screen. At first, it was bulky and could only work with thin walls. This generation is miniaturized and even works on metal walls. The disk on the window picks up conversations from the window vibrations. Impressed by my technical savvy?"

"Hmm, maybe. Tell me, did Torres show you how that worked back in Houston?" Seeing the look on Marc's face, she concluded, "Busted!"

"Okay, okay, so Torres may have schooled me on this a little," Marc admitted.

"Well, mister smarty pants, if that thing gives feedback based on water content, how could it work on the igloos?"

"It doesn't. I peeked in the back window of each igloo."

"Double busted!"

## Across the Canyon from the Pirate's Mine

Back on board, the lander, Marc, and Hilda gave their report.

"So, here's what we found. The mine has two workers that oversee the digging robots. I overheard them complaining about how unreliable their robots are. It seems the robots are obsolete, and the men feel they spend too much time just trying to keep the robots going. Also, their orders just changed from digging straight into the cliff to digging down. Straight down." Hilda said.

"I wonder why?" Marci said.

"Maybe the vein of ore they're following just turned downward, Ma'am," Marc suggested.

"That makes sense, Sarge. Go on, Gunny."

"I also heard them complain about having to wear terrestrial suits. Apparently, there's an 'inside' mine. There, the men don't need terrestrial suits at all."

"That doesn't make sense, Gunny," Marc said.

"I know it doesn't, Sarge. I'm just saying it's what I overheard. They also complained about the food, being hungry, and long hours. Curiously, as hungry as they were, they were not about to go out into the night. Not even a hundred or so yards to get food from the space transport that serves as crew quarters."

"Gunny's right. We didn't see anyone outside at all," Marc said. "No one was even standing guard," Marc observed. "For my part, the igloos are used to refine the ore. The men working that process are not thrilled. It seems the refined ore, they call PETN-A, is very unstable. One igloo, and those inside it, has already blown up because someone dropped some PETN-A."

"What's PETN-A? Has anyone heard of it?" Josh asked.

"I have. I learned about it in one of my explosives classes at the University," Marc said. "Come to think of it, I had a refresher course in a recent dream."

"Go on, Sarge," Marci said.

"There are two teams of two, one team per igloo, that do the refining. Six other pirates load and unload the Pirate landing craft, cook, and pull guard duty. The boss must be a piece of work. All he does is spend his time in the transport, taking reports, and drinking. Oh, there's also a radio operator. She spends her time communicating with the pirate ship our old man is watching. And, get this, she uses Morse code to communicate with the second mine."

"Morse code?" Josh asked.

"Strange but true. That's what I heard."

"From what you've said, I count twelve bad guys," Marci said.

Hilda said, 'That's correct, Ma'am. Twelve bad guys that are afraid of the dark."

"Good job, you two," Marci said. "I'm calling what we have into the Osprey. It sounds like no one's doing anything worth watching tonight. We want to be sharp tomorrow. So let's get some rest ourselves. Torres, take the first watch, then call me. I'll take the second watch."

The dim light of morning found Marci and her crew watching as the mining operation stirred to life. As a worker watched, robots unloaded more barrels from the lander that had come from the canyon on the previous day. Other men were gingerly loading boxes marked 'Explosive' onto a second lander.

"Think we should follow that lander back into the canyon, Ma'am?" Josh asked.

"Yes, we should, Ensign," Marci said. "Wait, I've got a better idea. Load up and strap yourselves in. We're taking off now."

"What're you thinking, Ma'am?" Josh asked.

"I think if we follow that transport down, someone, from down there or up here, who's watching the transport, might see us."

"Even in stealth mode, Ma'am?" Josh asked.

"Even in stealth mode. I'd prefer erring on the side of caution. If we proceed to the bottom of the canyon first and watch from down there, we'd have a better chance of being unobserved."

"Gunny and I can keep an eye out for that second mine on our way down, Ma'am," Marc offered.

"Sounds good. Thanks, Sarge."

Marci lifted the lander gently off the shelf and guided it slowly into the canyon. As it descended, the crew watched for some sign of another mining operation. None was found. Finally, the lander neared the bottom of the canyon.

"Looks like a lake at the bottom of the canyon," Hilda said.

"Can't be, Gunny," Marc corrected. "The gravity here is too weak to keep any water that makes its way to the surface from drifting off into space."

Hilda raised an eyebrow. "Then what is it?"

Marc said, "Ice. I'm sure the temperature down here is always well below zero."

"So, it's a frozen lake," Hilda persisted.

"Yeah, it's a frozen lake."

"So, it's a lake," Hilda stated with a triumphant smile.

"If that's the case, you'd think the lake would be smooth. This one has dozens of splash marks. They look like fountains that are beginning to form. How do you explain that, Mr. Geologist?" Marci asked.

"I'd say that's from a long time ago, when warm water, such as a geyser, broke through the ice and froze almost instantly," Marc replied."

"A long time ago? Not recently?" Hilda asked.

Marc said, "Yeah, Gunny. I'm sure the ice is way too thick for something like that to happen now. Those frozen plumes must be millions of years old. They—"

Josh interrupted. "I see the pirate lander approaching."

All field glasses, including Marci's, pointed up. "I see it, Ensign. It's coming down a little fast."

Josh watched the quickly growing speck. "A little fast? It's dropping like a rock!"

Marci shifted uncomfortably. "Faster than a rock, Ensign! Much faster! If the pilot doesn't pull up fast, it'll—" CRASH!

Before Marci could get her words out, the pirate lander plowed straight into the ice. Though there was no sound, the impact was so hard that it rocked Marci's lander and crew. She gasped as she watched the pirate lander disappear under the ice. It was replaced by a plume of water, which froze before it could fall back down.

"Holy crap!" Josh exclaimed. "What just happened?"

# Pirate Station

*"A man should look for what is and not for what he thinks should be."*
*Albert Einstein*

### Onboard, the Osprey – Parked on the surface of Mars

Barnabas noticed that Matt continued to stare after the receding lander containing four of his crew members long after it was out of sight. "They'll be okay, Sir," he said.

"Yes, Commander, I know they will."

"I hear a 'but' coming."

"They're heading toward the action, and we'll miss it," Matt confessed.

Barnabas turned toward Corporal Brady. "Kid, the captain hates waiting around. If he's not in the middle of the action, well, let's just say he's easily bored."

"I agree with the captain, Sir. I like being in action. Should we be calling NASA or the Space Force Command about now?"

Matt said, "Not just yet, Corporal. Like I said, I want to know more about the situation before calling it in."

Barnabas said, "I haven't had a chance to welcome you aboard, Corporal Brady. Is it Charles or Chuck?"

"It's Charles on my birth certificate, Sir. My friends call me Chuck."

"Around here, Charles, we'll be calling you Corporal or Mr. Brady," Matt said.

Barnabas said, "It's official, Corporal Brady. You're now a part of our crew. In honor of such a distinguished role, I want you to go back to the cargo hold. Double-check to be sure the crew stowed everything securely, in case we need to make an immediate departure."

"Yes, Sir, I'm on it," Chuck said as he moved toward the cargo hold.

Once he was out of earshot, Barnabas said, "You're not calling NASA, are you?"

"Nope."

"Not calling the Space Force headquarters either?"

"Nope."

"Thought as much."

"Would you?" Matt asked.

"What, call those geniuses that thought up the brilliant plan to invade Portae? Satan would be tossing snowballs in hell before I'd consider that option."

Matt chuckled. "Why, Commander, I didn't know you could be so sarcastic."

Barnabas's face broke into a huge smile. "Not sarcasm. Just the truth, Sir."

"It was pretty sarcastic."

"Well, maybe a little. Perhaps I've been influenced by my commanding officer."

"Perhaps you have. Your sentiments are well put, and I concur."

139

"Besides, calling NASA or the Space Force brass wasn't part of the orders we got from Taxiarchis," Barnabas said.

"You're spot on, Maalouf."

"While I'd love to see the look on Captain Lewis's face, getting a call from the Osprey that disappeared but was now sitting on Mars, staking out a pirate spaceship."

"I'd love to see the look on Admiral Robinson's face when he learns that his nemesis, Jacques Beauregard, is once again free as a bird," Matt said. "How the hell did he escape, anyway?"

"Had to have been an inside job," Barnabas said.

"Probably was. It seems that there is no end to Admiral Morris's influence."

"Where do you think Morris is hiding?"

"Don't know and don't care."

"Pretty cavalier, Captain. After all, he almost got us killed a couple of times."

"True, but he's not here, and that crazy pirate is. Say, what else do you see over there?" Matt asked as he looked through his field glasses.

Barnabas lifted his glasses. "I see the pirate spaceship tucked in the shadows. Wait, I see another, deeper in the shadows. Looks like a fueling tanker. It's set up to fuel two crafts at once."

"Yes, and to the right. What do you see?" Matt asked.

"Looks like an igloo-style ice house. I can barely make it out. Oh, there's a hovercraft parked just behind that igloo. Everything's tucked away from view unless you're on the ground. Wait, did you see that, Sir?"

"It was a person, bounding quickly from the igloo to the tanker," Matt said. "Moving fast and looking over his shoulder all the way."

"What do you make of it, Captain?"

"First, this place is set up to refuel two ships and has a semi-permanent dwelling. Perhaps more importantly, no one wants to linger outside. I wonder why?"

"Wonder no longer, Sir. Look at the ledge of the crater about 50 feet above them. In the shadows, there's some movement."

Matt switched to low-light vision. The area he was looking at was too bright. But, when he focused on the dark shadows, he saw a movement. He felt a chill as he brought the moving object into focus. "What the hell, Commander?"

"Looks like a huge flying-type creature, Sir. Wait, it just disappeared!"

"Can't be. Something like that can't exist in this hostile environment. Can it?"

"Whether it can or not, I know I'm not inclined to leave this ship," Barnabas answered.

Just then, Chuck entered the bridge. "Everything is secured, just as you asked, Sir."

"Thank you, Corporal," Barnabas said.

Matt said, "Perfect timing, Corporal. We need to set a watch schedule to keep an eye on things. I'll take the first watch. Commander, you take the second. Corporal, take the third."

Sometime later, Barnabas entered the bridge to assume his watch. "All quiet, Sir?"

"All's quiet, Commander."

Matt felt that he could finally relax. "I'd best lay down, Commander." He wandered back to the Crew Cabin and laid down. It seemed that he had just closed his eyes when Barnabas called him back to the bridge. He stood next to Barnabas. Looking out the window over the desolate landscape, he saw Jacques Beauregard entering the pirate spaceship. A flurry of activity around the ship signaled its imminent departure. He called Corporal Brady to the bridge and slid into the weapons officer's seat.

"Buckle up. Time to be on our way," Matt said as Brady slid into a passenger seat.

"Are you sure, Sir?" Barnabas asked.

"Absolutely. I'm not letting that scum-bag pirate escape again," Matt said.

"What about the rest of our crew, Sir?" Barnabas asked. "We don't have a—"

"Weapons officer?" Matt interrupted. "You're looking at him, Commander. Are you buckled in, Corporal?"

"I am, Sir."

They saw the pirate ship take off, stirring up a cloud of reddish-brown dust. "Let's get after it, Commander."

"Aye, Sir." Barnabas initiated the launch procedure. They felt themselves being pushed back into their chairs as the Osprey responded to her pilot's commands. "Where do you think he's going, Sir?"

"Have no clue, but we're losing him. Full power, Commander."

"Full power it is, Sir," Barnabas said while scanning the pre-flight checklist they should have followed first to be sure he didn't forget anything. The Osprey was slowly closing in on its prey. "Sir, we'll be passing painfully close to a large asteroid shortly," Barnabas said.

"Copy that, Commander. He's just within range."

The pirate ship began a series of corkscrew maneuvers, making it hard to target. Matt started sweating as he tried to squeeze off some quality shots. Three times the pirate was in his sights, but his reaction time was too slow. The pirate ship feigned a break to the right causing Matt to waste more shots trying to anticipate his moves. *Too bad the Corporal isn't trained on our weapons*, he thought, as the pirate began to make a gentle arc to the Osprey's portside. When the Osprey followed that arc, the pirate quickly fired several positioning jets to change its angle and slow its turn. The Osprey quickly passed their adversary.

"Rear shields up!" Barnabas said.

Matt tried to quickly switch from a weapons officer, firing at the pirate, to a tech officer, who controlled the Osprey's defensive shields. He was too late. Before the shields came up, the pirate landed a couple of shots. Alarms screamed, and the ship shuddered from multiple hits.

"Shields up," Matt said. "Finally," he added under his breath.

The damage was already done. The Osprey began to shimmy and slow as new alarms sounded.

"Captain, the fuel container is losing power!" Barnabas exclaimed.

"What does that mean?" the wide-eyed corporal asked.

"Our fuel is anti-matter. It's contained in a magnetic field. If we lose the magnetic field, the anti-matter reacts without control, and the engine blows up," Matt said.

"Container strength is failing, Sir. It's orange going to red," Barnabas said.

Matt took a deep breath. "Commander, prepare to eject from the engine compartment."

"Aye, Sir. I'm aiming toward the asteroid. We may be able to use it as a shield from the explosion."

"On my mark, eject us from the engine compartment. Three, two, one, MARK."

The Osprey sprang away from the failing engines. The engine compartment, a full kilometer away, exploded. Shrapnel from the explosion enveloped the Osprey. The sound was deafening. "This sucks!" Matt exclaimed, waking himself up. *Note to self. Don't chase a pirate without a weapons officer*, he thought.

He heard the voice of Barnabas over the intercom. "Captain to the bridge," it said.

Rubbing the sleep out of his eyes, he walked to the bridge. He was surprised to see Chuck there. "What are you doing here, Corporal? Your watch hasn't started yet."

"Actually, it just ended, Sir."

"Wow! Did I sleep through both watches?"

"You did," Barnabas affirmed.

Matt looked out the window. "Anything to report? Any activity?"

Both Barnabas and Chuck shook their heads no.

"Well, men, this is the perfect time to start the Corporal's training," Matt said.

"Training, Sir?" Chuck asked.

"Yes, Mr. Brady. You're about to become our backup weapons officer."

"He is?" Barnabas asked.

"No way, Sir! No disrespect, but I couldn't master the systems on this ship," Chuck complained.

"Did you receive several marksmanship awards? Are you questioning my orders?"

"Yes, Sir, and no, Sir."

"Good. While the rest of the crew is gone, you're the weapons officer, I'm the tech and defensive systems officer, and Commander, you're the pilot, of course."

"Of course, Sir," a bewildered Barnabas said.

"We'll start by running you through some training materials on the ship's computer. Once you're comfortable with that, the commander will fly us over the horizon briefly. There you'll target practice on a few of our drones."

"What about keeping an eye on our pirate friend over there, Sir?" Barnabas asked.

"We'll park a drone here to spy on him while we practice just over the horizon. If he makes a move, we'll be on his tail in no time," Matt said.

"Sounds like you've given this a lot of thought," Barnabas said.

"Let's just say I've been dreaming about this moment."

The wide-eyed corporal shook his head, "Awesome, Sir."

A shadow crossed over the portside windows. "What was that?" Matt asked.

"No clue, Sir," Barnabas said.

"Are we being watched by a drone?"

"I'm not picking up any radio signals that would suggest it's a drone, Captain," Barnabas said.

Carefully pushing himself from the window, Chuck said, "I only caught a glimpse of it. It looked greenish-brown and organic. But, that can't be."

"You're right, Corporal. Life, as we know it, doesn't exist on the surface of Mars," Matt said.

"Or hasn't yet been seen," Barnabas corrected.

"Oh, come on, Commander. You know what I mean. Mars's conditions and Life, as we know it, don't go together," Matt chided.

"There it goes again," Chuck said. "Didn't you see the shadow that crossed your console?"

Matt nodded. "Yeah, kid. I did. We're being watched, and I have no clue by whom or what.

"What does this mean?" Chuck asked.

"It means we can't let our guard down," Matt said.

This can't be good, Sir," Chuck said.

Barnabas agreed. "Got that right, Corporal."

# A Second Mine

*"You can't fix stupid." – Ron White*

### Bottom of a Martian Canyon

Hilda laughed. "So much for your theory about million-year-old water plumes, Mr. Geology Expert."

"Not to mention my idea about thick ice," Marc added with a smile.

"Do you think that was planned? Or was he just out of control?" Josh asked.

"Either it was planned, which explains the number of frozen fountains we see, or they've lost way too many landing craft," Marci observed.

Just then, another geyser erupted a hundred meters away from them. This one was topped by a small transport flying straight up. The column of water started to settle down and quickly froze to create a fountain of ice.

"That's it," Josh said. "The second mine is under the water. These ships are crashing through the ice on purpose."

"Why would you crash through the ice just to resurface a couple of minutes later?" Marc asked.

"Different ship, Sarge. The markings on the one that dove in are different from the one that just surfaced," Marci said.

"You've got a good eye, Lieutenant," Hilda said.

"Most importantly, blasting through the ice causes no apparent harm," Josh said. "The ice layer must be thin."

"That's surprising. Given that the temperature on the surface freezes the water so fast, you'd think that the ice cap would be thick," Hilda said.

"Unless the water underneath is warm enough to keep the water from freezing too deep," Marc said.

"There must be a mining operation underwater. Are the pirates mining the same stuff under the water as up above? Or are they mining for a second type of material and blending the two?" Marci asked.

"There's only one way to find out, Ma'am," Marc said.

Josh said, "Yeah, Sarge. But if we dive in, we'll lose our ability to communicate with the Osprey."

"Only until we surface again," Marc said.

"The lander is a spaceship. Will it even survive underwater?" Hilda asked.

Josh answered, "Good question, Gunny. This lander is designed to land on solid ground or in water. So, yeah, if we don't get too deep, we'll be okay. A couple of the landers splashed during our landing exercises, and they came up undamaged. I'd say we're good for about 20 to 30 meters."

"Lieutenant, what about it?" Marc asked. "Do we go for it? Or do you check with the captain first?"

"The last time I reported in, he gave us permission to seek out the second mine."

147

"Yeah, but underwater? Was he expecting us to go that far?" Marc asked.

"Good point. In this case, I'm inclined to ask forgiveness later rather than be denied permission now." Marci took a deep breath. "It's a risk, and we're all in this together. Does anyone have second thoughts about going in, other than the communications problem?" Looking around and seeing no objections, she continued, "Good. It would get mighty cold waiting on this ice for the rest of us to return. Ensign, contact the Osprey with our intentions, then turn our radio off."

"Done."

Marci steered the lander halfway up the canyon and paused. "Hold on, everyone. We're going in."

"Our lander isn't built for this kind of impact. Is it?" Hilda asked.

Sensing Hilda's concern, Marc asked, "What's the worst that can happen, Ensign?"

"The Lieutenant's insurance rate'll go through the roof," Josh quipped.

To which Marci responded, "Wrong, Ensign. I have an accident forgiveness policy."

"Seriously," Marc insisted, "what's the worst thing that can happen to us?"

"Not much, Sarge, unless we're not going fast enough to break through the ice. In which case we'd be stuck, with our ass side up," Josh said.

Hearing this, Marci took the lander higher still. Then she rolled it over and started a vertical dive at nearly full throttle. She winced as the craft approached the water. *I was never trained to fly into things. Fly around, fly above, fly below, but never crash into.* She braced for the impact. The jolting crash was deafening! The sound of ice scraping against the lander's skin was as shrill as someone scratching fingernails across a chalkboard. The lander slowed. *Damn! We are going to be stuck with our ass in the air. I'll never hear the end of it,* she thought as she pulled harder on the throttle. All went quiet as they cleared the ice and slid underwater. Josh began calling out the depth as he switched on the searchlights. Sure enough, the lake was shallow. The bottom came into sight after twenty meters.

"Where's the mining operation?" Hilda asked.

"Good question, Gunny. My scan shows nothing," Josh said.

"Wait! What's that about eight meters off the bottom to our starboard?"

"Looks like a cave, Lieutenant," Josh said.

"I'm going to ease into that cave slowly. Keep reading the depth, Torres. Gunny, keep a sharp eye on the roof above. Let me know if it starts to pinch down on us. Sarge, slide over next to Torres and be ready to kill the searchlights if we spot another vehicle or the mine."

Hilda said, "Aye, Ma'am. Is now a bad time to mention that I'm claustrophobic?"

The cave turned into a narrow tunnel. Surprisingly, it contained underwater life. There were outcroppings of pink and orange coral. Greenery, similar to what is known on Earth as seaweed, abounded. There was a variety of grasses growing from the floor of the tunnel.

"I'm not sure we can go much further without getting stuck," Marci said.

"Our sensors indicate that the tunnel should open soon, Ma'am," Josh said.

Marci brought the lander to a stop. "Kill the searchlights, Sarge."

"Aye, Ma'am," Marc said.

"Did you kill all of them?"

"Yes, Ma'am."

"Then what's that glow ahead of us?"

149

"Good question, Lieutenant. Could be the mining venture," Josh speculated.

"Only one way to find out." Marci edged the lander forward. "Be sure to keep our lights off, Sarge."

"Aye, Ma'am."

Marci continued to edge the lander forward.

"Sensors indicate we're clearing the tunnel now," Josh said.

The tunnel opened into a wider body of water.

"I'll be!" Hilda exclaimed. "The light's coming from above. We're in an underground lake."

"By the looks of it, I'd say they're artificial lights," Josh observed.

"I think you're right, Ensign," Marci said. "We'll take her up slow in stealth mode. Once we clear the surface, have our weapons online. I have no idea how unfriendly our reception might be if we're spotted."

The lander gently broke the surface of the water. Sheer cliffs rose on all sides. To their right, about a hundred meters up, was the source of the lights. "That must be where the mine is," Marci said. "We're going to ascend the opposite wall and see if we can find a spot from where we can observe what's happening."

Marci found a ledge running the cliff's length, about five meters above and opposite the lake from where the mine was. She parked the lander in the shadows. A narrow waterfall was on their right. To their left, as they faced the lake, was a natural bridge to the other side. The encampment consisted of half a dozen tents, several crude wooden huts, and stacks of drums. It was lit by several construction lights, similar to those used for night-time road work. Three landers were parked to the right of the huts. Finally, the compound featured two searchlights and guard towers. Occasionally, beams from the searchlights passed overhead and then settled on the tunnel entrance across from the natural bridge. Then the beams would move across where the Osprey lander was located, to another tunnel, by the waterfall. Fortunately, the lander was tucked far enough back into the wall's shadow to be mainly invisible to the light.

Marc looked around. "Beautiful. Absolutely beautiful, Ma'am. It's the most magnificent cavern I've ever seen."

Marci said, "Not interested in the cavern, Sarge. What do you notice about the encampment?"

"Sorry, Ma'am. I see … wait, look at those guys over by the mine entrance. They're not wearing terrestrial suits or helmets."

"Sarge is right," Hilda said. "They're all wearing regular clothes. How can that be? Everyone knows Mars is too cold and has too little oxygen for people just to walk around like they do on Earth."

"Yet, there they are. And they're human like us," Marc said. "I suspect the lake we just came through traps the air inside the cavern."

Josh disagreed. "Sorry, Sarge. That's just crazy. You know that the air pressure in underground caves naturally adjusts to match the air pressure outside. And Mars has little, if any, air pressure outside."

Hilda said, "If that's true, the lake, and all the air in here, would be siphoned off in no time. Why isn't it?"

Marc rubbed his chin. "What you say is normally true, Chief. It must be the ice. The temperature is so cold in the canyon, it keeps the lake's surface frozen. That acts as a bottle stopper, trapping the air in." After a few moments, Marc asked, "Permission to step out of the lander, Lieutenant?"

"Granted, Sarge. Use the starboard side door so the lander will hide you. Oh, and Ensign, put this lander into the fully cloaked mode. Those searchlights make me nervous," Marci said. "Everyone, grab your night vision binoculars. We're going to take a little field trip together."

"Now you're talking, Lieutenant!" Hilda exclaimed.

Positioned safely behind some boulders, Marci's crew spied on the encampment of tents, huts, and landers across the lake. They were clustered just outside of what Marci thought was the mine entrance. Sounds of the waterfall and work being done in the mine provided an unusual backdrop, as the vacuum of space carries no sound. The crew tried to make sense of what they were seeing.

Marci whispered, "This place reminds me of a prison camp."

Josh noticed the body language of the guards. "Why're the guards so nervous? They're carrying some mighty big guns."

"They also placed a checkpoint by their side of the natural bridge, running from our ledge down to theirs. And the whole compound is fenced in with nasty-looking razor wire and a mighty strong-looking gate." Hilda said.

"Weird," Marc said.

"What?" Marci asked.

"The first mine, on top, had no guards. Down here, I count an easy six heavily-armed guards. And they're acting like they might be attacked at any time," Marc answered.

"That, plus two guard towers and a gate at the entrance to the natural bridge," Hilda added.

"You'd think it'd be the other way around. Hell, no one on Earth even knows this place exists," Marc said.

Hilda said, "Looks to me like someone down here knows they exist. And is not happy about it. Whoever it is, they're on our side of the lake."

Marc said, "Meaning if hostilities break out, we'll be in the crossfire. You might say we're in the frying pan."

"You mean, between the frying pan and the fire," Hilda corrected.

Josh chuckled. "How about a rock and a hard place?"

Marci shook her head. "Stop with the clichés already."

Marc asked, "Could it be a prison, and they're trying to keep someone from escaping?" After catching skeptical glances from the rest of the crew, he added, "It's Just a thought."

"From the way the guards keep looking over here, Sarge, I'd say that's not likely," Marci said. "I need to call this in."

"How, Ma'am?" Josh asked. "We're too deep in the planet for any of our telecom equipment to work."

"Didn't think about that," Marci admitted. "I wonder if those folks over there have some way to communicate topside. Ensign, start scanning the radio frequencies. See if you can intercept any of their messages."

"Aye, Ma'am."

"Sarge, Gunny, I need you to reconnoiter the mining camp and mine ASAP."

Marc smiled, "Outta the frying pan, into the fire, Lieutenant."

Josh groaned at Marc's comment while Hilda said, "We're on it, Ma'am."

Josh and Marci watched as Hilda and Marc used their rock-climbing skills to traverse the side of the natural bridge. At one point, they stopped. Wondering why their pause, Marci scanned the top of the bridge. She gasped as she saw a couple of armed men leaving the camp and crossing over to her side. She motioned to Josh, who followed her lead, and ducked into a deep crevice in the rock wall behind their lander. Soon the patrol walked by, just missing the lander (still in cloak mode) by no more than inches. After they passed, Josh and Marci took up their old positions and looked across the lake. They saw that the Sarge and Gunny had traversed the bridge and were on the far cliff face. They made their traverse just below the shelf, housing the mining camp. Then the duo scrambled up the only place without a fence. It was where the landers were parked. Then they disappeared as they darted in and out of the shadows. *Just Waiting is the worst*, Marci thought.

153

## In the Martian Grotto

The traverse across the natural bridge was uneventful until Marc and Hilda heard some pirates talking right above them. They stopped and waited. Just when they thought all was clear, one of the pirates leaned over and spit out a wad of chewing tobacco. It landed right on Marc's black stocking cap.

"Crap!" Marc exclaimed as he felt the juice run down his neck.

"Shh!" Hilda whispered.

"Did you hear that?" one of the pirates asked his comrade.

"No," the second pirate answered.

"I could've sworn I heard someone say 'crap.'"

"You're just imagining things."

"No, it could be one of those beasts, and it's right below us."

"Those beasts fly and cling to walls. But they sure as hell don't speak. Let's move out and get this task done."

"I suppose you're right. The sooner we get the stuff and get back here, the better I'll like it." The two walked on across the bridge.

Hilda glared at Marc. "What?" he asked as they continued their traverse.

"You're a professional. Keep your mouth shut!" Hilda whispered.

Marc said nothing. *How can she make a whisper feel like a full-on smack-down?* He thought.

The duo finally made it to the other side. Then they began to traverse the cliff face. Razor wire and fencing ran along the edge until it reached where the landers were parked. That's where Marc and Hilda scrambled onto the ledge that held the pirate encampment. They moved quickly and quietly among the shadows. Even though the camp was well lit, there were plenty of nooks, crannies, and stalagmites along the back wall to cover Marc and Hilda's progress. They huddled behind a stalagmite abreast of the huts.

154

Hilda spoke softly, "They look occupied. There's light coming from the windows."

Marc whispered, "I'll take a closer look."

Looking to the left, then the right, Hilda tapped Marc on the shoulder and whispered, "Clear."

Marc dashed to one of the huts and hid by a stack of drums. He peeked in a window, then ducked back to the cover of the drums. Quietly, Marc opened one of the drums and reached inside. He pulled out a handful of white and blueish-gray residue. *This looks and feels a lot like contaminated PETNA*, he thought. *I didn't know you could mine it. I thought it was always created in a lab setting. If this is true, the pirates are collecting a powerful explosive at a fantastic rate. Why?* Marc looked around carefully. Seeing no one, he dashed quietly back to Hilda's position. "The huts are just the barracks where everyone sleeps and relaxes."

Hilda nodded and pointed to the tents.

"They're all yours, Gunny," Marc whispered.

Together, they worked their way over to the tents. The clanking, drilling, and hammering told them that the first tent was for machinery maintenance.

Marc whispered, "Did you notice that the repair tent over there is the only one being guarded?"

"Good point, Sarge. I'll give it a wide berth."

Back in the shadows, Marc checked his surroundings. When he saw no one, he tapped Hilda on the shoulder and said, "Clear."

Hilda darted across the open space, then settled in the shadow of the second tent. Marc could just make out a thumbs-up as she rolled over and scurried to the shadows between tents three and four. After a brief pause, she came back to where Marc was hiding. "Well, Gunny?"

"The first two tents were just a mess hall and supply tent. But, the fourth was their radio tent."

"Hmm. It could be interesting."

"Yep, Sarge. They were sending a couple of messages about mining robots breaking down and needing more food. Get this; they're using Morse code to communicate."

"Morse code. Now that's original. Of course. A radio down here's useless in communicating with the surface camp. But Morse code could be passed through the lake. All they'd need is a receptor here and one on the ice outside. That could work."

Hilda said, "They also talked about the workers refusing to dig further back into the mine. Something about it being too hot. They're planning to double their effort at digging a shaft upward and connect with the surface mine."

"What? Connect with the surface mine?"

"That's what I said, Sarge."

"That's just stupid! The minute those two mines connect, all the oxygen down here will escape! Anyone caught without life support equipment will suffocate!"

Hilda nodded in agreement. "Why would they do that? They can't be that stupid, can they?"

Marc shrugged and said, "We need to get word to the lieutenant ASAP!"

"Sarge, I want to check one more thing first."

"What?"

"In the mine. Who're the diggers that won't go further back?"

"I'm not following you, Gunny."

"Robots don't complain about the heat. They just break. And do you think any of these lazy pirates would be digging? I don't think so. I think they've got slaves doing their work."

"You sure about this? I don't think going into the mine is such a good idea."

"Humor me, Sarge. Just this once."

Marc shook his head no but said, "You lead the way, Gunny. I've got your back."

Creeping to the entrance, Marc peeked around the corner. Seeing no one, they slipped quickly into the main shaft, keeping against one of the walls. To their relief, the mine was dark once they got past the bright lights at the entrance. The heat became noticeable as they walked further into the mine. They found a shaft running to the right. Hilda shrugged and turned right. As they were walking, they heard some clanking and murmurs. They rounded a corner and were stopped by a gate that was made of iron rods. It was closed but not locked. They saw a shadowy figure using a large serving spoon to place something on tin plates, held by outstretched, hairy hands.

Marc whispered, "You're right, Gunny."

They crept back toward the mine entrance. Marc and Hilda had just stepped into the main tunnel when they heard footsteps. They ducked into the shadow of a couple of large support beams.

Just then, a voice rang out, "Hey, hold up, you two!"

Their momentum carried the duo into the shadows, where they froze.

"Yeah, you two. Don't ignore me."

Marc and Hilda looked at each other. They turned slowly, preparing to attack.

A second voice answered. "Hey, We're holding up right here, George. What's your problem anyway?"

"I found this guy slinking around. I think he's trying to escape. I've got him chained but don't have a key to the cell block."

George was holding a short manlike creature that stood about four-and-a-half feet tall. The stout creature was hairy all over with a full beard. It had big hands and big hairy feet.

"Jimmy's serving dinner right now, so the cell block is open. He's got the master key to the cells."

"Good enough. I'll take it back now," George said as he walked away.

"There goes part of our problem," the first pirate said to the second. "Those dwarves will only eat their kind of food. If it weren't for that, we wouldn't have to forage the land and fight those disgusting flying beasts."

"The boss ought to send teams of more than just two at a time. That place gives me the creeps."

"You got that right," the second pirate agreed as they walked out of the mine.

"Looks like we're clear," Marc whispered to Hilda.

They darted out of the mine and slid behind a nearby stalagmite. Two armed guards rounded the corner just as the duo made it into the shadows. Once the guards were out of sight, Marc called Marci.

Hilda kept an eye out for the guards as Marc placed his call.

"Lieutenant, here's a brief report," he whispered.

"Tell her about their slaves," Hilda prompted.

Marc nodded and continued, "First, this is a prison camp. They have some short hairy people held in cells and chains. Looks like the pirates are forcing them to do the mining work."

Marc continued, quietly describing his big concern that the miners might connect their shaft with the one from the first mine, which would rob the cavern of its air. Marc snapped his fingers. "Oh, and they're using Morse code for messaging the first mine."

Hilda nudged Marc and made a chopping motion with her hand across her throat; Marc cut off his mike mid-sentence, just as the guards got within ear-shot.

As the guards started to pass near the stalagmite hiding Marc and Hilda, the first guard said, "Hold up, I need to take a leak." He stepped into the shadows, where Marc and Hilda were hiding. He unzipped his pants and began to urinate on Marc's shoes.

"Shit!" The word slipped out of Marc's mouth before he could stop himself.

"What the hell!" the guard exclaimed as he jumped backward and pulled his automatic rifle off his shoulder. Marc would have taken that guard out before he could bring his weapon to bear. Unfortunately, he was already staring down the barrel of an automatic handgun, held steady by the second guard.

## Opposite the Pirate's Grotto Mining Camp

When Marci saw that Marc and Hilda were safely inside the pirate's compound, she said, "Ensign, let's get back to the lander. We need to see if there's some way to communicate with the captain."

"I'm on it, Ma'am."

Josh slipped inside the cloaked lander while Marci stood by the open door. "I wonder what would happen if that patrol came back and walked into the lander," she whispered.

Josh chuckled. "That would be a sight to see. Two guards fighting an invisible object," he whispered as he returned the lander to stealth mode and scanned the radio frequencies, looking for the one the pirates were using.

Finally, he sat up straight and whispered. "I got it, Lieutenant. I found the channel those guys are broadcasting on. The thing is, they're only sending Morse code. Why would they do that?"

"Hang on a second, Ensign." Marci scanned the surface of the lake with her low-light field glasses. "Yes, there it is."

"What?"

"There's a buoy floating down there. I bet it's picking up the Morse code and sending it along underwater. There must be a second buoy stuck up through the ice outside which rebroadcasts the coded messages."

"Sweet solution, but we can't use it without them overhearing what we say, seeing as we'd be using their frequency."

"Do you think the buoys are smart enough to pick up our messages and pass them along on our frequency?"

"Good thought, Ma'am. Maybe. I'm not sure their equipment's that sophisticated."

"Worst case, if we try on our frequency?"

"Most likely, our message doesn't get through. We can try by sending a generic message. Something like: 'FOUND SECOND MINE PLEASE ACKNOWLEDGE.'"

"I like it. How are your Morse code skills?"

"Rusty, but I'll get it done."

"Send that message. We'll wait for an acknowledgment."

"How long do we wait before we go to plan B, Lieutenant?"

"We'll wait 'til the Sarge, and Gunny get back. If we don't hear anything by then, we'll fly out to make our report."

Marci's earpiece crackled to life. It was Marc. "Lieutenant, here's a brief report," he whispered.

"Where are you, Sarge?" Marci asked.

"Gunny and I are hiding behind a stalagmite, just outside the mine entrance."

"You need to get back here ASAP."

"Will do. But you need to hear this first, Lieutenant."

"Can't it wait until you get back?"

"It's too critical. First, this is a prison camp. They're holding some short hairy people locked in cells and chains. Looks like the pirates are forcing them to do all of the mining work."

"How many are there?"

"At least two dozen. The creatures are being guarded pretty closely, Lieutenant."

"How many guards, Sarge?"

"A couple dozen. this camp has twice as many pirates as the one that's topside."

"Good to know. Now get back here ASAP."

"Wait, Lieutenant. There's more!"

"What?"

"The miners are collecting the same unrefined compound as the top-side mine. Now, they're digging upward. By my calculation, if they don't stop, they'll meet the other mine shaft. When that happens, the atmosphere down here escapes!"

listening in, Josh said, "You know what they say, Sarge. 'You can't fix stupid.'"

"Got that right, Ensign," Marc said.

"How close do you think they are?" Marci asked.

"Not sure, Ma'am. I'd say—" His transmission went dead.

"Sarge, do you read me?" Marci asked. "Sarge? Crap! Their com-link just died. Do you see anything over there, Ensign?"

"Nope, Ma'am. No sign of either of them."

### Onboard the Osprey – Parked on the surface of Mars

Matt had a brief conversation with Marci the night before she flew her lander through the Martian ice. Marci talked about what Hilda and Marc found and heard at the upper mine. She also mentioned a second mine, lower in the canyon. Matt didn't think twice about letting her look for the second mine. It seemed like the next logical step. *The more we learn about this operation, the better*, he thought.

"Remember, Lieutenant, keep a low profile. Don't draw attention to yourself."

"Copy that, Sir. Anything else?"

"Don't do anything I wouldn't do," Matt concluded.

"Roger that, Sir. I'm out," Marci signed off.

Barnabas laughed out loud.

"What's so funny, Maalouf?" Matt asked.

"You, Captain. 'Don't do anything I wouldn't.' Why, back in the day, you had a reputation for reckless abandon. You'd try anything at least once. 'Don't do anything I wouldn't' is like giving her carte blanche."

"Card what?" the Corporal asked.

"Permission to do whatever she wants," Barnabas said.

Matt frowned. "Corporal, don't believe everything Maalouf says. Remember, what I say goes around here."

"Don't mind the captain. He wishes he was in that canyon with our lander," Barnabas said.

"You got that right, Maalouf. I hate this waiting and wondering what's going on."

"You'll just have to trust Lieutenant Gonzales. She's top of her class and hand-picked for this mission," Barnabas said.

"I get it already, Commander. I just hate to wait," Matt said. "So, quit busting my chops already."

The night passed slowly for Matt. He tossed and turned but couldn't quiet his mind. *What's going on here with all those explosives? What does that crazy pirate plan to do?* Finally, Matt gave up on sleep and entered the bridge, where he found Barnabas humming a tune. "You're mighty cheerful, Commander. We've got quite a puzzle on our hands, and you're humming a tune."

"I think we've made some progress in solving our puzzle, Sir."

"What progress?"

Barnabas smiled. "At least we know where the second transport is. The one that would use this refueling station, Sir."

"Good point."

"Looks like he'll be loading up two ships with super high explosives, Captain. Where do you think he'll strike?"

"That's what kept me up all night. The colonies here on Mars are a logical choice because of their location, but …."

"But, what?"

"Each colony has a decent air defense set up. What Bauregaurd would gain by taking them on is beyond my paygrade," Matt said.

"You can be sure that whatever it is, he's going to do something very profitable or very big, Sir."

"Whatever he's planning, we need to dog him. When he makes his move, we need to take him down. Which means we need a first-rate weapons officer. Corporal Brady?"

"Here, Sir," Chuck answered as he entered the bridge.

"It's time for live-fire training. Commander, place our watchdog drone, and prepare to lift off."

"Aye, Sir."

Chuck whispered to Barnabas, "I like our captain, Sir."

Barnabas smiled. "So do I, Son. So do I."

Just then, a shadow crossed the window of the Osprey. Barnabas said, "Captain, something strange is happening."

"What?"

"The drone's not responding as it should. It acts like it's fighting a downdraft."

"Here on Mars, with a thin atmosphere? Makes no sense, Commander."

"No, it doesn't. I've got it in position, but it felt like I was maneuvering against a helicopter down-draft."

"Let's hope we can get this old bird up without so much trouble. Take us up, Commander."

Barnabas said, "Aye, Sir. We are beginning to lift—"

"Wait, Commander," Chuck interrupted. "I hear something at our port-side door."

"Too late, Corporal. We're on our way," Barnabas said as he accelerated. The ship rocked as if something jumped off its wing. *Strange, very strange*, Barnabas thought.

Matt asked, "What did you hear, Corporal?"

I heard tapping above the portal, like someone was on the wing, trying to get our attention."

"Don't worry, Corporal. It was probably just the metal creaking with the temperature change," Matt said.

*Like hell it was*, Barnabas thought.

# Shadow of Death

*"When you find a fork in the road, take it.". - Yogi Berra*

### Martian Grotto

Josh grabbed an assault rifle and his Glock as he scrambled out of the lander. Marci turned on the cloaking device and followed him, carrying her Glock and a pair of low-vision field glasses. She closed the door, which made the lander virtually invisible. Ducking behind an outcropping, the duo scanned the pirate's compound.

"Do you see anything, Torres?"

"Nothing. You?"

"No, it looks surprisingly quiet. Wait, I see Gunny and the Sarge. They're being taken to that lander over there." Marci pointed at the lander that was furthest away from the mine entrance. "Strange, they're only being held at gunpoint. There're no restraints on them."

"If they're put on that lander, we'll never get 'em back!" Josh brought his assault rifle up to his shoulder. "We've got to create a distraction."

"You're right," Marci said as she continued to scan the compound. "Okay, Take out the lights."

"Will do." Josh fired several rounds, dropped, and rolled to a different position. The sound of gunfire reverberated through the grotto. It sounded like a small army was on the loose. Several of the lights went out. Return gunfire erupted from one of the guards. Josh winced as ricochet bullets whizzed past him.

"That's not good enough. The Sarge and Gunny still aren't free. We need a bigger distraction." Marci squeezed off a couple of shots and rolled to a new position.

*What to do? What to do?* Josh thought as he looked intently at the compound. Just then, heavy gunfire came from the guard tower nearest the landers. Josh concentrated on that tower and its spotlight. Although he aimed at the light, his shots took out the stand that held the spotlight in place. It collapsed, freeing the light to fall out of the tower, knocking over a drum in a shower of sparks. The light, still connected to its source of power, shorted across the drum. WHOOSH. The drum erupted into a ball of fire. The concussion knocked everyone standing nearby to the ground. Josh and Marci felt the heat from their position across the lake. The drum itself was launched high into the air and bounced off a couple of stalactites.

"Incoming!" Josh yelled as he dove left. Marci dove right. The remains of the drum bounced between them and fell into the lake. The lander that had been next to the drum toppled over and caught fire. People were scrambling to control the fire. Someone shouted, "Get those other drums outta here before they blow!"

"How's that?" Josh asked.

"It was okay, I suppose."

"Come on, Lieutenant. That was better than just okay."

"Naw, that was just—" Marci started to laugh.

"What's so funny, Lieutenant?"

"I just remembered that the captain said to keep a low profile. I *don't* think this is his idea of a low profile."

Josh laughed. "Now that's funny, Lieutenant. I'd like to see—"

Gunfire erupted from behind Marci and Josh.

"Damn! We forgot about the pirates on patrol," Marci said as she took cover from the patrol. "Protect your rear, Torres!"

Josh dove behind a stalagmite. He landed face to face with a human skull. He jumped back, startled by its hollow eye holes and toothy grin. Resting on his knees, he struggled to control his breathing as he observed a pile of bones just behind and below the skull. He could detect a faint smell of burnt flesh. Josh shuddered and thought, *Someone must've disintegrated at this very spot.*

Just then, gunfire began from the natural bridge. Guards were moving across the bridge to take up positions behind Marci and Josh.

"Pirates advancing behind us!" Josh shouted.

"Protect your other rear, Torres!" Marci shouted.

"I've only got one rear," Josh yelled. He backed up, almost touching Marci's back.

The two pirates on patrol rushed Marci's position. An invisible fist reached out and knocked the first pirate flat on his back. The second pirate tripped over the first and fell face-first on the ground.

*So, that's what happens when someone runs into the lander. Cool,* Josh thought.

"Those two pirates are down, but not out," Marci said. "We gotta move quick!"

Josh scrambled up. "I've got an idea. Let's charge the guards on the bridge, then veer into the tunnel everyone avoids. Maybe that'll draw the guards toward us and free the checkpoint so Smith and McDermott can escape."

"You mean the tunnel across from the bridge on our left?"

167

"Yeah, that's the one."

Looking back, Marci saw the two grounded pirates start to get up. "Let's do it. Now!"

Josh and Marci jumped from behind their cover and headed toward the bridge, firing as they ran. The suddenness and ferociousness of their attack caught the guards by surprise. They dropped to the ground, uncertain what to do next. Just as Josh and Marci got close to the bridge, they veered into the mysterious tunnel. Seeing this, the guards scrambled up and ran after them. By this time, the two pirates on patrol got their bearings and followed Marci and Josh into the tunnel.

The tunnel was dark, and the path was narrow, with a steep drop-off to one side. There was a sound of rushing water far below Marci and Josh. "Watch your step, Torres," Marci said. The path led to a fork. There was an amber glow ahead to the right. The left fork appeared a little darker. Marci went left. She reached the tunnel opening and stopped at the edge of a drop-off. To her right, a trail ran upward, while on her left, a path led downward. Marci turned and looked back. She saw that Josh was right behind her. She also saw several figures heading their way and said, "I think it worked. I think we drew the guards away from their station."

Josh wasn't listening. He saw the red dot of a laser sight settle on Marci's heart. Without thinking, Josh threw himself at her. As he hit her in the chest, he felt a fist hit the back of his shoulder. Josh's impact pushed Marci off her feet. Together, they fell over the edge. As they fell, Josh heard the thunder of a gunshot and Marci saying, "Why the hell did you do that?"

Their fall of some two stories was broken by a deep pool of fresh water. As they both came up for air, Josh noticed a tinge of pink in the water. They drifted toward the far end of the pool.

Marci said, "What were you thinking, Torres? You could've killed both of us."

Just then, bullets began to rain around them from above. Josh pointed up and panted, "That's what I was thinking. They'd zeroed in on you, Lieutenant."

"Let's move before they get our range," Marci said. They began to swim with the current. "By the way, thanks."

"Don't mention it."

The current picked up speed as the edge of the lake flowed into a waterfall. It was more of a slide than a fall. Josh and Marci tumbled and rolled as they slid down. The tumbling water gave way to a lazy stream running through a flowery meadow. Josh and Marci scrambled out of the water, then dashed toward the cliffside of the stream. They crouched, listening for their pursuers. After a while, not hearing any pursuit, they began to walk along the base of the cliff. It was lined with what appeared to be blackberry bushes.

"Yum," Josh said. He ate a couple of dark berries.

"Ensign! You shouldn't eat those. You've no idea if they'll make you sick or not."

"Sorry, Ma'am," Josh said as he finished off the berries that were still in his hand.

"Where do you think those jokers who were shooting at us are?" Marci asked.

Josh said, "No clue, Lieutenant."

"Look, it's just the two of us, so we can drop the formalities."

"Works for me, Marci."

"Not that informal, Torres."

"As you wish, Gonzales."

"We need to keep close to the foot of this cliff. If the pirates are up there looking for us, they won't spot us from this angle."

"Think they'll keep following us?" Josh asked. "They didn't seem to be interested in straying too far from the mine."

"I hope you're right. In any case, we need to circle back to the lander."

"Do you think Gunny and Sarge got away?" Josh asked, trying not to give away how much his shoulder hurt.

"That's what I'm hoping," Marci said.

Josh grimaced. "Provided our diversion didn't kill them."

"Yeah. It did get a little out of hand," Marci agreed. "There must be a path somewhere around here that'll lead us back up to the tunnel we came from."

They walked along until there was a break in the undergrowth. The berry bushes gave way to some rocks that looked like a trailhead. Marci scrambled over the rocks while Josh tried to keep up.

"Here's a trail that looks promising," Marci said. "Hurry up, Torres."

Josh slipped and yelped in pain as he caught himself with his bad arm.

Marci looked at Josh. She gasped at what she saw. "You're bleeding, Torres."

Josh looked down and saw blood soaking through his shirt sleeve. "I guess I am."

"Here, sit here while I have a look." Marci cut away his shirt and found the wound. "You've been shot!"

"It's just a flesh wound, Gonzales."

"Like hell it is! We need to do something quick, or you'll bleed to death." Marci looked at the wound carefully. "It looks like the bullet went clean through. It left a nasty wound." She tore part of her undershirt into strips. "I'm getting as much pressure on this as I can. We must get you back to the lander," she said. She helped ease Josh to his feet. Josh felt light-headed and started to fall. Marci caught him and eased him into a sitting position. She jumped off the rocks and gathered as many berries as she could hold. Then she brought them to where Josh was, commanding that he eat them all.

Josh took the berries. "I thought you said not to eat—"

Marci interrupted, "That was then. This is now. You need the liquid, and the stream is no longer in sight."

After Josh ate the berries, Marci helped him up. Together, they began walking up the trail. The trail got steeper, and Josh got weaker.

"What if we meet those pirates on this trail?" Josh asked.

"We'll deal with it then. Now, we just need to keep going."

"I'm worried about the pirates," Josh persisted.

"Why?"

"I lost my weapons when we went over the waterfall, and I see your Glock isn't in its holster."

Marci looked down at her empty holster. "Crap! Let's just concentrate on getting you to the lander. Hopefully, those pirates gave up on us and returned to their mine."

One side of the path they were following hugged the cliff. The other side dropped off quickly into some underbrush. Then it dropped straight down. At times the trail would widen into an overlook as it curved to the contour of the cliff. Marci and Josh stopped at one of these overlooks. They surveyed the land. The amber sky seemed to sparkle and move like a river's current. The landscape, a peaceful valley of wildflowers and a few stands of oak trees, looked as if it had been painted by a Dutch master artist. It looked like a small column of smoke was rising from one stand of trees.

"Splendid countryside, isn't it?" Josh said. "I wonder if it's inhabited."

"Yeah, it's as pretty as any landscape I've seen on Earth." Marci lifted her viewer. "There, by that stand of trees. The one with the smoke. I see a trail, and I think I see a couple of houses there. To the right of the stand are a couple of farm fields. So the place must be inhabited."

Josh said, "Good to know. Hopefully, they're friendly. Look at the sky. There's a storm brewing, and it looks—" The crunching sound of boots interrupted Josh. He put his finger to his lips and motioned to Marci. Together, they melted into the underbrush. Looking out from under the bushes, they could see two pairs of legs.

"Luke, are you sure we need to follow those two? This place gives me the creeps."

Luke said, "Hey, I'm creeped out, too. But the boss said to catch or kill those two. And don't come back till we've got them or their bodies."

"I know what he said, but they must've drowned going over the falls. I hate being in this valley. We've already lost a couple of guys to those beasts. I don't want to be next."

Luke said, "You think? … That's why it's called the valley of death …. Look, we haven't spotted any beasts—"

"Yet."

"Yet. Let's just get down, find the bodies, and get back ASAP."

"Wait! Look at the ground."

"Is that blood?"

"It is. And it's heading down the path."

"Ha! I told you I hit one in the tunnel."

"Yeah, yeah. Let's get after them." The boots ran down the trail that Josh and Marci had just come up.

Marci got up. "We've got to move before they figure we're here."

A flash of lightning was followed by a clap of thunder so loud it hurt their ears. A torrential downpour began almost immediately after. The duo struggled up the hill against a strong wind and driving rain.

"At least our boot prints and blood'll be washed away," Josh yelled in Marci's ear.

Marci supported a weakening Josh. "Yeah, but we need to get out of this storm. I can hardly stand up."

It was now almost as dark as night. The two were barely making headway. Stopping to rest, Marci looked ahead and saw the glow of light coming out of the cliff. "Come on, Josh. Just a little further. Trust me."

They got to the glow and found the mouth of a cave. It was a welcome relief from the rain. Marci helped Josh stagger behind a couple of boulders just inside the entrance. Being soaked, they were both shivering from the cold. Even though the cave was warm and dry, it was uninviting. The cave was bathed in an eerie orange light. It ran back a little distance, then split into two chambers. The first chamber held the source of the glow and a flickering yellow light. From it came what sounded like a fire being stoked by a blacksmith's bellows. The second chamber was dark. From it came various noises, such as groans, chirps, scampering, and the echoes of distant screams.

"This place creeps me out," Josh said.

Marci surveyed the two chambers. "We should stay near the front of this cave. I think I spotted some eyes peering out from the dark chamber on the left."

Josh continued to shiver. "I do, too. They look like bat eyes that blink on, then off."

"If they're bat eyes, those are some big bats."

Josh pointed to the chamber on the right. "How about over there? It seems to be warm enough."

"I'm afraid the chamber on the right will be too hot, Torres."

"It sounds like the storm's letting up," Josh said. "Maybe we won't have to choose."

"With those two pirates lurking about, we should stay put for the time being."

"Works for me. What if those guys come in to investigate?"

"Good point. I'll have—" Marci fell silent as they heard footsteps just outside.

"Damn, Luke. Not in the cave. I hate this place."

"I don't like it any better than you. But those two couldn't have gotten around us without ducking in here. We have to look."

Marci got close to Josh's ear and whispered, "Follow my lead."

Josh nodded and watched Marci crouch on the balls of her feet. The two pirates crept into the cave, weapons at the ready. Even though the light was dim, it was easy to see that the pirates were jumpy and ill-at-ease. Marci nodded to Josh. Then she jumped up and screamed as loud as she could. Josh followed suit. They both continued screaming as they ducked behind the boulders. The cave echoed with their screams. Then, it erupted into other sounds of pained screeches and screams of its own. The pirates over-reacted. They sprayed the cave with automatic rifle fire until the ricochets started whizzing by them. Then they retreated from the cave, tripping over themselves on their way out.

Marci sighed with relief and gave a thumbs up to Josh. "That was almost too easy. I think they'll be back."

Just then, more gunfire erupted by the entrance of the cave. The two pirates were shouting and shooting. The sound of their battle moved down the trail. There was a loud swooshing sound, followed by a ball of fire stretching just inside the cave. This was followed closely by a second swooshing sound and another ball of fire. All was silent, except for the sound of flapping, like that made by an enormous bird. Marci looked at Josh and shrugged. She jumped up and paused for a few seconds. "Wait here," she said.

Josh didn't answer. He had passed out. After making sure he was in a comfortable position, Marci crept to the cave entrance. She looked up in time to see a shadow fly away. The air smelled of burnt flesh. She looked both ways on the trail. Seeing it was clear, she dashed out onto the path and up it. It led directly to a tunnel entrance. Thinking this might be the way back to the lander, she ducked inside. Her motion stirred up a hail of gunfire. Laying prone on the ground, Marci heard shouts of, "Get that beast!" and "Boys, hold your positions. Don't let that thing get any closer!" Marci backed herself out of the tunnel. *Well crap! This is the way back. But there's no way we're getting by that welcoming party,* she thought. *I can't just leave Josh in the cave. He's lost too much blood.*

Marci dashed back to the cave. She took a closer look at Josh. His face was ashen, and blood was still oozing out of his wound. She gently shook him awake. *"Come on, Josh, we need to get you to that farmhouse in the valley."* She helped him to his feet. Together, they staggered out of the cave and turned to go down the path.

"I sure hope the inhabitants around here are friendly," Josh said.

Marci stopped with a start. Looking down, she said, "It's not looking that way."

Josh followed her eyes. At their feet lay two skulls. Each was lying on a pile of scorched bones. Next to the bones lay two automatic rifles.

# The Pursuit

*"Let bravery be thy choice, but not bravado" – Menander*

### Martian Grotto Mining Camp

Marc whispered to Hilda, "How was I to know that the stupid guard was going to stop and take a leak where we were hiding?"

"If you'd not sworn, he might not have noticed us. You need to watch your mouth."

"Yeah, but he was peeing all over my best climbing shoes."

"Self-control, Sarge. You're supposed to be a seasoned and self-disciplined soldier. A little self-control. Is that too much to ask?"

"I know, Gunny. Just it's been a while since I—"

Their guard broke in. "Shut up! Both of you."

The sound of gunfire reverberated throughout the cavern. Marc, Hilda, and their guard instinctively hit the ground. Before Marc or Hilda could take advantage, their second guard reappeared and said, "Get up! We're getting into this lander, now!"

Marc and Hilda both moved slowly, acting as if they'd been hurt by their fall. Marc saw the source of the firing from across the lake. "I was hoping the kids could mount a better distraction than this," he whispered to Hilda.

Just then, WOOSH! Something exploded, toppling another lander and setting it on fire. Panic broke out through the entire compound. Someone yelled, "Get the rest of the drums out of here before they blow." Both guards ran toward the inferno.

Marc and Hilda melted back into the shadows. Then they began to move toward the gated bridge. "Is that diversion more to your liking, Sarge?"

"Most definitely! I underestimated how good those kids are. Remind me to thank them when we get back."

"Hey, Sarge."

"What?"

Hilda smiled. "I'm just reminding you to thank the Lieutenant and Ensign for their diversion."

"Not funny."

"I thought it was funny. Say, what do you suppose is in those drums?"

"Not sure. I think it's the explosive ore that's being mined. We're lucky that the drum wasn't full of the refined stuff. If it were, this whole compound would've been leveled."

"Us along with it?"

"Exactly. Look, Gunny, the bridge is clear."

"Yeah, and the checkpoint gate is up. Let's go."

Marc and Hilda sprinted to the natural bridge. They heard a second WOOSH! The remnants of another drum flew straight for them.

"Look out!" Marc yelled as he pushed Hilda to the ground. The drum hit the bridge a couple of feet before them and ricocheted where Hilda's head had been moments before. Hilda got up, grumbling at Marc.

"You're welcome," Marc said.

"Where'd the guards go?" Hilda asked.

"I think I saw them follow Gonzales and Torres into that tunnel ahead. We've got to catch them before they get to our guys!"

They ran after the pirates into the tunnel. One of the stunned guards by the gate came to in time to see them enter the tunnel. "You're not getting away that easy," he yelled as he got to his feet and staggered in pursuit.

In the dark tunnel, Hilda heard sounds of running feet and of rushing water. She ducked at the sound of gunshots. At the far end of the tunnel, someone yelled, "You go right, we'll go left." There was a fork in the path at the end of the tunnel. Hilda saw Marc run to the right. When she reached the tunnel opening, she followed Marc to her right. Failing to see Hilda turn right, the trailing pirate turned left at the fork in the trail. Hilda finally caught up with Marc. She stayed just behind him and followed the path that led first up, then down into a valley. The two men ahead of them came into view. Gasping for breath, Hilda saw the trail split into two. The first guard took the barren path up the cliff's side. Hilda and Marc followed his companion, who was running on the route which descended into a valley. The further they ran, the denser the vegetation became.

"We're gaining on him," Marc huffed.

*This sure seems familiar*, Hilda thought. *Have I been here before?* Without thinking, she drew her Glock and ran closer to Marc.

The trail took a turn and opened into a meadow beneath the cliff. Marc started to run through an archway made of two tall trees leaning together. Just as Marc got to the arch, Hilda went into a slide and leg-whipped him. He crashed, face first, onto the ground. As he hit the ground, multiple shots rang out. Hilda saw that the pirate they were chasing had turned and opened fire with his automatic rifle. Hilda rose to a kneeling position and heard three more shots. To her amazement, she saw three red holes appear on the pirate's chest. He dropped his weapon and fell to the ground. Hilda looked down and realized she had fired the deadly bullets. She ran to Marc and shook his body.

"What'd you do that for?" He complained as he sat up.

Hilda breathed a sigh of relief and pointed to the pirate in front of them. *Wait. Marc was killed by a pirate on the cliff in my dream*, she thought in a panic. Quickly, she drove her shoulder into Marc's chest, pushing them both flat to the ground. Hilda heard a series of shots and the bullets striking the tree behind them. Both she and Marc scrambled behind a couple of trees and started returning fire. Looking toward the ridge, Hilda saw the second pirate crouching behind a boulder and retaking aim.

"Are you okay, Sarge?"

"Other than a broken leg and two cracked ribs, I'm fine. You sure play rough."

"Stop complaining, you wuss. Do you see the pirate?"

"Yeah, I do, Gunny. Keep him occupied. I'll work my way back to the trail he ran up and get the drop on him. Oh, and thanks for saving me … twice."

"Anytime, Sarge. I've got your back."

"And my ribs," Marc replied as he headed back to the trail they'd passed earlier.

Hilda moved in the opposite direction, grabbing the fallen assailant's rifle, ducking under cover, and firing an occasional shot toward the pirate. *Just keep him occupied until the Sarge can get the drop on him. Whatever you do, girl, don't kill him*. Hilda and the pirate kept working their way down their respective paths as they traded shots. They wound up at the edge of a sea. Hilda could hear the sound of the surf beating against sand and rock.

The sound of an approaching storm came to her ears. She ducked behind a rock outcropping. The pirate was directly above her at the edge of the cliff. He was concentrating on shooting at her. After a while, she saw Marc moving into position. The pirate was maneuvering to his right, trying to get a better angle on Gunny. He'd not seen Marc running up behind him. Marc was just about to strike when the pirate spotted him. Without hesitation, the pirate jumped into the angry ocean. Marc stumbled to a stop at the edge of the cliff and looked down. The pirate had leaped off a hundred-foot cliff.

### On the Martian Coast

Hilda had moved further along the path and came upon a sea wall. She scrambled over it and arrived at the beach in time to see the pirate jump into the angry surf. Hilda saw Marc shake his head in amazement. He looked down at her and gave her a shrug. She waved at Marc. "Don't even think about it, Sarge!" she screamed into the freshening wind. She felt her heart sink as she watched Marc wave, step back, and take a running leap off the edge of the cliff. Hilda could barely make out his splash. The tide was coming in, and the squall was intensifying. Hilda ran along the beach to the foot of the cliffs. There she found a ledge rising about six feet above the sand. She scrambled onto the ledge and ran across it, dodging several tide pools along the way.

She stopped just short of where the waves were crashing onto the shelf and looked hard for the divers. She spotted a large rock, only a few hundred feet from the base of the cliff. Squinting through the rain, Hilda thought she could see Marc's head bounce up on one side of the rock. The pirate's head was bobbing on the other side. It looked like they were both struggling to reach the rock. She saw lightning streak across the sky, ricochet off the rock, and hit the top of the cliff. BOOM! The pressure from the thunder hurt her ears. Hilda looked again. She could see Marc was now away from the rock, swimming toward the shore. He wasn't making any progress. *Rip current*, she thought. *Be smart, Marc. Don't fight it!* Hilda was relieved to see Marc roll over on his back and slowly stroke along with the current. She looked for the pirate but couldn't find him anywhere. She looked back to Marc and saw he had turned parallel to the beach. She was almost knocked off her feet by a big wave. *The tide's moving in. I need to meet Marc when he gets back to shore,* she thought.

Hilda strapped the rifle over her shoulder and hopped onto the sand. She began running to where she thought Marc would return. The tide was moving in faster than Hilda expected. She had to scramble to get back onto the sea wall before being swept to sea herself. The storm was now in full force. Sheets of torrential rain pelted Hilda as she ran. It was the lightning that was most worrisome. Lightning was striking all around her. *I'm no good to Marc if I'm dead,* she thought. The lightning drove her inland, along the base of the cliffs. She found a shallow cave that would shelter her from the storm. She ducked inside, shivering from the cold. "God, I've never asked for anything. I don't even know if you exist. If you do and you care, please bring Marc back to me," she said.

Thankfully, the cave's sides and back were still warm from before the storm set in. At first, Hilda dropped her rifle and leaned exhausted against the back wall. Then she crept toward the mouth of the cave. *I'll wait here until the lightning passes. Then I'll look for Marc.* She noticed some bushes and flowers at the mouth of the cave. Blackberries were growing in the bushes. Only then did she realize how hungry she was. Taking a tentative bite, she found the taste better than she remembered. Soon she had picked and eaten her fill. Curiously, these bushes had no thorns on them. Looking further, she saw some poppy flowers. She leaned over and smelled the flowers. Their aroma was sweetly familiar. She couldn't quite put her finger on what it was, so she took several deeper breaths. A relaxing sensation passed over her. She retreated to the back of the cave and sat. Her eyes got heavy, and she could no longer keep her head up.

*Must stay awake for Marc,* she thought, as she laid down and drifted to sleep.

The following morning, she awoke to the chirping of birds. Light from the morning was shining in her eyes. Hilda stretched and walked into the bright light. She was refreshed yet anxious to know what had happened to Marc. She grabbed her rifle and walked briskly to the beach. The tide was on its way out, so she had no trouble hopping back on the ledge and looking around the shore. There was no sign of Marc. While she scanned the sea one more time, she caught a motion out of the corner of her eye. Instinctively, she dove off the ledge onto the sand and came to her knees. She felt a tug at her sleeve, then heard the crack of a rifle. She dove right. Another bullet ricocheted off the rock above her head. Then in one smooth motion, she came to her knee and squeezed off a couple of shots. It was the pirate. He had gained the upper ground.

Hilda dashed to the bottom of the cliff. A quick scan revealed a steep path that traveled up the side of the cliff. She scrambled up the trail, grabbing at the undergrowth to steady herself as she went. Her lungs were starting to burn when she reached the top. She moved behind a rock and aimed her rifle toward a spot where she thought the pirate would appear. He popped into sight, to the right of where she was aiming. He got off two quick shots before she could zero in on him. His attempts went wide. Hilda calmly sent a burst his way, hitting the rock he was hiding behind. Immediately after firing, Hilda ran right and dove behind a nearby rock.

She heard the pirate shoot again. His gun flashes came from the same spot as before. Hilda had a bad angle on him. Hilda took a couple more shots. She followed this by diving to her right and sheltering behind a fallen log. The pirate popped up and fired again at Hilda's original position. Hilda still did not have the angle she wanted. *Hmm,* she thought. *This guy's an amateur. He's not moving and isn't aware that I'm flanking his position. This'll be a piece of cake. I just need to make one more move, and I'll have him dead to rights when he pops up*. Hilda squeezed off three more rounds and ran to her final position. She knelt and aimed. Without warning, a giant shadow blocked the light from Hilda. She was pushed down by an invisible hand. Face in the ground, she heard the beat of a large set of wings.

Hilda wiped the sand out of her face and looked up. She saw the pirate yelling and spraying shots into the air. Only, he wasn't shooting at her. Instead, he was shooting at an enormous flying creature. It was the size of a man with four wings. It looked like a scorpion. What's worse, the pirate's bullets were just bouncing off the creature's body. The scorpion hovered about ten feet off the ground, halfway between Hilda and the pirate. Slowly, it brought its stinger forward as if to strike. *This can't be good*, Hilda thought. Frozen in place, she watched as the pirate continued to shoot at the scorpion. Undeterred, the scorpion took a steady aim. Hilda saw a thin stream of glistening liquid shoot from the scorpion's stinger and hit the pirate square in his chest. The pirate burst into a ball of flame. Hilda recoiled, then watched. When the flame went out, all that remained was a skeleton that immediately fell into a heap. Then, the scorpion turned and aimed at Hilda.

# Country Village

### Outside a Martian Cave

Josh stared at the bones on the ground. "Wow! Flame thrower? Laser
gun? A new type of energy weapon?"

Marci shook her head. "Whatever it was, it looks like they
didn't have a chance."

Josh said, "Judging from the angle of the burn marks, this attack
took place from the air."

Marci shook her head. "So, these beasts ... they're able to fly."

"Shall we grab those rifles, Lieutenant?"

"Didn't do them any good, and they'll only weigh us down. Let's
move out."

Josh nodded. Together they started down the path. The trail was
slippery, even though the rain had stopped. Josh and Marci slipped and
slid partway. They stumbled the rest of the way to the bottom of the cliff.
At the bottom, they stopped so Josh could rest. *This sucks!* Marci thought.

*Josh'll never make it to that village, and I can't carry him.* Marci helped Josh back up and supported him as they staggered across the meadow.

Thinking that all their pursuers were dead, Marci was not as vigilant as she should have been. Their passing through the meadow was seen by one final pursuer. The last pirate to give chase never caught up with any of his companions. He did succeed in tumbling and rolling down a path leading off the cliff. Initially stunned, he waited out the storm in a shallow crevice. He wandered for a while, looking for food. Wanting to avoid the flying monsters, he kept a sharp eye on the sky. He was just about to return to his base when he spotted his quarry. With renewed energy, he carefully followed Josh and Marci.

Marci and Josh finally reached the path leading toward the house she had seen earlier. The stream that they had previously followed turned away from the cliff. It was now following the trail. Marci and Josh crossed the path and went directly to the stream. Marci helped position Josh so he could drink some water. Then she took a drink herself.

Marci looked at Josh's wound. "This looks pretty nasty, Torres. Here, sit up while I clean it a little bit."

Marci ripped off the rest of her undershirt and used some water to clean Josh's wound. Then she rewrapped it. Marci bent over to take one last drink. That's when she saw, next to her reflection, another face, right behind her. It was gaunt, with long hair and dark, menacing eyes. Marci rolled quickly onto her back, kicking her foot up in the same motion. The stranger doubled over, holding his crotch, as Marci's kick landed home. She scrambled to her feet and kicked the side of the stranger's face. He lost his balance and fell to his side. He no more than hit the ground when he jumped up and started to run away, screaming, "Rabidus unam! Rabidus unam!" Only as she watched him run did Marci realize that he was naked except for a tool belt. He got to a cart and started to push away as fast as he could.

185

Josh started to chuckle.

"What's so funny, Torres?"

"He's calling you 'crazy one.'"

"No matter, we need that cart!" Marci sprinted and caught up. She spun the stranger around and shouted. "Stop, please stop. I need your help!"

The stranger, who was a good six and a half feet tall, held his arms up to ward off her attack. Instead of swinging, Marci repeated, "Help! We need your help." She pointed at the stream where Josh lay. The frightened man backed against his cart, almost whimpering, "Rabidus unam."

"Please, help!" Marci insisted as she grabbed his hand and pulled him to where Josh lay.

The tall stranger looked down and asked, "You hurt him, too?"

"No, I didn't hurt him. Bad men shot him. I need to get him to a doctor."

The stranger knelt beside Marc and examined the wound. "Don't know what 'doctor' is. The 'apron maker' needs to see him."

"Will you take us there?" Marci asked.

"Sure. If you don't hurt me," the stranger gently picked Marc up. He carried Marc to his cart and laid him down like one would a sleeping child. Then he went around to the back, lifted the handles, and began striding down the path. His stride was so long and quick, Marci had to jog just to keep up. The stream and path took another turn. This time it was into a wooded area. The trail and stream ran past a simple, well-crafted cottage. A footbridge led from the path, over the creek, to a flagstone courtyard in front of the white-washed structure. About twenty feet long and ten feet wide, the simple house with a stone chimney at one end had an open wooden door and two large windows. Under each window was a flower box full of colorful pansies. The cottage had two dormer windows set in its shingled roof and was framed by old oak trees. Marci could smell the jasmine in the air.

A dwarf, clad only in an apron, worked in the herb garden set to one side of the courtyard. He looked up at the sound of the approaching cart. When he saw the hand-cart, he grumped, "That's sure a lazy man, letting George push him around like that."

Marci bristled but said nothing.

George said, "He's not lazy, Gremli. He's hurt. It looks bad."

"Oh," Gremli said. He raised his voice and called, "Sabrina, we need your help!"

A tall, slender lady appeared at the cottage door. She had curly golden hair that streamed over her shoulders and covered part of her lavender gown. The gown extended to the top of her bare feet. Her face was young, yet wise, with large, kind eyes. The lacy wings on her back fluttered gently with every step she took.

Marci was caught off guard, despite her grave circumstances. "You can fly?"

The lady laughed. "No. I use my wings to keep myself from flying. I'm so light that if I'm not careful, I will float away. When I lose my footing, a couple of strokes from my wings keep me firmly on the ground." Her eyes fell on Josh. "Oh, dear. Let's get him inside." She motioned to George, who lifted Josh out of the cart and carried him into the cottage.

The cottage's main room was welcoming, with a stone fireplace at one end and large windows all about. The furniture was simple and elegant, much like that made by a Shaker. Her wooden framed bed had a firmly woven straw-like mattress and was topped by a colorful comforter.

"Here, George, place him on the bed, please. Gentle now. Careful of his shoulder," Sabrina directed. Then she asked, "What happened?"

Marci looked over Sabrina's shoulder. "We were attacked by pirates. They shot Josh in the back. He's lost a lot of blood and is going into shock."

Sabrina gently stroked Josh's forehead. "What are pirates?"

Marci pointed toward the cliffs they had just left. "Up there. Pirates are the ones that are mining something above the waterfall."

"Oh, at Cavern Lake. Are you one of them? I hear they often fight among themselves."

"She is. She's one of them!" George accused, pointing his finger. "She attacked me. She's rabidus unam."

Sabrina smiled and touched Marci softly on the cheek. "Now, George, Marci doesn't strike me as being loco."

Marci said, "I'm sorry, but you startled me when I saw your face reflected in the water. I thought you were one of the beasts."

Looking on from the door, Gremli frowned. "I'm not surprised. George, admit it. You do have a scary face."

"Excuse me." Sabrina stepped outside and whispered to Gremli, "Run as fast as you can and fetch Custos Vitae. Tell him to get here quickly. Tell him it's a matter of life and death." She returned and said, "Dear, we have no beasts living here. Only those who you call pirates are anything like beasts. They steal some of our crops from time to time."

"You're one of them. You're a pirate," George accused again.

Sabrina said, "Now, George, we must let Marci tell her story."

Marci looked closer at Sabrina. "That's the second time you've used my name. But I never introduced myself. How do you know my name?"

Sabrina smiled. "I saw it in your mind when I touched your face."

"What else did you see?" Marci asked.

"You think that your friend is in grave danger, and we are all strange creatures. I think that you and the pirates are more closely related than you want to admit."

Marci nodded. "You're right on all counts. My friend and I are human, just like the pirates. We're all from Earth. They cause much grief to those who travel from Earth to Mars. They steal, kidnap, and extort money. Josh and I belong to the U. S. Space Force that must stop them. We try to protect space travelers, not rob them."

George said, "Then, you're space custos? You don't look anything like our custos. If that is so, why are you here instead of in space protecting—"

"Hush, George," Sabrina interrupted. "We're wasting precious time talking." Sabrina began to unwrap Josh's wound. "We need to help this poor man. We need to move him to the courtyard table, and I need to sew up his wound."

Once Josh, who was now unconscious, was situated on a table in the courtyard, Sabrina set out her sewing tools. "You say he's lost a lot of blood. I don't know where we can find any."

Marci said, "I can help. My blood type is O-negative. That means I'm a universal blood donor."

"You would give him some of your blood?"

"I'm afraid that he'll die if I don't. I'm just not sure how we can safely transfer some of my blood to him."

"Custos Vitae will be able to help." Sabrina looked up. "Here he is right now."

Marci followed Sabrina's eyes and gasped. Just above her hovered a man-sized scorpion. It wasn't exactly a flying scorpion. It was half man and half scorpion. *This is the monster those pirates must have been talking about,* she thought.

Unperturbed, Sabrina said, "I'm glad you could come so quickly, Custos Vitae. This is Marci and her friend Josh, who is badly hurt. We have to help them."

Custos Vitae nodded but said nothing and continued to stare at Marci, who thought, *This isn't going well. At least he's not pointing his stinger at me.* She nodded to him and tried to smile.

"Marci, this is my good friend Custos Vitae," Sabrina said.

Marci reached out a tentative hand. "Pleased to meet you, Mr. Custos Vitae."

The scorpion-man took her hand. "I saw you and your friend being chased by two sons of Adam. Sadly, they attacked me also. I had to respond."

Marci nodded her head and thought, *They made a huge mistake.*

Sabrina's voice brought Marci back to the situation at hand. "Custos Vitae, I need you to help sterilize my tools, so I can safely sew up this poor man's wound.

"I can do that." The scorpion-man curled his stinger over his head until it was inches away from Sabrina's needles and knives. He gave a tiny squirt of flame over the tools until they glowed red. Then he withdrew his stinger.

"Thank you. Now please warm the water in my kettle, so we can wash up." Sabrina pointed to a nearby pot.

The scorpion-man immersed the pot in a more intense flame. Once again, Custos Vitae withdrew his stinger. Sabrina and Marci both washed their hands and began tending to Josh's wound. Finally, they had his wound sutured and bandaged.

Sabrina looked carefully at Marci. "Are you sure your blood will help your friend?"

"I'm sure it will. Josh'll die without it. How can we transfer—"

"Custos Vitae will help. Sit here and show him where to draw your blood." Sabrina pointed at a nearby chair.

Marci swallowed hard. *I didn't see this coming.* She sat in the chair and bent her left arm, resting it on the arm of the chair. Then she pointed at one of her veins. "Okay, take it from that vein right there."

"Please be still, daughter of Adam." The scorpion-man brought his stinger down to her arm. He held the stinger just above Marci's arm and squirted a little clear liquid on it. Marci, determined to watch, kept her eyes fixed on that menacing stinger. To her surprise, it slipped painlessly into her vein. The stinger was clear, so she could watch the blood being drawn. After ten minutes, Marci began to feel light-headed. "I think you've taken all I can give."

The Custos Vitae carefully removed his stinger. Then he repeated the process with Josh. Marci placed her hand on Josh's forehead. "He's too pale, and his breathing is too shallow. I think he's dehydrated. He probably also needs an infusion of saline."

"Saline?" Sabrina asked.

"It's water and just a little salt."

"I'll fix the solution. Custos Vitae can inject it," Sabrina offered.

Marci was puzzled. "How can Custos Vitae shoot fire, transfer blood, and transfer water with the same stinger?"

Sabrina said, "He has several chambers in his body to store various liquids. He's handy to have around."

Marci nodded in amazement. "I'll say."

George and Marci moved Josh inside and placed him back on the bed. Custos Vitae knelt beside him and administered the saline solution. Sabrina watched Marci sit next to Josh and take his hand. "You're fond of your friend. I can tell by how you look at him."

Marci stroked Josh's forehead. "He had just pushed me out of the way when he was shot. He saved my life, and this isn't the first time. I just hope … I get to tell him 'thanks."

Sabrina placed a hand on Marci's shoulder. "Gratitude expressed will bring joy to both of your hearts. Let's hope you have the chance to express your gratitude. Now that we've done all we can for your friend, perhaps you could answer George's question. Why are you here?"

"Taxiarchis sent us from Portae to help you and to fight the pirates."

The name 'Taxiarchis' caused a stir with Custos Vitae. "What did Taxiarchis look like?" he asked.

"When we first arrived, he looked like an angry red and yellow flaming column. But when we left, he was a dazzling ruby-colored column of light."

Sabrina placed her hand lightly on Marci's head. "Think about what he said and what he looked like when you last saw him. What did he say?"

Marci's mind replayed their departure. "Taxiarchis said he was sending us to your planet. That you are content, ingenious, and fulfilled. Now forces, of which you are unaware, are at work. You'll soon be in danger of losing all that you hold dear. Then he turned to Josh. He called Josh 'Qui Admonet.' He said that Josh must give a warning to the people of the Red Planet. If he doesn't: 'sanguis eorum sit super manus.'"

Sabrina looked at the scorpion man and nodded. "The daughter of Adam has indeed seen Taxiarchis. He did send her friend to warn us. 'Qui Admonet' means the one who warns. He also set an obligation on the young man's head. 'Sanguis eorum sit super manus' means our blood is on his hands if he fails to warn us."

Custos Vitae spoke up, "You know what this means, Sabrina?"

"It means he must be at the council meeting to deliver his message the day after tomorrow. We must see that he gets there if he survives."

Custos Vitae nodded in agreement. "It now makes sense why those sons of Adam wanted to kill these two. I must stay by his side and protect him, should more — what did you call them? — Pirates try to kill him. As much as I want, I can't go with you to the market today. Please give my regrets to the children."

Sabrina went to a closet and pulled out a light silk gown. "Custos Vitae will take good care of your friend. You and I can talk as we go to the market. First, you need to bathe in my pool out back and put this gown on. What you're wearing will never do. It makes you look too much like those terrible pirates. You'd scare all the poor children."

Marci looked surprised. "I'd scare the children, and Custos Vitae doesn't?"

"Oh no. The children love to crawl all over him. He flings them into their parent's arms with his tail. They'll be sorely disappointed that he won't be at the market today."

The path leading to the market wound its way through a grove of oak trees and over a small hill. Sabrina looked at her youthful companion. "Are you okay? You look worried."

"I am. Our two companions were being held prisoner by the pirates. We tried to create a distraction to free them. I've no idea whether they escaped or not. Now that Josh is under your care, I need to return to the cavern and find out what happened to them."

"You have no cause for concern. Custos Vitae told me that your friends escaped. Custos Maris is tracking them. Hopefully, you will all be united at the council meeting the day after tomorrow."

Marci still felt uneasy. *Can I trust these creatures? They seem nice enough. But are they for real?* "How did Custos Vitae hear from Custos Maris?" Marci asked.

"They have a unique language. It's a series of ultra-high-pitched clicks. We can't hear it, but the sound travels great distances. That's how all the Custos stay in touch. Even those who spend time on the surface in the dead-zone."

"Dead zone?"

"When the cosmic war swept over Mars, the entire surface became known as the dead-zone. Knowing this would happen, our Creator built Arcadia as a refuge."

"Arcadia?"

"Yes. Arcadia is this underground world. Those who believed followed Reuwel and were rescued from the destruction. We all live here as we did before on the surface. We only miss being able to watch the stars at night."

"Reuwel?"

"Reuwel is Our Circitor (Overseer). She usually presides over our council meetings. But she's away, meeting with our creator, and the council will meet tomorrow on their own."

"Is this unusual?"

"It's the first time that the council will meet alone."

"Why? Why not wait for her return?"

"Our situation with those you call pirates is desperate. They've stolen our food and imprisoned some of our dwarves."

"Why don't the Custos just attack and throw them out?"

"The Custos will never attack without permission from the council or unless they are defending themselves. The council received word that we're to be visited by one who is called the Great Dealmaker, with authority from Portae. He can resolve these difficult times without violence. The deal he's proposing can't wait for the return of Reuwel. You can imagine my surprise to hear that you have also been sent to us from Portae."

194

"Why would Portae send two different messengers to Mars?" Marci asked.

"Good question," Sabrina said.

The companions topped the hill that overlooked a sea of colorful circular pavilions. The small encampment bustled with activity. The aroma of bar-b-que rose to greet them. Marci paused. "It looks like a festival."

"It is a daily gathering to exchange goods, services, produce, and food. It's a time when everyone can enjoy each other's company. On some days, when the trolls add their music and sing their poems, it becomes a festival."

"Trolls?"

"Yes. George is a troll. He farms and also plays several instruments."

"Gremli isn't a troll?"

"Gremli is a dwarf. He's a carpenter. He's building a pergola for my front garden."

"How many kinds of intelligent creatures live here?"

"I've never given it any thought. I guess a dozen. Our leadership council has one representative from each kind of creature. There are a dozen members on our leadership council, plus Reuwel."

"You all seem to get along so well. How can that be?"

"I never thought about that either. It could be that we are all contented and enjoy what we do. Each kind, as you call us, has learned through the years what they enjoy doing. We all do what we enjoy. We find our greatest joy in sharing our skills to help each other out."

"No fights?"

"No need to fight."

"No rules?"

"Only one. We're free to do as we wish. We just can't sell the dirty chalk that those you call pirates are taking. You look puzzled, Marci."

"I am puzzled. No rules, no fights. Do you even have adversity?" Marci asked.

"We've faced adversity on several occasions. Once, the Evil One sent thousands of locusts to eat our crops and strip all our plants of their leaves. Another time, he sent an invasion of dwarf-sized poisonous spiders to try and kill us all. Both times, we were able to fight off the invasion with the help of our Custos."

"What about the pirates?"

"Times are distressful now because of these pirates. That's why the council will meet, as they have in other times of distress."

"What about the people like me who live on the surface of Mars?"

"We can't imagine why anyone wants to live in the dead zone. But if that's what those people wish, then who are we to stop them?"

"You're not afraid of them?"

"No, Custos Martis and his friends watch them for us. They've never made any effort to harm us until now."

"The Custos can live in the dead zone?" Marci asked.

"Yes, they can go for a while. You sure have a lot of questions."

"I'm sorry, Sabrina. It's just that the more I learn about your home, the more questions I have," Marci said. Then to herself, she thought, *This is surreal. This place is too peaceful. Its inhabitants are too friendly. What am I missing? What's wrong with this picture?*

The darkness of evening was beginning to settle in when the duo returned to Sabrina's cottage. The scorpion-man was standing watch at the door. "Our friend is sleeping well. I don't believe any son of Adam will be about tonight. I'll take some time myself and get something to eat." He took to the air and waved goodbye.

The following day Marci awoke more refreshed than she had been in several days. She rose and went to where Josh lay. She stepped to his bed, sat down, reached for his hand, and looked at his face. *His color is much better. I think the worst is over.*

Josh opened his eyes. They had a puzzled expression. Marci patted his hand. "You were shot and lost a lot of blood. We're in a kind woman's cottage. She and Custos Vitae helped fix your wounds. You passed out yesterday and slept through the whole night."

"You brought me here?" Josh asked.

"Yes, you need to rest and stay still so you don't reopen your wound."

"You saved me, Marci. Why'd you do it? I don't deserve it. After all, I failed to save HJ for you."

"I guess I have forgiven you," she looked into his eyes and remembered her dream. *What do I see?* she thought. *Gratitude? Yes, and love? No, it can't be that. But appreciation? Yes, appreciation.* The thought of being appreciated warmed her heart.

"You look beautiful," Josh said. Then he blushed. "My bad, Lieutenant. that was out of line."

"No worries, Josh. I appreciate the compliment and am glad to see you look much better." Marci helped Josh up. He was much stronger than she expected. "Let's go outside and get some fresh air," she suggested.

Together they walked out the door. Marci looked up. Right in the middle of the open garden gate stood a pirate wearing a goofy grin.

Marci said, "What the hel—"

"Surprised to see me?" the pirate interrupted. Mistaking Marci for Sabrina, the pirate continued, "Look, lady, I don't want to hurt you. So, hand over that guy, and we'll just walk away. If you don't, this here flash grenade in my hand will burn your house to the ground."

Marci's face grew dark with anger. "You son-of-a—"

"Which will it be, your house or my prisoner?" The pirate pulled the pin on his grenade and cocked his arm.

The sound of flapping wings filled the air. The pirate turned to face a hovering scorpion man. "Crap!" he exclaimed. He tossed the grenade toward Marci and Josh, then dove behind a rock for cover. Josh pushed Marci face-first to the ground, scooped up the grenade at their feet, and threw it high in the sky. BOOM. It flashed brightly. The shock wave pushed Josh to the ground.

Marci rolled over and jumped up. She saw the pirate rise from his position behind the rock, firing his automatic rifle at the scorpion man. Though the shots hit their target, the scorpion-man was unfazed. He calmly brought his stinger over his head, then shot a stream of liquid at the pirate. When the liquid hit his chest, it burst into a ball of flame. When the fire subsided, only a skeleton remained. It immediately fell to the ground in a heap. *I'm glad he's on our side,* she thought.

"Who's on our side," Josh groaned.

"You heard me, Josh?"

"I did."

"I'll need to think more quietly next time. Did you see what Custos Vitae did?"

"No."

"It was a thing of beauty … are you okay, Josh?" Marci knelt next to him, looking at his burnt face. A chill went down her spine.

# Marc's Epiphany

*"I never made one of my discoveries through the process of rational thinking."*
*- Albert Einstein*

## On A Martian Cliff

The sea was black and angry. The clouds over the water were an ominous gray, with the frequent glow of sheet lightning. Marc heard the rumble of approaching thunder. The wind was slapping at Marc's face. Standing at the edge of the cliff, looking down, Marc felt like he was a cliff diver in Mexico. The peak was higher than he anticipated. He looked for any sign of the pirate who had so recklessly jumped in. There, close to a rock, the pirate's head was bobbing among the waves. *I can't let him get away*, Marc thought. He backed up a few feet. He ran forward, and as he got to the edge, he jumped, aiming at where he last saw the pirate.

The water was cool but, surprisingly, not cold. Marc's feet first entry was off his mark by several yards. He landed with the rock in between him and the pirate. Marc swam back toward the cliffs. He saw the pirate swimming toward the rock, not the shore. Looking toward the shore, Marc noticed there was a shelf of rock. But there was no beach. The waves were pounding against the cliff—like angry fists. *Not good*, he thought. Marc swam toward the rock and the pirate.

Just as they were about to meet, Marc's hair stood on end, and he thought he heard a sizzle. There was a blinding flash of lightning and an ear-splitting boom of thunder. Marc fell back in the water, everything went silent, and his head ached. *Must have hit the cliff a couple of dozen yards away instead of the rock by me. Otherwise, I'd be dead now,* he thought. He started to swim toward the rock again. To his dismay, he was further away. The fact that he was still deaf from the thunder added to his sense of isolation. The harder he stroked, the further he drifted away from the rock and the coast. The pirate was no longer in his sight. *Riptide! Damn, I'm caught in a riptide!* Marc thought. Instinctively he rolled on his back to conserve energy—*only one thing to do now. I need to let this current carry me out until it weakens. Then I need to swim parallel to the shore until I'm free from it, then head back to a beach. I hope I have enough strength to do all this.* Marc was surprised at how calm he was. Tired and worried, sure, but not panicked.

Some time had now passed, as had the storm. Marc decided to start swimming out of the current. He looked back and was surprised at how far out the rip-tide had carried him. Marc began swimming slowly, using the backstroke. *This'll be a long haul,* he thought. *I could use some help.*

His skin crawled when he felt something head-butt him in the back. He jerked up. Treading water, he began looking around. *What the hell?* Directly in front of him, a giant sea turtle popped up. It even used its fore flipper to splash Marc in the face. *Is it smiling?* he wondered as he splashed back with his hand. It dove under him and surfaced behind him. Again, it splashed him with its fore fin. Marc turned and splashed back. *So, you do want to play,* he thought as he splashed back. A sense of calm had settled over him. He was no longer alone. His ears still rang, but he could hear the water slapping around him. The turtle dove again. This time it circled behind him. It then rose at an angle and cut Marc's feet out from under him. The result of this maneuver left Marc sitting on top of the turtle. Marc swung his legs to the side to ride the turtle—like he would ride a horse. The turtle was so broad, Marc felt like he was on the back of an elephant.

"Where are you taking me, little guy?" Marc said, not expecting an answer.

"Someplace special." The voice that responded made Marc jump.

*Did the turtle just speak to me? Or am I losing my mind?* Marc wondered. He looked back and saw that the beach was out of sight. The cliffs were barely visible. To his dismay, they were still heading away from the shore. The storm had passed. The swells were still running about ten to fifteen feet high. Even so, the turtle had no trouble navigating. It swam hard to reach each swell's crest, then coasted down into the following trough.

"Where are we going?" Marc asked again.

"Someplace special."

"Do you have a name?"

"Yes, it's Loggerhead."

"That's a type of turtle. What's your name?"

"What a strange creature you are," responded the turtle. "You ask me for my name. Then, you act like you know more about me than I do about myself. My name is Loggerhead."

"You're right, Loggerhead. My bad. How did you come about your name?"

"I guess it's because I gather up things in the sea."

"Such as?"

"Driftwood, bad swimmers, other stuff."

"I must get back to shore. I'd appreciate your help," Marc said. "It's urgent!"

"My Custodem Salutis said that you need to spend some time at my special place before you can be returned."

"Your Custodem?"

"Yes, he is one of the ones who keeps me safe. My Custodem Salutis."

"He's your protector?"

"That's what I said."

"Does he have a name?"

"Yes. It's Custos Maris."

"Did he say why I can't return right away? I need to stop a pirate from hurting my friends back on land."

"He didn't say why, only that you need to spend some time here first."

"I can't. My friends are in danger, and they need my help!"

"They'll be fine. Custos Maris will keep them safe, provided they don't do anything foolish. You need to rest here awhile. Custos Maris was most insistent. You're a funny creature. You're so stubborn."

"Okay, I give. Where is this special place?"

"In due time. First, look at our sky. Isn't it beautiful?"

"I suppose," Marc said. "The color's interesting."

"It is. The best part is that it changes hues, depending on which direction you look."

Marc looked up and saw an intensely bright yellow sky. He squinted and looked ahead. There the sky took on a yellow-orange hue. He looked behind him and saw the sky was a yellow-green hue. "Wow, that's interesting. I've never seen a sky like this before."

"I thought you'd appreciate that." They crested a swell, and the turtle continued, "Just ahead. Look, there's my special place."

Marc looked down into the trough. He saw what looked to be an emerald-green island. To say it was flat would not be entirely accurate. It seemed flat but followed the contour of the swells. It was lush with plant life and strangely inviting. He was beginning to realize just how tired he was. Loggerhead carried him down the wave they were on, right up to the floating island. It was a much larger close-up. The turtle slid easily onto the moss beach.

"Thanks, Loggerhead." Marc rolled off the turtle's back onto the soft moss. He sat up and asked, "Are there other places like this one?"

"There are. I use them as way-stops when I take folks to the other village, far across the sea."

"There's another village?"

"Yes, it's six way-stops from here."

"Do you bring folks here often?"

"Yes, I carry farmers to many of these places, so they can tend their crops."

"So, farmers raise crops on these floating islands?"

"You're a funny—"

"I know. I'm a funny creature that asks a lot of questions. I do this because I know very little about where you live. I've only been here for part of a day now."

"To answer your question, there are many of these islands near our village. Our farmers use them to raise all kinds of crops."

"So, this place is a farm."

"It's a vineyard. Its fruit is for eating and winemaking. I hear the wine is quite tasty. Not big on wine myself, though."

While the two were talking, their side of the island moved to the top of an ocean swell. This allowed Marc to survey the landscape, like someone sitting on a hillside looking down on a valley. Just as the turtle had said, Marc saw distinct straight rows of vines running the length of the island. To one side, he saw several structures. They looked like small huts that were made from woven vines.

"What are those?" Marc asked.

"Some are guest quarters for folks like you. They'll shelter you from the rain. Some are used to age and store the wine."

"So, they're locked."

"What does 'locked' mean?"

"It's what you do to a room if you want to keep the things in it from being stolen or vandalized."

"I don't know what you mean by 'stolen or vandalized.'"

"Stolen means to take without paying or having permission from its owner. Vandalize means to break or ruin for no reason."

"No one here would ever vandalize something. Of that, I'm sure. I don't know what paying means. Besides, anyone here can have what they want without asking permission. Anyway, make yourself comfortable. You might want to head for one of those huts. It'll probably rain after it gets dark."

"I will. Thanks, Loggerhead." Marc got up to walk, only to fall. He heard a chuckle behind him.

"Not funny, Loggerhead."

"Looked funny to me."

"Don't you have somewhere to be?"

"You're right. I do. Goodbye," Loggerhead said as she returned to the sea.

Marc sat there for a while. Then he slowly got back on his feet. Standing on the island was a challenge. The experience was like standing on a waterbed or a slightly deflated bouncy castle. Marc took a few steps, then he lurched to his knees. Falling did not hurt. The island had plenty of give. Once, Marc got quite a way toward the huts before he staggered, fell forward, and rolled on his back near a vine. He chuckled. *I bet I'm quite the sight trying to walk. No wonder that crazy turtle laughed at me*. He stopped and looked up at the sky. Several clouds were drifting by, but what caught his eye was the intense yellow. There was no Sun. Still, the yellow was so bright, one had to squint when looking at it. *What causes the yellow? It gives off warmth. These vines get enough usable light to grow,* Marc thought. He rolled over and got on his knees and examined the vine. He was surprised to see it had fruit in all stages of development. It had fruit blossoms and green, partially ripened, and ripe bunches of dark red grapes. Realizing he was hungry, Marc examined a cluster of ripe grapes. They were about twice the size of any he had seen on Earth. This made him wonder about the size of the farmers. If the scale of the fruit carried over to people, he'd be a midget in a land of giants. Marc plucked a single grape from the bunch and took a tentative bite. As he bit into the grape, it exploded with the most amazing flavor he'd ever experienced. In the beginning, it tasted like a cherry grape with a light after-taste of a cherry-berry tart. Marc eagerly ate the rest of that bunch of grapes. He was surprised at how quickly this little snack satisfied his hunger.

Marc so enjoyed the grapes, he failed to notice that darkness had fallen. He looked at the sky and saw it wasn't as black as he expected. It looked like the yellow energy he saw earlier activated fluorescent spots in the dark blue sky. The dots twinkled like dim white lights — almost like stars twinkling. The breeze picked up. As Loggerhead had predicted, it started to rain.

Marc was drenched and shivering by the time Marc made it, crawling and stumbling, to the nearest hut. *I don't suppose it would do to light a fire,* he thought. Inside it was dry and gave shelter from the wind and rain. Marc stripped off his wet clothes and hung them around the interior. He found a mattress of sorts with some silky soft sheets. Marc also found an elegantly woven towel. He dried off with the towel, sat on the bed, and looked around. He could just make out a bottle and a cup next to the mattress. *Is this the wine that's supposed to be so good?* He poured a quarter of a cup and took a sip. This was indeed a dessert wine. *Wow!*

205

*This is better than anything I've ever tasted.* It tasted like a cherry port with the aftertaste of cherry cordial. It also had a more potent kick than he expected. He finished off the cup of wine, wrapped himself in the sheets, and fell fast asleep.

Marc's head nodded. He came to with a jerk. Where was he? He was sitting at a desk in his old university's lecture hall. He was one of nearly a hundred students.

*My old physics classroom,* he thought. *My old astronomy 101 professor is handing out tests.*

Marc was comfortable enough listening to the lecture until he realized that yet again, he was wearing only his boxer shorts. Everyone else was fully clothed. No one seemed to notice his failure to dress, so he tried to concentrate on the test that had just been placed in front of him. It read:

How does the redshift of light relate to the doppler effect on sound?

What does a redshift in light from a star indicate?

What does a blueshift in light from a star indicate?

"Mr. Smith, what is your answer to question one?" his professor asked.

Marc looked at his blank paper. *I know this … I just can't think of the answer.* The professor nodded to a cute blond co-ed to his right.

She said, "The light waves from a star moving away from us lengthen and shift toward the color red. It's like how the sound waves of, say, a train's horn get longer apart or lower to our ears as the train moves away from us. Doppler effect refers to sound. Redshift and blueshift refer to light. Light moving toward us shifts toward the blue color, just as the sound from a train horn moving toward us has a higher pitch." When she finished, the co-ed flashed a self-satisfied smile in Marc's direction. *Oh, brother,* he thought, as he slipped back and fell out of his chair.

He woke with a start before he hit the ground. He was relieved to be out of his dream. He yawned, stretched, and sat up. The problem of the mine shafts jumped to his mind. But something else was wrong. He just couldn't put his finger on it. Marc's mouth was dry, and his stomach was growling. He looked for a drink of the wine like he'd had the night before. None was to be found. Marc got dressed and wandered out to the vineyard. Over to one side, he found some vines with football-shaped melons. There were a variety of colors. He picked one that was a pastel green with yellow streaks. Marc gave it a slight shake and heard fluid sloshing around. The skin was easily cut by his survival knife. Marc carefully cut a small hole at one end of the fruit and took a tentative drink. It tasted like the juice of a sweet honey-dew, with a slight aftertaste of coconut. After drinking the juice, Marc cut the melon into wedges. The flesh was thick, watery, and sweet. The texture was tender and chewable. It only took one melon to satisfy both Marc's hunger and thirst.

He laid on his back and watched the sky. Once again, the sky overhead was bright yellow. This time the color shift had changed. Looking toward the direction that had been yellow-green, Marc now found the sky to be yellow-orange. The direction that was yellow-orange the day before was now yellow-green. *How odd. Why would the light flow change like that? Could it be that the Martian 'sky' is a river of energy that courses along the top of this vast underground labyrinth? If so, what and where is the catalyst?*

Marc looked more closely at the sky. A cloud drifted overhead, allowing him to see the texture of the sky more clearly. It wasn't still like on Earth. Instead, it moved like the current of a river from one direction to the other. As Marc observed the current flow, his eyes traveled toward the mine he and his team had been watching. *Could the PETN-A be a kind of catalyst in all this? If so, what triggers the reaction?* He needed to get off this floating island (turned prison), find Hilda, and stop the mining activity as soon as possible. Marc made his way to the edge of the water and began to worry. *Where's that silly turtle? I could sure use a ride back right now rather than later.*

# The Seaside Village

*"God is subtle, but he is not malicious." – Albert Einstein*

### Atop A Martian Cliff

Hilda's mouth went dry as she eyed the scorpion hovering in front of her.

"Do you choose to also fight?" The beast asked.

Dumfounded, Hilda shook her head slowly, side to side.

"Then will you surrender?"

Quietly, Hilda flipped her rifle around and extended it, stock first. Now hovering just in front of Hilda, the scorpion took the gun from her hand with one of its claws, crushed it, and tossed it aside. Without taking her eyes off the scorpion, Hilda unholstered her Glock, twirled it, and held it out. The beast took the Glock in its right hand. Hilda then pulled her reserve pistol from her ankle holster and held it for the scorpion to take with its left hand.

"You have detachable parts?" the scorpion asked.

The question was so naïve, it struck Hilda as funny. She replied, "Yeah, and they're interchangeable as well."

She could tell immediately that the scorpion missed her meaning. She looked more closely and saw that this wasn't an actual scorpion. Instead of eight legs, it had four legs and two arms with hands. It had a head that resembled that of a man with unusually buggy eyes. She saw that the eyes were not blank. They were looking intently at her. She felt that the creature was deciding if it could trust her or not.

After looking over the pistols, the scorpion-man extended them back to Hilda and said, "Take these. You may need them."

Hilda took her weapons and holstered them. Her hands trembled slightly. It was hard enough to face a fearsome creature that was capable of such violence. To hear that same creature address her in such a matter-of-fact, calm manner was unnerving.

"Now that we've settled that, I need you to answer a few questions. Who are you?"

"I'm Gunnery Sergeant Hilda McDermott."

"You are with the sons of Adam, who are stealing our dirty chalk?"

Hilda wasn't sure if this was a question or a statement. "No, I am not," she said.

"But, you are a descendent of Adam. Do you deny that?"

"No, er, yes, I'm a descendent of Adam. But I, we … aren't with the ones who are stealing your dirty chalk."

"I saw you running after some sons of Adam from the mine."

"We were fighting them. We, my partner and I, were trying to protect our commanding officer. We were not with the pirates. As I said, we were fighting them."

"The fact you were fighting them doesn't prove you're not with them. I've witnessed many fights among those you call 'pirates.' The children of Adam are a rebellious lot. No good has come since they've arrived."

"Yes. But we didn't come with the pirates. We were sent to see what trouble they're causing. We're here to stop it."

So far, the scorpion-man was unconvinced. "You may have come at a different time. But you did come from Earth — like they did. Who sent you?"

Our commander on Earth has been pursuing an infamous pirate for years. We found that he is here on Mars. His crew is mining for some kind of explosive. We visited both mines and heard that they're planning to link the two together. If that happens, all the air here will be sucked into space, and no one will survive. I know this sounds crazy, but it's true. We need to let our captain know and get a team together to stop this. Can you help? You could help take out the pirates—"

The scorpion-man's lifted hand stopped the flow of words coming from Hilda.

"Please stop. My head is hurting. We are only allowed to fight those who first attack us. And you shouldn't either. I would take you to our Circitor (Overseer). She would know what to do. But she's away, so I'll take you to the Council. They'll tell us what to do. First, I must take you to the village."

"Before that, let me go to the shore to find my friend. I promise I will not leave."

"I must not leave you. It's not safe for you. Now that you've surrendered to me, I'm duty-bound to protect you."

"Then stay with me on the shore. I fear for my friend."

They walked together down a steep trail until they were on the path where Marc and Hilda initially chased the pirates. Walking along the way, they soon came upon the body of the pirate Hilda had killed.

"Please stand back," the scorpion-man said as he flew upward, pointed his stinger at the corpse, and fired. Once again, a stream of fluid hit the body, which burst into flames. When the fire was finished, only a skeleton remained.

Hilda's puzzled expression caused the scorpion-man to say, "I leave the bones as a warning to other pirates. When this trouble is over, I'll complete the job. That reminds me — I saw you shoot this one so fast; it looked like you already knew he would turn and attack your friend. How did you know?"

"You may not believe this. I had a dream that showed me this would happen."

"Tell me about your dream."

"It was the first evening that we were on Portae, in a garden—"

"Wait! You came from Portae?"

"We were sent from Earth to Portae. There we were treated to an evening in one of its gardens. That's where I had my dream. From there, Taxiarchi sent us here."

"Taxiarchi, from Portae, sent you here?"

"Yes. Taxiarchi sent us. His friends call him Uwriyel."

"Of course, Uwriyel, meaning 'flame of God'. Why did you not say so in the beginning? Reuwel told us to expect someone from Portae, sent by Uwriyel to help end our troubles with these pirates, as you call them."

"Reuwel?" Hilda asked.

"Reuwel is Our Circitor (Overseer). Reuwel is the Taxiarchi of harmony, fairness, and justice. I must say that seeing you with those pirates caused me great concern for the safety of my people."

"I'm sorry, Sir, I don't follow you."

"That's right. I've not introduced myself. Forgive me. My name is Custos Maris (guardian of the sea), at your service," the scorpion-man said with a slight bow.

"It's good to meet you, Custos Maris," Hilda said. She puzzled over the immediate change in his tone.

"I thought you would be causing more trouble as you traveled our land. But, if Uwriyel sent you, it must be for our help."

Feeling suddenly faint, Hilda sat on a nearby rock.

"You look tired. Are you hungry?"

Hilda simply nodded.

"Let me share some of my nourishment with you. Now hold very still and open your mouth and prepare to drink," the scorpion-man said as he backed away and brought his stinger over his head, aiming it directly at Hilda's mouth.

Hilda hesitated. "Isn't that the way you killed the pirate?"

The scorpion-man chuckled. "That was from a different storage sack. I think you'll find this much more enjoyable. See?" He brought the stinger all the way around to face his open mouth. A small milky stream shot into his mouth. He swallowed it as if it was from a drinking fountain.

Hilda noticed a sweet smell like caramel. She took one step back and opened her mouth. It took all of her self-control to just stand steady as the stinger came up next to her face. The stream that hit her mouth was surprisingly cool and rich. It tasted like a smooth, rich butterscotch milkshake. She noticed her strength renewing with every swallow.

"What do you think?" the scorpion-man asked when they had finished.

Hilda shook her head slowly and said, "That's the best drink I ever remember having." She thought that she saw a slight smile on the scorpion-man's face. "The Sarge and I saw the mine and the poor people that the pirates are forcing to work there. We want to help free the slaves and stop the mining before it destroys everyone."

"Who is this Sarge?"

"He's my friend and partner. He jumped into the sea, trying to stop the pirate you killed earlier."

"He will not return until tomorrow evening."

"How do you know this?"

"I spoke with Loggerhead."

"Loggerhead?"

"She's a friend of mine who's keeping an eye on your 'Sarge.' Another storm is moving in. We should stay here tonight."

The scorpion-man led Hilda to a cave that overlooked the sea. The wind was strengthening. By the time they got to shelter, the rain was coming down in sheets. The scorpion-man gathered a little driftwood and, with just one drop of fluid from his stinger, started a cozy fire toward the mouth of the cave. Hilda again found some berries not too far from the fire; she offered some to Custos Maris. He accepted and ate only one or two. As they ate, Custos Maris told Hilda about the root vegetables and chickens disappearing from nearby farms.

"The pirates travel in groups of two, stealing all this?" Hilda asked.

"Yes, and I wish they hadn't stolen our dwarves also," Custos Maris said. "Granted, the dwarves are often a cranky and ill-tempered lot. They still don't deserve the way they're being treated." The scorpion-man would have continued, but Hilda was fast asleep.

The following day, Hilda woke up refreshed. The scorpion-man was not in sight. She stretched and walked over to the berry bushes to grab some breakfast. She looked out over the calm sea. The water was a deeper color of yellow as it reflected the sky. *Hmm. The sky is more yellow-green than I remember,* she thought. Just then, she heard the beating of hefty wings. Custos Maris landed at the mouth of her cave.

"I'm glad you're awake. Did you rest well?"

"I did. Thank you."

"Good. We must be on our way to Cadgwith."

"What is Cadgwith?"

"It's a small fishing village, just a short walk over the hill from here."

Custos Maris and Hilda walked in silence along a path that led to the fishing village. As they crested the hill, Hilda surveyed the landscape. The road led to a natural harbor of small canoe-type vessels. Onshore were several rows of colorful tents, complete with flags waving from their tops. Some of the tents were red or green and white striped. Others were plain white. Still, others were brightly colored. All the tents were roughly ten feet in diameter, half-open for easy viewing of the produce and wares on sale. Or so it appeared. Inland, just off the beach, were several stone and thatch buildings that faced the sea. Just beyond the tents, the path dipped below the water level. A waist-high sea wall protected those standing on the track. *What a picturesque village*, Hilda thought. *It looks like a holiday at the beach, with all those colorful tents.*

Custos Maris interrupted her thoughts, "Here we are. Stay close to me. The locals are a little skittish with the strange things that have been happening around here."

Hilda noticed that once they were spotted, the locals moved away. Mothers gathered their children a little closer. Creatures — not quite human, not quite animal — shot worried glances their way. She saw dwarves standing four to five feet tall, with long hair and beards. Their hands and feet were large. They were big-boned and stout in stature. Hilda also saw a few trolls. Trolls were human-like, only taller, averaging six-and-a-half to seven-and-a-half feet tall. They had strong hands with long fingers. They were big-chested with slim waists and long legs. What surprised Hilda the most was that no one, male or female, wore clothes as expected on Earth. The only garments that were worn were aprons of various styles, with pockets and back sacks. The locals carried tools and semi-precious stones around in their apron pockets. Hilda thought it sad that the locals seemed so afraid of the scorpion man. *He's not that bad once you get to know him*. She would have liked to speak with some of them. Yet, they stayed their distance. Hilda and Custos Maris sat on a rock outcropping by the beach. The scorpion-man excused himself, saying, "Wait here. I have got someone there I want you to meet."

He got up and walked over to the nearest tent booth. Hilda was surprised to see the children descend on him like a long-lost uncle. They climbed on his back and clung to his claws. He'd jump, and they scamper away, squealing in delight. Some of the adults gathered around him to carry on friendly conversations. To her dismay, she realized that she was the one everyone was afraid of. They did not fear the scorpion-man. He was their friend. *They probably think that I'm one of the pirates who're causing such mischief,* she thought.

A female troll broke away from the group and walked over to Hilda. "Hi, I'm Lisa," she said, offering her hand. "Welcome to Arcadia."

"I'm Hilda. It's nice to meet you." Hilda held out her hand, and they shook. "I thought the name of your village is Cadgwith."

"Cadgwith is our village. Arcadia is the name of our entire land."

"Well, Arcadia is certainly a fascinating land, Lisa."

"Thank you. Custos Maris told us that you were sent to help us during this difficult and puzzling time."

Hilda said, "I hope my friends and I can help. I'm curious about what's happening. This looks much like the outdoor markets we have back home."

"This is where we come to trade and visit. What do you think?"

Hilda replied, "This is very festive. But I'm confused. I don't see any money changing hands."

Lisa looked puzzled. "Money? What's money?"

"It's coins and dollars. That's how we give value to what we sell. How do you buy and sell?"

"I'm not sure I understand 'buy and sell.' We trade. We trade potatoes for carrots, corn for fish, and so on."

"I understand trading things for things. We call that bartering. But, how do you trade work for things? What do you use for money?" Hilda asked.

"I think you mean stones. Each skill has a unique color stone. Carpenter stones are red. Farmer stones are purple, and so on. Stones are only reminders of promises made. If a carpenter builds a cart for a farmer, the farmer takes a red stone. This reminds the farmer that he needs to give the carpenter some of his produce when it's harvested. The stone is simply a reminder. When the debt is paid, the stone is returned to its owner."

"But, how do you decide on just how much produce pays for the new cart?"

"That's easy. We shake on it," Lisa said.

"What if the service rendered requires more than one person? How's that paid for?"

"Hmm, you mean helping build a cottage?" Lisa asked.

Hilda replied, "Exactly. If four people build a cottage, how much does each person get paid?"

"You're talking about a group. That's a co-op. They decide together what each gets for the work they do," Lisa said.

"Yeah, but how do they show they are agreed? What is their contract?"

"They shake on it."

"That sounds good. But what if someone cheats and doesn't live up to the handshake. How's it enforced?" Hilda asked.

"I don't understand the word 'cheat.' What does that mean?"

"That someone lies about what they'll do."

"I don't understand the word 'lie.'"

Hilda tried to explain. "A lie is when someone does not tell the truth."

"I don't know anyone who lies or even why they'd lie. I don't think I'd want to live where people lie and cheat. Is that what they do where you come from?"

"Sadly, many do. That's why we have money and a government. It's to keep people honest."

"What is a government? How can it keep people honest?" Lisa asked.

"A government is a group of people in charge of the rest of us people. It creates money and laws that we live by. It has a police force to enforce the laws and keep us safe."

"You mean like Custos Maris? He doesn't enforce anything. He just keeps us safe," Lisa said.

"Yes. Our government uses laws, the police, contracts, and the Constitution to keep us honest and safe."

Lisa thought for a while. Then she asked, "If your government, made of people, keeps you honest, who keeps your government honest?"

"That's a good question. I suppose it's only as honest as the people who run it."

"You said that your people aren't honest. Doesn't it scare you that dishonest people may be running your government?"

"You have a point. I never thought of it quite that way before. You have no government at all?" Hilda asked.

"We have our Circitor (Overseer) and our council. I don't think they make laws. I'm afraid I don't know what a law is," Lisa admitted.

"A law is like a rule—"

"Oh, we have a rule," Lisa interrupted.

"Only one rule?" Hilda asked.

"Yes. We can do anything we want. But, we are not to trade the dirty chalk that we call bitter-chalk. I don't think we're allowed to sell it either. It comes from that cave." Lisa pointed in the direction of the mine. "If we do, we will die. That's what the Circitor says."

"That's it?"

"Yes. We can use some as a fire starter. But, other than that, it's of no value."

"Interesting," Hilda mused. "What do you do if people disagree with each other?"

"We have judges, older people, that everyone respects. They listen to and settle any disagreement, what few there are. We also have a council of judges. They meet to decide what to do about things that affect us all."

"Such as?" Hilda asked.

"Such as, what to do when your people settled on the surface of our planet. Until now, we've avoided contact. But now your people are coming down here and taking our food without taking any stones. And they took several poor dwarves. I think they might also be breaking our only rule. Our council will be meeting soon to decide what to do about that. I'm happy you're here to help. I heard someone else, someone extremely powerful, is also coming to help."

"Oh, who?" Hilda asked.

"He's called the Great Dealmaker. He's supposed to be very old and truly wise. He invited himself to the council meeting."

"What does your Circitor think of him, Lisa?"

"We don't know. It just happens that our Circitor is away for a short time."

News of the Great Dealmaker left Hilda feeling uneasy. She wondered, *Did this dealmaker already know that the Circitor would be gone when he "invited himself" to the council meeting?*

"I must get back now. I enjoyed talking to you, Hilda. You're not as bad as I feared."

Hilda said, "Thank you for explaining your way of life, Lisa."

Lisa passed the scorpion-man, who had finished entertaining the children, as she returned to her tent. When he rejoined Hilda, he said, "It's time to go to the sea wall and meet your friend."

"Right now? Thanks, Custos Maris," Hilda gave him a big hug.

She ran to the sea wall with Custos Maris right behind her. When she saw Marc on the back of a giant sea turtle, she shouted and waved. Marc was stunned to see her.

*Crap! Hilda's being attacked by a giant scorpion*, he thought, as he jumped off the turtle, drew his Glock, and aimed at the beast.

Seeing this, Custos Maris took immediately to the air. Once airborne, he aimed at Marc. "Why is it you, sons of Adam, always want to fight?"

Undeterred, Marc shouted, "Get away from Gunny, you bast—"

Hilda interrupted him by waving her hands and shouting, "Marc! Hold your fire! He's a friend. Don't shoot!"

# Reunited

*"It is one of the blessings of old friends that you can afford to be stupid with them." - Ralph Waldo Emerson*

## Seaside Village Harbor

Something in Hilda's voice gave Marc pause. He looked at the threatening scorpion-man, with its stinger pointed straight at him. It took all of his self-control to not pull the trigger. He twirled the Glock and holstered it.

Hilda ran to him and gave him a big hug. "It's good to see you, Marc. Here's my friend and Guardian, Custos Maris."

The scorpion-man landed in front of Marc and stretched out his hand. "Give me your weapon."

Hilda nodded yes. Marc shrugged, drew his Glock, and handed it over, handle first. Custos Maris took the weapon, looked it over, and handed it back to Marc, who took the gun and holstered it. "Why did you take my gun only to return it?"

"If you intended me harm, you wouldn't have given me your weapon." This time the scorpion-man extended his hand. "I'm pleased to meet you, friend of Hilda."

Marc shook his hand, "We need your help. It's urgent! There's a group of pirates that are mining PETN-A."

"PETN-A?" Custos Maris asked.

"It's a powerful explosive. In quantity, it could destroy your world. The pirates must be stopped from mining it!" Marc explained. "We must attack—"

Custos Maris interrupted, "There'll be no attacks tonight. We know about what those you call 'pirates' are doing. Tomorrow, the council will meet and determine their fate. I see you're agitated. Don't worry; all will be made right."

Marc said, "You don't understand. We can't wait for another—"

Custos Maris held up his hand. "Enough talk. Come on, you both look hungry. Let's eat at the Fish Market. My treat."

They walked together along the path that ran by the harbor. Once again, parents steered their children away from the trio.

Marc whispered to Hilda, "It must be depressing to be the scorpion-man and have everyone afraid of you."

Hilda whispered back, "News flash — we're the ones they're afraid of."

"You're kidding?"

"I kid you not. The kids love to climb all over him."

"Wow. Who would've thought?"

The path dipped down to where a stone wall separated the way from the harbor. Above this waist-high wall, a cheerfully colored awning provided shade to both sides of the barrier. The wall served as a counter. Patrons stood on one side, ordering various seafood dishes. In contrast, Mermaids "stood" in the water, taking orders and cooking savory meals on hibachi grills from the harbor side.

The scorpion-man stepped up to one of the vendors. "Set my friends up with some lobster rolls and clam chowder. I'll have my usual."

The vendor smiled. "They're in luck. Our baker just paid for her meal with some fresh sourdough bread. They give a flavorful twist to our lobster salad rolls."

Hilda asked, "What is your usual?"

Custos Maris said, "Something you probably wouldn't want."

"Try me."

"Raw barnacles, roasted sea snails, and fresh seaweed salad."

"Point taken," Hilda admitted.

Marc asked, "When do we organize our resistance to the pirates?"

"The council is set to convene tomorrow afternoon. We'll set out first thing in the morning. In the meantime, we have a special treat tonight. The village is celebrating the meeting of the council with a fireworks display."

"Fireworks?" Hilda asked.

"A boat arrived earlier today carrying some bitter chalk fashioned by our friends, the goblins. We'll use them for our celebration."

When the evening turned dark, Custos Maris led Marc and Hilda to a hillside overlooking the village. Custos Maris stood beside them, with his stinger pointing to the sky. "I think you'll enjoy the celebration from here."

A couple of other scorpion men hovered, a dozen feet off the ground not far from him. Looking to their right, Marc and Hilda saw the silhouette of several trolls standing on the tallest cliff around. They had slings that they used to fling fist-sized bitter-chalk balls high into the air over the harbor. The scorpion men, Custos Maris included, took turns shooting flaming droplets from their stingers at the bitter chalk. When the droplets hit the bitter-chalk balls, they burst into a firework display of light and sparks, followed by a heart-pounding BOOM! Each burst was unique in color and style. The audience cheered and applauded with each explosion while children giggled and covered their ears.

Hilda said, "It looks like a fireworks scene at an old-fashioned country fair. What a great way to top off a fantastic meal."

Marc said, "I'll give you that. The lobster rolls and chowder were the best I've ever tasted. Still, what troubles me is their lack of urgency. These people are losing their life-giving energy as we sit here. It's being systematically stolen while they play. What's worse is that when those thieves are done, they'll destroy this place by blowing a hole in the mines and opening a hole to the surface. That'll suck the life-giving air right out of here."

"You speak the truth, son of Adam," Custos Maris agreed as he continued to shoot at the bitter-cake balls.

Marc was startled. "You heard me?"

"I did."

"You agree with me?"

"I do."

"Then, why the hell are you entertaining these people? Why aren't you saving these people by attacking those pirates?"

"It's not time."

"There's no time to waste! If you believe that I'm telling the truth, you'll do something now!"

"Truth is a funny thing. You can know the truth, but timing is also important. Truth spoken at the wrong time, in the wrong way, can do more harm than good. Trust me on this, friend of Hilda. The council must decide what the truth is tomorrow. Then they'll decide what to do and when."

Marc continued to insist, "How can you just wait? Time's running out. We don't need more truth. We know all we need to know to act now. I haven't even mentioned the poor dwarves that are being held in slavery. Don't you care about them?"

"I share your concern. But if we run off without permission, even to do what we think is right, are we any better than those stealing our food and energy? This land is at peace because we continue in our ancestors' ways, respecting and trusting each other. You said it yourself, Hilda. Our ways would not work on your planet because your kind is untrustworthy. If we attack on our own, even to save this world and break our trust with everyone else, will we not also be destroying life as we know it?"

Seeing that he was not getting anywhere with the Custos Maris, Marc asked, "Isn't there anything we can do?"

"Tomorrow, at the council meeting, a son of Adam will be asked to speak. I believe he's the one you refer to as Ensign Torres."

Marc perked up. "Josh will speak? Does he know what we know? Will I be able to talk with him first? I need to speak to him. He needs to know what I discovered, so he can warn the council."

The scorpion-man shrugged. "So many questions. We can try to get an audience with your friend. But I can't guarantee it."

That night they returned to the cave outside the village. Custos Maris stood watch as Hilda and Marc lay down to sleep. Soon, Marc could hear the steady rhythm of Hilda's breathing. He, however, could not quiet his mind. Marc didn't understand the indifferent attitude of Custos Maris. Obviously, he and his fellow scorpion-men could easily stop the pirates in their tracks. Custos Maris didn't seem to grasp the urgency of the situation. Nothing, Marc said, could spur him to action. Even Hilda didn't seem to understand what grave danger this peaceful land was in. *It's like watching a slow-moving train wreck, and I can do nothing to stop it. These gentle people are about to have a disaster overtake them, unawares, like a tsunami.*

225

# The Visitor

*"Things are not always what they seem; the first appearance deceives many; the intelligence of a few perceives what has been carefully hidden." - Phaedrus*

### On the Surface of Mars

Barnabas found Matt pacing back and forth in the cargo bay. "Can't sleep, Captain? What's on your mind?"

"Where to start? They were supposed to keep a low profile. Based on the chatter caught by Corporal Brady — explosions, gunfire, escaping prisoners — that's not my idea of keeping a low profile," Matt responded.

"I agree, and their last transmission is also troubling, Captain. Which is worse? The fact that they're on the interior of the planet? Or that the message was in Morse code? Why in Morse code?"

"Both, Commander. Things must've gone south on them, and now they're just improvising. I'd hoped to hear good news from them by now. I can't stop thinking about all the things that can go wrong."

"They're a well-trained crew. You should know. You're the one who trained them. So far as improvising goes, we'll just have to trust Lieutenant Gonzales' judgement."

226

"I know, but was I thorough enough?"

"From the way you've ridden our poor Corporal Brady, I'd say you're more than thorough enough."

"Do you think he's ready?" Matt asked.

Barnabas nodded yes. "He's no Lieutenant Gonzales. But under the circumstances, he's pretty darn good. Certainly, a site better than you, Sir. No offense intended."

Matt shrugged. "None taken. I know his natural skills are already better than mine. If we do tangle with Beauregard, we'll need to be at the top of our game."

"You're thinking we'll be fighting this guy again before all's said and done?" Barnabas asked.

"I do. Beauregard's just taken aboard what looks like loads of refined explosives. At least that's what Lieutenant Gonzales thinks. I'm sure that he won't be wasting time, sitting around and eating bon-bons."

"What do you think he's got up his sleeve?"

"If the stuff he's loading is as powerful as our crew thinks, he could be planning an attack on the settlements here on Mars," Matt said.

"Really?"

"Yeah. The settlers wouldn't expect an attack coming from this radiation zone."

"Why destroy the settlements? What does that gain him?"

"He probably wouldn't do that. He'll most likely take out each colony's defense installations. Maybe take out a full colony to terrorize the others into submission."

"We could counter-attack," Barnabas suggested.

"It would be months before we could organize and execute a counter-attack," Matt replied. "In the meantime, he'd strip each colony of all their wealth. Then disappear to some God-forsaken place elsewhere in the Solar System."

"Or here, in the radiation zone."

"That, too. Whatever happens, we can't let Beauregard out of our sight," Matt concluded.

A shadow crossed the console. Chuck jumped up and hit the intercom. "Captain, you're needed on the bridge ASAP!"

Matt quickly made his way onto the bridge with Barnabas close behind. "What's up, Corporal?" Matt asked.

"There's something just outside our portside door, Sir."

"What is it? Did you see it?" Matt asked.

"I saw a shadow," Chuck replied.

They heard a tapping sound. "What do you make of that?" Barnabas asked.

"We need to put on our EVA suits and get after whatever it is," Matt said.

The scratching and tapping continued as each man donned their EVA suit. Barnabas stopped. "Wait. Those aren't random sounds."

Matt still struggled to get his EVA suit on. "What do you mean, Maalouf?"

"Listen carefully. That's Morse code. It has to be. Listen to the pattern."

"You may be right. What's it saying?" Matt asked.

"S-O-S-N-E-E-D-A-I-R," Barnabas said.

"Maybe it's one of our crew members. Let's get out there," Matt bounded into the exit portal.

Barnabas followed. "Stay in for the moment, Corporal," Barnabas said as he secured the inside door behind him.

"I forgot my Glock." Chuck headed back to the crew cabin. He lost his balance and hit the emergency exit lever. The exterior door popped open, sending Matt sprawling backward onto the Martian soil. The pressure change sent Barnabas flying, face first, onto the ground. Matt looked up. He saw that he was face-to-face with a six-foot scorpion man, hovering just above the ground. Matt struggled to his feet and drew his weapon. Upon seeing Matt drawing a gun, the scorpion-man rose into the air and took aim with its stinger. Barnabas rolled over, saw the stand-off, and thought, *This isn't going to end well!*

Matt aimed his Glock, "We need to take this thing out, Commander!"

A vague memory came to Barnabas, who jumped ahead of Matt. Raising both hands, he said, "Don't shoot!"

Matt tried to push Barnabas to the side, "Outta my way!"

"No time to explain, Sir," Barnabas said as he kept his position between the two hostiles. "I know you," he said to the creature. "We come in peace."

Matt lowered his weapon. "That was lame, Commander."

"How do you know me?" the creature asked while lowering its stinger.

"I had a dream about you," Barnabas said.

"If you come in peace, why are your people stealing our dirty chalk?"

"We're wondering the same thing. I'm Commander Maalouf. This is my boss, Captain Dirksen. We are not with those who are stealing from you. We are here to help."

The scorpion-man landed in front of them. "I'm Custos Martis. I'm your sentinel."

"Our sentinel?"

"I'm assigned to keep watch over you. But I've overstayed my time on the surface and need to replenish my supply of air. May I come in? I'm in urgent need of air."

Barnabas turned to Matt and touched his firearm. "Trust me, Captain,"

Matt holstered his weapon and moved aside. "I hope you know what you're doing."

Barnabas motioned to the scorpion-man to follow as he stepped further into the portal. The portal could barely hold its three strange occupants. Soon the outer door was sealed, and O2 was flowing over the occupants. The scorpion-man took several deep breaths and exhaled. Barnabas coughed as the aroma of tar assaulted his nose.

Custos Martis said, "Thanks. I can go for a couple of hours with a store of air. After that, I need to breathe again."

The trio joined Chuck, who drew his weapon but set it aside when he saw Matt motion with his head.

"Perhaps more formal introductions are in order," Barnabas suggested.

"Quite so, Commander," Matt acknowledged. "I'm Captain Matthew Dirksen. I command the USS Osprey. The two crew members here are her pilot, Commander Barnabas Maalouf, and interim weapons officer, Corporal Charles Brady."

"My name is Custos Martis, the Guardian of Mars. I, and several of my kind, are charged with the safety and health of our land."

"Sounds like one of our police officers. I'll wager no one messes with you," Barnabas said.

"I'm not sure what you mean. I'm often invited to join families when they picnic or travel to market," the scorpion man said.

Matt said, "Here, Custos Martis, join us on the bridge. May I call you Martis?"'

"You may. I'm here to help if I can," Custos Martis replied.

Getting situated on the bridge was a challenge. The scorpion-man's wings folded down well enough. But his tail kept slapping things and people as he turned from side to side.

"Why're you out here in the first place?" Matt asked.

"I'm assigned to watch over the entrances to our land. If any of them are compromised, we will lose our air, and the land we live in would die."

Barnabas looked at Matt, who shrugged and motioned for the scorpion-man to rest at Marci's station. "Okay, Maalouf, how did you know Martis wasn't here to harm us?"

"I had a dream when we were on Portae—"

"You came from Portae?" Custos Martis interrupted. "Who sent you?"

"Taxiarchi," Barnabas replied.

"What did he look like?" Custos Martis asked.

Matt replied, "A flaming tower when we first met. But then a majestic beam of red light when he sent us here."

The scorpion-man looked puzzled. "Why did Taxiarch send you all here?"

"We were sent here to warn and help your people," Matt replied.

"Warn us about what?"

Matt said, "He said you are in great danger."

What kind of danger?"

"We don't know," Matt replied.

"Then how can you warn us?

Matt said, "Not sure."

"So, we're in some kind of danger, that you don't know, from what, you don't know. And you're sent here to warn us?" Custos Martis asked.

Matt shrugged. "Pretty much."

"And you said Taxiarchi from Portae sent you?"

"Yes, he did," Matt affirmed.

"Sent here from Portae, by Taxiarchi, with an obscure assignment," Custos Martis said. "Fascinating. That actually makes sense."

"When we arrived, we found our nemesis, Jacques Beauregard. He and his crew are dangerous. They cause much grief to those who travel between Mars and Earth. He was arrested a while ago and should be in jail. He must've escaped. So, we, my crew, and I are quietly observing him and his crew of pirates," Matt explained.

Custos Martis chuckled. "Blowing up part of their camp and shooting at them doesn't seem all that quiet. Fortunately, they've slowed the mining of dirty chalk to a crawl, so it can't be all bad. Those sons of Adam running the camps are our current threat.

"Sons of Adam?" Matt asked.

"That's what we call people that came here from Earth," Custos Martis said.

"Do you know who they're connected with?" Matt asked.

"Not sure. At first, we thought the Sons of Adam were connected to the camps your people set up on the surface of our planet. But only a couple of people came here from there. The others came directly from other places in space. The fact that you and your crew consider them dangerous confirms our suspicions."

Matt rubbed his chin. "Tell us more."

"My people have been in danger several times. First, when the great war of rebellion swept over our planet. At that time, Custos de Caelos, our overseer, moved all who were willing to follow her to safety. A subterranean land had been prepared especially to protect us, as the surface was destroyed by the battle."

"It must be a big space," Barnabas observed.

"It's vast and beautiful," Custos Martis replied. "We call it Arcadia."

"So, your entire population lives below?" Matt asked.

"Yes, everyone must live inside of our planet. No one would survive being on the surface. We call it the great wasteland. Because of our hard bodies and ability to hold much air, we're the only ones who can survive being on the surface. Our land below is safe and has only been threatened two other times. The first was a scourge of man-sized locusts. They were released by the one we call the Great Destroyer."

"Great Destroyer?" Matt asked.

"He's the leader of the rebels," Custos Martis replied. "The locusts threatened to eat all of our food. We fought them off. Finally, we destroyed the last of them and sealed the entrance by which they came."

"Your second threat?" Matt prompted.

"It was worse than the first. It was an army of man-sized spiders who had a poisonous bite. We had to fight them and treat those who were bitten. Finally, we prevailed and sealed that entrance to our land. Now only three entrances remain. The one in that shadow, over there. One is far to the north. And the one your crew and those, you call pirates, used to gain access to our land."

"And how's my crew?" Matt asked.

"They're all well. A couple of my companions, Custos Vitaes and Custos Maris, are watching over them," the scorpion-man replied. "This third threat is different. Your people, the ones you call 'pirates,' are a puzzle. They've not invaded by force. Instead, they've set up two camps where they are taking dirty chalk from the ground."

"What is dirty chalk?" Barnabas asked.

"It is a substance that gives energy to our land. It's fun to play with. It can be dangerous if not handled properly, as the pirates discovered," Custos Martis said.

"Why don't you just destroy them?" Matt asked.

233

"We keep them isolated but are not allowed to destroy them unless they first attack us. I'm not sure what danger these pirates pose or how to handle their presence. Our council is meeting shortly to determine what to do. We've received word that the Great Dealmaker is coming, sent by Taxiarchi, to help us solve the problem. My friend and I are to wait here for his arrival and escort him to the meeting. Your crew will be able to attend and speak of their concerns also."

"What concerns do my crew have?" Matt asked.

"The one they call Sarge is convinced that continued mining could cause our land harm. He's most insistent. He'll want to argue against any solution that does not include an immediate and permanent end to the collecting of dirty chalk."

Matt nodded his approval. "Sarge knows his stuff. If he's concerned, the council should pay attention. "How's the Great Dealmaker going to make a difference?"

Custos Martis shrugged. "He's supposed to be very powerful and wise. Word is, he has a compromise that'll satisfy both the pirates and us. I'm afraid that your friend over there will do something destructive with all the dirty chalk he has in his spaceship; if he doesn't like the outcome of the council's meeting."

Matt nodded in agreement. "We're keeping an eye on him. We'll interfere with any plans he has to destroy anything. Is there any way I can speak with my crew?"

"I'll speak to one of your crew and relay any messages back and forth as needed—"

The scorpion-man was interrupted by a rising cloud of reddish-brown dust outside the Osprey that drew their attention. A large Cruiser Class ship was landing beside Beauregard's space frigate. "That's my cue," Custos Martis said as he prepared to exit the Osprey.

He turned so quickly, his tail hit Chuck, knocking him against the ship's bulkhead. The scorpion-man turned back to apologize, swinging his tail into Barnabas.

"Whoa, Martis," Matt chuckled. "Let's get you on your way."

The awkward dance continued until Custos Martis was curled up in the Osprey's portal entry chamber. Then Matt hit the release lever. The scorpion-man flew out of the Osprey, over to where the space cruiser had just landed. The trio watched as another scorpion man flew out of the shadows to join his companion. Once the dust settled, out of the space cruiser stepped a tall and powerfully built man, wearing a gleaming black cape with red trim instead of an EVA suit. Beauregard and two crew members, wearing EVA suits, stepped out of their frigate to greet the Great Dealmaker. The two scorpion men then stepped forward to greet everyone. Beauregard's crew drew their weapons, but the mysterious visitor waved them aside. The two crew members returned quickly to their ship. The caped visitor stepped forward and shook hands with the scorpion men. They all turned and disappeared into the shadows.

Barnabas frowned. "What do you make of all this, boss?"

Matt took a deep breath and let it out slowly. "I'm not sure what it is ... something's just not right. We need to be extra vigilant."

### Staging for the Debate

The amphitheater was impressive. On one side, it was a three-quarter bowl, stretching from the crown of a hill down to a narrow lagoon. The lagoon separated the hillside from an island. The island held two stages, each with a clam-shell backdrop. A particular area was set apart for the council members at the base of the bowl. Marc was surprised by the number of creatures that were already settling in for the event. Some were families that brought picnic lunches and snacks for their children. Even the lagoon was teeming with sea life, as turtles and mermaids found places from which to watch the Great Dealmaker.

The amber sky accentuated the yellow, golden orange of the Citrine outcroppings. Marc was struck by their size. As was the case on Portae, Citrine on Earth never occurred as such large, uncovered outcroppings.

Hilda interrupted his thoughts. "Look, Marc. Here comes the Lieutenant with a scorpion-man of her own."

Marc could barely give Marci the appropriate greeting. "Hi, Lieutenant. Where's Ensign Torres?"

"It's good to see you too, Sarge," Marci mocked. "The Ensign is with Custos Vitae. He is behind the curtain to the platform, on your left. Right now, He's preparing to speak to the council."

"I need to talk to him before this show starts. It's urgent! Is there any way you can pull some strings, so I could see him now?"

Marci shook her head. "Not possible. I'm just a spectator, like you, Sarge."

"Lieutenant, this place is in grave danger! But, no one seems to know or care. I've got to get this info to Torres, pronto!"

"I'd help if I could. But it's out of my hands." Marci gestured toward Custos Vitae.

Marc turned toward his escort. "Maris, I know you said we must stay here until after the debate. Are you sure there isn't any way for me to get a message to Torres before he speaks?"

"No, there isn't. After the debate, I'll ask the council to listen to you and consider your request."

"Yes, but by then, it may be too late!" Marc insisted.

"I'm sorry, that's just the way it has to be."

Marc spotted Josh walking to the stage. *This sucks!* he thought. *I can't just sit here. I've got to get to Torres.* He stood up and started to jump the barricade beside him. He was halfway over it when a sharp sting hit his right buttocks. He felt himself go limp and start to slide back to the ground. His mind was relaxed. He knew he should warn someone of something, but he was unable to focus. The funny thing was that he was fully aware of what was happening. He just had no control over his body other than breathing.

"I'm so sorry, Sarge," Custos Maris said. "I can't let you break our protocol. You must remain in the audience and let the debate go  on without speaking with either of the debaters."

Finally, Marc was able to shake his head and clear his mind. *Without my information, I can't see this ending well at all.*

# The Debate

*"Has God really said, 'You shall not eat of any tree of the garden?'"*
*Satan - Genesis 3:1 [WEB]*

### Martian Amphitheater

J osh had been ushered to a small anti-chamber, just to the left of where he was to stand when addressing the council. He was accompanied by Sabrina and Custos Vitae. Josh's mind wandered back to the evening before when he had recklessly picked up and tossed the pirate's grenade. His body was still sore from being blown to the ground. He knew that the flash-bang grenade had blinded him. He remembered little else other than being carried back into Sabrina's cottage. He heard, rather than saw, Sabrina and Marci fussing over him. He also remembered hearing the low voice of one they called Custos Vitae. Josh felt a solution being poured over his eyes. That night he had not slept well. He'd heard that the council was meeting today and that he needed to speak. The idea disturbed him. He'd even dreamt that he had a conversation with an old friend. Josh couldn't place his finger on who it was. He — or was it a she? — seemed real enough. They had said, "Remember, Qui Admonet, you must give a warning to the people of Arcadia."

238

Josh took a deep breath. *I can't do this*, he thought.

"No, you can't," the voice said. "I'm here to help you."

*What to do? What do I do?* Josh thought.

"Just relax. I'll bring the right words to your mind."

"That's easier said than done," Josh said out loud.

"In the morning, you'll see. It will be the sign that I am with you."

The morning came, and Josh could see, partially. He could not make out distinct features or details of those around him. He could see well enough to keep from walking into things. *It's a start*, he thought. Still, he felt like he was looking through a mist that clouded his vision.

Sabrina's voice brought him back to the present. "It's time. Are you ready?"

"I am," Josh said, as he thought, *Is a mouse ever ready to face the hungry cat?*

### In Front of the Martian Council

Josh peered into the mist — that was his vision — and saw two great stages. Below the platforms were a dozen thrones, on which a variety of creatures sat. Some looked familiar to Josh. Others didn't. Behind the thrones was a crowd of creatures. Josh could make out the forms of trolls and dwarves. An inlet of water separated the thrones from the rest of the amphitheater. In it were vague shapes of mermaids and sea turtles. On the far stage, a tall and imposing man stood. Josh imagined he was magnificently dressed. He couldn't be sure, as his eyes were so clouded.

Marc, on the other hand, could see all too well. *The dealmaker looks like a Roman god. He's certainly more impressive in appearance than Josh.*

The president of the council began the proceedings. "You all know that we've been troubled, for some time now, by the sons of Adam. They've traveled from a place called Terra and are taking our dirty chalk without asking. They've even taken some of our dwarves as slaves. Today, we'll hear from the Great Dealmaker, who comes to us from Portae, to present a solution to our dilemma. We will then hear from a son of Adam, who also says that he comes from Portae, with a warning. First, we'll hear from Factorem Plurimum, the Great Dealmaker."

The dealmaker stepped forward, opening his previously folded arms with a gesture of generosity. "Thank you, Madam President. I've been pondering your problem ever since I heard of it. It strikes me that the solution is quite simple. So simple, I'm surprised that your Custos de Caelos hasn't suggested it before now. You could visit the sons of Adam and offer to sell the dirty chalk to them."

A hush fell over the audience. *That guy's smooth*, Marc thought.

The council president spoke up. "That is not an option. Custos de Caelos has said that we are not to sell the dirty chalk."

"Surely, Custos de Caelos wasn't serious when she told you not to sell the dirty chalk. Was she?"

"I'm afraid she was," the president said. "This was the one negative command that came straight from Alpha Omega."

"Are you sure about that, Madam President?" asked the dealmaker. Without waiting for a response, he continued, "Perhaps Custos de Caelos is holding out on you. She knows that selling the dirty chalk will make you both wealthy and wise."

"I don't understand 'wealthy.' We have everything we need now."

"Do you? Can you enjoy the beauty, that is, the surface of Mars?"

"The surface of Mars is barren," the council president said.

"Is it? Have you seen it recently?" As the Great Dealmaker spoke, the clamshell behind him became a screen showing images of majestic mountaintops overlooking lush forests. The scenes changed and showed stunning sunrises and flocks of colorful birds rising from picturesque lakes and streams. There was a murmur of approval from the audience. *He's very smooth*, Marc thought.

"It's a shame you must spend your whole lives down here, with amber-shaded skies, and never get to see the truly remarkable range of colors in the sky above Mars."

"Not true!" Josh interrupted. "Those are images of Earth. The surface of Mars looks nothing like that."

"You're wrong, son of Adam. These are images of Mars. Some of you in this audience remember what Mars was like before you were forced to live down here. Are these images correct?"

Marc winced as he heard a murmur of approval from the audience. *There goes your credibility, Josh.*

"Okay, Son of Adam. Show us how Mars' surface looks now, according to you."

Josh said, "I can describe it, just not show it."

"Possibly because you can tell a lie but not show a lie," suggested the dealmaker.

Sabrina flew up behind Josh and whispered, "I can help you. Just think in your mind what images you want to share."

She placed her hands on Josh's head. Immediately, the clamshell behind Josh became a screen showing the actual Martian surface, just as Josh had seen it. It was reddish-brown and desolate, with a black sky. The audience caught their breath.

The Great Dealmaker smirked. "You, who cannot even show your thoughts on your own, question me?" Turning toward the audience, he continued, "Think of what you're missing." Turning back to face Josh, he said, "Think on this, oh, Son of Adam — why do other sons and daughters of Adam, even now, live on the surface of Mars?"

The audience gasped, and Marc shook his head. *This is going sideways fast! The dealmaker is smooth, with warm words of comfort, positive, and giving hope for a quick resolution of the Martian's dilemma. Josh's delivery is halting and awkward. He's not prepared. I wish he knew what I know.*

241

"Tell me, Son of Adam, if Terra — the place you call Earth — is so beautiful and Mars is so ugly, why would your people leave Earth to live on Mars? Why would they want to live on the surface of someplace as ugly as you pictured? Do I not speak the truth when I say that sons of Adam live on the surface of Mars?"

The audience leaned forward in anticipation. Josh nodded. "You speak the truth about a few people from Earth living on Mars. They must live in shelters, caves, and lava tubes because the surface of Mars is too desolate and hostile to live otherwise."

"I repeat my question. Why would your people leave Terra to live on the surface of someplace as ugly as you say?"

"Because, as barren as it is, the surface of Mars is different. Some are curious. Others are sent there as punishment for the crimes they committed on Earth."

"Crimes? Punishment? What does that mean?" The council's president wondered.

Marc could see the genius of the Great Dealmaker's approach. Many, other than the Custos, had never seen the surface of Mars. Those that had, were ushered below before the surface, as they remembered it, was wiped out. And the Custos, Marc had been told, were barred from even speaking at council meetings. The Martians had no reference point from which to judge the truth of what was being said. He wanted to jump in and help Josh's argument. Still, though his mind was clear, his body was frozen. Other than breathing, he couldn't move.

"Nice try, Son of Adam," The Great Dealmaker said in a low voice. He then spoke louder, "The truth is that there is something the Alpha and Omega didn't want you to know. He knows that if you step out onto the surface of Mars, you'll be free. Oh, it's pretty, down here. However, it's nowhere as pleasing and freeing as it is on the surface. It's so easy to achieve. All you have to do is sell the dirty chalk to the sons of Adam.

They're already taking it, anyway. You can trade access to the magnificent surface, which belongs to you, for the dirty chalk they've already taken. It's not actually selling. It's trading, after all." Encouraged by a murmur of assent, he continued, "You're at the crossroads of your history. You can decide for yourselves if it is right or wrong to sell the dirty chalk. Do you really need to defer to Custos de Caelos? This is your chance to be like a god, or a man, such as the sons of Adam."

The phrase "sons of Adam" triggered a memory deep within Josh. "Oh yes, I remember a story of when my forefather, Adam, was offered a similar deal. He and his wife lived in a beautiful garden full of peace and tranquility. They also had only one rule. The offer — given to them — was that if they broke that rule, they'd receive what had been denied them. They believed the lie and lost their garden of tranquility. Our world hasn't had peace ever since."

The dealmaker laughed. "Adam was a fool. He should have stood up on his own. But he couldn't because he was too weak. You, my friends, are not like him. You are strong. But you are fools if you believe this little man. The sons of Adam have achieved great things." As the Great Dealmaker spoke, scenes of massive bridges and tall skyscrapers flashed across the screen.

Simultaneously, scenes of Holocaust death camps and cities bombed into ruin ran across Josh's screen. "Don't make the same mistake my forefather made. Ours is a cursed rebel planet because Adam failed to trust Alpha Omega, who even had to send his son to begin to set things right."

The dealmaker smirked. "Did you hear that story? Alpha Omega sent his son to save the poor little sons of Adam. Has he ever sent his son to visit you? Have you ever seen Alpha Omega? Maybe he's only a story Custos de Caelos invented to keep you all down here." The dealmaker turned toward Josh.

Marc noticed that the dealmaker had grown. He was now at least nine feet tall and had a dreadful, yet regal, air about him. "Tell us, little Son of Adam, have YOU ever seen Alpha Omega? How do you KNOW he exists?" the Great Dealmaker asked.

Josh paused. Surprisingly to Marc, he did not shrink from his now-massive adversary. "While I have not seen Him, I have faith that he exists."

"Faith. What is that?" The president of the council asked.

"It was once said, 'Faith is being sure of what we hope for and certain of what we do not see.' It was also said, 'Without faith, it is impossible to please Alpha Omega because anyone who wants to meet him must believe that he exists and that he rewards anyone that earnestly seeks him.' I urge all of you to have faith in your beloved Custos de Caelos. And trust that there's a good reason for Alpha Omega to forbid selling dirty chalk. Have faith that they know what is best for you," Josh said.

"There you have it, my friends. Straight from the little son of Adam. Trust and stay in line. I say trust but verify. How do you know selling dirty chalk is wrong if you don't try it? How do you know if the story about the supposed destruction of Mar's surface is even true? But nooo, this mere mortal who, by his own admission, comes from a rebel planet, says that you cannot solve your difficulty. Really? You have what it takes to stand on your own. You don't need Custos Caelos' permission. Stand up. Tell that little son of Adam you don't need his advice."

Josh shook his head. "Let's talk about trust. Sabrina creates meals for George and Gimpy. They each have different ideas about what tastes good. But they trust Sabrina's ability to give them what they each enjoy. Sabrina says she will sew you a fine and useful apron. You believe her. Why? Because you trust her. Custos Vitae tries to inject you with his stinger. You let him without fear because you trust he's doing it to help you, not hurt you. Your whole society is built on trust. And your life is good because no one has ever broken your trust."

Marc heard a murmur of agreement. Josh continued, "Words like 'lawyer,' 'cheat,' 'contracts,' 'courts,' and 'war' make no sense to you. They never made sense to my forefather or my foremother until the day when the Great Deceiver offered them a deal. They did what he suggested. Breaking that rule brought pain and death to their world."

Marc thought he heard a slight gasp in the audience. Josh wasn't finished. "This dealmaker accuses your guardians of keeping you deprived and naïve. Until now, you've trusted that your creator made you as rich and wise as you need to be. You've trusted that the Custos care only for your safety. Your problem now is ... who will you trust? Your Custos de Caelos or ..." Josh gestured toward his opponent, "this one. He says he's the Great Dealmaker. I say he's the Great Deceiver. The same father of lies that brought my forefather such grief. NO! He's not just the Great Deceiver. He's the Great Destroyer!"

Marc heard the audience gasp. *You're on quite a roll, kid. But is it enough? I'm afraid it isn't.*

The Great Dealmaker just laughed. "That's rich. Aren't your own brothers, other sons of Adam, that, at this minute, are in the mines, robbing these good people of what is rightfully theirs? We both know that breaking the one rule of not selling dirty chalk causes no harm. Instead, it will expand their horizons. They'll be able, once again, to live on the surface, enjoy its beauty, and look out at the stars. Would you deny them that? Must they always be cooped up inside the planet? Perhaps it's you who is the Great Deceiver and Destroyer come in disguise, to deny them what is rightfully theirs. That's the truth of this matter, isn't it?"

Marc winced as he heard the Great Dealmaker's skillful flip of Josh's argument.

The President of the Council rose to her feet. "Thank you both for your advice and warning. You both claim to come from Portae with conflicting stories. We're simple creatures. So, I have only one question. Dealmaker, when Taxiarchi sent you to us, what did he look like?"

"Why, Madam President, we all know Taxiarchi appears as an all-consuming fire." As he spoke, the screen behind him showed an immense column of angry fire.

The President nodded her agreement. She then turned to Josh. "Son of Adam, when Taxiarchi sent you to us, what did he look like?"

"Madam President, at first, he was a tall column of angry fire. But when he sent us, he was a column of ruby-red light. He was so magnificent I couldn't stop looking at him." As Josh spoke, his screen first showed a column of fire, similar to that of his adversary. Then it went blank.

"I make a pretty poor Qui Admonet," Josh said under his breath.

"A what?" Josh's fairy helper asked.

"Oh, it's just a name Taxiarchis gave me on Portae."

"He gave you the name that means 'he who warns'?"

"Yeah, but I'm bad at it. I don't know why he chose me."

"Josh, listen to me. I need you to recall in your mind when he gave you that name."

"Recall?"

"Yes, think about it, visualize the moment Taxiarchis named you Qui Admonet."

Just then, Josh's screen turned into a magnificent column of ruby-red light.

"Thank you both." The President turned to the council. They began conversing quietly among themselves. Marc's heart sank as he heard the murmurings among the audience. To him, Josh wasn't as convincing as the Great Dealmaker.

After a long time, with animated discussions, the council president stood, and the audience fell silent. "It is the judgment of the council that you have both made strong cases for your points of view. But only one of you could have come from Portae. I have never seen Taxiarchi myself. But I've often heard Custos de Caelo speak of him as a being full of grace and truth." She turned toward the Great Dealmaker. "According to her, the Taxiarchis you know is one of anger and judgment, not grace and truth." She then turned toward Josh. "The ruby column you described is the Taxiarchis of grace and truth. Your message must be true and the one that guides us." She turned back to the dealmaker. "You, then, are not sent from Taxiarchis to help us."

The dealmaker's face darkened. "You're making a grave mistake. My proposal is reasonable and desirable. Can you give me one good reason not to believe me over this sniveling son of Adam?"

"We, despite your dispersions, chose to trust the one who Taxiarchis sent. That is not you. Therefore … you must be, as the son of Adam says, the Great Destroyer, come on your own, to do us harm. You must now leave."

The Great Dealmaker became enraged. "You think you chose life. The truth is, you chose death. My destruction will rain down on you, as surely as this will consume that son of Adam." With those words, the dealmaker hurled a ball of energy right at Josh and disappeared.

# Jail Break

*"The paradox of courage is that a man must be a little careless of his life even in order to keep it." - Gilbert K. Chesterton*

### In Front of the Martian Council

The energy ball never made it to Josh. Four scorpion men fired energy balls of their own. These intercepted the first one, halting it, mid-course, in a bright flash. The Martian audience sat in stunned silence. They had never witnessed an outburst of anger like that before. Much less one of such violence. Someone seated near the council asked, "What does this mean?"

One of the council members replied, "It means we chose wisely."

Marci noticed that Josh was lying on the ground backstage. Hovering over him were Sabrina and Custos Vitae. She rushed over to where they were. "Is he okay?"

"He's okay," Sabrina replied. "We're working to finish repairing his eyes."

Marci winced as she watched the scorpion-man bring his stinger over his head to within a fraction of an inch from Josh's right eye. She watched a stream of liquid hit the eye causing, a frothing reaction. The process was repeated on Josh's left eye, with the same result.

"We're softening the covering on his eyes. Now we'll wash it away."

Custos Vitae again aimed his stinger at Josh's eyes. This time a clear stream flooded the eyes, washing the foam and debris out.

Josh said, "I don't know what you're doing, but it feels good."

"Can you see anything?" Sabrina asked.

"It feels like I'm underwater looking at a bright sky."

Sabrina knelt to dab Josh's eyes dry. Marci also knelt beside Josh. "Here, let me," she said.

As Marci dabbed, Josh smiled. "I can see now." He looked directly into Marci's face. "Gosh, you're beautiful!"

Marci blushed. "Then your eyes are still not as good as you think they are."

"No, my eyes are clearer now than before the accident. And you're so beautiful I can't take them off you."

Marci felt herself blush again. "Ensign Torres, you're out of line! Now get up. We've got work to do."

Josh struggled to his feet and turned toward Custos Vitae. "I don't know how to thank you for bringing my sight back."

The scorpion-man nodded. "You can start by ridding us of your people who are holding the dwarves as slaves."

Hilda walked up. "Lieutenant, you've got to come to the council right away."

"What do they want?"

Custos Maris and the Sarge just finished talking to them about the pirates' threat in the mines. The council wants you to get rid of the pirates, pronto."

Marci and Hilda arrived in time to hear the head of the council address the audience. "The sons of Adam are a greater threat to our world than were the spiders and locusts. We're asking the team from Portae to remove that threat from Mars. Will you do this for us?"

Marci nodded. "Yes, Ma'am, we will remove the pirates right away."

Upon hearing this, the audience applauded politely.

"Is there anything that you need from us?" the president asked.

"We could use the help of your Custos," Marc answered.

The president smiled. "That's an excellent idea. Custos Maris, will you accept the challenge?"

"On behalf of my friends, we accept the challenge," Custos Maris said as the other scorpion men nodded in agreement. To this, the audience broke into cheers and enthusiastic applause.

"Good." The president gestured toward Marci. "I will put the daughter of Adam in charge." She motioned to the Custos. "You four are to do as she says, but do not forget the code you live by. Godspeed." With that, the scorpion-men and crew of the Osprey were sent on their way.

Marci signaled for her crew and scorpion-men to regroup among a stand of live oak trees. "Custos Martis, you must get word to our captain immediately about what happened down here. Tell him that we need to stop the mining operation ASAP. He can't leave our unhappy visitors that just left to their own devices. When you're done speaking with the captain, please join Custos Maris at the surface mine. Now, hurry!"

"Yes, Lieutenant." The scorpion-man flew off.

"Custos Maris, you must get to the surface mine as fast as possible. Keep those pirates from getting to their transport ship. I don't want them to team up with Beauregard against the Osprey."

"You forget, Lieutenant, that I cannot harm anyone except for self-defense."

"I'm not asking you to hurt the pirates. Just keep a line of fire between them and their space vehicles."

"Oh, I've got it. I'm on my way." Custos Maris flew off.

Marci sent Custos Pago and Custos Vitae ahead to reconnoiter the pirate's defenses of the grotto mine. She and her crew ran as fast as they could toward the cliff.

Custos Pago met them at the base of the cliff with his report.

"The pirates are guarding the nearest cave entrance and the bridge to their mine. The second cave entrance is free of guards. Of course, you must pass by the first entrance to get to it."

Marc said, "Ma'am, we need to stop the pirates from connecting their mine shafts!"

Hilda exclaimed, "We need to rescue the dwarves!"

Josh asked, "How'll we keep the pirates from escaping to the surface?"

"We must stop the mining ASAP! What's our strategy?" Marc insisted.

Marci motioned for silence. The idea that she was now in charge slapped her like a splash of ice water. It invigorated her. A plan was starting to come together in her mind. She held her hand up to give her time to articulate their subsequent actions. A tug at her sleeve stopped her.

Custos Vitae said, "I'm afraid that if we attack the pirates in the grotto mine, they'll harm the dwarves, Lieutenant."

"That is a real possibility," Marci admitted.

"Perhaps I could enlist the help of the gremlins," Custos Vitae suggested.

"The gremlins?" Marci asked.

"They inhabit all of the caves and dark places of our world. They're normally painfully shy. But they're friends with the dwarves. I think they'll be able to free the dwarves before we attack—"

251

"Not before we attack," Marci interrupted. "They need to do it while we attack. The sound of our attack will draw the guard's attention to us. That way, the gremlins can help the dwarves slip out without being detected."

Custos Vitae nodded in agreement. "You're quite right, Lieutenant."

"Go and tell the gremlins to get in position, but not move until they hear the first shots fired."

"I'm on my way, Lieutenant." Custos Vitae flew off.

Marci welcomed the responsibility for this endeavor. "Okay, team. Here's the plan. Custos Pago will give Torres and me cover fire as we work our way through the first cave entrance. While we're occupying those guarding that entrance, Gunny and Sarge will slip behind us and enter the cave through the second entrance. Then, they'll traverse the far cave wall, going behind the waterfall. This will bring them in behind the pirate landers." Marci turned and faced Marc and Hilda. "Your goal is to capture those landers. We want to trap the pirates here below and keep them from escaping."

Marc and Hilda both smiled. "Now you're talking, Boss!" Marc exclaimed.

Marci smiled, despite herself. "Torres, we'll work our way into the Grotto. Then, you'll cover me by concentrating your fire on the guard tower nearest the bridge. I'll re-enter the Osprey lander and use its firepower to take out the radio shack and bridge blockades. Once we've secured the pirates' surrender, you'll send a Morse code message to the upper mine that our mining equipment is broken and that we need help. We'll capture those who come to help. Finally, we'll take on the remaining pirates, topside. That's our plan A … questions?"

"If plan A doesn't work?" Josh asked.

"Then we'll go with plan B."

Josh looked perplexed. "Plan B?"

Marci smiled. "We improvise. Now let's move out."

Josh grinned. "Captain Dirksen'll be proud of you, Lieutenant!"

"Or he'll have your bar," Hilda added with a smile.

Thanks for your encouragement, Gunny," Marci replied.

"Anytime, Lieutenant," Hilda said. "Anytime."

Custos Pago led the way. He hovered as he entered the first tunnel leading to the cavern. The beating of his wings sounded like a helicopter slowly landing. The sound terrified the pirates, who began shooting and retreating from the tunnel toward the grotto. Marci and Josh dashed into the tunnel, staying low. Josh stayed to one side — Marci stayed along the other. They advanced quickly as the pirates retreated. Sparks flew around them as the wild firing of the pirates ricocheted off the tunnel walls and ceiling. Marci thought, *Note to self — next time, don't forget about the ricochets*. Marci and Josh resisted the urge to fire so as not to give away their positions. The pirate fire was concentrated on Custos Pago, who was, by now, hovering just inside the cavern, shading his eyes, his only weak spot.

"Custos Pago, spray your fire around the mine entrance to keep anyone from entering," Marci commanded.

The scorpion-man complied. In response, the pirate camp erupted into more gunfire and frenzied motion. The pirates that had been guarding the tunnel entrance broke into a run for the bridge. They yelled at the bridge guards to open the gate as they ran. Marci and Josh ran for the Osprey lander. Josh forgot that its cloaking device was still on. He ran right into it, falling back, stunned by the impact.

Marci laughed. "Thanks for finding the lander, Torres. I couldn't remember exactly where it was." She found the entrance pad and activated it with her palm print. Once inside, she tossed a weapon to Josh. "Concentrate on the watchtower lights and the bridge. I'll take out the radio shack." Flipping to stealth mode, Marci aimed at the radio shack and fired. It lit up like a bonfire.

Meanwhile, three pirates assigned to guard the dwarves inside the mine had just finished locking them up when they heard the gunfire.

"What the hell?" the first pirate exclaimed.

They rushed toward the mine entrance only to be stopped short by the fire coming from Custos Pago.

"What's that?" one pirate asked.

"Looks like flame-throwers in the air," another said.

"What do we do? We can't make it to the landers from here."

The first pirate held his hand up. "Do you hear that?"

"Hear what?"

"It sounds like the clanking and squeaking of cell doors back in the mine."

"Did they circle behind us?"

"The first pirate spat. "Don't be stupid. This is the only way in or out. Wait, there it goes again."

Another pirate exclaimed, "It's the dwarves. They're escaping!"

"No way! I locked their doors."

The first pirate snapped his finger. "That's it."

"What?"

"We'll use those little buggers as hostages. We'll bring them up here and threaten to kill them if we aren't let out."

"Great idea! Let's get them."

The pirates rushed back to the makeshift jail. They found that the main gate was lifted from its hinges and set aside. Walking more cautiously, the pirates rounded a corner. They saw that all the cell doors were also off their hinges and lying open. They saw a couple of dwarves running toward the far corner.

The first pirate aimed his assault rifle. "I've got one in my sites." Just as he squeezed the trigger, the lights went out. The sound of the rifle shots was deafening. "Damn, I missed it!

The guards flipped on their helmet lights and ran back to the main shaft. "Where'd they go?"

The first guard said, "My money's on them wanting to get higher. Follow me."

He led the others to the antechamber at the bottom of the only vertical shaft in the mine. "I bet they're up there somewhere."

During the confusion, Marc and Hilda had run, undetected, down the second tunnel. "Ready for some bouldering, Gunny?"

"You forgot your makeup, Sarge." Hilda pulled a stick of camouflage face paint out of her pocket. She began to apply it to Marc's face, more gently than she needed to. When she was done, Marc applied it to her face, his hand gently brushing her cheek when he'd finished. They gazed briefly but intently into each other's eyes. "It's time, Sarge."

Marc nodded. "Let's do this, Gunny."

They began traversing the cave wall across the lake. "Careful, Sarge. Or you'll be swimming over."

Marc laughed. "No worries. It's not time for my Saturday bath just yet."

Once Marci took out the radio shack, she concentrated on the guard towers. Josh aimed at the guards that were retreating across the bridge. Instead, he hit a barrel of dirty chalk. Whoosh! The barrel launched like a rocket and bounced against a grotto wall, then fell like a ball of fire. Seeing the watchtowers in flames, Marci turned her attention to the space that separated the landers from the rest of the pirate camp. This kept anyone not already on a lander at bay. Hilda felt the heat of combat on her back. "It feels like Dante's Inferno, Sarge. We'd better move it if we're to keep those landers from taking off."

Marc clambered off the wall, not twelve feet from the nearest lander. "Roger that!"

In no time, he was pounding on the lander. A voice from inside yelled, "It's open. I'm trying to get a bead on that gun across the lake."

Marc opened the door in time to see the speaker taking aim at the Osprey lander. Wasting no time, Marc grabbed his knife and threw it at the pirate. It hit him in the temple, handle first. When the pirate slumped in his chair, Marc retrieved his knife and zip-tied the pirate. "Gunny, take the second lander."

"I'm on it," Hilda yelled as she pounded on its door.

A pirate opened the door and said, "Hurry! We're gettin' the hell outa here." He stopped when he saw Hilda. "Who are—" Her rifle butt ended their conversation. As she tossed the unconscious pirate to the ground, she felt the ship shudder and begin to lift. Jumping through the doorway, she leveled her rifle at the head of the lander's pilot. "Set her down gently, or you'll be sporting an extra hole in your head."

"No way in hell am I doing that," the pirate said as he looked her way. It wasn't looking down the barrel of an assault rifle that unnerved him. Instead, the cold, grim expression on the face behind the rifle caused him to raise one hand while gently setting the lander back down with the other.

"Now shut her down."

He complied.

"Hand me the radio mike."

He handed the mike to Hilda. Obeying her motions, the pirate backed up, knelt, and placed his hands on his head.

Hilda grabbed the radio mike and spun the dial to the Osprey lander's frequency. "Lieutenant, both landers are secure."

"Excellent work, Gunny!" Marci quit firing and lifted the Osprey lander until it hovered above the middle of the cavern lake. Turning on its powerful landing lights, she caught a handful of remaining fighters. "Throw your weapons down, put your hands above your heads, and drop to your knees," Marci ordered over the lander's external speaker. The pirates complied. Marc strolled over to them and zip-tied each of the pirates. Running in from the other side, Josh found one last pirate hiding among the watchtowers' debris.

"Sarge, secure all the prisoners on the lander. Torres, get yourself on this lander as soon as I set her down."

With the prisoners secured, the crew assembled by the Osprey's lander. Marci said, "Now for phase two. Torres, send a distress message to draw those topside pirates to us."

"Aye, Lieutenant." Josh tapped out the first message. "I told them we have serious mechanical problems."

When the reply came back, Josh frowned and sent a second message.

"They said 'fix it yourself.' So, I sent an S-O-S an attack is imminent —message."

Another response came in. Again, Josh frowned and tapped out another S-O-S message. "They said they can't help. We've all been ordered to evacuate, and they're busy packing. I sent a more urgent message."

A final message came in, causing Josh to pound out three letters.

Marci saw the look on his face. "They're not coming."

"No, they're not. The message read, and I quote, 'Get your butts up here or you'll be left behind.'"

Marci said, "Your last message didn't sound like a typical S-O-S."

"It wasn't. It was 'S-O-B.'"

"Crap! So, the pirates at the upper mine aren't going to get drawn down here. Torres, take the pirate lander with our prisoners and get topside to help out the scorpion-men. If those pirates get any of their ships in the air, it'll be bad news for the captain. Take the Sarge with you. Gunny and I'll be along shortly."

Custos Pago spoke up. "I'm getting a report from Custos Maris. He's watching a couple of pirates pull two barrels off their lander and are rolling them toward the mine. What should he do?"

"Tell him that they're going to blow that hole Sarge was worried about right now. Torres, get going! Custos Pago, tell him not to let them get those barrels into the mine!"

## Surface Mining Camp

Men at the first mine were scurrying back and forth, dodging fireballs from Custos Maris. While no one was hit, the rain of fire had everyone on edge. Their anxiety deepened when they received word that the mine in the cavern was about to be attacked. No one volunteered to help their companions trapped in the cavern. Instead, the news was passed on to Pierre Beauregard. His response, though detailed, gave no mention of the pirates in the second mine. It read, "Use a barrel of refined explosive to blow a hole in the down shaft. Position it so that it will finish connecting with the upward shaft from below. That'll suck the life out of that hell hole. It'll be our parting gift. Once that's done, load the lander into the transport and head toward me. I need you to take out a pesky NASA ship."

The pirates at the first mine weren't completely heartless. They sent a second message that they were evacuating. Their message, which was never received, read, "If you want off this rock, get your asses up here, NOW!"

Two pirates began following Beauregard's order. They rolled a barrel of PETN-A to the mine entrance. "What're you waiting for, Greg?" one of the pirates asked.

"Two barrels are better than one, I says. Let's get one more." Greg scampered back to retrieve one more barrel from the lander.

"Shouldn't we leave time for the lower mine to be evacuated?"

Greg spit out a wad of tobacco. "To hell with them. They always get the best of everything, anyway. Let's blow the damn mine shaft and get out while we can!"

"Pago, this is Maris. Tell the lieutenant I'm watching a pirate roll a second barrel to the mine. What should I do?"

"The lieutenant thinks that's refined cake," came the response. "If they get it positioned just right, it will blow a hole in the floor of the top mine. That'd create a way for all the air in Arcadia to escape. You can't let that happen!"

Custos Maris hesitated. "I'm not sure, Pago. Those men aren't shooting at me. I promised not to hurt anyone that doesn't attack me."

Custos Pago replied, "Think about it. They're attacking every living thing in Arcadia, just as the spiders and locusts did. What these people are doing will take away all the air you and I need to breathe. In that way, they're attacking us. So, shooting them doesn't violate our rule of engagement."

"I see your point, Pago. I just don't feel right doing it."

"Don't forget, we're under the Lieutenant's command, so the choice is for her to make, not us. She says they must be stopped. I can't stop them, so you must!"

"You're right, my friend. I didn't think of it that way. Still ...."

"Why isn't Custos Maris firing?" Josh asked as he steered his lander up the canyon.

"I don't know," Marc said. "He's just hovering."

"Damn!" Josh exclaimed. "It looks like they're rolling some refined cake into the mine. If Maris doesn't do something quick, it'll be too late!"

"Can't you take them out, Ensign?"

259

I'm out of position. By the time I get lined up, it'll be too late!"

The two pirates were just entering the mine with both barrels when a stream of fire hit. The explosion lit up the Martian sky. The flash, observed from miles away by the Delta colony, was attributed to a meteor. The mine entrance disappeared as the mine collapsed utterly. Starting from the lower mine, the vertical shaft was clogged with piles of rubble throughout, stopping any possibility of air escaping. The explosion almost rocked Marci off her feet.

"Well done!" she exclaimed. "Tell Custos Maris he just saved Arcadia and us."

Upon hearing this message, Custos Maris shrugged, "It wasn't me." Looking back, the scorpion-man saw the Custos Martis, hovering just above. "Thanks, Martis. I couldn't bring myself to kill them."

"No problem," Custos Martis replied. "We had no choice. Their actions would have sucked the life out of Arcadia."

Josh and Marc arrived on the scene just in time to see the fireball, followed by the mine entrance collapse and a slide of rocks, as the mine became sealed off.

Marc gave a low whistle. "Wow! That settles that. No more mining for those guys."

Josh agreed. "I pity anyone down below in the cavern mine. If they were in that vertical shaft, they didn't have a chance. You've got to hand it to those scorpion men. They sure know how to handle themselves. What do you make of the camp, Sarge?"

"It looks abandoned. There're probably a couple of pirates in the lander. Perhaps a couple more in the transport. Scorpion-men are laying down some heavy fire in between the two ships."

"That's good. It'll keep those clowns from combining forces."

"Which do we take on first, Torres?"

Josh watched the lander begin to rise from the ground. "There's our answer."

"How do you plan to stop them?"

"Easy. It's a maneuver I call 'couch potato.'" Josh brought his lander to a stop just above the pirates who were trying to flee. Then he lowered his lander onto theirs. And applied more power. Over the radio, he said, "Shut her down, boys, or I'll crush you."

The pirate lander shut down, and Josh smiled. "They're the couch. I'm the potato."

Marc grinned. "Well played. You've got game, Torres."

"That was easy enough. The main thing is to keep that transport over there from taking off. If it does, things will get scarily complicated for the Osprey and our captain."

Marc smiled. "'Scary complicated.' That's an interesting way of putting—" He glanced at the transport. "Shit! They're taking off right now!"

"Crap, I went after the wrong ship. Now the captain's screwed!"

# The Dilemma

*"Life is a matter of really tough choices." - Joe Biden*

## On the Surface of Mars

Aboard the Osprey, time seemed to drag on slowly ever since the caped stranger and his entourage entered the shadows.

"I need to get some shuteye, Commander. Take over for a while." Matt closed his eyes and relaxed. He drifted off into a dreamless sleep.

After a short time, Barnabas, who was sitting next to him, said, "Hey Skipper, looks like there's activity by the pirate ship."

Matt woke up and rubbed his eyes. He looked out the window across the reddish-brown expanse toward Beauregard's ship. He saw a flurry of activity around the spaceship, signaling its imminent departure. The scorpion men were nowhere to be seen. The caped stranger and Beauregard were involved in an animated discussion. After some final words, the caped stranger stepped into his ship. Soon it disappeared in a cloud of dust. Beauregard entered his vessel as his crew completed the ground activity, then joined him.

Matt slid into the tech officer's seat. "Buckle up, gang. Time to be on our way."

"Are you sure, Sir?" Barnabas asked.

"Absolutely. I'm not letting that scum bag escape," Matt replied.

"Corporal, take the weapons officer's seat and buckle up. You're now our weapons officer. Make your shots count."

"Will do, Sir."

They saw the pirate ship take off from where it had just been parked, stirring up a cloud of red dust. "Let's get after it, Commander. Start our departure protocol."

Just then, they saw a scorpion man flying directly toward them. "Hold off. Shut her down," Matt directed. "Let's see what he has to say."

Once onboard, Custos Martis spoke of how the debate ended and the pirates' danger at the two mines. He concluded, "It turns out, Captain, that the Great Dealmaker is the Great Destroyer in person."

"Meaning?" Matt asked.

"Meaning that everyone on Mars is in extreme danger!"

"What makes you so sure?"

"The Great Destroyer is, as is your pirate friend, a mighty warrior who became too proud. Now he's roaming about, destroying anything that blocks him from what he wants."

"Doesn't sound like he got what he wanted from your council," Matt said.

"No, and he'll waste little time in showing his retribution. He'll probably leave the dirty work to your friend, the pirate. It's clear to me, you were sent here to stop him."

Matt nodded. "Roger that."

"And your crew needs to help shut down the mines."

Matt hesitated, then said. "You're right, Martis. Tell them to contact me ASAP."

263

Barnabas extended his hand. Custos Martis shook it awkwardly. Then he did the same with Matt. "Odd custom you sons of Adam have. Anyway, Godspeed."

"Be safe," Matt responded.

Once the Scorpion-man was off the Osprey, Matt said to Barnabas, "Let's go."

"Aye, Sir. Beginning launch sequence now."

They felt their bodies being pushed back into their chairs as the Osprey responded to her pilot's commands. "Where do you think he's going, Sir?"

"Have no clue, but we're losing him. Full power, Commander."

"Full power it is, Sir," Barnabas said. He scanned the pre-flight checklist he didn't initially follow to be sure he didn't forget anything.

"Keep the pedal to the floorboard, Commander."

"Don't you mean metal? You gotta get your clichés right, Sir."

"Whatever. At least Beauregard's pulling away from Mars. So, our colonies should be safe."

"Can we catch them?" Chuck asked.

Barnabas replied, "Our Z56 Positron Reactor engine has more than enough power to catch any craft known to man."

"That's an anti-matter engine. Isn't it dangerous?"

Barnabas chuckled. "Only if the magnetic field holding the anti-matter fuel fails."

"What then?" Chuck asked.

Matt shrugged, "Nothing too bad unless you're in the kill zone."

Chuck looked worried. "How large is the kill zone?"

Barnabas smiled. "It's only a few kilometers."

"Somehow, I'm not feeling well," Chuck concluded.

Matt could see the Osprey slowly closing in on its prey. "I think we're close enough. Let's hang back and see where he goes, Commander."

"Aye, Sir. Where's he headed?"

Matt shrugged. "Your guess is as good as mine."

They raced on for a day. Partway through the second day, Corporal Brady broke the silence. "Our long-range sensor is picking up a contact."

Barnabas observed, "It looks like our friend up ahead is adjusting his course, and he's reducing his speed."

Matt asked, "Any sense of what that contact is, Corporal?"

Chuck replied, "Too big to be another spaceship. It's huge. Must be a comet, or a huge asteroid, Sir."

Barnabas agreed. "The kid's right, Sir. At our rate of travel, we'll be passing uncomfortably close to it shortly. That thing must be at least a mile wide."

"Slow up, Commander. What's Beauregard up to?"

"Looks like he's intercepting that rogue asteroid. We're coming in at an angle. I think he's circling to match its speed and direction. We'll have to turn hard then punch it if we are to keep up with that thing."

"Do what you need to do to keep up with them," Matt ordered.

The astronauts were slammed around in their harnesses as Barnabas hit the retro rockets, made a sharp U-turn, then accelerated to full speed. His maneuver placed the Osprey in front of his target. The grayish-green asteroid passed on their port side as the Osprey picked up the pace.

"What a weird shape. It looks like a lopsided peanut or maybe a roughly shaped bowling pin," Chuck said.

"It's huge," Barnabas said.

Matt was suddenly worried. "Anybody have eyes on Beauregard? We need to get eyes on that pirate ship."

Chuck said, "Don't see him, Sir. He must be somewhere on the other side of the asteroid."

"Damn it!" Matt exclaimed. "Put us in stealth mode and get eyes on that pirate!"

"Stealth mode is on, Sir," Barnabas said.

"There he is, Captain!" Chuck said. "He's on the other side, next to where the asteroid narrows in its middle."

"I see him. He's moving alongside the asteroid. I don't think he sees us. What's he doing?" Matt asked.

"Looks like he's attacking the asteroid, Sir," Chuck said. "I know it sounds crazy, but that's what it looks like. He's forming a landing party."

Four landing craft dropped out of the pirate ship's rear cargo door and headed toward the heart of the asteroid.

"Those are the same landing craft that we saw on Mars. Why land on an asteroid?" Matt asked.

"Don't know, Sir," Chuck replied. "Two orange landers are heading into a crevasse that runs through the middle of the asteroid."

"I'm tracking the other two. The red lander is headed for a cave on the leading edge of our asteroid. The blue one is landing on the trailing edge," Barnabas said.

Several minutes passed, with all eyes on the asteroid. Finally, one lander flew out of the crevasse. It disappeared into the same cave that was occupied by the red lander. After a few minutes, it reappeared and flew to where the blue lander was parked. Matt enlarged the image on his console. He saw a pirate in a spacesuit launch himself out of the blue lander. He scrambled into the orange lander. Once the door was closed, the orange lander took off and flew toward the pirate ship. Warning bells went off in the back of Matt's mind. *Something's wrong with this picture. What is it?*

"Sir. Why leave three perfectly good landers on this hunk of rock?" Chuck asked.

"Good question, Corporal," Matt answered. "Keep a close eye on that pirate ship. Something's not right."

"The lander's being retrieved by the pirate ship," Chuck reported.

Just then, the pirate ship reversed course and accelerated away from the asteroid. Matt watched the maneuver. *Looks like he's trying to get away from here fast. Why?*

Barnabas said, "Sir, should I bring the Osprey around and follow our friend?"

"Yes, Commander. Swing in behind him. Don't let him get too far in front of us."

"Coming around now," Barnabas said.

A thought struck Matt. *Of course. He's unloaded his explosives on this asteroid.* "We've got to get out of here fast!" He yelled at Barnabas, "Full speed! Get us the hell out of here now!"

An explosion in the crevasse ripped through the asteroid, breaking it into two separate asteroids, each over a half-mile in diameter. The force of the blast pushed the rear half of the asteroid into the path of the Osprey. Collision alarms sounded as the Osprey braked and kicked up to avoid the obstacle that was now looming large in the window.

"I don't think we'll clear it, Sir. We've got too much forward inertia!" Barnabas said.

There was a second explosion on the asteroid that was menacing the Osprey. Miraculously, that explosion pushed the asteroid down and away. The Osprey, now slowing to a near standstill, missed the asteroid by several feet, at most.

"I said to step on it, Commander," Matt ordered. "Don't let that pirate get away!"

"I'm on it, Sir. Just giving something bigger the right-of-way, first."

"If we'd moved out faster, the asteroid wouldn't have been a problem," Matt said.

Barnabas said nothing. But he caught the Corporal's eye and raised an eyebrow. Soon they spotted the pirate ship. Being out of danger from the asteroid, the pirate ship had slowed some. This was the opportunity Barnabas needed. He brought the Osprey just within striking distance behind the pirate.

"Sir, we've closed the gap."

"Copy that, Commander. He's just within range. Open fire at will, Corporal."

Chuck took careful aim and let loose a series of bursts from his weapon's system. The pirate ship began a series of corkscrew maneuvers, making it hard to target. Chuck started sweating as he tried to squeeze off some quality shots. The pirate was in his sights three times but never long enough for his attempts to be effective. The pirate ship feigned a break to the right, causing Chuck to waste more shots, trying to anticipate his moves. The pirate began to make a gentle arc to the Osprey's portside. As the Osprey followed that arc, the pirate quickly fired several positioning jets to change its angle and slow its turn. The Osprey quickly passed the pirate ship.

"Rear shields up!" Barnabas said.

"Rear shields up!" Matt replied as he brought the Osprey's defensive shields online. He was just in time. Even though the pirate landed a couple of shots, the shields held, and the Osprey was unscathed. Barnabas accelerated, pulling straight ahead of the pirate ship. The pirate was landing shots consistently. Fortunately, the rear shields continued to hold. Barnabas began to make a gentle arc to the Osprey's portside. The pirate ship dropped back and followed on a parallel course.

Barnabas smiled. "He thinks I'm going to try the same maneuver on him that he just pulled on me. I have something better in mind, Captain. Override the crash avoidance system. Corporal, stand by to fire on my command. Captain, if we were to change course, say, stop in front of the pirate, how long before his ship would be on us?"

Matt ran the calculations. "You've got 180 seconds."

"Captain, on my word, activate the cloaking device and set it to full cloak."

"You're flying blind?" Matt asked.

"Only for 172 seconds. When time is up, disengage the cloaking device."

"Roger that, Commander, if you're sure," Matt said.

"Trust me on this, Captain." Matt heard Barnabas and nodded but thought, *I sure hope you know what you're doing.*

"Let's do this on my mark. Three, two, one, MARK!"

Matt activated the cloaking device, which made the Osprey invisible to the pirate ship. It also made the universe invisible to the Osprey. Flying blind, Barnabas made a sharp change in course, fired his retro-rockets, slowing the Osprey to a crawl, and turned her to face their enemy. The strain of such radical moves almost caused the crew to pass out. Matt started the count-down. "I'm deactivating the cloaking device in five, four, three, two, one, NOW!"

Matt gasped as he saw the pirate ship fill their window, heading straight for them. Instinctively, he braced for impact. The pirate ship quickly shimmied to a stop while it kicked up and to the right, just missing the Osprey.

"Commence firing at her under-belly," Barnabas ordered.

"Aye, Sir," Chuck said as he began firing.

Barnabas guided the Osprey under the pirate and reversed the Osprey again to face the pirate's rear. Alarms sounded off to warn that the Osprey was still within the kill zone. If the pirate ship were to explode, both it and the Osprey would be destroyed. Slowly, the Osprey drifted just out of the kill zone.

"Aim at their engines, Corporal," Barnabas directed.

The pirate ship finally got underway, but Barnabas still had the advantage. He had no problem keeping up with his adversary. The pirate ship maneuvered back and forth, causing Chuck to miss his target. Finally, Chuck found a rhythm, and his shots started landing home. At first, the pirate shields glowed as they absorbed the Osprey's fire. Soon, however, they faded, and the starboard engine began to glow, then burn. "Nice shooting, kid — don't you think, Captain? Captain, are you paying attention?"

Matt wasn't. He was deep in thought. His head snapped up, and he swore. "Break off contact, now! Follow the course I just entered into the computer."

Barnabas said, "But, Sir, we haven't finished off the pirate shi—"

Matt cut him off. "There's no time!"

"All the Corporal needs is a few more second—"

"Just do it, Commander! NOW!" Matt interrupted.

"Bringing the ship around now, Captain."

"Good. I just hope we're not too late."

"Too late for what, Sir?" Chuck asked.

"To save Mars and the Earth. I've been wondering why someone would go to so much effort to blow up an asteroid. I ran the new trajectories of both asteroids. One's on a collision course with Mars, the other, with Earth."

Barnabas groaned. "The results'll be catastrophic. We're one ship. How do we stop both asteroids?"

Matt's heart sank. *At the speed that these two rocks are drifting apart, it'll take a miracle to stop both.* "I'm working on it, guys," is all he said.

# Off to Save?

*"If you think you're too small to make a difference, try sleeping with a mosquito." - African Proverb*

### The Upper Mine

The pirate transport ship was lifting off.

Forgetting that his voice wouldn't travel into the grotto, where he had left the Osprey lander, Josh hit his mike. "Those cowards. They're not even waiting for their teammates from the lower mine."

He jumped as he heard Marci's reply, "Not to worry, the Cavalry has arrived." Marci had blasted through the ice lake and was flying as fast as her lander would allow. "I'm coming in hot," she warned.

Just as the transport began to inch forward, building up power, Marci screamed by. She missed the vessel by inches. This move caused the transport pilot to hesitate, hovering over his ship for a few moments. Marci looped back and halted, facing it nose to nose. "You have a count of ten to set her back down, or I'll blast you," she challenged.

"You're crazy!" the pilot said. "If you shoot at this range, we will both die."

271

"Ten."

"You're bluffing."

"Nine."

"You wouldn't—"

"Eight."

"You'd best do as she says," Josh interjected. "She never bluffs."

"Seven."

"I'll drive this transport right through you."

"Six."

"Listen to reason, lady."

"Five. Arming weapons."

"Let's be reason—"

"Four."

"Okay. Okay! I'm setting her down."

"No talk. Just do it! Three."

The transport cut power and settled back to the ground.

"Now listen to me. First, open your starboard side door. Then, have everyone in your ship come out unarmed and lay face down on the ground. Be quick about it!" Marci commanded.

The pirates complied. Marc jumped from Josh's lander, zip-tied their hands behind their back, and then had them sit up. They were then joined by the two pirates that had almost been left behind. With that, the upper mine settlement was secured.

Marci set her lander down. "Well done, everyone. Now, all we need to do is kick back and wait for the captain to check-in."

"What about the prisoners, Lieutenant?" Hilda asked.

"We'll find a spot for them in the cargo bay. Oops, there's the call from Captain Dirksen. Gotta take it."

## Somewhere Above Mars

Matt could feel the thrust of the Osprey pushing him hard against his seat. Sweat was forming on his forehead. He drummed his fingers impatiently as he pondered their situation. *A killer asteroid headed straight for Mars and my family. Another more dangerous asteroid headed on a collision course with Earth. If either hit their target ... I'd best not dwell on that. What to do?*

Barnabas interrupted Matt's thoughts. "Orders, Boss?"

"First, we need to at least catch up with them, Commander."

"She's flying as fast as she can, Sir. I think we're gaining on them, but they're diverging. I don't think we can stop both of them. We'll have to choose. Which one do we concentrate on, Captain?" Barnabas asked.

"The first one we can catch, Commander."

Barnabas altered course slightly to zero in on the asteroid headed toward Mars. "You've got an idea, Sir?"

Matt frowned, thinking hard. Then an idea came to him, *That's got to be it. It's our only chance.* "You've heard of killing two birds with one stone? It's a long shot. But, let's kill two rocks with one bird. We'll take out the smaller asteroid headed toward Mars with four of our missiles. Then we'll swing around the planet and use its gravitational energy to propel us even faster toward the asteroid that's bound for Earth. We'll use our remaining eight rockets on that one."

Barnabas nodded. "Good. That's good, Captain. What if that pirate tries to re-engage us?"

"Good point. We'll keep our rear shields up. Corporal, make yourself useful. Pull up a training video for launching the missiles. We've only got twelve, and we've got to make every single one count."

Chuck started to bring up the training video. "Aye, Sir. Just one question."

"Yes, Corporal?"

"Why didn't we use a rocket on the pirate ship?"

Matt said, "These things are old technology. They aren't always reliable and need to be used at a distance. To keep them from exploding prematurely, they're set to auto-arm eight to ten seconds after launch. Hitting your target before the rocket arms itself isn't very effective. In theory, the rocket is self-guiding, but there are well-known counter-measures that fool it into missing its target."

"Gotcha, Sir. Thanks."

Chuck set about his task with grim determination.

Barnabas noticed Chuck's body language. "You all right, Corporal? You look like something the cat drug in."

"I screwed up, and that pirate is still out there in one piece because of me."

"What? No way. The captain called us off before we could finish the job."

"If Lieutenant Gonzales had been shooting, she would've hit him right away."

"You do realize that you're comparing yourself to an experienced weapons officer? She's hands-down the best in the entire fleet. Don't beat yourself up, kid. What's really eating at you?"

"I joined the service to make a difference. So far, all I've done is bumble around. I'm not much of a difference-maker."

"Hey, Corporal, here's an old African proverb you need to embrace — 'If you think you're too small to make a difference, try sleeping with a mosquito.'"

"I'll keep that in mind, Sir."

The Osprey was gaining on the asteroid. But its progress was way too slow to satisfy Matt, who wished he could get up and pace. *The one bad thing about space flight is that no pacing is possible,* he thought. His mind raced ahead. *What if the rockets don't do the trick? What then? Do we keep*

274

*trying to save Mars and forget Earth or ...?* He remembered the rest of his crew and picked up his radio microphone. Praying that the team was on the surface, he pressed the transmit button.

"Lieutenant Gonzales, Captain Dirksen here. Do you read me?"

Silence.

"Come in, Lieutenant Gonzales, Captain Dirksen here."

Silence.

"Crap. Get on the line, Lieutenant," Matt thought out loud.

"Captain Dirksen, Lieutenant Gonzales here. We're Dealing with a little crap of our own, Sir."

"Who said anything about crap?"

"You did, Sir."

"I'm sure I only thought it, Lieutenant."

"With all due respect, Sir, you may want to think more quietly. What do you need?"

Matt chuckled. "Lieutenant, I need your help. There's a killer asteroid heading straight for you."

"Really? Crap!"

"My thoughts exactly, Lieutenant. It gets better. There's a second, larger asteroid heading to Earth."

"Holy crap!"

"I plan to use four rockets to take out the asteroid heading toward you. Then whip around Mars. I'm hoping that'll gain us enough speed to catch the one heading toward Earth. Thoughts?"

"Ambitious, Sir. What can we do?"

"If our rockets don't do enough to push this asteroid off course, I need you to finish the job. Sadly, I don't have any idea how you'd do that."

Marci looked over the remains of the upper mine, the handful of shuttles, and the pirate's transport ship. "No worries, Captain. I've got a couple of ideas. How much time do we have?"

"A day. Two at most."

Marci whistled. "Wow, we'll have to bust our butts! But we'll be ready, Sir."

"Thanks, Lieutenant. Dirksen out."

"Good luck, Sir. Gonzales out."

"Captain, we're in missile range of the asteroid," Barnabas said.

Matt looked up and saw the brown-grey mass filling the Osprey's windshield. "Ease up, Commander. We don't want to be too close. Corporal, prepare to fire your missiles."

"Aye. Where do you want me to place them, Sir?"

"Looks like a crevice running up and down, along the center. What do you think?

"I see it, Sir. I can place them all along that crevice."

"Aim all four of the missiles at the same spot along the center of the crevice. The combined blast should push that sucker off course."

"I'm lined up for the shot, Sir."

"Good. On my mark, fire all four rockets simultaneously. three, two, one, fire!"

The Osprey gave a slight shudder, and the screen filled with smoke. "Missiles away, Sir. Estimated time to impact is two minutes."

A warning buzzer sounded. "What's that?" Matt asked.

"One of the rockets failed to arm, Sir," Chucked groaned. "Will three armed missiles be enough?"

"It'll have to be, Corporal," Barnabas replied.

Matt tapped his foot impatiently as the seconds ticked slowly away. Finally, the center of the asteroid burst into a bright orange-red flash. Grey dust shot out in all directions. The dust cloud cleared enough to see that the asteroid had broken into two roughly equal halves.

"Great shooting!" Matt exclaimed. "Commander, get us slung around the red planet so we can take out that second rock."

Barnabas sent the Osprey hurtling in between the two halves and speeding toward Mars. "I'm on it, Sir. Are you running the new projected paths of the two halves?"

"I'm running the projections now, Commander. Oh, crap! We broke that sucker in two, but both pieces are still on target to hit Mars. What's worse, given the rotation of Mars, they'll hit damn close to our colonies."

Matt hit the transmit button on his mike. "Osprey Lander, this is the Osprey. Over."

"Osprey, this is Lieutenant Gonzales. What's up, Captain. Over."

"Lieutenant, we've got a problem!"

## At the Surface Mining Camp

When the crew heard from Marci, they noticed the sense of urgency in her voice. "Okay, team. There's an asteroid heading our way. The captain is trying to take it out with four missiles—"

Josh interrupted, "Why only four missiles, Lieutenant? He's got twelve on board."

"Saving the other eight for the bigger asteroid heading toward Earth, Ensign."

Hilda winced. "Not sounding good, Lieutenant."

"Got that right," Marci said. "We may need to go after a couple of asteroids ourselves if the captain fails. Suggestions?"

"First, we need to pull the prisoners off the transport and let the Martians watch them," Marc suggested.

This was overheard by the prisoners, who nearly panicked. "Please no! Anything just not that!" They pleaded.

"How about we load them all on a lander, send it to the wormhole, and ask Josh's friend to pass it on toward Earth?" Marc asked.

Though the prisoners didn't know about wormholes, the idea of heading to Earth sounded better than the first alternative. They cheered and pleaded that Marc's idea be adopted.

Marci smiled at how just the thought of being around the scorpion men kept the prisoners in line. "It's settled. We'll send the prisoners toward Earth. Now for the hard part. How do we destroy an asteroid?"

Marc spoke up, "The transport has enough refined cake to blast several asteroids. We have two pirate landers that we can load with that stuff, and they will become the delivery system."

"Two? You forget that we need one to transport the prisoners."

Josh said, "There's one already in the cargo bay of their transport, Ma'am."

"Excellent! But, do we have room for our Osprey lander?"

"More than enough, Lieutenant," Marc replied.

Marci was encouraged by the confidence in Marc's voice. "Good. One lander for the prisoners. One lander to blow the asteroid. One lander as a backup if either of the first two fails. Let's do it!"

The work went on for several hours. It was sped up by some prisoners who were more than willing to help if it got them off Mars sooner rather than later. Finally, the second call came in from Captain Dirksen. Marci relayed the bad news. "Well, team, that asteroid is heading our way. I should say we now have two smaller asteroids heading toward us. We've got, at most, two days to catch them and take them out."

"Two asteroids. It's a good thing we've got two landers, loaded with refined cake," Josh observed.

"We need to move if we hope to be of any use," Marci said. "As it is, we won't be able to deposit the prisoners at the wormhole and get to the asteroids in time to make a difference."

"Lieutenant, I have an idea," Josh said.

"Go ahead."

"With the Sarge's help, I might be able to fly the prisoner's lander to the drop-off point remotely. Once it's there, I can kill the engine and leave them floating without power. Maybe the Watchers will suck them into the wormhole and deposit them by Earth. If so, great. If not, we'll swing by in a couple of days and pick them up."

"How'll NASA know what to do with them if they are deposited by Earth?"

"I'll code a distress message with instructions," Josh said.

"Do it! And hurry. When can we leave?" Marci asked.

"Just as soon as the Sarge and I check out one thing, Ma'am."

"Be quick about it, Torres."

"What're we looking for?" The Sarge asked as he and Josh crawled through an air duct alongside the transport's crew compartment.

"Red cabling patch cords."

Marc asked, "Why do you need me?"

"Simple." Josh opened a junction box and pointed inside. "I'm color blind."

"Oh, sorry about that," Marc said as he shined a light in the box.

Josh said, "Look, here are nine red cables connected at this junction. There's also a grey cable. That means this ship is rigged for remote/hologram control."

Marc said, "In English, please."

"The grey cable is for simple radio communications. But, the nine red lines bring multiple data streams together simultaneously. This enables us to remotely control the landers and lock them away from local control. Our landers are configured the same way.

"So, you can fly the landers while you're on board this ship?"

"Yes, as long as all of the red cables are patched correctly into our network panel. Let's tell Gonzales that we are free to fly."

Josh took up his position at the Tech Officer station of the transport. After engaging the remote piloting system, he passed the word to Marc to load their prisoners onto the lander.

Custos Martis hovered nearby. The sight of him encouraged the pirates to file into their transport with only a little prodding from Marc, or Hilda, who was eager to help.

"Thanks, Gunny, but I've got this," Marc said.

Hilda smiled. "You can use a hand in keeping the prisoners calm."

Something about Hilda's smile stopped Marc. "What're you up to, Gunny?"

"You'll see."

As the last prisoner was seated, Marc and Hilda stepped to the portal doorway. Just before they closed the door, Hilda reached into both of her thigh pockets, pulled out some brittle, brown pods, and threw them on the floor. Upon hitting the floor, each pod burst, releasing a fine powder into the air. Marc gave her a strange look.

"What? Sarge, it's an experiment." Hilda quickly shut the door.

Once Marci had the transport ship underway, Josh began flying the prisoners' lander toward the wormhole. The prisoners saw, in the pilot's seat, a perfect hologram of Josh at the controls. When the lander approached the wormhole, a beam of shimmering light appeared to the right of Josh's hologram. The two conversed briefly. Then Josh turned toward the prisoners, waved farewell, and disappeared. The lander then took them on the ride of their life through the wormhole.

Once Josh was done, he signaled to Marc. "I'm setting the two landers to intercept the asteroids, Lieutenant."

"Very good, Ensign," Marci said as she concentrated on charting the fastest course to the two asteroids.

Marc followed Josh as he hopped into the first lander. "Aren't you going to fly them the same way you flew the prisoners' lander?" Marc asked.

Josh replied, "No. Any interference from a solar storm could degrade our remote connection and leave the lander in a neutral state."

"Again, in English, please."

"If our signal breaks up, I may not be able to fly the landers remotely. That's why I'm pre-setting them to fly themselves into the path of the oncoming asteroids. Once they get on the path, they turn toward the asteroid and hit it head-on."

Marc said, "Boom! The refined cake turns the lander and asteroid into dust."

"Something like that."

Marc's face lit up. "I like it!"

Josh laughed. "I forgot that you like to watch stuff blow up."

The crew settled in for a long flight toward the asteroids. Marci used the time to familiarize herself with the transport controls while Josh refreshed his control station's knowledge. The asteroids showed on the transport's sensors after a day of flying. Marci gathered her team on the bridge.

"We'll start to decelerate soon, deliver our packages, then turn away to stay clear of the asteroids," Marci said.

"Sounds easy enough," Hilda said.

Josh agreed, "Piece of cake, Lieutenant."

Marci snapped her fingers. "You think we have enough explosives to do the trick?"

"Marc laughed. "Based on what I know about PETN-A explosives, we've got more than enough."

"Good. I've given this approach a lot of thought and can't see it going awry," Marci said. "Any questions?" Hearing none, she said, "We'll remain on this course for another fifteen minutes. Then we'll begin executing my plan. What is it, Sarge?"

"Permission to leave the bridge, Lieutenant?" Marc asked.

"Why? What do you need to do?" Marci asked.

"Uh, I need to relieve myself, Ma'am. I'd rather do it in private if I may," Marc said.

Marci smiled. "Permission granted, Sarge."

Hilda laughed. "That's a sure sign you're getting old, Sarge."

"You're not funny, McDermott," Marc said as he pushed himself through the bulkhead door.

"We thought it was funny, Sarge," Marci giggled.

An alarm screamed. "Incoming missiles!" Josh shouted.

"I've got a bead on them," Marci said. Her voice was ice-cold. "Locate the ship that fired them."

The alarm changed tone, becoming a rapid series of high-pitched beeps. "The missiles acquired us as their target!" Josh exclaimed.

"I can hear that," Marci growled. "Just locate who fired them!"

Marci angled the transport upward. The two missiles adjusted their course to stay with her trajectory. "Damn." She feinted her ship to the right. The missiles again altered their course.

Just as they were about to hit, Marci jerked the transport hard to its port side and dove downward. The missiles were unable to adjust fast enough, so they overshot their target.

The transport's erratic motion caused Marc to bounce around like a pinball.

Josh said, "I found the ship that's firing on us!"

Marci said, "The missiles will re-acquire us shortly. Then we'll lead them back to their mother ship."

"It's Beauregard's ship. I've got the course set to bring us up on his underside."

"Good. Start shooting as soon as we're in range," Marci ordered.

"Roger that." Josh brought his weapons systems online.

The pirate's shields lit up, but not as strongly as Josh expected. "They've lost shield strength. I might be able to finish them off."

Marci shook her head. "No time! Those missiles are running up our tail."

The transport was now so close to the pirate ship that the crash avoidance alarms started sounding. Marci put the vehicle into a violent maneuver, which caused the missiles to overshoot again. This time, however, they locked onto Beauregard's ship as their target.

"Well played, Lieutenant!" Josh exclaimed as he watched the pirate ship go into its own set of maneuvers, trying to shake the missiles.

Marci smiled. "Enough of that. Let's zero in on those asteroids."

"Yes, let's do that." The voice came from a middle-aged man in a NASA flight suit, who had just appeared in the copilot's seat next to Marci. The man was looking straight ahead and seemed not to notice anyone.

Marci jumped and said, "What the hel—"

"Oh, don't mind me, I'm just taking over this ship. My friends call me 'the Boss.'"

Marci frowned. "Could've fooled me. You look just like James Morris, and you're not taking over anything."

"My dear Lieutenant, as lovely as ever. It's already done." The hologram watched as Marci tried in vain to steer. "Your station is now under my control."

Josh tried to override the ship's controls but failed. "Your station is locked out also, Torres. You should've left well enough alone when you had the chance. Now you're all my passengers as we take on the asteroid."

Josh started to leave his station. "Hold it right there, Torres. I've locked you all in. No one leaves the bridge. Don't worry. I'm going to fly this bird right into the nearest asteroid. You'll get to see it until the very end. Unfortunately, this is only one ship, so the other asteroid will go on to destroy Mars. Oh well!"

"Why are you doing this?" Marci asked. "A lot of innocent people will die if we don't stop both asteroids."

"You should've thought of that when you started messing with my little operation, Lieutenant. I had a corner on one of the most powerful explosives known to man. I was on my way to becoming insanely rich. That is until you came along with your team of misfits and screwed everything up."

Marci said, "You could at least let the Sarge and Gunny go in an escape pod. You've got no beef with them."

"Oh, but I do. They're part of your team. You can consider them collateral damage."

The sound of Marc trying to re-enter the bridge caused the hologram to look around. "Where is the sergeant?"

Marc, who was unaware of what was happening on the bridge, flipped his mike to Hilda's frequency. "Hate to bother the others, but the door's locked. Can you let me in?"

Hilda said nothing as she flipped her mike on so Marc could hear what was happening.

The hologram said, "I hate repeating myself. Where is the sergeant?"

"He had to take a leak," Josh said as he eyed the asteroid bearing down on them.

The hologram said, "Oh, he did now. That's too bad. He's missing the party."

"You could unlock the door and let him in," Josh suggested.

"So, he could help you slip out and cause some mischief? Not going to happen, Torres." Morris's hologram continued, "I know you want to get in, Sarge. However, I have a better idea."

Marc asked, "What do you have in mind, Sir?"

"Simple. You like to watch things blow up. I'm giving you that chance. Next to the crew's quarters are the captain's quarters. When you get in there, you'll find a two-way mirror overlooking the bridge. It'll give you a great view of the asteroid we're flying into. You won't want to miss the fun."

"On my way, Sir," Marc said while thinking, *What does he have up his sleeve?*

"Are you there yet?" the hologram asked.

"I'm grabbing a drink," Marc said as he grabbed some duct tape.

"Well, hurry, or you'll miss the show," the hologram urged.

Marc slid some duct tape over the door latch as he entered the captain's quarters. "Wow, that rock sure is getting bigger!" Hearing the door latch engage, he thought, *I hope I used enough duct tape.*

Hilda tried to slide out of her harness, to no avail. "That bastard locked our harnesses!" She whispered into her mike.

Marc heard and thought, *She sure is cute when she's angry. Bet she hates the fact that she's a helpless bystander. I wish that she was here next to me.* "Say Gunny," Marc whispered. "I just want you to know that I—"

"Think that I'm cute when I get mad. You've said that before."

"No … I mean you are cute, but what I was going to say was—"

"Unless it is to tell us how to get out of this mess, now's just not the time."

Josh was sweating. He tried to slip out of his harness.

"No use in trying, Torres. You're locked in. Of course, you can always close your eyes if you can't bear to watch," the hologram taunted.

Not one to give up, Josh scribbled a note on his white pad and held it, unseen, toward the captain's quarter's window. "So, you're going to see us all die," he said. "Bet you've been waiting a long time for this."

The hologram nodded in agreement. "Yes, I have — and now that it's here, I'm enjoying every moment."

Marc read Josh's note and moved to leave the quarters. The door wouldn't budge. *Crap, I didn't use enough duct tape!* He positioned himself against a support beam and pushed with both feet. The door still didn't budge. Marc continued to push as he looked out the window. *We're done for. That rock is right on top of us!*

"Pardon me, Mr. Boss, Sir. As a condemned man, may I be excused to have one last cigarette before I die?" Marc asked.

"I see no reason why not. You're running out of time, so make it quick."

"Uh, I left them in the crew cabin." Marc heard the latch unlock. "Thanks," he said as he tumbled out the door.

"I'll let you get them. You must hurry, or you'll miss the grand finale. And don't try to escape. The escape pods and landers are locked down as well," Morris' hologram said.

After Marc departed, Morris' hologram turned to Marci. "None of this had to happen, if only you had followed my advice and testified at Torres' trial. Now Torres will meet the justice he deserves."

Marci noticed that the asteroid filled the entire windshield. "I don't think this is what HJ would have wanted."

"You're right … HJ … Want you to <static> live … <static>." As quickly as it appeared, the hologram vanished. "I've got my controls back, Lieutenant!" Josh said. "I'm deploying the landers as I speak."

"What just happened?" Hilda asked.

"I don't know." Marci steered the transport hard to the starboard. "We're not out of trouble yet!" she said as the collision alarms sounded. "Torres! Fire all of our bottom positioning thrusters, NOW!"

"Aye, Lieutenant. Firing them now."

"Drop our shields and give me all the power you've got," Marci commanded. "I'm accelerating to full thrust!"

"Shouldn't we be braking, Lieutenant?" Hilda asked as she watched the asteroid become a blur.

Marci shook her head. "Nope. Just basic law of physics. Slowing when you see an object coming toward you gets you hit. Speeding up gets you out of harm's way."

Marc floated through the bulkhead door, holding a handful of red cables. The collision alarm fell silent, and Marci asked, "What gives, Sarge?"

Josh smiled. "Welcome back, Sarge. Nice job in disconnecting the red cables."

Marc grinned. "Good thing I'm not color blind."

"Thanks, Sarge," Marci said. "Torres, are those landers launched?"

"They're on their way, Lieutenant. I suggest that we put some distance between us and those rocks."

Invisible hands pushed each astronaut hard against their seat as Marci accelerated the transport to full power, away from the asteroids. Even so, as the first fireball erupted, breaking up the closest asteroid, a cloud of debris rained down on their ship. Shortly after, a second fireball erupted, breaking up the second asteroid.

Hilda nodded. "Looks like this one bird got two rocks."

Marci smiled. "Ensign, were we able to blow those rocks off course?"

"Running the calculations now. One is totally off course and broken up pretty well. The second has broken up, but it's still a threat. With luck, those pieces will skim the surface and not cause too much damage."

"That'll have to do. We're going to swing around Mars and slingshot after that pirate ship. Hopefully, we'll catch it before it gets to the Osprey."

Two evenings later, say some of the Martian colonists, asteroid remnants rained down. While its atmosphere wasn't strong enough to give total protection, the debris did only minor damage to the colonies and none to Arcadia. Those who witnessed the event saw a spectacular show of fireballs.

As Marci was slinging the transport around Mars, using its gravity to give her more speed, she asked, "What're the odds we'll catch up with the Osprey in time to help?"

Josh asked, "Honestly?"

"Honestly."

"Odds are slim to none. And slim is waving goodbye."

# The Sacrifice

*"Greater love has no one than this, that someone lay down his life for his friends." - John 15:13 [WEB]*

## Somewhere Between Mars and Earth

Speeding toward the rogue asteroid, Matt tried to concentrate on the task ahead. But his mind kept drifting back to his wife and son. He'd failed to keep them safe. His most valuable possessions ever. Not that he could possess his wife. She was a free spirit with a passion for helping others. She shared his enthusiasm for space exploration. This is probably why she signed on to be a physician at one of the Martian settlements. No, he didn't possess her. But he did love her and couldn't get his mind off her.

Barnabas saw the concern on his face. "Captain, she's in good hands. You know the lieutenant will do everything possible to keep those rocks from hurting her or your son. Gonzales won't let you down." As he said this, Barnabas thought, *Dear God, help Gonzales not to let him down.*

Matt looked over at Barnabas. "You're a real mind reader, Commander. Let's get after our target before it's too late."

Swinging around Mars helped the Osprey make up for the time it lost chasing the asteroid that menaced Mars. Still, its progress was painfully slow. Finally, Barnabas announced they were within missile range of the asteroid. With no pirates around to interfere, the Osprey's crew was able to concentrate on their objective.

"Corporal, aim all of our missiles at the dead center of that monster. The combined blast of all eight missiles should edge that thing off its course. At this distance from Earth, even a slight variation in course should do the trick."

"I'm lined up for the shot, Sir."

"Good. On my mark, fire all missiles simultaneously—Three, two, one, MARK!"

The Osprey gave a slight shudder, and, again, the screen filled with smoke. "Missiles away, Sir. Estimated time to impact is three-and-a-half minutes."

Matt thumped the console with both his index fingers as the seconds dragged on. Finally, the center of this asteroid blossomed into a bright orange-red flash. Grey dust, again, shot out in all directions.

Matt straightened in his seat. "Direct hit, Corporal! Nice shooting!"

"Thanks, Sir. I suspect hitting the broad side of a barn would be tougher than hitting that rock."

The dust slowly dissipated. Matt and Barnabas looked at the shallow cave Chuck had just blasted out of the asteroid. "Did our blast give us enough push to shove the asteroid off course, Sir?" Barnabas asked.

"I'm running the projections now, Commander." Matt took a deep breath. "Damn! It wasn't enough. That rock is still headed directly toward Earth. We're out of options."

"What about Lieutenant Gonzales?" Barnabas asked.

"I doubt that any explosives she has left, after blowing the Mars-bound asteroids, will be enough to make a difference. I'll radio NASA and warn them. Even with our warning, an asteroid this size is pretty much unstoppable, even for their asteroid-protection system." Matt slumped back in his seat. "Looks like we've failed."

Barnabas shook his head. "Look, Captain, you've done everything in your power to stop this thing; you can't—"

"Did I?" Matt interrupted. "I wasted four rockets on the asteroid headed to Mars. We didn't stop it. Those extra four rockets might have been enough to save Earth."

Barnabas said, "You don't know that, Sir."

Matt looked down. "Doesn't matter. We failed … I failed."

"It's too bad we can't use the anti-matter from our engine," Chuck mused.

A big smile broke over Barnabas's face. "Son, you're a genius! An absolute genius!"

"I am?"

"Absolutely! We can back the Osprey into that cave and kill the magnetic field surrounding our fuel. That's one blast that'll carry this rock far off course, if not outright destroy it!"

Matt's face lit up. "I'll be damned, Commander. That's exactly what we'll do. Great idea, Corporal. It'll gain you a promotion, for sure. It may be posthumous. But, by God, you've earned it!"

Chuck frowned. "If it's all the same to you, Sir, I'd rather just skip the posthumous part if I can."

Barnabas laughed. "So, would I, Kid. So would I."

"How does killing a magnetic field cause a big explosion?" Chuck asked.

Matt said, "Simple. The anti-matter fuel for Our Z56 Positron Reactor is kept in a magnetic field. If we lose the magnetic field that

291

contains it, all the anti-matter reacts without control, and the engine blows up," Matt said.

Barnabas added, "We're talking big explosion—something the size of a small nuke. It'll have a kill zone of several kilometers."

"Seriously, I'm too young to die," Chuck worried.

Barnabas laughed again. "Nobody's going to die. Least if we plant the engine properly."

"If the engine blows, don't we go with it?" the wide-eyed Corporal asked.

"Not to worry. Our ship has an escape rocket that pushes it beyond the kill radius of the anti-matter. We'll only lose our engine and its compartment. Everything else should remain intact. If—"

An alarm squealed. Barnabas gasped. "It's our threat indicator alarm!"

Matt looked at the monitor. "Damn! We've got two incoming rockets."

"I see the frigate that fired the rockets in my rear scanner, Sir," Chuck reported.

The Osprey's radio sprang to life.

"I've got you now, Dirksen! You've been a pain in my ass long enough."

Matt said, "It's Beauregard. That figures."

Beauregard continued, "I'm sending you straight to hell, you son of a bi—"

"This is a first," Matt interrupted. "I've never talked to someone I was about to kill."

"You don't stand a chance," Beauregard snorted.

Matt killed the radio. "Enough with the trash-talk. I'm releasing a couple of drones. Commander, take evasive action, NOW!"

"I'm on it, Sir." Barnabas flipped the cloaking device to full cloak mode. Then he steered the Osprey into a blind ninety-degree dive for thirty seconds. He followed this by a hard turn toward the last known location of the pirate frigate. "Why attack us with rockets? Barnabas asked. "That was way too easy to evade. He could have at least sent some drones our way."

"My guess, Commander, is that our boy, the Corporal here, did way too much damage to his shields for him to risk a close-in dogfight. His drone-release system is probably damaged as well. Get in on him as close as you can."

Barnabas continued for fifteen seconds, then switched back to normal mode. Coming out of cloak mode returned the Osprey's sensors to life. Alarms screamed, warning of more rockets.

"Incoming!" Chuck shouted.

"I'm on it!" Barnabas aimed the Osprey right at the rockets.

"What the hell?" Matt asked. "How'd he know where we'd be?"

Barnabas winced as he watched the missiles growing more prominent on his screen. "Must've been a lucky guess."

The radio sounded. "Ha! I saw you use that maneuver before. You can't play that same trick on me twice." Beauregard sounded triumphant. "Any last words, Dirksen?"

"Screw you!" Matt said, then hit the mute button. "Full power ahead, Commander. If we can hit those rockets before they arm themselves, we may just survive!"

"Aye, Sir," Barnabas said.

"How many seconds do we have before they arm?" Matt asked.

"Seven or eight seconds, give or take a second or two."

"Yeah, at our closing rate, the missiles won't have to explode. Won't they fly right through us, Sir?" Chuck asked.

"So, noted Corporal. Now read off the seconds before impact. And let the Commander do his thing. You do know what to do, Commander?"

Barnabas grimaced. "Yeah … I think."

"You could at least try to sound a little more reassuring, Maalouf. Corporal, seconds to impact?"

Chuck said, "Sir, we're at second five, four, three …."

A couple of seconds before impact, Barnabas used his thrusters to push the Osprey straight down, as if it were descending to a landing pad. The rockets had no time to react. Instead of slamming into the front of the Osprey's wings, they ricocheted off the top, setting off a couple of collision alarms."

Matt said, "Well played, Commander."

"I've got our friend in my sights!" Chuck said.

"Then let him have it, Corporal."

Just as Chuck began to fire on the pirate frigate, alarms sounded again. "Incoming from our rear!" Barnabas shouted.

"What? Who the hell's shooting from our rear? Matt demanded.

"It's the same rockets that just missed us. They've re-acquired us and are making another pass." Barnabas answered.

"Evasive action would be good, Commander."

"Taking evasive measures now, Sir. If I play my cards right, I can lead them toward our friend, Mr. Beauregard."

Chuck tried to sound calm. "Impact will be in twelve seconds, Sir."

"Count them down, Corporal," Barnabas said.

"Eleven, ten, nine, eight, seven, six, five, four …."

Barnabas steered hard down and to the right, just as the missiles flew by, missing the Osprey by inches. They were now heading straight toward the pirate ship. Beauregard released some chaff, then broke to his right and up. The confused missiles wandered off course after the chaff that the pirate vessel left behind.

Barnabas shook his head. "Almost got him, Sir."

"Nice try, Commander. Where'd he go?"

"I think he dodged them and flew over the asteroid, Sir," Chuck answered.

Barnabas agreed. "He doesn't show on my scanner either."

"He wants us to follow him in a game of cat and mouse. He'll keep firing those missiles at us, from a distance, to keep us guessing where he'll be next."

"That's for sure, Captain. He'll never let us in close enough to engage the way we want," Barnabas said.

Matt sighed. "He'll run us around to keep us from attacking the asteroid. We don't have time for this. Every minute we let slip by means, the asteroid will be harder to knock off course. Forget the pirate. Let's blow that rock."

"Aye, Captain. Once we're in the cave, I'll put the Osprey in cloak mode. That pirate will never see us until it's too late."

"Good call, Commander."

Barnabas brought the Osprey to a halt just above the asteroid cave. He reversed engines and backed the Osprey, as far as he could, into the cave. Under his breath, he said, "Μεγαλύτερη αγάπη που έχει κανείς από αυτήν που κάποιος καθορίζει τη ζωή του για τους φίλους του."

"What?" Chuck perked up. "What'd you say, Commander?"

"Nothing."

"No, Sir. I heard you give some kind of chant or something. What was it?"

"It was Greek. It means 'Greater love has no one than this, that someone lay down his life for his friends."

Chuck said, "With all due respect, Sir, I don't find that reassuring."

Barnabas smiled. "Captain, we're in position."

"Good, Commander. Everyone, switch to your local air supply on your suits. I doubt the life support system will support us once we kill the engines. Come with me, Corporal. I'll need your help in the engine compartment."

When Matt and Chuck got to the engine compartment, Matt licked his lips. "Corporal, I have to be sure the magnetic field fails. When it does, I won't have enough time to get back through the bulkhead door, then secure it once I get into the cargo hold. I need you to hold the door open for me, slam it shut, then secure it as soon as I'm through it. Got that?"

"Aye, Sir. Uh, can we practice once?"

"Wish we could, Kid. But we're outta time. So — no pressure — just get it right on the first try."

They opened the heavy door, and Chuck held it while Matt went into the engine compartment. Matt turned the communication link on. "Can you hear me, Commander?"

"Loud and clear, Captain."

"Good. I'm about to flip the master power switch to 'console control only.' On my command, turn the master power off at your console. That should do the trick."

Matt turned the master power switch to "console control only." "OK, Commander, kill the power."

"Done, Sir."

Matt looked at the magnetic field strength dials. They were still holding steady. "Come on. Die already." Slowly they started falling.

"Captain, the fuel container's losing power!" Barnabas exclaimed. "Container strength is failing. It's orange going to red."

Matt took a deep breath. "Commander, on my mark, give us a count to five, then fire the ejection rocket and get us away from the engine compartment."

"Aye, Sir. I'm standing by."

Matt saw the needle pause before passing into the red. *I was afraid of this. It'll take more than Maalouf's command to kill the containment field. Sure wish Torres was here. He'd know what to do.* Matt scanned the engine room console. Then he saw it. There was a warning message asking if all the power should be killed. Matt keyed in "YES." He said, "Remember, a five-count from my mark. Then separate us from the engine compartment. Three, two, one, MARK." Matt hit the "ENTER" key (activating total power down) and dove through the open hatch. Chuck immediately slammed it shut and secured it closed.

"Corporal, brace yourself against the back wall. We're about to get quite the jolt. We—" Matt was interrupted, by a series of loud bangs, reverberating through the rear of the cargo hold.

Chuck gulped air. "What's that, Sir?"

"Don't worry, Kid. It's just the explosive bolts blowing to release our ship from the engine compartment."

There was a slight pause. Then the escape rocket roared to life. The Osprey sprang forward, away from the failing magnetic containers. Matt and Chuck were pressed hard against the rear wall of the Osprey. There, they stuck like glue.

*We're on our way!* Matt thought. *I hope those "kill radius" calculations the engineers made are correct.*

The rocket burn ended, returning the Osprey to a constant speed. Matt and Chuck floated free, just above the floor, then made their way to the bridge. "What's our status, Commander?" Matt asked.

"It's both good and bad news, Captain. The good news is, we got away clean, and our life-support system is still working. Plus, we are barely clear of the kill zone."

"Great! Switch off your local support systems, guys. The bad news, Commander?"

"Our cloaking device won't function without the engine compartment intact, Sir."

Matt asked, "Can we at least go into stealth mode?"

Barnabas replied, "I'll switch it on. But no guarantees."

"We're going to be sitting ducks," Matt said.

Barnabas nodded his head in agreement. "Looks as if. And I've only got my thrusters for maneuvering."

"Let's hope that the engine blows before Beauregard finds us."

"What difference will that make, Sir?" Chuck asked.

"If the blast stirs up enough debris and dust, and if our stealth mode works, he may not see us."

"That's a lot of 'ifs,' Captain," Barnabas noted.

"It is. Let's hope the cavalry arrives in time."

"The cavalry, Sir?" Chuck asked.

"Lieutenant Gonzales and the rest of our—"

Barnabas interrupted. "No such luck, Sir. I've just picked up Beauregard on my rear scanner."

Over the radio, they heard Beauregard gloating. "This'll be easier than shooting fish in a barrel."

"Nuts to you," Matt answered before hitting the mute button.

"That's lame, Captain," Barnabas said.

"Lame?"

"Yeah. 'Screw you' and 'nuts to you.' Really? Captain. You've gotta be more creative than that."

"Sorry to disappoint, Commander. I have a few other things on my mind, like staying alive. Creative trash talking just isn't high on my list."

Barnabas chuckled. "By the way, Sir, he's still in the kill zone."

Matt hit the transmit button. "You can't hit the broad side of a barn from there, Beauregard. You need to get in closer. Much closer."

"I can hit you from here, or even a couple clicks further away."

"That's bull. You're a lousy shot," Matt taunted.

"He's stopped!" Barnabas whispered.

Matt hit the mute button. "In the kill-zone?"

Barnabas gave him the thumbs up. Matt smiled. "Come in close. I dare you. You're a coward."

"Naw, I'll just sit here and pick you off with a couple of rockets. I'll even let you hear my launch count, so you'll know when you'll be blown to hell."

"Dear God, please let our engine blow before he gets those missiles launched," Barnabas prayed.

*Crap!* Matt thought. *I didn't think to pray.* "What he said, God!"

"Nine, eight, seven, see you in hell, Dirksen! Four, three, two—"

FLASH! The engine compartment, an entire three kilometers away, exploded silently.

"I suspect you just beat me there, Beauregard," Matt said.

"Uh, Captain, we're out of the kill zone. Of course, no one mentioned the damage zone," Barnabas said.

"Crap, Commander, I forgot, the damage alone could take us out. Everyone, switch to local life support, NOW!"

Debris from the explosion rained down on the Osprey. The noise was deafening, like heavy hail on a tin roof.

Aboard the Pirate Transport Ship

"I see the explosion!" Hilda exclaimed, looking at the long-range scanner. "Looks like they set off quite the blast with their rockets."

Marci nodded. "No surprise there, Gunny. Eight Hellcat missiles hitting the same spot simultaneously ought to light things up. Run the calculations, Ensign. See if that didn't do the trick."

"Running them now, Lieutenant. CRAP! There's a slight adjustment to its trajectory, but it's still on course to hit the Earth."

"Wow! If that didn't do the job, I doubt that the few barrels of explosives that we have here on board will make a difference."

The transport's radio came to life.

"I've got you now, Dirksen!" It was Beauregard's voice. "You've been a pain in my ass long enough."

"This is a first," Dirksen's voice replied. "I've never talked with someone I was about to kill."

Beauregard said, "You don't stand a chance."

"Where are they? What do you see?" Marci asked.

Hilda replied, "They're straight ahead in a dog fight!"

"How soon before we can join it?"

"We're a solid fifteen minutes out of range, Lieutenant," Josh said.

Marci's frustration overflowed. "Dammit! See if you can squeeze more power out of this tin can, Ensign!"

"Aye, Lieutenant. I'm on it," Josh said.

Marci wondered how, in the past, Captain Dirksen seemed so collected when approaching combat. She changed positions in her seat. If she could have, she'd have gotten up and paced. Mentally, she calculated the best method of entering the fray. *This heap won't do much up against a pirate frigate. But we've got the element of surprise on our side,* she thought. *If we closed in fast and latched onto the pirate vessel, the Sarge and Gunny could board them. It might just work.* "Gunny, Sarge, prepare to board an enemy vessel," she commanded.

Marc grinned, "Aye, Lieutenant."

"Now you're talking. I mean, Aye, Lieutenant," was Hilda's response.

Marci smiled. "I'm going to bring us in hot. I'll swing behind the pirate ship and land us on top of their emergency escape hatch. That way, you two can drop in on them. Let's hope they'll be preoccupied with the Osprey and won't notice us until it's too late."

"We're almost in range, Lieutenant," Josh announced.

"Great! Let's get after him." *Hold on a little longer, Captain* Marci thought as she raced toward the two combatants. The asteroid was now looming large on their screen.

Josh was concentrating on the long-range scanner. "I lost the bogie, but I see the Osprey, Lieutenant!"

"Where?" Marci asked.

"It's just below the asteroid, angling quickly down. We'll pass over it in two to three minutes! There's the bogie. I see it now!"

"Where? Where's the pirate ship?"

"It's topping the asteroid bearing down on the Osprey," Josh said. "No. Wait. It's holding its position. I think Beauregard's lining up to fire his missiles."

"Crap!" Marci exclaimed. "We're too late for my plan to work."

Josh said, "Worse yet, the Osprey's drifting. She's a sitting duck!"

Marci looked hard at the Osprey. "There's something wrong with her. She's too short. It looks like she's lost her engine and engine compartment."

Josh blinked. "That means they've jettisoned their engine compartment."

Marci asked, "Why would they? Damn! Reversing engines now."

The change in acceleration threw everyone hard against their harnesses. The transport vessel groaned under the charge of direction. Alarms screeched.

"What the hell!" Marc exclaimed without thinking.

Marci ignored his comment. "We're backing off! The only reason the Osprey would abandon her engines is that—"

WHOOSH. A brilliant flash of light obscured the asteroid and the two dueling spaceships. The intensity of the flash nearly blinded the transport crew. When they finally looked, they saw rubble and dust expanding from where the asteroid had once been. There was no sign of either the pirate ship or the Osprey. The conflagration died into a series of smaller fire blossoms as the anti-matter residue continued to react with nearby matter. The transport crew sat in silence, stunned by what they had just witnessed.

Marci broke the silence. "Did that push the asteroid off course?"

Josh shook himself out of his stupor. "I'm running the calculations now. Whoa! Half the asteroid is now rubble. Projections show that the one big rock that's left will hit the Earth's atmosphere at such a shallow angle it'll skip back into space. The rubble that gets drawn into the atmosphere will put on a spectacular but harmless, light show."

Marci gave a brief fist pump. "He did it! That crazy captain did it!"

"Where is he?" Hilda asked. "Does anyone see the Osprey or the pirate frigate?"

"It's hard to tell with all that rubble and dust," Josh admitted. "I don't think the Osprey survived—"

The radio crackled to life. "Transport, Osprey here, do you read me? Over."

Marci grabbed the mike. "Osprey, transport here. We read you, Captain! Over."

Marci thought Matt's voice never sounded so good as he said, "It's about time you kids showed up. Over."

"I see them!" Josh exclaimed.

Marci flipped the radio over to the cabin speaker. "Osprey, transport here. We have visual contact with you, or should I say, what's left of you. Over."

"Transport, Osprey here. We're a little beat up at the moment. Were we able to push that rock off course? Over."

"That's affirmative, Captain. Mission accomplished!" Marci could hear relieved cheers from the Osprey. "Josh isn't picking up any sign of the pirate ship, Sir."

"He won't, Lieutenant. Beauregard was in the kill zone of the anti-matter when it went off. It's a lousy way to go."

"Any way is a lousy way to go," Josh said.

"Got that right, Ensign," Marci agreed.

"Transport, one last question. How's my wife?"

"She's safe, Captain. All the settlements are safe."

"Thanks, Lieutenant. You'll never know what that means to me."

Marci choked a little. "I'm sorry we were so late to the party, Sir."

"You're not late, Lieutenant; you're right on time."

"On time for what, Sir?"

"To give us a tow back to Mars, of course."

# Epilogue

*If I can put one touch of rosy sunset into the life of any man or woman, I shall feel that I have worked with God." – G. K. Chesterton*

### The Courtyard to Sabrina's Cottage

The wedding was a simple affair. Held at Sabrina's courtyard, it had an intimate air about it. Captain Matthew Dirksen, wearing his dress blues, officiated. The bride was dressed in a simple white silk gown provided by Sabrina. The groom was also wearing his dress uniform, as was his best man. The maid of honor wore an airy pastel green gown, also provided by Sabrina. Barnabas and Chuck sat on the front row, along with Matt's wife and son. Several Custos and other Martians provided the rest of the audience. Once Matt introduced the newlywed couple, the audience broke into spontaneous applause.

After the ceremony, the wedding party and guests journeyed to the seaside village and lagoon. They sat together at tables just outside the fish market.

Barnabas stood up. "A toast to the beautiful bride and lucky groom." As glasses raised, he continued. "Tell us, Sarge, how did you know that Gunny was the one for you?'

Sarge laughed. "We've got a lot in common – interests, background, and outlook on life. The clincher is my memory of some advice I got from my dad. I remember several occasions when I was dating a girl. We'd date for a while. Then I'd ask my dad, 'How do you know you're really in love and she's the one for you?' He would always answer, 'When you're actually in love with the right one, you'll not need to ask that question.' He was right. It took me much longer than I expected, but Hilda's the one. And I'm one fortunate fella."

Hilda smiled at his words. "It took him a while to convince me. Then I realized that Marc's the only man I've ever trusted enough to say, 'I do.'"

"What about you two?" Marci asked. "Tell us – now that you've tied the knot, what's in your future?"

Hilda looked at Marc. "We're taking a week or two to explore this fascinating land. Those at our Mars base think we're on a geological expedition on the surface. Instead, we'll be down here."

Marc nodded his head in agreement. "After our time here, it happens that a southwestern university is pursuing both of us. They want me to do geological research for them."

"And they want me to seek grant money to research plant life particular to the southwest," Hilda added. "The southwest is logical for both of us."

"Why the southwest?" Barnabas asked.

"It just makes sense. It's where I feel closest to my Grandfather and Marc to his Dad," Hilda answered, looking at Marc. "We both enjoy camping, hiking, and fieldwork. We'll be doing as much as we can of that together."

"We'll sure miss you from the Space Force," Barnabas said.

"Oh, we're not leaving entirely. We're joining the Space Force Reserves," Marc replied. "What about you, Commander? What do you plan to do now that you don't have a ship to fly?"

Barnabas rubbed his chin. "I'll be taking some time off to reconnect with my daughter and her family. I'm expecting a chilly reception."

"Chilly reception?" Hilda asked.

"We were estranged when her mom passed. I was off fighting when it happened. My daughter felt I should have been with them at the time."

"That's rough," Hilda commented.

"I knew she was ill. Sadly, no one told me *how* ill. I ended up losing a wife and daughter at the same time."

"You think your daughter's ready to reconcile?"

"Not sure. I let way too much time slip by, But I need to try. Her mom would want me to."

Hilda nodded in agreement. "I hope it works out. What will you do after that?"

"Word is that Captain Dirksen is in line to become the Top Gun Flight School's Commander. If he does, he wants me to sign on as one of his instructors. Speaking of the captain, he's been a lot more human lately.

Marci said, "I guess it's because the captain finally reunited with his wife and son. Now, he's a changed man."

"He sure is," Barnabas agreed. "I even caught him laughing a little while ago."

"A smile hardly makes him a changed man," Hilda challenged.

"Trust me — for him, that's being downright giddy," Barnabas countered. "What about you Chuck? Now that you're officially part of the Space Force and free of the Army, what do you plan to do?

Chuck smiled. "I'm applying to get a degree in Engineering from the Academy. Captain Dirksen agreed to sponsor me."

Barnabas quipped, "Brave to let your name be attached to the captain."

Chuck frowned. "That's not funny, Sir."

"I thought it was funny," Marc said.

"It was a little funny," Hilda agreed. "Say, Corporal, uhh, I guess it's now Chief Bradley. When you get your degree, become an officer, and rebuild our dearly departed Osprey, sign us up. We'll fly with you again."

Barnabas laughed. "Sounds like a tall order to me."

Chuck spoke up. "I'd like to try. I really would."

Josh tugged at Marci's sleeve. "May I have a word with you, Lieutenant?" He motioned toward the top of the hill.

Marci stood up and smiled. "Sure, Ensign."

As they walked, Josh argued with himself. *She's way outta my league. Yeah, but you'll never know if you've got a shot unless you ask.*

They walked a little further. Josh found her hand. She didn't resist when he held it. Feeling encouraged, he said, "Lieutenant, uh, Marci—"

"Yes?"

"It's been quite an adventure. Uh, the last several days."

"That's an understatement."

Josh chuckled. "It sure is. The main thing is, you had my back and saved my life. Thank you."

"We had each other's back. You saved my life, also."

"We make a good team."

"Yes, we do."

Josh stopped and faced Marci. He felt his heart begin to pound. *Gosh, she's terrific.* He felt his courage start to ebb. "You're one helluva pilot," he blurted out. *One helluva pilot? That's just lame.*

Marci smiled. "Why, thank you, Ensign."

*Just say it, stupid!* "You're the most beautiful Lieutenant I've ever seen." Inside, Josh groaned, and he felt his face blush. *This isn't going well at all.*

"Aren't all the other Lieutenants you know men?" she shot back.

"Not fair. You know what I mean."

Marci gave an innocent smile. "Do I?"

*She's enjoying this way too much,* Josh thought.

They turned and walked a little further in silence. The couple stopped and viewed the grand Arcadian landscape.

It seemed, to Josh, that Marci was patiently waiting to hear what he had to say. The problem was Josh was now at a loss for words. His mouth was dry. He cleared his throat. "Have you heard what your next assignment is?"

"No word yet. I hope to hear something when Captain Dirksen is finished meeting with Captain Wright. You?"

"Oh, I was granted a month to 'explore Mars.' Custos Maris told me where there's a secret passage back underground. I'll spend my time helping the Martians repurpose the old mining equipment."

"Repurpose?"

"Yeah. The Martians plan to use the equipment to build two observatories. They'll be able to look at the stars and the surface of their planet."

"That's ironic. They'll see that the Great Deceiver was lying to them all along."

"Custos Maris isn't sure that the old-timers — the ones that saw the surface before when the great war swept over it — will want to see what it's become."

Marci looked thoughtful. "That would be hard. What about you, after helping the Martians?"

"I don't know. Maybe our paths will cross again?"

"I'd like to think that they would, Josh."

"Perhaps our paths don't have to part at all."

"Maybe. That would be nice."

Encouraged by her words, Josh said, "You know, Marci, I'm glad we're friends."

"I am as well."

"What I mean is, I … I feel more for you than just friendship. Would … uh … do you think we could be more than just friends?" *There, I said it. What do I see in her face? Fondness? Yes? No? What?*

Marci smiled, and Josh felt his heart melt. "Josh, I've come to be fond of you, just not in the same way as you feel about me. You're a nice guy, and I hope we can always be friends. Good friends, but no more. I need to concentrate on my career. You need to find someone who can love you back. I'll always have a warm spot in my heart for you. But only as a friend. I—

She was interrupted by Chuck, who jogged up. "Lieutenant! Lieutenant, the captain's looking for you, and he seems pretty excited. Or agitated. I'm not sure which."

The trio returned to find Matt with their friends. "Glad you could finally join us," he said.

*Doesn't sound like a new Dirksen to me,* a dejected Josh thought.

"I just finished a secured call with Captain — soon to be Vice Admiral — Wright. Here's what's in store for us, post-Osprey. "I've accepted an appointment to command the Space Force Flight School. This includes the Top Gun Flight School and NASA's Western Region space flight simulator training."

"I never thought you'd leave the bridge, Captain," Marc said.

Matt chuckled. "I didn't either. But I'll still get into space on occasion, and this assignment is as far from Washington as I can get. Now, for some of the rest of you: Commander — soon to be Captain — Maalouf,

Wright approved my request to bring you to the Top Gun school as an instructor. He also supports *your* admission to the Space Force Academy, Chief Bradley. Ensign Torres, when you're finished helping out here on Mars, I'm putting you in charge of our simulator labs. Finally, Lieutenant Gonzales, you are being appointed to head the Ninth Space Fighter Squadron."

"Don't I have to be a captain to head a squadron, Sir?" Marci asked.

"You do, and you will be promoted as soon as you and I return to Houston to present our official report on what just happened here."

Barnabas gave a low whistle.

"Won't be that bad, Commander. We'll be in Houston, not Washington," Matt said.

"They're not interrogating all of us like last time?" Hilda asked.

"Nope, Gunny. They just want a report from me and Lieutenant Gonzales, as we were the two officers in charge of our little adventure."

"Going to include the part about Portae, Captain?" Josh asked.

"A little hard to leave it out, given the way our assault went sideways," Matt replied.

"Any casualties on the assault team?" Barnabas asked.

"Just some bruised egos," Matt answered. "The whole thing is being reported as a training exercise. Our excursion to Portae is being filed as 'top secret.' Not even Admiral Robinson wants to talk about it. I think Lewis Wright mentions it just to get under the admiral's skin."

"What about the Martians? What are you going to say about them?" Marc asked.

"No need to mention them or anything about the interior of the planet, Sarge."

Marc pressed. "Not even the second mine?"

Matt smiled at Marc. "We'll just say that we discovered a second mine in a large cave. No one needs to know that it is also part of the planet's interior."

"Good point, Sir," Marc said.

"Given the mindset of Washington, I'm afraid that if they were to find out about the Martians, they'd ..." Matt paused midsentence. Then he said, "Well, let's just say that opens up a can of worms." Matt heard a murmur of consent and watched heads nod their approval. "We're agreed, then? No mention of the Martians, to anyone?"

His question was met by a chorus of "Yes, Sir's."

"Good. If the Martians want to reveal themselves to our colonists, they can pick their place and time. That's their right."

Marc spoke up. "We agree, Sir. But what if our colonists begin mining Mars themselves. Won't that be stealing from the Martians?"

Matt nodded. "According to Custos Maris, the Martians are keeping a close eye on the colonists. If the colonists begin mining, it'll either be okay with the Martians, or they'll put a stop to it. Either way, it'll be their call. As it turns out, they've asked me to make Josh available to help refurbish the mining gear left behind by the pirates. They'll use it to create a couple of safe surface-level observatories for themselves. Sarge, Gunny, you both could pitch in and help if you wish."

"Won't the colonists get suspicious?" Hilda asked.

"I've gotten NASA approval for the three of you to spend a month exploring Mars. I'm sure the Custos will get you quietly underground."

Hilda slapped her hands together. "Hot dog! This'll be fun."

"Marc, you're not smiling. Don't you want to be part of the fun?" Matt asked.

"I do, Sir. I'm just worried that the pirates we captured will blow this whole thing wide open with tales of flying scorpions, grottos, and an interior full of life."

311

"Funny story about those pirate prisoners. Captain Wright said that the Marines, who boarded their lander, found them high on what seemed to be peyote. They were either pretty chill or thoroughly disoriented. One pirate was wandering around saying, 'What do you think I am? A tube of toothpaste?' So, no one is taking their babblings about flying beasts and intelligent life seriously. Would anyone happen to know how peyote found its way onto the lander?" Matt asked while looking straight at Hilda.

Hilda's face flushed as she smiled. "Why Captain, If I can put one touch of rosy sunset into the life of any man or woman, I shall feel that I have worked with God."

"What does that have to do with putting peyote in the pirate's lander?" Matt asked.

Marc started laughing. "Nothing, Sir. Unless you think of peyote as a rosy sunset."

"No matter how it got there. It's discredited anything the pirates may say about Mars. The Custos will torch the remaining above-ground evidence of pirates. So, if anyone goes looking, they'll never find a trace of where we've been. The secret of the Martians' existence is safe, for now."

"Any idea of where 'the boss' is hanging out, Sir?" Marci asked.

"He's still on your mind?" Barnabas asked.

"And in my dreams. I just can't shake the bad feeling I have about him," Marci answered. "I still wonder where he may be lurking."

"Your guess is as good as mine, Lieutenant. I'd like to be hopeful that we've heard the last of him. But that would be foolish thinking."

Marci's face clouded. "Well said, Captain."


THE END

# An Excerpt From THE RESURRECTION OF THE OSPREY

## By DJ Albrecht

### Ill-Fated Flight

*"Et Tu, Brute?" – Julius Caesar*

### In the Sky Above Kepler 186f

Marci was amazed at how green the world below her was. The sky was its usual overcast gray. Marci guided her scout fighter over several meadows into a series of foothills. She made a lazy turn to follow a river upstream. *Josh said that upstream is the source of the toxin that's troubling the villagers.* As she traveled further, she found that she was flying up one fork of the river. It joined another river branch. So, the river had two divisions. The one she had been following fed the village's water supply. Where did the second one go? She'd follow it on her way back. Right now, she needed to find the source of the toxin.

Marci dropped her fighter closer to the ground and rounded a bend in the river. There it was — a reddish-orange scarred stream fed the river. Marci set her starfighter down in a nearby clearing. After a short walk, she found the source of the toxins. It was dozens of rusted-out drums lying about and leaking a putrid-smelling liquid. This foul stream ran down a bank into the river. Looking around, Marci found a trail leading from the dumpsite into the forest. *Must be heading through the woods to a road*, she thought. Glancing back, Marci saw a flash of light. She looked closer and noticed that the source of the glint was a couple of new drums. From the way they lay on the ground, it was apparent that someone had intentionally poured them into the river. Then she noticed the tire tracks. *Hmm … these tracks are made by a large truck. Josh said that the only trucks here are owned by the government. That makes no sense. Why would the government poison its own citizens? I think I'll see where that trail leads.*

Marci mounted her fighter and guided it upward. She hovered over the sight briefly, then began to fly above the road. Her ship shuddered, and several warning alarms sounded.

*I'm being attacked!* Instinctively Marci avoided the incoming fire from another scout fighter. Her maneuver caused her to rise quickly and roll over, reversing direction. In so doing, she spotted what looked like her wingman pass just below her. He quickly changed course to bring him in on her tail. Marci raised her rear shields. *Damn! I should've had those shields up, to begin with.* She started a series of corkscrew turns.

She tried to raise her assailant on the radio. "Jake, what are you doing?" But there was no answer. Every maneuver she made was skillfully matched by the opposing fighter. *It's got to be Jake. No one else knows my moves as well as he does. What won't he expect?*

Marci stood her fighter on its tail and accelerated straight up in an apparent effort to out-climb her opponent. He took the bait and fell in behind her. Marci hit her air brakes, causing her opponent to overshoot her. Once he'd passed by, she opened fire and began to accelerate again. This time her ship began to shudder and shake. A quick check of her gauges confirmed that her engine was starting to fail. *It must have been those first hits before I got my shields up,* she thought ruefully. Marci tried to site her opponent in for a missile shot. But the ship's erratic motion made it impossible to lock in on her target. She fired both her missiles anyway. *That should keep him busy for a while,* she thought.

Marci noticed that their flying put them above the mouth of the second river branch. This branch descended quickly into a ravine. *I need to set this puppy down quick before it dies altogether.* Marci rolled to her left and dove into the gorge, brushing the treetops along the way. By now, the ship was shaking violently, and Marci struggled to control it. Then, as quickly as it started, the shuddering stopped. The engine died. Her maneuvering thrusters were also dead. Looking ahead, Marci found a slight clearing and aimed for it while bracing for a "dead-stick" landing.

The thought ran through her head; *he'll get turned around soon enough and will be looking to finish me off. What to do? Hopefully, this looks enough like a fatal crash to keep him from checking too close.* She released her chaff and smoke cylinders just before her fighter hit the ground. This created smoke and debris that hid her point of impact.

*I'm coming in too fast!* The ship hit the ground hard, sliding and starting to turn toward one side. A stand of small trees stood in her way. As her vessel hit the trees, its wings sheared off. Somehow the cockpit was untouched and spun to a stop. Marci unbuckled her harness, grabbed the emergency kit, and jerked the lever, which pops the canopy, only to find that it was stuck.

Marci could smell the smoke that signals the start of a fire. *Gotta get outta here.* While the canopy was unlatched, it was held in place by a tree branch. Marci swung her feet up against the canopy and pushed with all her strength. It opened partway, then fell back. She pushed again. This time the branch slid to the side, and the canopy popped open.

Marci struggled to get out of the cockpit. *Must hurry! He'll be by soon.* She jumped to the ground and scrambled, fighting through the underbrush along the ravine, until she found a rock outcropping. She clawed her way up the ravine side until she could slide in behind the outcropping. She wasn't a second too soon. She heard her adversary streaking past her position as he searched for her ship.

Marci settled in to watch. She saw that the ship which attacked her was indeed her wingman's ship. "Et Tu, Bute?" She said under her breath.

It circled above the crash site and fired two missiles at her ship, which erupted into a ball of fire, spewing shrapnel everywhere. As she ducked, she heard pieces of her starfighter bouncing off the rocks that sheltered her. Her assailant slowed and hovered until the fire subsided. Then he flew slowly over the conflagration, checking for any sign of life. From her angle, Marci could see, even though it was Jake's ship, Jake wasn't flying it. She was both relieved that Jake wasn't her assailant and worried about how his fighter was taken. The pilot must have been satisfied that he'd killed her because she saw him give a little fist pump before he flew off.

Marci stood up and began to look for a path or some other way down. Without warning, a secondary explosion released a fireball that shook the ground. Marci lost her balance and began to fall. She grabbed at a nearby shrub. That held her for only a moment. Then it gave way, pitching her backward into the ravine ....